The Quiet Unraveling of Eve Ellaway

Books by Melanie Hooyenga

The Campfire Series
CHASING THE SUN
CHASING THE STARS
CHASING THE MOON

The Rules Series
THE SLOPE RULES
THE FRIEND RULES (short story)
THE TRAIL RULES
THE EDGE RULES

The Flicker Effect Trilogy
FLICKER
FRACTURE
FADED

Anthologies
LOVE ON MAIN
THE ART OF TAKING CHANCES

Praise for The Quiet Unraveling of Eve Ellaway

"A twin win: It's hard to put down and stays with you after you finish." *—Kirkus Reviews*

"This is truly a one-of-a-kind novel with an unforgettable ending." *—The BookLife Prize*

"Prepare to lose sleep—Eve's story will keep you up late into the night as you question both her reliability as a narrator and the people around her." — *Kellie M. Parker, author of YA thriller* Thin Air

"An emotional roller-coaster ride you will not soon forget. Simply terrific!" — *Alan Orloff, author of the Anthony and Agatha-Award winning YA thriller,* I Play One on TV

"An emotional riptide from beginning until its shocking end." *—Heather Levy, Anthony-nominated author of* Hurt for Me *and* This Violent Heart

"This book is a whirlwind emotional ride. Impossible to put down, with shocking twists and heartbreaking truths, it's truly an unforgettable story." — *Michelle MacQueen*

"...a gripping exploration of identity and mental illness. This dark, psychological novel is a raw journey that will captivate readers who enjoy stories that blur the line between reality and delusion." — *NetGalley review*

The Quiet Unraveling of Eve Ellaway

MELANIE HOOYENGA

Left-Handed Mitten
Publications

THE QUIET UNRAVELING OF EVE ELLAWAY

Published by Left-Handed Mitten Publications
ISBN-13: 9798330430468

UPC

Book design, cover design, and ebook formatting by Left-Handed Mitten Publications. Author photo by Jenn Marie Photography.

Author website: melaniehoo.com
Email: melaniehooyenga@gmail.com
Facebook: facebook.com/MelanieHooyenga
Instagram: @melaniehoo
Threads: @melaniehoo
Newsletter: melaniehoo.com/hoos-letter

Melanie Hooyenga
PO Box 554
Grand Haven, MI 49417

To my friends and family,
who've kept me from unraveling
more times than you know.

One

To wish away everything you know—everyone you know—for a chance at something better is a dangerous daydream. Does it make me a bad person? Maybe. But eighteen years of putting my mother's well-being before mine has earned me the right to a little selfishness.

My bag lands with a thump on the floor next to the kitchen table. Dad's still at work and Mom doesn't come downstairs, so right now, in this moment, I'm alone. I can finally be just me. With my eyes closed, school and this house and the charade of every day fall away, leaving room for something else.

Hope.

The briefest brush of anticipation at what life will be like next fall when I start college on the other side of the lake at Northwestern. Maybe even a little optimism that things might change.

I grab an apple from the bowl on the counter and take bite after bite as the silence wraps around me. Softens the edges of the secrets hiding in the corners.

A seed falls to the floor, and I stare at it. If you dig too deeply into anything, it'll start to fall apart. Break into pieces until it no longer resembles what you thought you knew to be true. Until it's nothing but fragments on the kitchen floor.

My twin sister disappeared when we were babies, and it still seems impossible she could have vanished so completely. Her disappearance shattered our family, the fragments sprouting into a darkness from which we've never recovered.

In five more months, I'll get to leave this all behind. But there's nothing I can do about it right now. I nudge the seed under the edge of the cabinet, grab my bag, and head upstairs.

Mom's door is cracked, but no sound comes from inside. I knock lightly on the door and poke my head in. "Hey, Mom."

She looks up from her knitting and smiles. "Hi, Eve. How was your day?" She moves her yarn to the floor to make room for me on the loveseat and nods at the TV, which is paused mid-show. "Do you mind?"

I shake my head and Ross and Rachel—two characters from Friends, the only show she watches—spring to life. "It was fine. It was good to see everyone after break. I'm ahead on my feature articles, and we get to write a short story for English."

"That's nice." She pats my knee before resuming her knitting. The long needles click-clack against each other, a sound so ingrained in my memories of her I doubt I'll ever manage to separate the two. My eyes drift to photos lining the windowsill but I force myself to look away. To avoid the framed family photos hanging above the TV. Except for the addition of new photos each year, her room has barely changed since 2007—the year I was born. When I was younger, I thought it was because my birth was so important to her and she wanted to remember every detail. And I was partly right.

But so very, very wrong.

I press my shoulder against hers. "You seem quiet. Are you okay?" She always gets like this when our routine changes. Having me home all day during spring break, filling her normally quiet hours with conversation and activity, is great while it lasts. But then she slips.

She touches my cheek, and for a flash of a heartbeat I catch myself hoping for something that will never come. Recognition. Realization. Clarity. Then she slides back into the safety of the cocoon in her mind. "Just a little sad today."

Stories about my day—embellished with my writerly flair—collect on the tip of my tongue, but I keep them to myself. Pretending to be happy to cheer her up requires an energy I don't have right now. And I need to save whatever energy I do have for later.

So we sit quietly side by side, her knitting needles clicking on a new project—it's too soon to tell if it'll be another scarf or sweater, or something more ambitious—while the pretty actors perform on TV. Mom has watched these episodes hundreds of times. She knows every word and she mouths them as she knits, purls, knits, purls, but somehow she never tires of watching the same stories over and over. Some days I feel like that's what I am to her. A performer who delivers exactly what she expects, what she needs to finish off her day and go to bed with her mind at ease.

While mine spins uncontrollably.

A leaf slaps against the window overlooking the backyard, and a strong wind shakes the pane. She leans past me to look outside, in the direction of the high school. "I hope Gen's warm enough at practice. It's supposed to storm pretty hard tonight."

At school, we have a whiteboard in the *Sabre* office that tracks the news stories and assignments for each weeks' issue, and every Friday we take turns wiping it clean. There's something incredibly satisfying about erasing the past with a swipe of your hand, creating a blank slate for the next week. That's what my mind does now. Wipes clean. Erases the past fifteen minutes.

Because our time together isn't about me.

It's about Gen.

It's always about Gen.

Mom doesn't even notice I've shut down.

Physically I'm still sitting next to my mother as she loses herself in her show, but mentally I'm already at Lake Michigan, running on the beach until my lungs feel ready to explode.

Because only when I've pushed myself to complete exhaustion do I get a moment's rest.

When the show ends, I rise from the couch and stretch my arms over my head. "I better get started on my homework."

Mom rests her needles in her lap and looks over my shoulder out the window before settling her gaze on my face. "I think Old Sherm died."

"What?"

She points a needle at the window. "Our neighbor. I think he died." Her face falls, her deeply creased skin hanging loose beneath her watery brown eyes.

Since Mom never leaves her room, her only contact with the outside world is our creaky next-door neighbor. Our houses sit side-by-side at the end of an otherwise forested road, close enough to the lake that I can easily go there for runs, but not so close that our houses are worth much. Based on the depth of weeds in Old Sherm's yard, he hasn't set foot back there in at least a decade. I don't think they've spoken in as many years—I certainly haven't—but she talks about him like they sit on the porch swing, sipping lemonade and spinning yarns about the other neighbors. I peer outside, prepared to humor her, but the yard looks untouched and the light that constantly burns over the weather-worn deck still shines.

"What makes you think he died?"

"An ambulance came without the sirens and took him away."

I whip around to face her. The driveway isn't visible from her window. "How—"

"You can see the street from Gen's room," she says.

Her words are a blow to the chest. My breath stops. My back hits the edge of the window and my fingers reach behind me until they grip the smooth wood, but the room is still off-balance. "Do you go in there a lot?" My voice is a whisper. If I speak too loudly or sound like I'm accusing her of something, this delicate charade will splinter, leaving us both devastated.

She shakes her head. "I saw the lights on the side of his house."

The rest is left unsaid.

When I was little, I didn't understand why my mom didn't take me places like my friends' moms did. Or drive me to school. Or bake cookies. Or cook at all for that matter. With each passing year, her isolation became normal—but the kind of normal that knocks you off your feet if you step back and think about it too long. I take it for granted that she doesn't leave their bedroom, but if she's exploring the house, I'll need to be more careful.

Mom moves to the window, oblivious to my unease. "I hope they clean up the backyard. It'd be nice to have a prettier view."

We might get new neighbors.

They might be curious.

My secret might get out.

And that would be very bad for Mom.

The thoughts come so quickly I have to shake my head to focus on what Mom's saying.

"Dad used to bring you girls over there to play with his grandson when you were little." She clutches the edge of the window frame and rests her forehead against the glass. "Gen liked Old Sherm better than you did."

Of course she did. She does everything better.

"My short story awaits." I let out a sigh so she doesn't realize she's made me uncomfortable, but I'd rather lose myself in a creative writing assignment than watch her stare out the window.

She turns and smiles. "I'd like to read it when you're finished."

For the briefest moment, a lightness lifts my heart. She's not a terrible mother. She loves me and wants me to be happy. "Sure, Mom."

Her gaze returns to the window, but she's looking beyond Old Sherm's house in the direction of the high school, where the girls' soccer team is practicing.

To Gen.

My twin sister who was kidnapped when we were barely a month old.

And was never found.

Two

Dad comes home while I'm working on my short story, a fantastical tale about a sorceress and the havoc she wreaks on the world around her. Based on the sounds coming from the kitchen, he's starting dinner before greeting Mom. Which means he's exhausted—or stealing a few moments for himself.

As if he deserves a reprieve.

Dad claims Mom went to therapy the first year but she refused to accept that Gen was gone, and at some point he stopped trying. Now there's an ebb and flow in our house, the years of resentment acting like magnets that push Dad and me to opposite corners of the house to suffer through our existence in solitude. Except for breakfast and dinner—the only times we land in the same part of the house.

The sorceress turns two men to a pile of ash and the clenching around my heart eases. I lose myself in her wrath until the alarm on my phone gives me the ten-minute warning.

Gen flashes across the screen and I silence the alarm.

Like I could ever forget.

Mom's delusions didn't come about entirely on her own. Dad helped put them there, and I'm complicit. And that's why 6 p.m. is the hardest part of my day.

I bid farewell to my sorceress, pushing my laptop against the books lining the back of my desk and trailing my fingers over my collection of thesauruses and style guides. Mr. Barney, the newspaper advisor, insists on AP Style because he's a purist and most of Europe apparently hates the Oxford comma, but my English teacher, Miss Emory, understands the need for clarity and requires that we follow the Chicago Manual of Style. More books fill the shelf above the desk, nonfiction accounts of political turmoil resting side-by-side with epic fantasies, and centered above the desk, a poster of my idol, British-Iranian journalist Christiane Amanpour. Cal surprised me with her last year, long before our friendship turned into something more, and she displaced Ruth Bader Ginsburg to the wall above my bed.

I turn off the string of Christmas lights that snake around the edge of the ceiling, softening the edges of my world, and cross the hall to Gen's room.

Dad's rules from years ago echo through my mind.

Don't talk about Gen at school.

Tell people Mommy is sick and stays home.

And the biggest one: Save stories about your day for your "special time" with Mommy.

I squint against the harsh overhead light in Gen's room. We used to turn on the lamp on the nightstand, but the bulb is long gone, taken when mine burned out and it was easier to steal hers than find another one in the basement.

I ditch my pleated skirt and Chucks for leggings and a bulky University of Virginia sweatshirt. They're known for their women's soccer program, and even though Mom and Dad don't love the idea of Gen going so far away, it was too easy to buy the sweatshirt online and announce that she was accepted. I put my hair in a high ponytail, swap my contacts for glasses, and confirm in the full-length mirror that my Clark Kent transformation is complete.

This time when I open Mom's door, she's ready for me. A new episode is cued up and her knitting is tucked away in the basket near the window. Steam rises from a fresh cup of tea on the low table in front of her. And her face lights up in a way it only does for her favorite daughter.

For my twin sister, Gen.

For the other me.

"Hey, Mom." I take my same spot on the couch, but this time I let myself look at the pictures. At myself in duplicate. At me dressed as myself and Gen as we grew up. Dad learned Photoshop so he could create pictures of us together, and they're spread throughout the room, a constant reminder of the charade he forced me into.

You can't miss what you've never had, so while I never wanted for anything as a young child, my life was not ordinary. Having a mother who goes to the park—or even the grocery store—was something out of TV shows, something to daydream about while playing with my dolls.

"Gen." Mom's voice is a content sigh, her day complete now that Gen's here. "How was your day? Were you warm enough at practice? I keep thinking it'll get warmer, but you know spring in Michigan."

I smile while she rambles, softening the scowl that lives around my eyes. "It was great, Mom. Audrey and Lissa have awesome tans from Florida"—a detail I wish I didn't still notice about Lissa—"so they wore shorts to practice and froze their asses off."

Gen gets to swear in front of Mom. I don't. It's a rule I've tested.

She touches my arm. "You had your sweatshirt?"

"Yeah, thank god."

"I wish Eve had something to join like you do."

My stomach clenches but I force my voice to stay upbeat. Bubbly. "She's got the newspaper."

She shrugs and picks up the remote. "Ready?"

"Sure, Mom."

My feet carry me the couple blocks to Lake Michigan while my mind uncoils. Replays the past twenty-four hours. Searches for moments where I slipped. Because pretending to be two people requires constant vigilance, a stamina that leaves me raw by the end of the day.

It's hard on Dad, too, but he only has to pretend that he's a loving father and husband.

If Mom's venturing out of her room, I'll have to do a better job making Gen's room look lived in. Or at least slept in. Dad bought a new comforter when we started high school, and I haven't changed the sheets since. The hoodies and yoga pants I wear during our evening chats get washed at least once a month, but beyond that, her room never changes.

Dad started serving Mom's meals in her room when I first began school. Gen and I took turns eating with Mom off the special tray in her room while one of us was "busy," but as we—I—got older, it shifted to special occasions, then major holidays, and now we never eat together. But she always stayed in her room.

Or so I thought.

The sound of crashing waves greets me like an old friend, and I inhale deeply. Glance into the distance. Northwestern is near the shore on the other side—it's one of the things that drew me to the school. Sometimes my daily runs are the only thing that keep me sane, and knowing I'll be able to continue this in the fall is one more perk to leaving.

The ground changes from pavement to sand and my body comes alive. This is how I imagine Gen feels when she's sprinting down the soccer field, the ball at her feet, defenders on her heels. Full of adrenaline, mind focused on one thing and one thing only—scoring the goal. Or in my case, running until my lungs burn and my legs shake and the only thought in my head is how exhausted I am.

This place on the edge between land and water feels more like home than the place where I have two bedrooms, two wardrobes, two lives.

Here I'm allowed to have one singular dream. One singular life.

I don't have to think about my missing sister.

Three

"Last night was amazing." Cal's dark hair is artfully tousled, his political t-shirt and skinny jeans completing the image of a budding journalist. He pulls me into his arms the moment I step into the *Sabre* office, and my eyes close. Last night was no different than any other time we've slept together. His room is in the basement, and not only does it have a full bathroom and living room with a flatscreen and a couch, it has a separate entrance. He lets me shower from my run, then I stay undressed until I go home.

It's one of the few places where I can be myself, and as much as I hate letting anyone get too close, he is my safe space.

For all the times I've been there, his parents have only appeared a handful of times, and never unexpectedly. It's like they have so much trust in Cal they never considered he could be doing something unholy.

His hand trails over the hem of my pleated skirt. We've got ten minutes before the rest of the newspaper staff arrives. Not enough time for what I'd like to do, but more than enough for a few harmless kisses.

But kissing Cal LeBlanc is never harmless. He'll always want more than I can give. Each kiss ties him closer to my heart, to finding out my secret, and no one can ever learn the truth or what's left of our family will be destroyed. Dad says Mom could be taken away and that he—I don't know what will happen to him without this life he's fabricated.

We may be a mess, but it's the only family I have. And I'll do anything to keep Mom with us.

I murmur a non-response, nuzzling my face into Cal's neck, and his embrace tightens.

Suffocates.

The seconds tick away and I begin counting. At ten I step back. Smile up at him. For all his bravado, he's a sensitive guy and while we don't agree on what we are—exclusive, dating, friends with benefits—life would suck considerably more without him. His eyes betray his thoughts, so I rest my hand on his chest to stop him from pulling me closer.

"I came up with an idea for my next feature."

"Besides the ones you've already written?" he asks.

The corner of my mouth lifts and I tap the side of my head. "It never turns off."

"As your editor, I approve. And as your whatever," he shrugs at my unspoken insistence that we're not an official couple, "I'm glad."

If I could, I'd write every article on mental illness, but not only do the people at school get tired of it, I worry each piece lures Cal closer to discovering what lurks beneath my smile. So instead, I sprinkle in other fun topics, like the growing suicide rates among teens in our county.

My lips brush his cheek, but I put distance between us when my best friend Ember Chen busts through the door. Her eyebrow quirks when she sees us, but she keeps her thoughts to herself. She's one of the few people who knows about me and Cal, and the only one I trust enough with details.

Ember lowers into the chair next to mine and rests her messenger bag on the floor. Her straight black hair has streaks of teal racing through it, and her black and white plaid pants and neon green top scream that she belongs in a bigger city, not in our sleepy lakeside town.

I run a finger through a strand of her hair. "This is fun."

"Claire finally came over last night." She twirls a strand of teal hair around her finger. "I'm still bummed she had to stay home for break. It would have been awesome to bring her along, but there's no way my parents would let that happen."

"I'm sorry they still haven't come around."

"Yeah, me too." Ember and Claire have the healthiest relationship of anyone I know. It sucks that her parents won't accept them together.

Cal inches closer to me in his seat but I pretend not to notice. He'd never be so bold as to rest a hand on my thigh with others around, but it's like my skin can feel his touch anyway. I cross my legs away from him, focusing on my Chucks—today they're gray—to push away temptation.

By the time the rest of the *Sabre* crew arrives, my fingers are flying over the keyboard. I smile a hello as they settle in around me, but don't stop writing until Mr. Barney grabs a chair near the proofing table. He flips it around and straddles it, beaming at us until Ember finally asks, "What?"

He rubs his hands together like a mad scientist. The blue frames of his glasses pop against his dark skin and complement the blue and pink checkered pattern of his dress shirt. "I have exciting news."

"Ugh, dude. Tell us!" Aiden, our resident photographer, throws his hands in the air.

Mr. Barney grips the top of the chair and leans back, straightening his arms. "Your favorite teacher has helped coordinate a multi-school competition—"

"Miss Baker did that? Sweet!" Ember smirks, waiting for the roll of his eyes we all know is coming. Mr. Barney is by far the best teacher in the school, at least as far as we're concerned, but we show it with teasing and jokes.

"Of course you go for the female teachers." Aiden's comment is low enough that Mr. Barney doesn't hear, but Ember and I whip around to glare at him as he bumps fists with Kevin, the bigoted graphic designer who outed Ember to her parents last fall.

"Ignore him," I whisper.

"Why do there have to be two of them?" she says.

Kevin leans toward Aiden and they look our way and laugh.

Mr. Barney must not have heard what Aiden said, because he rolls his eyes and relaxes his shoulders. "As I was saying, a three-school multimedia awareness competition. Our esteemed Spring Haven, plus Traverse City and Bay City. You'll each be teamed up with a student from the other two schools and tasked with a project to present at a competition at Grand Valley State University the second weekend of May."

"That's so extra extra," says Ember.

I smile at our favorite response to everything. It's a combination of the old-school newspaper kids who'd yell "Extra! Extra!" on the street corner and just being, well, extra.

"We have a month?" Cal asks. He's a planner—it's what makes him a good editor—and he needs to know every detail of everything around him. It's what drives him so crazy about my refusal to commit. If he had his way, I'd already be sporting a promise ring and we'd be saving for a down payment on a house. But I want something bigger than that. Than him.

Mr. Barney waves him off. "All in good time, sir." He clears his throat. "Each team will have a writer, a photographer, and a graphic designer, so your strengths will be on full display."

"I know what else will be on full display." Kevin and Aiden high five.

This time I roll my eyes.

"What's the topic?" Ember asks. She's leaning back in her chair, seeming disinterested, but the idea of a competition has brightened her eyes, putting her on alert.

"You know that recent report about the issues facing teens today? The youth assessment survey?" Mr. Barney asks. When we nod, he continues. "Each group will choose one of those issues, then develop a project that helps raise awareness of the issue to your peers. The winning team—" he pauses, swiveling his head to look at each one of us—"gets to attend a one-month intensive at Grand Valley State University this summer," he pauses again, but my heart's already galloping out of my chest.

A college campus. For a month. This summer.

Leaving home before Northwestern.

I could get out sooner. GVSU is barely half an hour away, but it'll be good practice for Mom. And me.

But from the excited chatter around the room, that's not the grand prize.

"—the commercial will air regionally, and you'll get the chance to work with the local media, including the TV station in Grand Rapids."

Ember jumps out of her seat and paces around the editing table. My dreams of being a journalist who travels around the world are matched in intensity by hers to be a world-renowned graphic designer. Cal looks just as eager, but years of discipline have taught him to channel that energy inward. His elbows rest on his knees, his clenched fists propping his chin, but he can't hide his full smile. He catches my eye and my stomach flips.

He really is handsome, in a geeky-chic sort of way, and seeing him this happy reminds me why I was first attracted to him all those months ago.

Mr. Barney raises a hand to quiet us. "The majority of the work will be done online in a forum we've created. Groups will be assigned randomly and will each have shared folders where you'll collaborate. To keep things interesting," he smiles, and the nerves in my stomach stop. "You won't meet until the day of competition."

"Why?" I don't mean to speak, but the word leaves my mouth before I can stop it. Based on the murmurs around me, I'm not the only one wondering.

"In journalism, you'll often have to work with sources whose identity will need to be kept secret, or some other parameter that will make your work more difficult. The other two advisors and I thought it would make the competition more interesting."

Interesting indeed.

Ember settles back into her chair. "This is pretty cool, right?" It's not like her to seek my approval, especially on the coolness of anything. She's twisting her hands in her lap like she's trying to contain her excitement.

"Yeah. Definitely."

"What do you think about being paired up with people we don't know?" she asks.

It's perfection.

I shrug. "It'll be fun."

But fun hardly gives it justice. Thoughts buzz through my head so loudly I can barely hear anyone else. I'll be working with people who don't know me. Who won't give me pitiful looks when I pass them in the hallway. Who don't know my history or the sad tragedy that scarred my family.

They won't know about Gen.

Four

HOW LONG CAN YOU KEEP A SECRET BEFORE IT CHANGES YOU? BURROWS INTO YOUR SUBCONSCIOUS AND WORMS THROUGH THE FOLDS OF YOUR BRAIN THE WAY THE SAND AT THE EDGE OF THE LAKE ENVELOPS YOUR TOES, THREATENING TO PULL YOU UNDER.

EVERYONE KNOWS I DON'T GO ANYWHERE BECAUSE MOM, WELL, MOM DOESN'T GO ANYWHERE. LIKE, DOESN'T LEAVE THE UPSTAIRS OF OUR HOUSE GO ANYWHERE. ALTHOUGH NO ONE KNOWS THAT PART. I'VE BEEN HIDING IT FOR SO LONG THAT THE THOUGHT OF ANYONE FINDING OUT NEARLY DESTROYS ME. I JUST NEED TO GET THROUGH THE REST OF SENIOR YEAR, THEN I CAN START MY OWN LIFE.

ONE HUNDRED FORTY DAYS.

MOST KIDS SEE COLLEGE AS A NEW BEGINNING. FOR ME, IT'S AN ESCAPE.

NO ONE KNOWS I'M COUNTING DOWN THE DAYS. THEY WOULDN'T UNDERSTAND. COULDN'T.

ONLY ONE HUNDRED FORTY MORE DAYS TO FAKE MY WAY THROUGH. THEN I'LL FINALLY BE FREE.

—EE

My mind's still buzzing when I open Mom's door later that night. A new episode is cued up and she's waiting for me on the couch.

She gives me a tender smile. "How was your day?"

I sit next to her, tucking my legs beneath me. "Good. It

was warmer today, so practice was more fun. And school was school." Thoughts of the competition fight for my attention, but I already told her about it during my time, and she didn't seem very interested. Of course, I left out the part about leaving for a month over the summer, but even without that detail, I thought she'd be more excited for me.

"I think someone's moving into Old Sherm's house." The casual comment makes my heart race. It'll be nice for Mom to have something new to keep her imagination occupied, but complicated for me. For us.

"Did you see them?" Please be another old couple. Or people with tiny kids. People who keep to themselves and don't wonder about the strange family living next door. Anything but—

"It looked like a single mom with a son about your age."

The absolute worst possible outcome.

"You probably know him. He looked popular."

"Cool." Never mind that popularity isn't a physical characteristic like hair color or height. If he's popular, he won't know who I am and my secret should be safe. My shoulders relax and my smile appears automatically. "Hopefully they're nice."

She pats my hand. "Is Lissa having her party this weekend?"

My head bobs with an enthusiasm I don't feel. Putting Gen on the soccer team seemed like an easy way to explain where she was after school. Having her be best friends with two of the most popular girls came naturally after that. I really was BFFs with Lissa for two weeks in sixth grade—just long enough for me to memorize the way her cheeks dimpled when she smiled and be completely confused by what that smile did to my insides. But our friendship ended with a non-invite to the first of an endless string of parties, and she's belonged to Gen ever since.

Now, as our—my—senior year winds down, keeping track of my lies is second nature.

"Cal's picking me up, but I'm not sure how long we'll stay."

She touches my cheek, her eyes on mine. They're just as watery as they were earlier but there's a brightness to them that only comes out when Gen's in the room. "I wish Eve would find a nice boy like Cal. You two seem so happy."

Fury bubbles to the surface, my blood burning through my body and years of pent-up venom threatening to spew all over my oblivious mother as she strokes her knitting needles.

I did this. This is my fault.

Not hers.

But she's my mother. She should know.

You've been too careful. She never will.

What if I slip? There's a lot to keep track of. And you don't know Cal like I do.

Maybe I'd like to.

How would Mom like it if Eve stole Gen's boyfriend?

She'd just push me higher on the pedestal.

My fingers are so tangled in my ponytail that hair knots around the silver ring on my thumb. It frees with a yank, and the sharp pain in my skull settles my thoughts. A smile surfaces. "You know Eve. She's too busy with the paper. Until she finds a boy who loves words as much as she does, she'd rather be alone."

Cal loves words.

So why do you keep pushing him away?

Shut up.

Mom sighs, an exhalation of her hopes and dreams for her younger daughter. Her only daughter. She grips my hand, her bony fingers surprisingly tight around mine. "Maybe you could set her up with one of your friends? A boy from the soccer team."

Never mind that the majority of the boys on the soccer team think oppression and regime refer to a killer offense. The odds of me having anything in common with one of them are about as likely as Mom snapping out of her eighteen-year fog and realizing her precious Gen doesn't exist.

"I don't think she'd go for that."

"It was just a thought." She squeezes my hand and the claustrophobia sets in.

One.

Two.

Three.

"I just want you both to be happy."

My interests don't matter.

Four.

Five.

"Do you want a new outfit for the party?"

I exhale. "Nah, that's okay." The urge to take advantage of her is strong, but this practiced discipline applies to more than just keeping my secret. Besides if I really press Dad, he'll buy me whatever I want.

To keep me happy.

Compliant.

Mom releases my hand and pats my knee. "Just promise you'll wear something besides yoga pants to the party."

The unexpected dig is a shot of adrenaline. Mom almost never criticizes Gen. My lower lip pushes out and my lashes flutter. The expression feels forced, but whenever Lissa does this to her flavor-of-the-month from across the cafeteria, it usually earns her a sympathetic smile. "I don't wear this on dates, Mom."

She smirks, and for a second, I peer through a window to what she must have been like before. Teasing, playful. Was she popular like Gen? Or quieter like me? Dad so rarely talks about their lives before us that I have to piece together these rare moments before the window into her life shatters around me.

"I know, sweetie."

The TV erupts with laughter and the moment evaporates, leaving me with the niggling concern that I'm jumping through hoops for a woman who I might have hated if we'd gone to school together.

One hundred forty days.

"Ten bucks says Mom's knitting a scarf." Teasing about her knitting is an easy way to avoid conversations with substance.

Dad spears a piece of meatloaf with his fork and drags it through the glob of ketchup on his plate. "Nah, it's almost summer. It's probably something bigger for the fall."

"Blanket?"

"Could be."

"Insider trading?" He spends more time with her so odds are he already knows what she's making.

He smiles, but it doesn't reach his eyes. "Mom said you were quiet tonight."

He doesn't say that about Gen. He never does. Because Gen's the star, the one they both adore.

And my penance for being the daughter who's left is doing whatever Dad says to keep Mom happy.

"I'm tired. It was a long day. And Mom's not interested in stories about the newspaper. She prefers soccer and Lissa and Audrey." Plus I'd really like to get out of here before it gets any later. I usually run between visits with Mom, and not just because it makes me sweaty while Gen's at practice. Running after dinner blows.

Dad chews slowly, watching me. My long dark hair and athletic frame are from Mom, but the penetrating stare is all him. Although mine's gotten progressively meaner as his has weakened, like eighteen years of this charade has depleted his will to care, while strengthening my resolve to get the hell out of here. "You know how hard it is on her after you girls have been home on break."

My glare narrows. "Me. Just me."

"You know what I mean."

If only the sigh that rushes out of me could knock him out of his chair.

Stop, he's just worried about her.

But he's always worried about her. When will he be worried about me?

"Yeah, Dad. I do." Frustration trembles through me and I

set my fork on my plate to keep myself from throwing it across the table. "How can we possibly maintain this?"

Confusion and alarm flash across his face but are quickly replaced with the calm patience I've grown to expect. "We've talked about this."

"And maybe some day you'll give me a different answer." Because nothing he's ever said will make me understand how a father could do what he's done to his daughter.

After years of trying and a difficult pregnancy, Mom and Dad were mentally and physically stretched to their limit and facing the harsh truth that perhaps they'd waited too long, that forty-five was too old to have a baby. But the eggs stuck, so to speak, and nine months later, Gen and Eve—named for Mom's grandmother Genevieve—screamed into the world.

The double blessing of twins was more than my parents expected, and after Mom's history of multiple miscarriages and two failed in-vitro procedures, her struggle with postpartum depression was just one more thing to push her over the edge. Dad was no stranger to a fractured mind, but his would manifest in different ways.

His gaze drops to his plate. "I did what I thought was best for your mom. You know that."

Mom. Not me.

My chair shudders against the wooden floor as I stand.

"Where are you going?"

"For a run."

He looks out the window, a piece of meatloaf dangling from his fork. Grease drips onto the plate, sliding around the ketchup. "It's getting dark."

"I'll wear my light."

Pushing boundaries with him isn't new, but since my eighteenth birthday last month he seems more hesitant. Like he's afraid to push back. While I count the days until I leave for college, I imagine he's consumed with the fear of what my leaving will do to Mom. Each new day brings us closer to finding out.

But I don't have the energy to worry about that now. After I change into my running clothes, I text Cal to let him know I'll end my run at his place, then tuck my phone into my jacket pocket and step into the crisp night air.

Five

"Journalist309?" Cal's cheek brushes mine as he peers over my shoulder, a light graze that reminds me of other, more private moments, and my skin warms. We're creating our profiles on the Interschool Project Forum, or the IPF as Mr. Barney keeps calling it. "You don't want to use your real name?"

Being forced to work with strangers is doing a weird thing to my body. A slight tremble has taken over my hands since Mr. Barney announced we're starting the project today, and I have the sudden and distinct urge to use the bathroom. Like now. But I mentally block it out.

I shrug, and he brushes a kiss against my shoulder before leaning back. "Anonymity has its perks. Plus, I figure this way there's no questioning where my strength lies."

"Anyone who knows you knows that," he says.

True, but I can list on one hand the number of people who know me. And even they don't know the real me. "I'm using this." My head leans toward him, seeking the security of his warmth, but he's too far away. "What about you? Please tell me you're not using plain old Cal LeBlanc."

"What's wrong with my name?"

"Nothing. But what about ProtestantBoy, or TheologyisMyJam?"

He rolls his eyes. "I'm surprised you didn't say Joey."

The irony that he has the same last name as one of the actors on Mom's show is too much for me to keep to myself. My fingers trail over his knee, the smooth fabric of his pants catching on my nail. "That name's mine."

By refusing to be something more than what we are, I don't have the right to be possessive, but Cal LeBlanc has found a soft spot near my heart—not quite my heart, maybe my spleen—and I want to protect it. To hang onto the one person who sees me. Eve.

His fingers find mine, and for a moment the rest of the room drops away and it's just us. No *Sabre*, no pressure to move away, no Gen. Just this sweet boy who's too good for me.

Whose heart I'll soon shatter despite my attempts not to.

"What about MrEditor?" I ask.

His chuckle makes me smile. "That could work."

I turn to look at him, and our quiet bubble pops. Kevin is watching us, his gaze anything but friendly. My smile fades and I blink him away. "Only if you want to."

Mr. Barney's voice further breaks Cal's spell. "Once you've created your profile, select your area of expertise—writer, photographer, or designer. The system will randomly assign the groups, and then we'll get started."

"Will we find out today?" Ember asks from my other side. A chunk of her black and teal hair is twisted around her fingers, but I can't tell if she's nervous or excited.

I'm terrified.

This town, with its sidelong glances and opinionated whispers, is all I've ever known. While getting out is my number one goal, nerves threaten to shut me down if I dwell on what leaving actually means. No more Mom or Dad. Or Cal. Or Ember. This project feels like a trial run for reestablishing myself, and I'm not ready. My new persona is still a rough draft.

"We'll email your group assignments by the end of the day," says Mr. Barney. "So please be sure to check your email. By this time tomorrow, each team will have a password-protected room where you'll do your work."

"Ooh, fancy," says Kevin.

"We've also created chat rooms everyone can access, and we encourage you to spend time there as well. Brainstorming as a group can be helpful, especially with the parameters we've placed on you. Short deadline, unknown partners, all that. But please remember the golden rule."

"Be respectful," we say in unison. The collective eye roll is our personal touch on his mantra.

He claps his hands together. "Great. I'll give you a couple more minutes to finish up, then we've got baseball playoffs to discuss!"

Ember slides her chair closer to mine. "I keep wishing we could pick our partners, but I guess it doesn't matter, right? It's not like we know anyone."

My eyes meet hers, our mutual uncertainty calming me. If Ember, who doesn't let anyone or anything dictate what she thinks, is nervous, then it feels okay for me to be nervous, too. "They're probably just as freaked as we are. I just wish we could know now. I hate waiting."

"What if—" she pauses, her fingers twisted in her hair again. "What if they don't like my style?"

My hands fall to my lap harder than necessary, and the slap makes several heads turn our way. "What are you talking about? You have an incredible eye." Ember's never been a traditionalist—it's why she's the only real friend I have—and her digital compositions are nothing like what the wannabe artsy kids put together. Hers jump off the screen, grabbing you by the throat and punching you with emotions that stay long after you've looked away. "And since when do you care what anyone else thinks?"

"The prize is huge. Getting partnered with someone who's more traditional would make it challenging."

"Challenging, sure. But not impossible." My shoulder brushes hers. The bump of solidarity is the closest I get to physical contact—at least with anyone but Cal. "They'll be as amazed by you as the rest of us."

Aiden hangs over the back of his chair and sneers at Ember. "Until they find out you just like girls because it's trendy."

"What the actual hell are you talking about?" Ember's voice slices the smirk off his face, which he covers by rubbing his nonexistent scruff.

"I'm an amazing investigator," says Aiden.

Ember throws a scowl toward the back of the room at Kevin. "It's been six months since douchebag let it slip."

"You're full of shit," I say to Aiden. "And you're a photographer. Not an investigator."

"Why can't I be both? You afraid of a little competition?" He stares into the proverbial distance. "The New York Times just needs to stay in business long enough for me to get my degree."

If he hasn't figured out Cal and I are whatever and we're right in front of him, his hopes for investigating global crises might be short-lived. "There's always the Daily Beast or New York Post," I say. "They're always looking for click-bait stories and photoshopped pictures. You'd fit right in."

Mr. Barney raps a pencil on his desk to get our attention. "Because of the shortened timetable, you'll need to choose your topic by the end of the week. There will be an outline with weekly goals on the general forum and I strongly encourage you to follow it if you want a shot at the grand prize." He paces the front of the room, tapping his pencil against the palm of his hand. "We've already posted the most recent youth assessment survey. That's where you'll get your topic. We'd prefer each group does something different, but given the other restrictions, we're capping duplicates at three per topic."

"Dibs on texting while driving!" shouts Kevin.

"It doesn't work that way, Comic Sans," says Ember.

"Who put you in charge, snowflake?" His harsh tone bites in a way that feels unnatural in this normally cozy room.

"Hey!" Mr. Barney slams his palm against the whiteboard. A dry erase marker bounces to the floor and no one moves. "What—" the word is crisp, staccato, "—is my number one rule?"

"Be respectful," we parrot back.

There are no eye rolls this time.

"Kevin, Ember, I will not tolerate disrespectful behavior in this room." His glare cements them to their chairs, any anger that simmered between them gone. "You two have a beef with each other, save it for later. In here, you act like adults."

"Yes, sir," Kevin murmurs.

"Sorry," Ember says, but it's directed at Mr. Barney, not Kevin. She'll never apologize to him.

"What if we don't like our partners?" asks the quiet reporter behind me who happily covers the student government meetings and anything else so boring it'd make your eyes bleed. Her highest ambition is to work for our local paper, covering city council meetings and the occasional flare-up over the boundary between the separation of church and state.

"I trust you'll find a way," Mr. Barney says. "There will be no switching teams."

Ember raises her brows at me as if to say, "oh shit."

Mr. Barney's moods run on a ninety-five to five split of good versus bad, and when a bad mood strikes, it's miserable for all of us. He shifts the conversation to regular *Sabre* news, including the baseball team advancing to the regionals.

"Calvin, you want to take it from here?"

All eyes are on Cal as he takes Mr. Barney's place in the center of the room. I'd rather shrivel into a ball and die than have the spotlight on me, but Cal revels in it. He dreams of being the editor of a major newspaper some day—assuming they still exist in another ten years—and he's already got the calm commanding presence thing down.

It's what draws me to him.

As for his name—Calvin—his parents named him after the French theologian who created the Protestant faith, and as far as they're aware, he lives his life to that standard. His mom's the head minister at the wealthiest mega-church in town and their lives revolve around their flock.

Her words.

Their expectations of Cal and his demeanor align with their beliefs, but they're so rarely home they leave their precious son to himself.

To me.

Cal ticks through his checklist, handing out assignments to each of us. It's like he's channeling his namesake and we're his flock, hanging on his every word. My ears perk when I hear my name. I may not care about much, but the things I do care about—like being a journalist far away from this claustrophobic town and everyone in it—I'm nearly obsessive about.

My attention drifts until he mentions topics closer to my heart—a recent report on the percentage of teens dealing with depression and anxiety—and Cal smiles at me. His encouragement is what first drew me to him. He's attracted to my mind—something practically unheard of in high school—although if he knew the depths of my depravity, he'd run the other way without looking back.

I sneaked glances at the youth assessment thing throughout the day, so even though Mr. Barney hasn't emailed our team assignments, when I turn onto our street after school, I feel lighter than I have in a long time. While the issues facing teens in our area are depressing, being able to report on something meaningful has energized me like nothing else.

Betty, my ancient hand-me-down car from Mom, grumbles into the driveway and jerks to a stop at the end. A white semi-truck fills Old Sherm's driveway, back doors flung open, spilling the contents of someone's lives onto the front yard. Bulky men the size of grizzly bears carry stacked boxes through the front door while a blonde woman with a no-nonsense haircut directs them.

"Be careful with that one!" Her voice carries through my closed windows, turning my stomach to knots. This isn't a person who will keep to herself, content to worry about her own problems and her own life. No, she's the type who notices things, then doesn't let it go until she's turned your life inside out.

The man carrying a box with FRAGILE scrawled across the side nods at her and follows his partner into the house.

If only it were that easy.

Betty eases into her spot on the side of the driveway, but I don't get out. Not yet. Meeting the new neighbors wasn't on my mental playlist today and I need more time to perfect our story. To craft how she'll see us from this day forward. Because unless every detail is flawless, she'll find out the truth.

Mom mentioned a teenaged son, but the blonde seems to be the only one home. Or at least outside. Betty's door normally creaks when I open it, but today she's a good girl and stays quiet. If I time it right, I can get inside without her seeing—

"Oh, hello there!" Without the window to muffle the noise, the blonde's voice is shrill, almost ear-piercing.

I already miss Old Sherm.

My hand lifts in a polite wave, followed by my courteous smile. Gen's smile. "Hi."

"We're just moving in," she says with a wave at the moving truck. "But I guess that's obvious." She crosses her arms over her chest while she assesses me.

My breath comes slowly and my shoulders remain relaxed—a practiced skill a decade and a half in the making.

I'm a stereotypical teen.

No one to worry about.

My impression should be minimal, no more than a blip before real problems barge back into her mind.

"Welcome to the neighborhood."

"I guess you don't remember me," she says.

There is something familiar about her, but I move toward the door and pretend I don't hear her.

Don't be a bitch.

I'm not ready.

You could at least pretend to be nice.

My head shakes slowly from side to side. I welcomed her. Any more and she'll get curious.

Maybe I want to meet more people.

The metal handle of the front door is cool in my hand, and I pause before stepping inside. If I start a conversation now her son could come home and, while I can't avoid the inevitable, I can put it off until I'm better prepared. The latch on the door clicks as I push it open, then again when it's shut behind me. The woman's voice is silenced, but I can't turn off Gen.

You're a fricking wimp.

Not a wimp. Cautious. You don't know how difficult this is.

It doesn't have to be.

I—I can't.

I dare you.

My bag slips through my fingers to its usual spot next to the island. How different would things be if Gen hadn't disappeared? Mom would have a job and a life beyond our family. Or maybe she'd have afternoon snacks ready for us when we got home from school. We'd tell her about our day, fighting over each other to talk instead my evening performance of the theater of the absurd.

As I move upstairs, my mind drifts through the what-ifs.

What if Dad hadn't fallen asleep that day at the park?

What if Mom didn't lose her grip on reality when Gen was taken?

And the question that buries me in guilt when the darkness creeps too close: Why didn't they take me?

My laptop hums as I open my short story. Biology and history can wait until later. Today Miss Emory encouraged us to explore an emotion within our characters that's the opposite of how we've portrayed them so far. My sorceress kills any man who looks at her wrong. Giving birth is too extreme for her story, but she could find love. Or at least lust.

The words fly from my fingers, the clicks of the keyboard the only sound until a car door slams outside, luring me across the hall to Gen's window. A tall, lean boy with his mother's hair and an athletic build stands next to a beat-up pickup truck, watching the movers.

Wes Sherman.

Old Sherm's grandson.

We haven't spoken since we were kids. The only time I see his name is at the *Sabre*. He's been a starter on the varsity soccer team since freshman year, and we recently ran an article about him getting a scholarship to play at Hope College, a small school half an hour from here. From what I've witnessed he's still a nice enough guy, but aside from a courteous hello in mutual classes, it's like we never knew each other. He's been a big deal his whole life, the kind of guy most people gravitate to like deer to the hosta plants Dad keeps planting in the backyard.

The kind of person Gen gravitates toward. Not me.

My breathing slows. Wes is safe. If it had to be someone from school living next door, at least it's a guy who's so wrapped up in his world he no longer knows I exist.

New Sherm nods to the movers and walks to the house, never looking my way. Which is exactly how I want it.

Six

The email stares at me from my laptop.

<u>Group 5</u>
Noah B, Traverse City High School, photographer.
Eve E, Spring Haven High School, journalist.
Willow K, Bay City Central High School, graphic design.

Noah and Willow. Two strangers who hold the power to either help me escape for a month this summer or screw things up so badly that this opportunity is snatched away. If they're on their newspapers as seniors, it's fair to assume they have a modicum of ambition, but I don't intend to wait to find out.

I switch tabs to the Interschool Project Forum. IPF blazes across the top of the page, and I scroll down to the section for group five. Start a new thread. Take a deep breath.

And channel Gen.

`Journalist309: Hey! This is Eve. I'm super excited for this project! Should we throw out ideas to figure out our common interests?`

Hit enter.

`Journalist309: This is going to be great!`

Roll my eyes at myself.

But this forced exuberance is necessary. When I go to college, I'll be able to reinvent myself, to step out of Gen's shadow and the tragedy of her disappearance and just be Eve. It's too soon for a complete transformation, but their first impression of me will affect the outcome of this project.

"Just a reminder that we'll be monitoring the forum." Mr. Barney sits at his desk at the front of the room, watching us over the top of his glasses. His arms cross over his broad chest and he catches my eye. "We want you all to get to know each other, but remember Big Brother is watching."

We read George Orwell's *1984* freshman year, so the reference gets the appropriate snorts and giggles. But his words make me pause. Will he notice a shift in my personality? And if he does, will he care? Last year, Mr. Barney recommended an article about cultivating sources that explained how sometimes you have to tell small mistruths to earn a stranger's trust.

That's when I knew I was on the right path.

Mistruths are my specialty.

If he says anything about the difference in my behavior, I'll tell him I'm practicing my journalism skills.

My laptop dings with a new message.

`NoBPhoto: Hi Eve and Willow. I'm Noah. Do either of you have a passion project?`

`WillowRicha: This is Willow (duh). What about drunk driving.`

In middle school, I inhaled every quirky grammar book I could find and had a special fondness for those that explained the intricacies of the English language using humor and word play. While I understand few people share my passion for proper punctuation, a small part of me dies when I'm forced to interact with people who use it improperly.

I wait a beat for Willow to add the question mark.

`WillowRicha: Or do you think that's overplayed.`

Dead. I am dead.

What kind of monster doesn't use proper punctuation?

```
Journalist309: Yeah, maybe. Did you look
through the survey?
```

And do you see how the squiggly mark at the end of my sentence indicates it's a question?

I thought you were channeling me?

It's not like she can hear me.

```
NoBPhoto: Drugs and all that are boring. What
about mental illness? We could actually help
people with a project about that.
```

The tension in my chest eases.

```
Journalist309: I like that idea. I've written
a few pieces on mental illness for our paper.
We could compare the increase of depression
with suicide rates.
```

Not that I'm afraid to do more work but having a base understanding of the data will make starting that much easier.

```
WillowRicha: Did you see the data about human
trafficking.
```

The lack of a question mark doesn't lessen the nausea that sweeps through me. We don't talk about where Gen may have ended up, what she went through, or what she might be going through if she's still alive, but that doesn't mean I haven't imagined every dark, twisted thing humans can inflict on one another. The first time I researched human trafficking was after I overheard dad on the phone with a detective. I was too young to know what it meant, but not too young to look it up online. My research concluded she was most likely taken to be adopted for profit, and while it sparked my journalistic tendencies, it didn't silence the internal longing for my sister.

Because I never knew Gen, I don't know if the occasional tugging on my heart and prickle of my skin are her communicating with me, that twin ESP some people talk about, or just an eternal longing for the connection that was severed much too soon.

The soft conversations around me mix with the roaring in my head until all I hear is Gen's voice. The voice I've created.

That could be interesting.

NoBPhoto: Yes. Let's do that.

WillowRicha: Was there enough data to do a whole project.

NoBPhoto: That's why they invented the internet.

Journalist309: So no to depression and suicide?

NoBPhoto: Trafficking is unique. Since we'll have to do more research, it's unlikely another group will do it.

WillowRicha: Eve, you good with that.

Hey, Willow, the question mark is on the right side of the keyboard next to the period. But more importantly, how am I supposed to write a piece about exploited children without completely losing my grip on reality?

I thought you were trying to be nice?

Why do you care?

Eye on the prize. Winning will get you away sooner.

Journalist309: Sure, it'll be fun.

WillowRicha: I have so many ideas already! We could do a flyer that goes on the inside of bathroom stall doors. I've seen those at the hospital.

Oh, sure. She has no problem with exclamation points. If this is what I'm working with, my eyes will be permanently locked at the top of my skull before the project is over.

By the end of the period, we've agreed on Willow's idea and outlined each of our assignments. Despite her complete disregard for punctuation, Willow's ideas are solid, and Noah seems really dedicated to creating a piece that helps people.

Cal's arm brushes mine as we step into the hall. "Did you pick your topic?"

My eyes meet his and I let out a breath. Moments like these, when he's watching me with heavy interest, not caring about the students jostling us in the hall or the group laughing nearby, make me second-guess my decision. We could be good together. We are good together. The distance I keep between us is for his benefit. When I leave for college, I'm leaving everything behind.

"Human trafficking."

He touches his chin. "Woah, heavy."

"Willow, one of my partners, suggested we highlight how it's more than just teens being forced into sex at the Superbowl. The survey data shows it's happening here, but not in the ways we assume." And if I concentrate on the data, maybe the image of my twin having sex with strangers to stay alive will stop haunting me.

Cal studies the people around us, as if he's wondering if any of them could be suffering. The edge of his lip catches between his teeth and his nostrils flare, then he purses his lips and nods.

I know that look. "No. You're not stealing our idea."

"Not for the project."

"Not for the *Sabre* either."

"But if it's as critical as you're saying, people need to know."

"You're not winning your first Pulitzer with my project idea." Because I truly believe he'll win awards some day. People with his ambition and intelligence don't fade into the background, they climb to the top where everyone can see them shine. It's what keeps me in his orbit, despite my determination to not let anyone get too close.

Be honest. That's not why you don't want him to write it. You're afraid to find out what happened to me.

A shiver runs over my skin, breaking me from my future-Cal daydream. When I pause, I inadvertently make eye contact with my new neighbor. Wes Sherman. New Sherm.

His gaze skims past me, the lack of recognition clear on his face, before nodding at Cal. "LeBlanc," he says.

Cal returns the head nod. "Sherman."

Deep breath. "You know him?"

"Same as anyone else. How do you not know him?"

"He moved into the house next door to mine."

"Huh." We're almost to first period, our classes across the hall from each other. While we see each other throughout the day, this is usually our last time to talk. "Can you come over tonight? And not after a run. For dinner."

Shuffling the schedule with Mom can wreak havoc, as proven by her mood since spring break ended, but as I keep telling Dad, I have a life to live and I'm not spending my last few months here playing make-believe with my mother.

"I'll pick you up."

"Marking your territory now that there's a boy next door?" My harsh tone is the opposite of how I feel, and I regret the words as soon as I say them.

You don't deserve him.

His face falls. "You know it's not like that." He closes the space between us until our toes touch. "I want more from you than just sex." His voice is so low I almost don't hear him. Almost. His thumb brushes mine, the gentle caress too intimate for the crowded hallway, and I try to blink away the images that flash through my mind.

Us at college, walking hand in hand across the quad.

Late nights at the college newspaper, stealing kisses while researching stories that will actually change the world.

Sitting across from each other in our first apartment, sipping coffee as we read the morning paper.

Someone bumps me as they pass, and I take a step back.

"Don't tell me you don't want that, too," he says. "I can see it in your eyes. You might have everyone else fooled, but you can't hide it from me."

But I have to. My lips curl in a smile. "Only if your mom's making mashed potatoes."

He smiles back. "I'll text her now." As part of their mission to be the most devout people in Spring Haven, his parents volunteer at several places after work and are rarely home until well after dinnertime. Which leaves a lot of unsupervised time for Cal. But once a week, the LeBlancs have a Pleasantville family dinner before retiring to their respective rooms—den for him, living room for her—where they read or meditate or do whatever it is married couples who are only together for appearances do. And her mashed potatoes are worth the awkward tension that inevitably surfaces when his dad brings up the seminary for the millionth time, even though Cal would rather uncover the truth in the form of hard facts.

"Thanks, Joey." My fingers graze his arm. "And I'm sorry. I know you aren't like that, it's just—"

"You're hard-wired to push people away. I know."

My head jerks back in surprise, but it shouldn't. Cal LeBlanc is one of the smartest guys I know—it's the main reason I'm in this non-relationship with him, aside from his killer smile and grippable hair—and he's hard-wired to find the story in everything. In everyone.

"One of these days, you'll trust me enough to let me in."

Cal can never know about Gen. He says he's understanding, but if he knew how messed up I really am, the softness in his eyes, the private touches, the whispers about how we'll take over the world—it would all end. And while I'm planning to end things before we leave for college, it needs to be on my terms. I need to be the one in control.

"Don't give up on me," I say, hoping it's enough to keep him.

My visits with Mom follow the regular script, with a few asides about the New Sherms next door. Since the moving truck left, it's been quiet. Calm. Just the way I like it.

Gen's visit got bumped up because "practice was cancelled," so when Cal pulls into the driveway, I'm back in my regular clothes—my favorite purple and teal pleated skirt, a white t-shirt, and gray Chucks. He's at the door before I get there, and the next thing I know he's standing in the front hall.

This isn't the first time he's been inside, but Dad's not here to run interference. Mom rarely ventures downstairs, but if she hears a strange voice, she might.

"What's up?" My fingers trail the length of his blue FIRST AMENDMENT shirt, stopping at the belt loop on his gray skinny jeans. Like me, he's wearing Chucks, but unlike me, his are always white. Notes of citrus from his body wash reach me and I inhale, closing my eyes. The combination of lemon and grapefruit has a Pavlovian effect and before he can answer, I'm pulling his head toward mine for a kiss.

He looks over my shoulder at the staircase before our lips meet. "Are your parents home?"

Pointless question since Mom's always home, but he doesn't know the severity of her seclusion. "Just my mom. She's upstairs."

He rewards me with his lips, soft and gentle and unhurried. Kissing Cal LeBlanc is one of my favorite pastimes. His lean arms wrap around me, his bare skin brushing against my upper arms, and my body shifts gears, pushing the kiss deeper.

We could sneak upstairs. He's never been in my room.

My heart races at the thought of sharing another piece of me. Of letting him in. Of inching toward that next step.

If we were quiet, she wouldn't even know we're here.

He'll see my room.

I break the kiss. Our breaths come quickly, his lips still inches from mine. "We should go."

"Can I get a glass of water?"

"Now?"

"That's why I came in."

My gaze drops to the floor as a blush creeps up my neck. Sometimes I wonder what's wrong with me, why I'm always the one thinking about sex first, emotions later.

He touches my chin so I look at him. "I will never complain about kissing you." The corner of his mouth lifts in the smirk that first captured my interest. "I forgot my water bottle at home."

My shoulders relax. What teenage boy would turn down a make-out session, even if he is dying of thirst? "Stay here, I'll go grab a glass."

Leaving him unattended?

She won't leave her room.

At least, I don't think she will. But just in case, I skip the ice maker and pour cool tap water into a glass. I'm turning off the faucet when I hear her voice.

"Oh, hello. And who are you?"

Nooooooooooo no no no no no no no. Thoughts fly through my mind as I race to the stairs.

"I'm Cal, I'm—"

"Hey, Mom. This is Cal LeBlanc."

She's at the top of the stairs, her hand resting lightly on the railing as if she might venture off the second floor. A delighted grin creases her face. "Joey."

Cal laughs. "Eve calls me that sometimes."

"I was just getting him a drink."

"Does Gen know you're here?"

"Mom, we're good. You can go back to your room."

She glances over her shoulder, as if realizing how far from her room she's strayed. "Oh. Yes. My show is about to start."

"It was nice to meet you, Mrs. Ellaway." If Cal's confused, he's covering it well.

"You as well. Eve, can you come with me for a moment?" She turns toward her room and I squeeze Cal's hand.

"Be right back." I take the stairs two at a time, not caring that my skirt flips up. Maybe the brief glimpse of my underwear will make Cal forget what Mom said.

Mom's already in her room, pacing in front of the TV. "I thought Gen was dating Cal?"

"She is. But Cal and I know each other, too."

She stops. "You do?"

"It's a small school, Mom." I don't mention he's on the newspaper because she thinks Gen dates jocks. Athletes. And while Cal runs for exercise, he's about as likely to letter in a sport as I am.

"I remember that from when I was in school. But the different groups didn't mix."

"Now they do." We're face to face, and I'm struck at how much we—I—resemble her. Same height, same dark hair—although hers is streaked with gray. But the distrust in her eyes is new. "Gen and Cal are going to dinner and I'm hanging out with a friend from the paper." Not a lie.

She pats my arm. "Don't be too late, dear."

Mom's never had a say in my curfew, but I smile like the placating daughter that I am. "Of course."

My descent down the stairs is slower.

Cal's waiting in the same spot I left him. "Why did she mention Gen?"

I imagine the wheels in his brain turning as he pieces together the fragments of what I've told him with what he's seen for himself, and realizing they don't match.

I think he'd like me better.

Don't.

You already told Mom I'm dating him.

Let me have this one thing.

"Sometimes she gets confused. It's easier to just go with it." The things I leave unsaid nearly bury me where I stand.

He drags a hand through his hair, making it look better than it did before. "Man, your family is so extra extra."

"No."

He smirks. "I can't pull it off?"

"Not even close. But nice attempt." I move toward the door. "Can we go?"

He sets his glass on the side table near the door, and we step outside. I stumble as I lock eyes with Wes Sherman, who's watering a patch of grass seed in front of his house like he has nothing better to do. Cal catches me with an arm around my waist, and Wes stares like he's piecing together a story that's been right in front of him all along.

"Hey, man," Cal says, ruining any chance for Wes to pretend he didn't see us.

Wes waves, so I wave back.

Aren't you the friendly neighbor.

Fuck off.

If only it were that easy.

Cal opens my door, drying the ink on whatever story Wes has imagined, and I climb in. He's quiet as he backs out of the driveway, perhaps recognizing that I need a moment after the encounter with Mom. Or maybe he's just being an eighteen-year-old boy and thinking about something else entirely.

His hand finds mine in my lap, his thumb stroking my bare leg while he holds my fingers. "You okay?"

I feel like I'm already losing control.

My voice cracks. "Yeah. I can't wait for your mom's mashed potatoes."

The pieces of my carefully constructed world tumble around me, falling beyond my grasp, and no amount of lies will put them back the way they belong.

Seven

APRIL 9

AS A JOURNALIST, THERE'S NOTHING WORSE THAN WHEN YOU'RE ON DEADLINE AND DISCOVER A KEY PIECE OF INFORMATION IS INACCURATE—OR WORSE, A SOURCE LIED—AND THE ENTIRE FOCUS OF THE STORY HAS TO CHANGE. THAT'S HOW I FEEL NOW. A FEW CASUAL WORDS FROM MY MOTHER THREATEN TO UNRAVEL THE HOURS, MONTHS, YEARS I'VE SPENT METICULOUSLY WEAVING MY STORY AND NO MATTER HOW HARD I TRY TO HOLD IT ALL TOGETHER, IF SHE KEEPS UNEARTHING PLOT HOLES, EVEN THE BEST EDITING WON'T KEEP OUR NARRATIVE FROM DISINTEGRATING AROUND ME.

—EE

On Thursday, the sun chases the chill from the air, teasing the first hint of flowers from their winter hibernation and activating a switch in every teen for a hundred miles. Spring fever is real when you live in a place that spends half the year buried under snow and clouds, and a restless energy pulses through the school. Through the students.

Through everyone except me.

Getting swept up in crowd exuberance can be dangerous, especially when one slip can undo years of vigilance. But that's not why I'm resisting nature's pull to let my inner flower child run free. Cal and Ember are the only ones who remember the significance of April 9, the only ones who treat me more gently than normal and allow me to wallow in my darkness.

Because eighteen years ago, on our one-month birthday, my twin sister was kidnapped.

It's hard to blame Dad. Taking his newborn daughters to the park so his wife could rest seemed like the right thing to do. The loving thing to do.

From what I've been told, it was a warm spring day like today, and putting a sleep-deprived parent on a blanket warmed by the sun can only have one outcome. He swore he'd only closed his eyes for a moment, his body wrapped around the wheels of our stroller, as if that could protect us.

Gen never made a sound.

I sometimes wonder if I saw her abductor. If deep in the recesses of my mind lives the face of the person who Picassoed our family, turning us into a splintered, broken imitation of what we could have been.

Even though I was too young to protect her, I live with the regret that I likely watched my sister spirited away from our stroller and out of our lives.

When Dad woke, he didn't know right away that anything was wrong. The typical baby noises coming from my one-month-self assured him we were okay. It wasn't until he sat up that he realized Gen was gone.

And we've been living with the shrapnel of that day ever since.

"Eve, hi. How was your day?" Mom's waiting on her couch, the significance of today's date stopping at the threshold to her room.

Shaking off my true feelings has gotten easier with time, but not today. The ache of longing worsens as I sit on the couch, wrapping around my chest and squeezing until I can't breathe.

Longing not for the sister who barely was, but for my oblivious mother to just once recognize the histrionics I put forth every day. This day. For her.

Gen smiles for me. "It was fine."

"Just fine?"

How can you not comprehend what I'm going through? How Dad and I quietly suffer to protect your fragile mind?

It's too late for that.

Is it?

Deep breath, in and out, while Mom fusses with a ball of orange yarn that even through my desperation, I hope is not for me. The lack of sleeves means it's not a sweater, and I hope it's not yet another scarf.

"This interschool project is really cool. I'm still not sure teen drunk driving was the best idea, but I was outvoted."

Why are you lying about the topic?

It's not worth the risk triggering her by explaining what human trafficking is.

Mom unravels a knot before looking at me. "And you haven't actually met the other kids? That seems strange."

A side effect of Mom secluding herself in her room is she's missed most of the technological advances since 2007. The internet existed, but not the way it does now. Smart phones would blow her mind more than it already is.

"I don't know what they look like. The instructors thought it would be more productive if our work is based purely on our minds and isn't influenced by appearance." I shift so I'm facing her, and her brown eyes meet mine. To the untrained eye she seems properly enthused, but her eyes don't light up the way they do with Gen, and she's gripping her knitting needles like she's waiting for me to leave. The differences are so subtle no one else could possibly notice. My heart insists she isn't aware she's doing it, but I stopped listening to my heart a long time ago.

She unclenches the needles to pat my hand. "I guess I have to take your word on that. Is drunk driving still a problem with teens?"

My eyes close, and I weave another story filled with half-truths and soft corners meant to protect her from the cruel world that took one daughter and has nearly destroyed the other.

Later, after I've changed into Gen's favorite sweatshirt and leggings and am pulling up my hair, grief closes in. Eighteen years. This charade has been my reality for eighteen years.

After that fateful afternoon, Mom and Dad's sleep-deprived worlds went over a cliff and landed in an alternate universe of police reports and news stories and flyers that cried Have You Seen My Baby? For a time, they suspected Dad, as is apparently common with all domestic cases, but reports of an unfamiliar couple trolling the park and a car with out-of-state plates led to the conclusion Gen had been taken. Her kidnapping never reached Jon Benet status, but Baby Gen and Michelle and Larry Ellaway became minor celebrities in the twisted, morbid way tragedies do. People almost forgot they still had a baby at home.

My life has never fully been my own, always shadowed by the almost-sister who has somehow become the center of my universe, and not only does my mother not know the truth, she prefers the sister I invented.

Quit being a baby.

My gaze locks on the mirror, and for a moment I see her. Gen. Not Eve.

You only have yourself to blame.

They started it.

But you made me.

What if I don't want to do this anymore?

You don't have a choice.

With one motion, I yank out my ponytail. My hair falls in messy waves over my shoulders, brushing the top of the word UNIVERSITY on Gen's UVA sweatshirt.

Ooh, you really showed me.

Just stop. Today sucked and I don't need you making it worse.

Better buck up before she catches on.

Deep breath. One. Two. Three. Four. Five—

You can't meditate me away.

I control you. Not the other way around.

That's cute. Now fix your hair and play nice with Mom before she thinks something's wrong.

Six. Seven. Eight. Nine. Ten. With shaky hands I pull up my hair, straighten my sweatshirt, and slap the light switch on my way out of her room.

Mom's in the same spot on the couch, but her knitting is resting in its basket beneath the window and a fresh cup of tea steams on the table in front of her. Some days I wonder how much of her life revolves around waiting for Gen and me, or if her mornings and afternoons have their own routine apart from us. But asking could lead to a spiral that neither Dad nor I can handle. Best to play my part and get out.

"Hi, Mom."

And for the six thousand-five hundred sixty-eighth time, I dance my way through a choreographed routine meant to protect my mother's psyche. And for the four thousand-three hundred-eightieth time, I watch for a sign—any sign—that she sees me.

Eve, not Gen.

And for just as many times, I bid her good night with a smile while my soul screams out for a mother who isn't broken, who can see the world for what it truly is, not an alternate reality created by her grieving husband and unwitting child.

Dad explained that Mom's history of mental illness caused her break with reality, but this type of lie could only happen with his encouragement. Changing a baby's outfits fifteen times a day is common, so he claims he didn't realize what was happening, how she was coping, until she was so far gone there was no turning back. By the time he understood how deeply her mental schism ran, she'd convinced herself I was both Gen and Eve.

Any rational person would march his wife back into her therapist's office and insist that this time the woman he loves would get the help she needs. If not for her, then to protect his remaining daughter. But Dad's guilt over not protecting Gen overshadowed any rational thought, and instead, he played along. What's the harm? They're just babies.

Baby.

Singular.

Most people assume how they're raised is normal. It's not until friends enter the picture and innocent chatter reveals that perhaps what seemed normal is quite the opposite, that the fuzzy edges become clear.

I close Mom's door behind me and hesitate outside Gen's room.

Her silence since our argument feels fragile. History has proven it won't last long and avoiding her room won't keep her quiet. A simmering fear creeps through my chest, wrapping around my lungs until my breath comes in broken gasps. I lean against the door frame—shoulder then head—and close my eyes against the darkness of her room. My pulse races, and the lack of oxygen makes my head spin. Standing on her threshold, I feel caught between two worlds, two realities, and I wonder for the millionth time if it would be easier to just stop. To let her go.

You can't.

You aren't real.

I could be.

This isn't the first time we've had this conversation, but her recent aggressiveness scares me.

I'm not trying to be scary.

Why have you changed?

I want more.

More how?

There's a hesitation, a beat only I can feel.

I want to go outside.

Eight

It's too risky.

Who will see?

The neighbors.

We live on a dead-end street.

No.

Let me take the trash out.

Gen, I can't.

You can. It'll take two minutes.

No.

I want to breathe the night air.

Giving in feels like letting go, but not the way I crave. Taking Gen outside will make her bolder, less compliant, and my grip is already so tenuous.

You're already dressed.

Why can't you understand that it's dangerous?

Why can't you understand that it's such a non-issue?

She keeps arguing, and while I can't block her out, I can refuse to respond. To do whatever it takes to maintain my barely balanced life with Gen trapped inside my head. My hand finds the light switch, and I'm pulling her sweatshirt over my head when the yelling stops. The sudden silence is deafening, intriguing, and my curiosity gets the better of me.

Please.

Her voice is soft. Gentle. Pleading.

The difference in our voices is subtle and this doesn't sound like her. The desperation sounds like me.

Just for a minute.

Fine.

My heart thrums, excitement and anticipation coursing through me. But it feels separate, like it's not actually my body responding.

Thank you.

One. Two. Three—

Don't think. Just go.

My feet carry me down the stairs and into the kitchen. Dad's still at the table and his presence startles me out of Gen's trance. The light is low, the dishwasher humming in the background. Most families would hug to mark the passage of another year, or at least share a moment of grief, but he's focused on the tablet resting on the table alongside an empty whiskey glass. If he's surprised to see me dressed as Gen, he doesn't show it.

"I'm taking the trash out."

His eyes flick to the calendar hanging on the wall, confirming tomorrow is trash day. It's a weird thing to notice, a weird thing for him to check, but perhaps my mounting panic is sharpening every detail.

Or perhaps he's offended a chore as insignificant as taking out the trash must happen on this most ominous anniversary.

Even though I've read every detail in old newspapers, Gen's boldness urges me to ask about that day. But we don't talk about that anymore. When I was little, Dad seemed to be the devoted father I needed, when in reality his focus was on keeping our secret safe, on directing me in what would become the never-ending performance of my life.

He made the rules when I started preschool. Not talking about Mom or Gen was easy enough. It's the special time that's spiraled into something neither of us could have ever imagined.

Dad looks up, his bloodshot eyes unfocused. "Thanks." The near-whisper sounds abrasive, like he hasn't spoken in awhile and has forgotten how to form the simplest words.

Go.

I remove the full bag. Tie it off. Replace the fresh bag. All the while waiting for Dad to swim to the surface of his grief and Spot the One Thing That's Wrong With This Picture.

His gaze never fully focuses—not on me, not on anything—and soon drifts back to his darkened tablet.

Quit stalling.

With a shaky breath, I pick up the bag and step into the night. A near-full moon lights the porch and the tree in the front yard drooping with spring buds.

Is it everything you hoped for?

And more.

My eyes roll. No one can see me, but she knows.

Thank you.

The softness in her voice tugs at something deep inside me. As much as we bicker, I don't know how I'd get through the day without her.

Awwww.

Shut up.

The trash bin sits on a cement pad next to the garage. It's only half-full, but there's no turning back now. I toss in the bag, then pull the bin down the long driveway. My breath hitches with each squeak of the wheel until my pulse roars in my ears.

Someonewillsee.

Someonewillsee.

Someonewillsee.

You're being ridiculous.

You don't understand the lengths I've gone to, the lies and deceptions and half-truths that have kept you a secret. To make people forget about Baby Ellaway.

Dad coached you well.

I still have his rules in my nightstand drawer.

The trash bin shudders to a stop at the end of the driveway, settling into the groove separating our white concrete from the blacktop of the street with a raspy scratch of plastic on pavement.

Was that so hard?

Harder than you know.

The moon winks behind a cloud and I look up at the same moment a door slams. My internal voice—not Gen, my voice—yells to run, but I freeze as plastic drags across the concrete. Wheels squeak. Footsteps grow near.

The cloud shifts and Wes Sherman appears in the bright moonlight as if some omniscient director decided he deserved an entrance worthy of the star he is. He pauses when he sees me, our hands locked on the handles of our respective trash bins.

"Hey." I've heard him speak at school, but his voice has never been directed at me.

He could be fun.

No.

Say hello back.

"Hi."

He gives me a once over that makes my skin crawl. Do girls usually go for that? "You look cute like that."

My head drops to look at my outfit, as if I could forget I'm dressed as Gen. "Of course you'd think so."

His head cocks. "What's that supposed to mean?"

"Nothing." Just that you've only ever seen me in my uniform of skirts and Chucks and now you decide to comment on my outfit?

"I was just trying to be nice. You know, since we're neighbors." He nods at my chest, at Gen's school of choice. "I thought you got into Northwestern?"

Heat rushes through me as questions tumble over each other. Why does he know that? Why does he know anything about me? Why is he watching me with a casual smile, like this is the most normal thing in the world? Regardless of his motivation, his proximity is dangerous. And the longer I stand outside dressed as Gen the slipperier my control over the situation gets. Nothing good can come from Wes Sherman infiltrating into my life and he needs to know that now.

"Don't waste your energy." The bin shudders as I shove it into place, my footsteps echoing off the pavement in a staccato that matches my racing heart. I don't turn around to see if he's watching me flee. I don't want to know if I'll stay in his mind after he goes inside. And I don't want to imagine what could happen if he keeps asking questions.

Dad doesn't move when I burst into the kitchen, so I bypass him and sprint upstairs. Slam Gen's door behind me. Rip out the ponytail and yank off her traitorous UVA sweatshirt. Tears burn but the rage bubbling inside me stops them from falling. This is my fault. I created Gen. I'm the one who made her a better version of myself, so it shouldn't surprise me if people like her better. Wes Sherman has never so much as glanced at me but the moment I step outside dressed as the figment of my imagination, he suddenly wants to be friends.

Calm down. He was just being nice.

I hope you enjoyed that because it's never happening again.

A beat passes. Then another. I can feel her thinking, calculating, waiting.

Her silence feels weighted. She has more to say but it's like she recognizes that anything that rolls through my head right now is likely to push me off the deep end.

And we both know how that works in our family.

I wake with a start. Hints of the sunrise streak across unfamiliar walls and it takes me a moment to realize I fell asleep in Gen's room. Mine gets the sunset. My phone blinks with unread messages—probably Cal with his usual goodnight texts—and I turn off the alarm that's set to go off in another ten minutes.

Her room feels different in the morning. It's never been cozy, but the muted sunlight diffuses the sharp edges that threaten to trip me up, unravel my lies, and leave me naked and alone on the beige carpet. In this moment, the constant worry that SOMEONE WILL FIND OUT shifts from a roiling boil to a slow simmer. My neck's stiff from sleeping curled up at the end of the bed, but I feel rested. Ready to finish the week strong.

My newfound confidence stumbles when I see Wes at school before first period. Cal and I pass him at the same spot as before, they exchange their bro-code head nods, but then he pauses and smiles at me.

"Eve," he says, like we're old friends and I didn't leave him gawking in his driveway last night.

My exhale speaks for me as I hurry down the hall.

"What was that about?" Cal asks.

"I don't need another friend."

His hand grazes my elbow. "Did something happen?"

My forced smile—a Gen smile—smooths the crease between his brows. "He was just trying to be nice. I wasn't in the mood."

He snorts a laugh. "I almost feel bad for him."

I stop abruptly. People move around me like I'm Moses parting the Red Sea, but it takes Cal a second to realize I'm no longer next to him. When he turns around, his face wears a mask of apology.

"I just mean—"

My raised hand stops him. "Don't."

"Eve, you know I didn't mean anything. It's hardly a secret you like to be left alone." His words spill over themselves. "That's all I was trying to say."

It's taken years to get everyone to leave me alone so I can't get mad when they take the hint. People glance at us as they head to first period, and their curiosity makes my cheeks burn. Journalism first appealed to me because it keeps me behind the scenes while the attention-seekers bask in the spotlight.

So why'd you put me on the soccer team?

Momentary weakness.

You can lie to yourself all you want. I know the truth.

I don't want to be popular.

But you want to be seen.

The warning bell rings. Cal's still watching me.

I shake Gen away. "I'm sorry I overreacted. I know you didn't mean anything by it."

"You know I'd never hurt you, right?" He reaches for my arm, but I pull back.

"I just can't right now." One of my rules is no PDA and even though he's subtly touched me a million times, there's a difference between in the *Sabre* office and standing in front of half the senior class.

His lips form a hard line and his gaze settles on something over my shoulder. "Well, I can't deal with you when you're like this." Then he walks away before I can stop him.

Friday night carried me down an internet sub-forum wormhole filled with stories of trafficking survivors, some of whom are still trapped in their hellish realities. Even though it's less common for kids to be trafficked from the child welfare system, I can't stop wondering if that's what happened to Gen. People don't typically steal babies to force them into servitude, but who knows if she's with the same person who took her or if she's been passed along a string of miscreants since she was taken. When I came across one girl's account of being kidnapped as a child, I return to the safer topics in my New York Times daily emails.

All while assuring Cal I don't hate him, which inevitably led to me promising we'd hang out Sunday.

But for now, Saturday belongs to me.

After our morning check-ins with Mom—one hundred thirty-six days until that's over—I slip on my running shoes and head for the lake. Running tights and a fitted jacket will keep me warm once I get into a rhythm, but right now my hands and cheeks sting with the cold.

I'm on alert during the two blocks to the lake. The same people have lived in our neighborhood since I was a child, so obligation and familial respect force me to say hello to anyone I pass. Dog walkers, fellow joggers, and the occasional neighbor doing yard work each chip away at my reserve of energy until I'm almost depleted. When my feet hit the sand, I can breathe again.

The air is still, the lake flat. Some days it's churning so violently I want to fling myself into the water to forget about life, but other days, like today, the calmness centers me. Years of waves have eaten away at the dunes that creep toward the lake, creating a six-foot cliff that blocks out the rest of the world. Seagulls hover lazily over the beach grass dotting the land above me. Aside from tire marks from cyclists, there's zero evidence of human life.

My thoughts volley between Cal and the project with each slap of my shoes on the sand.

For not wanting to be in a relationship, I sure spend a lot of time worrying about his feelings and imagining what our lives could be like if I stopped holding back and let my emotions get the best of me.

Considering my sister was kidnapped, researching human trafficking should be freaking me out more than it is. The writer in me fills in the gaps of any story, and the mystery of Gen's disappearance is no different. Odds are she's safe and happy and living in Arizona or Kansas with a family who adores her. It's doubtful she's been forced into slave labor, working and living in a darkened room with no hope for a better future. But it's impossible not to picture her face—my face—with each story I read.

The frigid lake water laps inches from my feet as the sun warms my cheeks, and I push out thoughts of Cal and human trafficking. My ponytail swings low against my back—the opposite of Gen's perky style—and soon my breathing levels and my mind clears.

Until footsteps sound behind me.

I move closer to the sandy cliff so the person has to run closer to the water, but they don't pass me. A glance over my shoulder wipes away my good mood.

Wes Sherman.

He's wearing an outfit similar to mine and an infuriating half-smile that probably makes other girls swoon.

"Quit stalking me."

"Get over yourself." Despite what I deserve, his tone isn't harsh or angry. He sounds amused. And he's matching my stride.

I pick up the pace, stretching my legs as far as they'll go until we're sprinting side-by-side along the shore. The wooden steps of an overlook dangle over the sand a hundred yards ahead. If he's still with me when I reach it, I'll talk to him.

Seventy-five yards.

Fifty. And he's pulling ahead.

Shit.

At twenty-five, he's a length ahead of me with no sign of slowing down.

I dig deep and push with everything I've got, but he passes the overlook two strides before me. We slow in unison, coming to a stop beneath a tuft of beach grass clinging to the edge of the dune. My hands drop to my knees as I catch my breath.

"How the fuck are you so fast?"

He mirrors my stance. If my language bothers him, he doesn't show it. "Soccer. How are you so fast?"

My hand gestures at the lake stretched out as far as we can see. "This is my soccer field."

"You out here a lot?"

"That depends."

"On what?"

"If you plan to keep stalking me."

He laughs under his breath. "I go for long runs on the weekend. When we lived near Hofma, I ran there." He shrugs. "Now I run here."

"I'm out here at least five days a week." I brace for a witty comeback, but he straightens and stares over the calm water.

"It's gorgeous out here."

"Yeah."

"I can see why you love it."

Did I say that? No, but it's simple to deduce if I run here almost every day.

"So what's the deal with your mom?"

My blood turns to ice. Goosebumps race up my arms and I'm sure my pupils are twice their normal size. When I first started school—when the rules were brand new—the adults knew better than to press a four-year old about her missing sister and my fellow paste-eaters were the only ones who'd never heard of Baby Ellaway. Sometimes I stumbled, but instead of ostracizing me, my friends included my imaginary friend in our games.

Acting as if Gen never disappeared got easier.

Wes is still facing the water, unaware of the reaction his words have caused. I clear my throat. "What do you mean?"

"They're not divorced, right?"

My head shakes on its own. "No." Where is he going with this?

Another shrug from shoulders that have never born the weight of the world. "I haven't seen her since we moved in. But as far as anyone knows, you still live with her."

"You asked about me?"

"I didn't send out a survey or anything. Just asked a couple friends."

"We don't have the same friends."

He shrugs again, and everything about him is relaxed. The way his weight is on one foot, his arms loose at his sides. His hair messy with sweat but still somehow styled. "So are you and Cal a thing?"

"What did your friends say?" The word "friends" comes out on a sneer, and I kick sand into the water to cover my lapse of control.

"The guys think you're dating. The girls think you need to stop stringing him along."

My head snaps up. "Who said that?"

"Lissa and Audrey."

Hahahhahhahahahahhahahahahhahahha.

Shut. Up.

My BFFs hate you.

That's not what he said.

"Why are they wasting their energy on me?" The irony is too much. Of all the people for him to bring up, it has to be her. I turn so he can't see my face, see the anger and frustration mounting with each passing breath.

"They're not bad people."

"Yet they spend their time ruminating about who I am or am not dating."

"People talk. Get curious. They don't mean anything by it."

I whirl back on him. "So now that you live next door, they've put you up to asking?"

"It's not like that." He pushes a hand through his hair. "We're neighbors. No ulterior motive. Believe it or not, I'm trying to be friendly." The redness of his face is no match for mine, but it's clear this isn't how he saw our conversation going.

That doesn't mean I'm going to make it any easier on him.

I tap my nonexistent watch, my fury rising with each beat of my heart. "By my count you've got eighteen more questions. What else do you need to know? My bra size? Favorite fruit?"

He steps back and rests a foot on the sandy cliff behind him. Crosses his arms. Doesn't leave. "Is this where I'm supposed to run away?"

"Yes."

"Not happening."

"Why?" I cross and uncross my arms. My body's recovered from the sprint and I still have another couple miles left in me. Standing at the edge of the lake arguing with a guy who seems completely unflustered when I can't manage to get through a conversation without being pissed off is not how I plan on spending the morning. "Because we're not friends. You—" I wave a hand at him, dismissing his general state of being, "—do not fit into my world."

"What's wrong with making new friends?"

Of course everything comes easily for Wes Sherman. He doesn't have to worry about people discovering his secrets because he doesn't have anything to hide.

"You can't be serious."

The creases around his eyes deepen as he watches me, and his mouth tightens into a firm line.

"We graduate in a month and I'm getting the hell out of Dodge. What's the point?"

He shrugs, and I want to shake the gesture out of his system. "You seem like you could use a friend."

Everything about him seems genuine, from his unassuming pose to the way he watches me without coming too close, but letting someone in goes against every fiber of my being.

He could be good for you.

How?

I dunno. Get you out of your shell.

The mocking in her tone makes me want to claw at my ears until I can never hear her again. But her words linger, settling against my racing heart until I look up at Wes. "Why would you want to be friends with me?"

His relaxed smile steals its luminance from the sun. "I like to know people who are real, and you're about the realest person I've ever met."

Nine

IN THE MOMENTS WHEN I LET MYSELF WORRY ABOUT WHAT EVERYONE THINKS, I WONDER WHAT THEY WONDER ABOUT ME. IF THEY HAVE A CLUE ABOUT THE TWISTED GAME I'M FORCED TO PLAY. IF THEY HAVE ANY IDEA THAT SOME DAYS IT TAKES ALL MY STRENGTH JUST TO BLEND IN.

TOO MANY PEOPLE ARE TRYING TO GET PAST MY DEFENSES. BETWEEN THE FORUM AND NEW SHERM, I'M MIXING NEW LIES WITH OLD AND SOONER OR LATER I'M GOING TO SLIP. DESPITE WHAT GEN THINKS, THIS SECRET CANNOT GET OUT. NOT JUST FOR MY SAKE, BUT FOR MOM'S.

FIVE WEEKS UNTIL GRADUATION. ONLY ONE HUNDRED THIRTY-FOUR MORE DAYS UNTIL I CAN STOP PRETENDING. UNTIL I CAN FINALLY BE FREE.

—EE

Wes's comment about Lissa and Audrey thinking I'm stringing Cal along followed me all weekend, so much that I canceled our Sunday plans. Maybe they're right. He's made it clear he wants more, however pointless it may be, so I should give him the chance to have the clichéd end-of-the-year romance before we leave for college.

"Mom's latest project is starting to take shape. Care to change your wager?" Dad's watching me over his cup of coffee, eyebrows raised. This is standard morning banter for us. Don't ask for details. Keep things light as we eat our bowls of cereal. Never address the one-hundred thirty-five-pound elephant pacing upstairs.

"I still say scarf."

He nods. "You ready for the new week?"

A lie forms in my mouth, something easy and casual to keep him at arm's length, but Mom's indifference over the forum project chooses that moment to sneak up my back and dig its claws into me. "This has to stop."

"What?"

My chair squeaks as I push away from the table. "This." I stab a hand at the ceiling and yell loud enough that she could hear me if she tried. "This can't go on forever."

The thunk of Dad's coffee cup on the table, followed by a sigh that says he's carrying eighteen years of worries on his shoulders, sets my nerves on edge. Just once I'd like him to raise his voice and yell back.

To apologize for not trying harder to help Mom.

To care about me.

"Seriously, Dad. How long can this go on?" My feet carry me in brisk circles on my side of the table, my breathing as labored as my thoughts. "I've already made up the bullshit about Virginia. Am I supposed to get two degrees? Have two Zoom accounts? Don't you think my roommate will think it's weird if half my room is a shrine to UVA, just so my crazy-ass mom doesn't realize Gen is calling her from Northwestern?"

I honestly hadn't thought about the room situation until I said it out loud, but hearing the words proves how unsustainable this charade is. Dad's hand hovers next to his coffee cup like he planned on taking a drink but is too stunned to move. But I'm not done.

"Then what? Two careers? Ooh, and two husbands? Two families?" A maniacal laugh bubbles to my lips, but the disbelief on Dad's face stifles it. "Some people are into kinky stuff, but

I don't think anyone will tolerate this house of horrors you've created." I stop in front of my chair and level my gaze on his. "Why don't we just kill Gen off? Like they do on TV. Then Eve goes off to college and lives happily ever after."

You wouldn't dare.

At first, I'm not sure if it's Dad or Gen who spoke, but Dad seems frozen in place.

"I never imagined it would get to this point. I—I didn't know..." His gaze drops to the table.

"Didn't know? What exactly do you think about when you're sipping your coffee and gazing out the window? About how perfect your family is? Because I gotta tell you—"

He holds up a hand. "I had the best intentions when I... when we—"

"When you gave me a list of rules about my nonexistent sister?"

"I didn't know it would turn out this way. I know it's been difficult, but—"

"Difficult? Calculus is difficult. The SATs were difficult. This is a lifetime of manipulations with no end in sight. A psychotic freak-show no one would ever believe."

His eyes widen. "Have you told anyone?"

And like that, my anger deflates. It doesn't matter how much I rant or rage or threaten to end my performance, in the end his primary concern is Mom.

Mom.

Not Eve.

I'm nothing more than a puppet that role-plays as her missing sister whenever they command.

"No, Dad. I haven't told anyone."

But maybe you should.

"We'll figure out a way to... to let you have a life." He doesn't continue, because every scenario ends with Mom suffering, and we both know that will never be an option.

My foul mood is noticeable at school. Cal keeps his distance in the *Sabre*, barely saying hello when I arrive and getting right to business on this week's assignments. His indifference piques my interest, and what does that say about how horrible a person I am? We lock eyes during a discussion about the baseball team's advancement to regionals, but he breaks it with a heavy sigh and a hand through his hair. His lean arms flex when he does it and I kick myself for canceling on him. Relationship or not, Cal's hot and spending up close and personal time with him is the best distraction I have from my screwed-up life.

"I'm sorry I bailed yesterday," I say as we step into the hallway.

His eyes stay trained ahead of us and his elbow doesn't bump mine. "You keep saying we're not dating. Maybe it's time I listened to you."

My stomach flips. This is what I keep insisting I want, so why does this feel like when Dad took away my favorite blankie?

Because you're selfish. Set the blankie free.

I risk a look at him. "Is that what you want?"

His jaw ticks while he considers my words. Finally, his shoulders relax and he stops to face me. "No. What I want is for you to get your head out of your ass and realize how good we are together. I don't know what spooked you this weekend, but nothing has changed."

Everything has changed.

Wes Sherman chooses that moment to appear. "Hey, Cal. Eve." He nods as if him greeting both of us is a normal thing. "Great run Saturday." Then he's gone.

If I watch closely, I can see the trajectory of Wes's words as they leave his mouth and travel the space to Cal's brain, see their meaning settle into him and jealousy flare from his nostrils. He takes a step back. "I see how it is."

My eyes roll on their own and it only increases his anger. "We were both running on the beach. Separate. We stopped and talked.

End of story." Explaining myself, trying to ease his jealousy, feels like a slippery slope into couplehood. But it's the truth.

"But you won't run with me." He pushes a hand through his hair. "You can be so hot and cold. Some days you act like you only keep me around to sleep with me when it's convenient for you."

"Is that really how you feel?"

He nods, a quick jerk of his head.

I reach for his arm, and he doesn't pull away, but he also doesn't look at me. "Things are shitty at home. I was just trying to spare you my mood yesterday. Wes Sherman is a non-issue."

"Can we go for a run tomorrow?" He's so used to the excuse he's stopped asking for details because he knows I won't elaborate. But right now, his trusting eyes leave only one option. If I say no, I'm saying goodbye to al for good, and as much as I don't want to admit it, I need him. When I'm with him, I believe the goodness he sees in me and sometimes that's the only thing carrying me through the day.

"Yes."

When I see Wes before lunch, my temper simmers to a rolling boil. The only reason I don't shove him into the bank of lockers he's casually walking by with two friends is to avoid the gossip that would follow. The last thing I need is my name linked with Wes Sherman's.

"Wes."

My tone stops him. He waves his friends off and his smile falls as he approaches. "Why do I feel like I'm in trouble?"

"Don't act like you didn't do that on purpose."

He looks around like an explanation for my attitude is on the prom posters plastered to the walls. "Actually, going to lunch was one hundred percent on purpose. I didn't realize I needed your permission." He crosses his arms over his chest, relaxed and ready for whatever I throw back at him.

"I'm talking about what you said in front of Cal."

His brows raise. "About running?"

My glare should send him on his way, but he just stands there, all casual with his cocky smirk that makes me want to claw out his eyeballs.

"If you're not really dating, what's the difference?"

My pulse roars in my head. I'm starting to sweat, and I hate that he's causing this reaction in me. Wes Sherman hasn't earned the right for my headspace. "Is that what this is about? Are you trying to prove a point? Maybe free him up for Lissa or Audrey?"

My insides still for a moment, like Gen wants to say something but has chosen to hold her tongue, then my frustration whips my insides into a frenzy. The edges of my vision get fuzzy and the only thing I can hear is my pulse roaring in my ears.

He reaches for my arm but wisely stops before making contact. A few heads turn our way—Eve Ellaway and Wes Sherman live in separate worlds and this conversation has already lasted too long to go unnoticed. "Eve, I swear I didn't mean anything by it. I had fun running and this morning was the first time I've seen you since then. If LeBlanc has an issue with us being friends, that's on him."

"We're not friends."

"You keep saying that."

"So why won't you listen?"

This time he does touch my arm, a gentle brush that directs me out of the flow of traffic and against the lockers. "I meant what I said Saturday. You seem like you could use a friend."

"And why is that your concern?" I've spent half my life pushing people away to keep my secret safe, but being the angry girl whose sister was kidnapped gets really lonely. Ember's my only real friend, but I still keep her from getting too close. And Cal, well, Cal may know me the best physically, but he's barely scraped the surface.

"Because we're neighbors."

"And that's it?"

He smirks. "What, you want a fling before school ends?"

A laugh escapes me, a short burst of air that surprises us both. As cute as he is, cocky soccer players aren't in the same solar system as anyone I'm romantically interested in. Even if he does seem sincere.

"Absolutely not."

But having another person around to talk to, who doesn't want anything from me other than friendship, might be nice. At some point, I have to stop pushing people away, and it'll be good practice for when I go to college. "This doesn't mean you're suddenly my best friend. But I'll try not to be a bitch when I see you."

"You have a strange definition of friendship."

"This was your idea."

A darkness flickers over his face, aging him for a moment before his smile returns. But it's not the cocky smile from before. It's gentler, like he's trying to lull me into trusting him.

You should tell him.

My breath stops short. Gen's comments tend to be contrary or manipulative, like she can't stand not being a full part of the conversation and wants to see me flail in front of the unknowing twits—her words—I call friends. But this feels different. Dangerous. Like she's setting me up for something and I can't feel deep enough inside myself to know what it is.

"I—I have to go." Our shoulders bump as I step past him and hurry to lunch.

Ember's already at our table when I slide my tray next to hers, and she watches me with a practiced patience while I unwrap my sandwich. "What happened?"

"Wes Sherman."

She cocks her head and scans the cafeteria until she spots him at his usual table. "The soccer player?"

I nod while I take a bite.

"How do you even know him? Beyond the fact that he's Wes Sherman."

"He's my new neighbor."

"And this displeases you because?"

"He wants to be friends."

"And you don't like people." It's not a question, and it stings more than it should.

"I like you."

She smiles, but there's a hesitation to her movements, like maybe she isn't sure what I truly think of her. A strand of freshly dyed hair—purple this time, which matches her skirt—falls forward, shielding her face. "And I like you."

Our words hangs between us, mingling with the seriousness in Wes's eyes before I left him, and I need a moment to straighten out my thoughts. "Can I ask why?"

"Why I like you?"

"Yeah. As you said, I don't like people. I push them away. So why are you my friend?"

She slides her tray toward the center of the table and rests her elbows on the edge. "He really screwed with your head." When I don't contradict her, she continues. "You don't take anyone's bullshit, but more than that, you call them out on it. You stick up for people when they deserve it and you encourage me when I don't." Her gaze drops. "When things got bad with my parents, you helped me more than you realize."

A lump catches in my throat. The weeks after Ember's parents found out she's gay, a darkness overshadowed her love for Claire. The longer her parents didn't speak to her, the more she feared she'd have to choose between her relationship with Claire and the relationship with her parents. Some days I'm still not sure both will survive.

Ember sniffs, then her smile brushes away memories of last semester. "You're an amazing writer with a brain that frightens me. And you're funny when you don't let that brain get in the way."

My mouth lifts in a smile. "My brain frightens you?"

If she knew the half of it.

She tucks her hair behind her ear. "Only some of the time." Her fingers trail over the edge of her tray. "You're the most genuine person I know and I respect that."

My stomach knots. Genuine means free from pretense, authentic, real. And while my opinions are certainly authentic, the layers to my true self are so deep and convoluted it'd take an excavation team years to reach my soul.

Ember's watching me, waiting for a response. Her normally smooth forehead is creased, her lower lip caught between her teeth like she's not sure how I'll react.

My pulse slows until I feel almost relaxed.

"Now do me!"

I choke on my water. "I'm sorry, what?"

Ember's laughter causes heads to turn our way. We're one of the quiet tables—part of our unspoken agreement to let the popular clique horde the attention so we can get through high school under the radar. Changing hair colors notwithstanding.

"Tell me why you're friends with me."

"This is easy." I lean back in my seat and count off on my fingers. "You follow your heart even when your family makes it impossible. You're loyal and funny and smart and an amazing designer who's going to crush it in a big city where I can come visit." The smile that brightens her face fills me with a lightness that burns away the bitterness from earlier, and I don't look in Wes Sherman's direction a single time.

But that lightness doesn't last.

The residual indignation from this morning's argument with Dad reignites after lunch and I take it out on my afternoon run. The lake accepts my deepening fury like she always does, absorbing my unspeakable thoughts like an old friend who's seen it all, heard it all, and offers only comfort and acceptance. My anger lifts as I pound my feet on her shore until all I feel is my breath expanding my lungs, filling me with a glimmer of hope that soon, soon, this will be over and I can start my new life.

That hope crashes when I round the corner onto my street. Wes Sherman is stretching in his front yard with his back to me. Unless I cut through the woods and approach the house from the opposite side, he'll see me. I don't have the energy to deal with him but I'm too tired for a hike through the woods.

My feet slow.

Maybe he won't see me.

With careful steps, I approach my driveway. And kick a stone, which ricochets off Betty's hubcap.

Wes turns. "Eve, hey." His tone is unassuming, like he's tired from practice and is just being polite. His arms hang at the side of his sweaty T-shirt, and he does the single nod that's become the standard greeting among guys my age.

Give him a chance.

What do you see in him that I don't?

He seems genuine.

That word again.

It feels risky.

Live a little. You'll be gone soon so what difference does it make?

What if he finds out?

What if you tell him?

Why the fascination with Wes Sherman? You've never cared about the people in my life.

Maybe I want a friend.

Curiosity gets the better of me and I pause in front of Betty. "How was practice?"

He crosses the yard, stopping at the edge of his property. Close, but not too close. "Brutal. Coach Hendricks assumes we slack off on the weekends and runs our asses into the ground on Mondays."

"But since you don't slack off, it shouldn't be so bad, right?" He was fast as hell sprinting on the beach but right now he looks like he ran a marathon.

"Hendricks brings new meaning to the word sadistic."

"Ouch."

"Yeah."

He lifts his arms over his head and leans from side to side, revealing toned abs. "Want to see something cool?"

My arms cross over my chest. “Is this a ploy to get me in your room? I told you, I’m not interested.”

“Relax. It’s in the backyard.” His hand runs through his damp hair, making it stand on end. “And I know you’re with LeBlanc. I swear I’m not looking for anything but friendship.”

“Because you think I need a friend.”

“Do you trust me?”

“Not really. But I believe you.”

“Is there a difference?”

“There is to me.”

“Come on.” With a jerk of his head, he moves toward the space between our houses, his lifetime of kept promises and minimal disappointments assuring him I’ll follow.

Which I do.

Ten

The backyard, once an overgrown jungle of weeds surrounding an abandoned garden, has been hacked and groomed until it resembles something almost suburban. Plastic Adirondack chairs ring a stone fire pit a few steps from the small wooden deck. Dark soil fills the garden, like it's ready for a fresh start. The manicured lawn makes our yard look unruly, and my gaze travels over the similar deck to my house. From here, the secrets that usually feel all-consuming seem tucked away, less scary. Standing in this yard, my neighbor's yard, our house looks like any other house.

"Wes, this looks great! When did you do all this?"

"Not that," he says over his shoulder, still moving across the yard. "Up there." He nods at the large maple tree at the far edge of the yard. A series of two-by-fours create a makeshift ladder up the trunk, leading to a wooden structure nestled in the lower branches.

"It's still there?" Grainy memories of playing in the treehouse as a child flash through my mind. Each wall has a small window, perfect for surveilling from any direction, and a hatch on the bottom serves as the entrance. The wood is worn, the paint long gone, but it's solid. Safe.

Was I Gen or Eve on those days? And how did I not realize it's still here?

"I loved playing up here when I was a kid." He studies the boards nailed into the trunk like he's making a decision. "I haven't been up since we moved in."

Vague memories of a younger Wes running around the backyard flit through my mind. Does he remember us playing together? I push those thoughts away, my innate curiosity to learn every detail of a story tugging me toward the tree. My hand reaches for a board that's chest-high, and my foot steps on the lowest rung. Years of snow and ice have worn the wood to a smooth finish. "Want to check it out?"

His laughter behind me makes me pause. I glance at him over my shoulder, expecting the usual mocking expression I've come to expect from people at school, but a soft smile warms his face. "Just when I think I've got you figured out."

The anxiety that lives in my every interaction relaxes, just for a moment.

"But let me go first. If these boards don't hold, I should be the one to fall."

"How gentlemanly of you."

"My mom would kill me if you got hurt."

Mom. The word rolls out of his mouth like an afterthought, like breakfast or sleep or TV. A part of the greater whole that makes up his life, not the center of his universe around which every decision, every deception, every lie, is based.

I step back from the tree and wave my arm with a flourish. "Well then, by all means."

He starts slowly, tugging each board to see if it'll support his weight before climbing higher. "Gramps knew what he was doing. These aren't going anywhere." When he reaches the top, he punches the hatch open and pulls himself up in one fluid movement. Then his head appears in the opening. "Your turn."

My ascent is slower. Even though he made it up safely, I don't trust easily and I need to see for myself that the boards will hold. When my head pokes through the opening in the floor, he offers a hand. His skin is warm against mine, and I'm grateful for the lack of fluttering butterflies or other blood-pumping reaction. Wes Sherman can only fit into my life as a friend.

A pair of plastic chairs sits in a corner surrounded by dead leaves and a platoon of dusty Army men long defeated by harsh Michigan winters. Wes uprights the chairs and sets one near the window facing our backyards. He sits in the other and waits for me to join him.

My focus stays on the room, this childhood haven that hasn't been touched in years, because I'm terrified to look out the window. To discover what he might be able to see.

"Sit." It's not a command or a question, merely an invitation to come to his level in the cramped space.

My perch in the chair by the window gives me a direct view into Mom's room. The house looks smaller from this perspective, but the normalcy I felt while in the yard evaporates the longer I stare. "Did you spend a lot of time up here?"

"When I was a kid, yeah." Caution laces his words, like he realizes something serious lurks beneath my question, even if he isn't sure what it is. "When my parents first split up, I spent a lot of afternoons up here hiding from the world."

Did I not notice him then? "When was that?"

"Seventh grade."

Around the time Gen made her debut in my mind. No wonder I didn't realize there was a boy next door. "Do you still see your dad?"

"Not if I can help it."

Eye contact feels too personal for this conversation, and my gaze drifts out the window.

He nods at my house. "Is that your room?"

He could be looking at any of the second-story windows, but intuition warns he's focused on Mom's. "Mine's the one in the middle, next to the bathroom. My parents' room is on the end closest to your house."

"Cool."

Because how else do you reply to a completely mundane report of facts.

My eyes find his and I force a smile. "Thanks for improving

the view. From the window, I mean." A blush heats my cheeks and he laughs softly.

"My pleasure." He leans forward, elbows on knees. "Actually, it's my pleasure now that it's done. I think Gramps fed those weeds just to mess with us after he died. It was like a frickin' jungle back here."

His words wash over me, tickling away my concern. He's just a nice boy who thinks I need a friend. He's not a threat. Talking to him won't hurt anything.

A movement in Mom's window catches my eye and my body stills. She's facing our backyard, one hand resting on the window frame, too far away to tell where she's actually looking. If she sees us. I push my chair away from the window. The wooden wall scratches my bare arm and I lean into it, grateful for the tactile sensation, for the distraction from wondering if Mom's looking for me or for Gen.

"Tell me what's going on."

My previous impression of Wes as a dumb jock who's only concerned with sports and being popular is clearly inaccurate. He's still leaning forward, hands clasped in front of him, eyes on mine like he can draw the truth from me if he stares hard enough.

But I've got years of experience resisting people who just want what's best for me. "I can't."

"I thought we were friends now."

"I don't even know you."

He looks at his hands, giving me a break from his sudden intensity. "Maybe it's better that way. Sometimes it's easier to tell your secrets to a stranger." His words carry the heaviness of a truth he hasn't yet shared. He lets out a breath like he's deciding something. "What if I share something first?"

My sarcastic laugh breaks the tension. "You show me yours and I'll show you mine?"

He leans back in his chair and runs a hand through his drying hair. "Something like that."

"Whatcha got, soccer boy?"

He raises an eyebrow, and I want to lunge at my words, pull them out of the air and his brain and stuff them back in my mouth where they belong. Because my cavalier impulse to impress him, to be seen as more than the angry reporter girl, just agreed to tell him a secret.

His gaze explores the small room, a space built for holding confessions about petty vandalism and other eight-year-old secrets, not the psyche-bending enigma that has become my reality.

"When my dad left," he pauses and I sit upright. He's not wasting time. "He didn't just leave us, he wiped out the bank account. Mom's got a good job but we've struggled ever since. Gramps kept telling us to move in with him, but she was too proud. Said she wasn't moving back home."

"But then he died."

"He'd been sick for a while so it wasn't a surprise, but she's taking it pretty hard. The house is paid for so..." he trails off, leaving the rest unspoken.

"I'm sorry. That sounds rough." With everything that's bad in my life, the one constant is my parents' love for each other. They may have split my life in half, but I've never doubted the impetus behind Dad's decisions or had to worry if we had enough money to pay the bills. Wes's beat-up truck takes on new significance. In the odd moment I allowed myself to speculate, I assumed its condition was a reverse status thing. Like he was telling everyone he doesn't need flashy things to be popular, that his sparkling personality and skills on the soccer field were enough. But I was projecting my own issues on him. He's just a guy trying to get through high school like everyone else.

He watches me with a wary expression, but I can't tell if it's because he's worried I'll tell his secret or that I won't reciprocate.

"My turn, eh?"

When Cal and I started spending more time together, it became impossible to hide that my mother had become her own version of Miss Havisham, minus the decrepit wedding dress. He's only been in the house a handful of times, quick visits to appease his curiosity and maintain his interest in me, and there's no easy way to explain why she doesn't leave her room. So I went with the truth. At least the beginning.

Wes's body language whispers "trust me," from his relaxed limbs and open expression to his eyes that never leave mine. He'd be a great therapist someday. Or detective.

"You know about my sister." It's not a question. Everyone in Spring Haven knows.

He nods.

My heart pounds.

"My mom didn't handle it very well. She has a history of mental illness and when Gen disappeared, something snapped." The images running through my mind are not my own, but I believe they're as close to the truth as I'll ever get. Dad's frantic search at the park. Mom's breakdown. Me, alone, crying for my other half. When you spend nine months spooning with someone, you feel their absence immediately.

Wes opens his mouth like he wants to say something. The space between us feels charged with an electricity that's pulling the truth from me, tickling at the secrets that have never passed my lips. Or maybe it's my aching desire to finally tell someone.

Guilt pricks at my conscience and I glance out the window. Mom's no longer watching, but I feel her presence. My betrayal. "Basically, she never leaves her room." His eyes widen and I rush to explain. "It's a big room. With a sitting area and bathroom and all that. She keeps busy. Knits, watches Friends." Stares at Photoshopped pictures of me. Obsesses over her daughter who no longer exists.

"How—" He stops. "Does she—" Pauses again, rubs a hand through his hair. "But she cooks and grocery shops and stuff." Not a question. His jaw ticks as I shake my head.

"She's only left the house a handful of time since Gen vanished." Saying her name out loud lifts the weight from my chest long enough for me to take a breath. But I can feel her waiting, watching. Wondering how far I'll go. "And not since I was little."

He exhales and I imagine his breath stirring the dust and leaves until they fill the air, surrounding us in everything left unsaid. Instead of feeling relief for confiding a sliver of my truth, a heaviness from deep within slams to the floor, taking my energy with it.

Questions light his eyes and his studied calm is replaced with curiosity. "That's got to be hard."

"You have no idea."

"Thanks for trusting me."

Thanks for believing I told you everything. "I'm still working on that."

"I won't tell anyone."

My hand trails over the windowsill, rubbing a crack in the smooth wood until I find my next words. Something that will convince Wes I've shared my full story and now we're friends and there's nothing else to worry his pretty soccer-playing mind. My fake smile—Gen's smile—forms on my lips and he smiles back. "I hope not."

He leans forward, the calm confidence returning, but I stand before he can say anything else.

"I better get going. I visit with my mom at the same times every day and she gets out of sorts if I'm late."

Times.

Plural.

But he doesn't seem to notice the slip.

"Oh. Yeah." He moves to the opening in the floor and lowers himself to the ladder, the power of my half-confession still holding him. The sound of nails squealing against wood snaps me out of my fog and I follow him down.

Back on solid ground, we stand a foot apart, something unspoken hovering between us. While I'm familiar with this unsettled feeling, he seems confused, like he just woke from a deep sleep.

Gen smiles up at him. "Thanks for listening. I'll see you around."

He's still standing beneath the tree when I go inside.

Mom's pacing in front of the TV when I enter her room, her hands clenched against her stomach. "Gen, where have you been? I was worried." She chews her lower lip, her eyes watering. While Mom doesn't remember Gen was taken, her subconscious does. Anytime I'm late or the schedule changes, the terror of that day and the years that followed creeps its way through her and reduces her to the broken woman she's become.

"Sorry, I took the long way home." Even though I changed into Gen's hoodie and leggings, the encounter with Wes lingers on me like the earthy smell after a hard rain. My semi-confession left me off-balance, and his concern worries me. He may not realize how much I left unsaid, but with every inch I give him, the harder it'll be to push him away.

Mom pauses by the window and stares out at the yard. "I saw Eve talking to the neighbor boy. Do you think he likes her?"

Not "does she like him." Because my interests don't matter. She only cares about how I'm perceived by others. I bite back a snide retort about how I've chased everyone away, including the only boy who likes me, and channel the perkiness of the popular girls.

"I hope so. It'd be good for her to have a boyfriend before she goes to college."

Shit. College has always been a far-off future thing I avoid talking about to prevent Mom from panicking. Even though I received my early acceptance to Northwestern last semester and Gen's been wearing a sweatshirt from her school of choice since the fall.

Mom's hand flutters over her heart and I sense the tears before she sniffles. "Life will be so different when you girls go off to college." She faces me, her smile wobbly. "I'm proud of what you've both accomplished, but I'll miss you so much."

I cross the room and wrap my arms around her, settling my head against her shoulder. We're the same height but we could not be more different. A strange sensation fills me as she pulls me tight to her spindly frame. My whole life I've felt like she holds the power over our family, that her well-being is more important than mine or Dad's, and my purpose in life is to make her happy. But standing next to her window while she cries, I realize I'm the one with the power. My cooperation is the only thing holding this charade together and with three heartbreaking words—Gen doesn't exist—it could all end.

As if sensing my discord, Mom pulls back and looks directly in my eyes. Touches my cheek. "You know you're my favorite."

My grip tightens and she gasps. Fury burns through my body and a roaring scream fills my head and so much anger, anger, anger fills my lungs that I'm going to explode from the inside. I've never been a violent person but my hands itch to smash her face until she can no longer speak or smile or breathe. I step back, breaking contact so I don't hurt her, but she mistakes my rage for affection.

"Don't tell Eve." Her face lights up in a way it doesn't for me, like we're best friends sharing a secret.

She doesn't know what she's saying.

Easy for you to say.

She's a crazy old lady.

This needs to end.

Breathe.

My hands drop to my sides and I lean my head against the window.

One.

Two.

Three.

"Oh, there's the boy Eve was talking to. Do you know him?"

I open my eyes and my gaze locks on Wes. He's in the same spot I left him, leaning against the tree like his mind is a million miles away.

As if he can feel my eyes on him, he shifts so he's facing my house. Looks up. Tilts his head as he sees me. Lifts his hand to wave, but I turn away without waving back.

My mind's on the treehouse and our conversation, but I force my shoulders to relax and give a Wes-inspired shrug. "He's on the boys soccer team, so yeah."

"He's cute."

He is, but I don't see him that way. We may barely know each other, but I'm starting to trust him and his looks have nothing to do with who he is to me. "Are you ready for your show?"

She hesitates at the window a moment longer before moving to the couch. "This is the one where they go on a break."

I recently did the math and determined I've seen the entire ten-season show almost nineteen times. Two-hundred thirty-six episodes times twelve years, when we switched from my cartoons to her beloved Friends—give or take a few movie nights—and I can recite every. Single. Line.

Even though inside I cringe because the jokes that were popular before I was born are incredibly offensive now.

My lips move with the dialogue—just like Mom—but I'm still thinking of the treehouse. Of the sense of calm that stayed with me even when I told Wes my half-truth. How I felt grounded despite being twenty feet in the air. Cal's room is the only place where I ever feel that safe, and I've always assumed it was because of his presence. Having another safe place close to home could be useful.

Mom giggles along with the show and another thought strikes me: Gen didn't speak the entire time we were up there.

I didn't have anything to say.

I don't believe you.

My entire life, Gen has followed me wherever I go. Her voice has strengthened as we've gotten older, whether arguing with or encouraging me, and as much as I'd love to have my headspace to myself, the idea of her being quiet is as far-fetched as Mom suddenly realizing she only has one daughter.

I'm not that intrusive.

Keep telling yourself that.

You'd be lost without me. You've said it yourself.

Okay, fine. I do need you. But let me get through this. Please.

Mom's shoulder presses against mine for the rest of the show, and when it ends, she stretches. My cue to leave. "Tell Eve to give that boy a chance."

I have a fucking almost-boyfriend and if you weren't so self-absorbed you would know that. Rage colors everything red. To try and try and try to be good, only to have it slapped back in your face—this must be what it feels like to truly lose your mind. The threads of lies disintegrate into a boiling cesspool in my belly. My breath sticks in my throat, catching the hurtful words I long to scream at her.

Eve.

My feet carry me from the couch to the door. My arms cross themselves. My lips somehow lift in a smile. My voice doesn't scream or shout or crack, it simply functions as it has every day before. "I'll try."

The door shuts with a click behind me and I slide down the wall.

"This has to stop."

One hundred thirty-three and a half days.

I didn't know you were keeping track.

It's all you think about. How can I not?

Do you really think this will end with graduation? Or me going to college?

Her silence is heavy.

Gen?

My pulse speeds then slows, speeds and slows, as if beating for the both of us. Her, calm and calculating and unconcerned with what the future holds. Me, gripping the final delicate thread keeping me connected to reality like a string to a balloon that's being ripped from my hands, shredding my flesh until I'm forced to let go.

My hands burn. Half-moons pierce my palms, perfectly matched with my fingernails. I stretch my hands open and blood colors the moons, tangible evidence that this is real. That I'm real. That my actions have consequences.

Gen hovers nearby but she's not sharing her thoughts.

I place one hand on the floor, then lean forward and rest the other next to it so I'm on my hands and knees. When I lift the first hand, bloody half-moons stain the carpet.

Satisfaction pushes away Gen's indifference. I control what I do. Not her, not Dad, not Mom. Me. For too long I've tiptoed through this hall, letting Mom's delusions dictate my life.

Dad's somewhere downstairs, oblivious to this precipice I've found myself on, so I crawl to Gen's room, carefully pressing my hands into the carpet. Leaving marks that prove I exist.

Me.

Eve.

Her door is open, the light off. Across the hall in my room, the faint pinks and purples of the setting sun do nothing to soften this newfound resolve pulsing through me. My heart's still racing but adrenaline lifts me to my feet instead of crushing me to the floor. The carpet absorbed most of the blood, but I drag a hand across her door anyway. Claim her room as mine.

Inside it looks like it always does. Bed made, photos of her friends swiped from social media taped to the mirror, random crap Dad bought to decorate her room lining the dresser and windowsill. I turn on the light and pause in front of the pictures, my reflection looking nothing like the cheerful selfie taped in the top corner. In the photo my ponytail is smooth, a fitted t-shirt showing off my body in a way only Gen can pull off, but in reality, pieces of hair hang around my face, Gen's baggy sweatshirt concealing the sculpted body only Cal gets to see.

The picture peels away from the mirror with a tug, tears in half with a twist of my fingers. The other photos follow until Gen's friends lie shredded in a pile at my feet. With each rip the knot in my chest loosens and my breath comes easier. I look around for more. My hand wraps around a stuffed unicorn, hurls it against the wall.

Not enough.

A book about soccer rests on her nightstand and makes a satisfying thump against the baseboard. The bookmark flutters in the air, a small detail Dad must have added. Has he moved it to mark her progress every night, too?

Another book follows, its pages fluttering as it slams against the wall above her bed.

Why are you doing this?

Stuffed animals and soccer cleats and other stupid crap that has nothing to do with me laugh and jeer and taunt until the roaring in my head drowns them out. I grasp and heave without aim, the frustration and fury building with each insignificant plot point Dad added to this room.

Gen but not Gen whispers "Is that all you've got?" and I attack the dresser. Unworn clothes land on the unused bedspread and a strangled cry rips from my soul. I expect footsteps on the stairs, a knock on the door, but the only sound is my inner voice urging more, more, more. Not Eve but not Gen. My movements become frenzied, unrecognizable, until every piece of minutia in her room is scattered on the floor.

Still not enough.

I yank the elastic out of my hair. Pull off the sweatshirt and fling it at the window. The hood catches on the miniblinds, a small detail that slips past my wrath, freezing me as the scene splits in two. Into a new Before and After.

Remnants of my lies litter the carpet and nothing but the sound of my heartbeat fills my head. I slip off the rest of Gen's clothes. Naked and shaking, I drift down the hall to the bathroom. Turn on the shower.

Let the water drown away my despair until the trembling finally stops.

Eleven

The beauty of my secret is no one knows when days like yesterday happen. Mr. Barney and Cal are at the front of the room, yammering about prom- and sports-related articles for this week's issue while I troll the forum. There are a dozen threads about time management and other tips to keep us focused, but until today I haven't gone beyond my project page. Noah and Willow have been surprisingly capable and things have gone smoothly since the initial tension while choosing a topic, even if Willow is a bit chatty for my taste.

"Have you checked out the Dr. Seuss thread?" Ember whispers next to me. She points at a link near the bottom of my screen. "It's pretty funny."

I'm careful not to reveal my palms as I click the One Fish, Two Fish link. Ember's never questioned any of my idiosyncrasies, but she won't hold her tongue if she thinks I'm hurting myself. Our school takes mental illness seriously, and we've been drilled on what to do to help someone who's struggling. There's even a club called Operation Sunshine that emails motivational quotes and tips on meditation.

As if I want to spend more time with my thoughts.

```
WillowRicha: Okay! Let's have some fun!
WillowRicha: One fish, two fish
Aiden22205: Red fish, blue fish
```

k-shizzle: Old fish, gnu fish

Twilight: Bark fish, moo fish

A giggle escapes before I can catch it.

Aiden22205: I have a bird I like to hold

Twilight: Good for you man

Aiden22205: it's from the book

NoBPhoto: My fish just died. This is sad.

Twilight: Ooh that reminds me of this amazing trout my mom made.

NoBPhoto: Smoked fish, stewed fish

The other students ignore Twilight's borderline trolling in favor of the more obvious euphemisms, but their sense of humor is drier than the others and I laugh in spite of myself.

"Told you," Ember says.

I click Twilight's name, pulling up their profile page. Apparently, Twilight is a female designer from Traverse City named Sky. "Ha, Twilight." The play on words makes me instantly like her.

Another tap and the public conversations she's commented on fill the screen. She's social without being showy, engaging with the more thoughtful students and seeming to ignore the douche canoes, even when they bait her. An urge to connect with this girl starts in my belly and builds until I'm typing a private message to a complete stranger. "It's just practice for college," I whisper to myself. It's not like I'm going to be BFFs with a girl from halfway across the state.

The room erupts in applause before I can hit send and I jump in my seat. Cal's watching me from his spot next to Mr. Barney, a private, Joey-style smile on his face despite standing in front of the room.

"What'd I miss?" I ask Ember.

"Baseball advanced in the playoffs."

"Woohoo." I smile back at Cal, feeling like I missed something more, but my attention returns to my laptop.

Journalist309: It's nice to find someone with a sense of humor. And clever screen name.

My lame attempt at an introduction would be embarrassing if I was actually trying, but it's practice, nothing more.

Twilight: the evening sky is my favorite so—

My back straightens. When I made the connection between her name and her screen name, I pictured the soft light as evening fades to night, but hadn't thought of my name as part of it.

Journalist309: Mine too.

A moment passes. Then two.

Twilight: hold up, your name's Eve?

I'm not sure if I'm pleased or freaked out that she looked up my profile, even though I just did the same to her.

Journalist309: Yeah

Twilight: we're like complementary parts.

Twilight: also, SO glad you didn't think it was for the book.

Twilight: you didn't think it was the book, right?

This feels rushed. I lean back in my chair, Sky's unanswered question staring at me. Her unspoken "hello?" rings in my ear, followed by a desperate uncertainty that I've said too much and wish I could rein in my enthusiasm.

If it's practice, then practice.

Journalist309: Never read it.

Twilight: I wish I could say the same. I'll never get that week back.

Journalist309: lol

Is this what everyone else does? Mindlessly chat about nothing until that nothing forms a friendship?

Journalist309: What's your topic? If you don't mind sharing.

She doesn't know me from the jackwads in here and has no reason to trust—

Twilight: abusive and co-dependent relationships.

Journalist309: Wow. That sounds heavy.

Twilight: things are different this close to the arctic.

I snort. I actually snort. Loud enough to get Mr. Barney's and Cal's attention. Mr. Barney raises a warning brow, and I rest my hands in my lap while I compose myself.

Journalist309: Genuine LOL. And you just got me busted.

Twilight: sorry not sorry. ;P

Twilight: so what's your topic? if you don't mind sharing?

Not, "because I told you mine." It's simply the next step in the conversation.

Journalist309: Human trafficking.

Twilight: egads!

Journalist309: It wasn't my first choice, but I think our project will definitely help people.

Twilight: cheers to making a difference!

Twilight: gotta run, getting the death stare from our advisor.

Twilight: nice meeting you Eve. talk soon?

The simple request says so much about her personality. Can I really be friends with someone who doesn't overthink each moment of the day?

Yesssssssss.

Journalist309: Nice meeting you! Talk soon!

Nailed it, lol.

Shut up. I'm trying.

A new message blinks in my group thread. Mr. Barney's stepped aside to let Cal lead the discussion, and despite the quizzical look he throws at me, I click on the thread.

NoBPhoto: Took a couple shots last night. Think these could work?

The backgrounds of the pictures are fuzzy, and they're shot from waist height so they don't show faces. The first picture shows a girl behind the counter at a diner with cash in her hand. A man, presumably much older, has one hand on the money and the other on her hip.

The next shows a boy in jeans and a hoodie with his back pressed against a brick wall in an alley. While a dumpster casts a shadow on him, a single stream of light draws attention to another guy, not as old as the creeper in the first photo, reaching for the boy's waistband.

The third shows a girl sitting on a couch with her head in her hands. A blanket and pillow rest neatly next to her. A blurry couple lurks in the background, arms crossed.

Alone, they spark curiosity, a need to know what happens next. Together they paint a powerful image of the different ways some teens struggle to get by. Heat flushes my cheeks and I'm filled with an unnamed emotion, an urge to do something beyond myself, which I suppose is the point of the multi-media awareness campaign. Reading about and being lectured on the issues facing our peers is different from seeing it.

Journalist309: Noah, these are phenomenal.

NoBPhoto: You mean it?

It's the first sign of uncertainty he's shown, and it triggers an urge to protect him.

Journalist309: You've taken a vague concept most people our age don't understand, or even know about, and you've humanized it. These show what some people are forced to endure just to survive, but you've done it in a way that makes it impossible to look away.

NoBPhoto: Thanks Eve. That means a lot.

NoBPhoto: How's the research coming?

Journalist309: Depressing.

In the past week I've learned that seven hundred teens in our county say they've been trafficked for sex or work; one in one hundred teens said they were given money, shelter, food, or something of value in exchange for sex; and one and a half in one hundred said they were forced to do work or something illegal by someone who received money or something of value for what they did.

In our county.

Where I live.

Journalist309: But I think this could actually make a difference.

NoBPhoto: Nobel Prize for Group 5? ;)

I laugh.

Journalist309: It could happen.

WillowRicha: OMG! Noah, these are so good! Eve, how many stats do you think we should include on the flyer.

Gen snorts in my head.

Journalist309: Three? One for each picture?

NoBPhoto: Yeah, we don't want to put too much on there. Our oral presentation will be where it's at.

Journalist309: We can get into the signs that someone's being trafficked and how people can help.

WillowRicha: We could do a series of flyers. Then we can show more data but keep the design clean.

Journalist309: I like that idea. One could include myths, like how it's not always about sex or violence. Or how people use threats and isolation to control victims.

WillowRicha: Woah.

NoBPhoto: That's heavy.

WillowRicha: Noah, can you email me the pics and I'll start designing the comps.

NoBPhoto: On it.

WillowRicha: Great work guys!

NoBPhoto: Hey Willow. Can I ask you a question?

Look at that beautiful question mark.

WillowRicha: Anything!

NoBPhoto: I thought we weren't supposed to use last names.

WillowRicha: Yeah, and.

Journalist309: Isn't Richa your last name?

WillowRicha: No, duh. It means bear in Punjabi.

NoBPhoto: So why didn't you just go by WillowBear?

WillowRicha: Because now you know more about me.

Punctuation notwithstanding, I'm really starting to like her.

Cal slides into the chair next to me. "You cool with that?"

My stomach drops and I get that panicky feeling like in the nightmare where I have to take a final for a class I never attended.

He smirks and presses a hand to his chest. "Miss Future Journalist of the Year wasn't paying attention?"

I nod at my monitor. "I was working on my project."

"Woah, those shots are badass." He leans closer and I catch a whiff of his body wash. I like to think I'm better than the girls who swoon over pretty-smelling boys, but I know what's beneath his HUMAN RIGHTS T-shirt and skinny jeans. Even though it's too early in the morning to think about such things, my heart rate picks up. He glances at me over his shoulder and must see something on my face because he shifts so his leg presses against mine. "Your partner took these?"

"Yeah. I have to admit I was skeptical about our topic at first but—"

He gives me a look that says, "What, you?" and I elbow his side, nudging him away. The scent of his body wash lingers.

"But this could turn out really well." My hand drops from my lap to the open space between us. I itch to touch him—his arm, his leg, his hair, it doesn't matter—but I made the rules so I need to follow them. "What did you sign me up for?"

His lips pull into a grimace that shows his teeth. "Baseball game."

I sit upright. "As in the playoffs?"

He nods once, then his neck sinks into his shoulders like he's bracing for my reaction.

"You want me to cover the biggest game of the season?" Someone less self-aware might take the assignment as a compliment, as confidence in my reporting skills despite the fact that I've never written about sports in my life. But I know better. "Who's sick?"

"It's a perfect storm of family birthdays, a robotics competition, and the prom committee." Cal's far too professional to verbalize that I'm the last choice, but he also wouldn't give me this assignment if he didn't trust me.

"Which leaves me."

"Do you want me to come with you?"

"Absolutely not." If he's able to go, he may as well cover it himself.

"You'll be fine. Review the coverage of recent games to get an idea for the flow, and I can help you piece it together afterwards."

I won't need his help.

He hesitates. There's more.

"Out with it, Joey."

His expression softens at the nickname, then quickly goes back to business. "Aiden is going, too."

"Fantastic."

"And *Sabre* staff usually rides together for away games."

"There's no way in hell I'm getting in a car with him."

This time his smile stays. "I figured as much."

"When is the game?"

"Thursday."

"So I've got two days to learn the fine art of sports reporting."

His knuckle grazes my bare knee. "I'm happy to help."

My fingers hook through his for a beat, then I lean back in my chair. "This'll be good practice." For what exactly, I'm not sure, but teachers are always telling us to step outside our comfort zones and team sports are so far beyond my zone they may as well be on another planet.

The warning bell for first period rings. Chairs scrape as everyone stands, and Mr. Barney shouts over the burst of chatter. "Just a reminder to be respectful. The conversations on the forum are not private." A hush stills the room. Eyes meet and dart to the next person, as if we can tell with a glance who prompted the warning. Mr. Barney points two fingers at his eyes, then at all of us. "Big Brother is watching." A smile breaks over his face and he chuckles, but none of us join his laughter.

Ember slides between Cal and me as we step into the hall. "What do you think that was about?"

"I heard Barney say something about people talking about partying," Cal says. "Are they really stupid enough to put that on a school forum?"

"You give your fellow students too much credit," I say. As stupid as they are, I'm glad for the reminder. My conversation with Sky was completely mundane, but in the short time we chatted, I'd already forgotten the advisors could see our conversation. If we keep talking, we might need to switch to another platform.

Ember waves before turning down a hall toward her class. "See you at lunch."

Cal bumps my shoulder and nudges me to the side of the hall. "Running this afternoon?" He stares down at me, his eyes narrowed like my next words could destroy his trust.

"Yeah. Is 4:30 okay?" That'll give me time for both visits with Mom, and then I can go to Cal's afterwards guilt-free. "Can we meet at the beach?"

"Text when you're leaving." He leans into my space like he wants to kiss me, but I've already maxed out my comfort zone.

I press a hand to his chest. "See you then."

Twelve

The beach is deserted when I arrive. Storm clouds smudge the horizon, their darkness reaching deep inside me and wrapping around my soul, rubbing against the fury from yesterday that still simmers beneath my skin. Whitecaps break along the sandbar, then again at the shore, wetting the sand at my feet.

I move to the softer sand to wait for Cal. As my hand pulls my sneaker against my butt to stretch my quads, the rough material catches on the half-moons on my palm. No one noticed them at school. And when I came home, all evidence of my rage had been put away. Like it didn't happen.

But it did. My hands prove it.

My gaze settles on the clouds and the sound of the waves soothes my thoughts. The students from Operation Sunshine are really into meditation and on more than one occasion have cornered me after I've snapped at someone in class, insisting I need to rebalance my chakras, but this right here is all I need. The water and the sky and the sound of the waves crashing on the shore, leaving no room for dark thoughts or concerns about the future.

"You been here long?"

Cal's voice startles me and I lose my balance. My shoe scrapes against my tender palm, catching the deepest cut and ripping my flesh. I press my hand to my mouth, sucking away the blood.

"What happened?" He's at my side in a flash but I shake him away.

"I cut my hand. It's no big deal."

His fingers are gentle on my wrist as he lifts my hand, but I slip from his grasp.

"You ready?"

He nods and we fall into a steady rhythm. My favorite part about running is it's one of the few activities where it's perfectly acceptable to be alone. No one questions my desire for solitude and other runners don't try to make idle conversation. We pass with a nod and continue on our way. Cal's taller than me so I expected his stride to challenge mine, but our bodies are so in tune with each other that we find an agreeable cadence with little effort.

The waves grow in intensity as we run, lapping closer and closer until we're forced off the hard-packed earth and into the looser sand. Cal's form is different than Wes's—less showy, more practical. Wes runs like he's got a soccer ball attached to his feet, but Cal's reasons for running are more like mine—exercise and clearing his head—and he runs like no one's watching. The loose sand slows my pace and the euphoria that usually settles over me lingers beyond my grasp.

Our pace slows further when we reach the pier that juts into Lake Michigan. The Grand River runs through our tiny town, dumping into Lake Michigan between two concrete piers. The south pier, the one we're facing, is the bigger, iconic structure. A red wooden fog house sits at the end, tethered to land by a steel catwalk that runs the length of the pier, intercepted by a red lighthouse at the midway point. Fishermen line the south side of the pier, their backs to the channel, but aside from them and a few people with dogs, it's nearly empty.

"Want to go out there?" Cal asks.

It's either that or follow the boardwalk along the river into town, and the fewer people the better. I nod, and we jog alongside the catwalk. Cal weaves through the supports but I maintain a straight line until we reach the fog house at the end.

A couple our age snuggle against the front of it, clearly expecting privacy, but this is my lake as much as theirs.

Cal slips his arm around me and for once I don't push him away. His skin is warm on mine, a sensual promise of what's to come. "Thanks for agreeing to run with me. I know this is your special time."

His words hit me in the chest. I've never spoken the words "special time" aloud outside my house, and yet here they are, hanging in the air between us.

I force out a response. "This was fun." My voice sounds flat, so I tighten my arm around his waist. Take a shallow breath. Maybe running with Cal isn't so bad. He didn't try to talk and I could tell he was holding back as we ran. My pace could improve with him pushing me. "I could do this again."

He pulls his head back so he can look at me. "Eve Ellaway, did you just make plans more than a day in advance?"

I smile against his arm. "Stop or I'll take it back."

A wave crashes over the surface of the pier and we jump apart. The water is high this year, lapping over the metal lip that edges the concrete, teasing me closer. Unlike piers in ocean towns, which are built on stilts to account for tides, ours sits barely a foot above the surface. On calm days, the water looks like an extension of the concrete, a gray-blue glass you could almost walk on. But on days like today, the lake becomes a tumultuous sea, raging and thrashing against anything that stands in her way.

This is my favorite version of Lake Michigan.

I inch closer to the edge, transfixed by the predictable way the waves crash into the concrete. If you watch long enough you can find the pattern, but most people are too impatient and scream and squeal when a spray of water arcs over their heads.

They also don't comprehend how dangerous it is. Every year, the lake pulls a handful of people into her depths, some swept from the pier, others engulfed by the riptide that lurks just past the shore. Locals understand her power and give her the respect she deserves, but that doesn't mean we can resist her.

Another wave surges over the edge, soaking me from the knees down.

"Eve, you should get back."

He knows I know this, but the concern in his voice outweighs my irritation at being told what to do. Being nice to the boy who likes me shouldn't be a constant struggle, especially when he genuinely cares for me.

Maybe that's the problem.

You don't think I deserve someone nice?

I don't think you think you deserve that.

My feet carry me back to Cal's side, to his warmth. "It's like a magnet sometimes."

"The lake?"

He gets it. He gets me. "Yeah. I feel like the stupid moth to a flame. Its beauty eclipses the danger."

Sounds like someone else I know.

Cal brushes a piece of hair from my cheek. The tender expression on his face warms my belly. "I know what you mean."

He does get you.

I push to my toes and press my lips to Cal's throat. He's sweaty and salty, but notes of his body wash still cling to his skin. His arms tighten around me, holding me close, letting me take the lead. He's been turned down too many times to initiate anything beyond casual touching in public. My lips drift over his jaw to his mouth, and it's like I uncorked the tension in his body. He relaxes into me, still not pushing but returning my kiss until I forget about everything around us.

Another wave breaks over the pier and we step apart.

"Ready to go?" he asks. His eyes lock on mine and his hands continue their looping pattern over my hips.

I nod, and without a word, we run in the straightest direction possible to his house.

His car is the only one in the driveway when we arrive, despite it being after five o'clock, something that's always seemed convenient, but today strikes me as sad. Like something

I should have asked about before now. Cal's always accepted his parents' devotion to their flock—to them choosing others over him—but what toll has it taken on his life? Their example to always see the best in people and help them even at your own expense is probably why he sticks with me even when I don't deserve it, but who's looking out for him?

"You okay?" he asks, his brows furrowed.

The question "are you okay?" lingers on my lips, but I swallow it and nod my head and follow him inside.

Even though I shower here at least once a week, I don't get my own spot on the towel rack. The LeBlancs may be oblivious, but they're not stupid and there's no point disrupting their apathy this close to graduation. Cal grabs me a fresh towel from the closet while I turn on the water. He touches my hip, turning me to face him. Heat turns his eyes liquid and my pulse quickens. Since we've never run together before, we've never needed a shower at the same time, and a fresh wave of desire washes over me as I realize what we can do. What he's thinking. We slip out of our clothes, eyes never leaving e ach other. He steps into the shower first and watches me, waiting, as if after all this time he's still not sure if I'll follow him or run away.

The water slides over me, washing away school and the constant uncertainty that haunts my every breath. Cal's hands are gentle, unhurried, the physical contact exactly what I need, but I can't shake the niggle in the back of my mind that I'm just using him. His lips trail over my shoulder until he finds my mouth, and I push away my thoughts. Lose myself in him. In how he makes me feel.

Before things get too heated, shampoo finds its way into my hair and we step apart to do the showering part of the shower. I've never bathed with another person, and while I'm not shy about my body—especially not with Cal, who's seen every inch of me—washing in front of him feels like I'm exposing myself in a way I can't take back.

He tilts his head back to rinse soap from his hair and I run my hand down his stomach. A smile touches his lips while his eyes stay closed, and a rush of power energizes me. He trusts me completely. He doesn't just care about me, he would do anything for me.

We switch spots so I can rinse off, then he hands me a towel and walks naked to his room. To the one place where my nightmare isn't real.

He's already got the condom ready when I join him in bed. Our bodies move together in the same rhythm from our run, him keeping pace with me, never pushing farther than I'm willing to go.

Is this what love feels like? This yearning for a connection with another person, to feel so intensely it blocks out everything else? Everyone else? His gaze meets mine, and while he's never said the three words, I see it in his eyes. Feel it in the way his hand cradles my face. In the way he always knows exactly what I need when I need it.

My eyes close, shutting out his intensity. The emotions on his face are too much. Will I ever be able to care for him that way? For anyone? I throw my head back, but it's not passion or ecstasy moving me against him. My body switches to autopilot, touching him where he likes and making the noises that'll bring him to the edge.

Afterwards, he's even more tender.

The girl who ends up with him will be very lucky.

When he drops me off at home, Wes is standing in his open garage. Cal acknowledges him with a quick nod, then turns to me. "Have a good night."

Kissing him is easier than speaking. Safer. Because seeing Wes shattered the safety from Cal's room and I don't know how much longer I can stay silent.

Thirteen

My navigation insists I take the exit before the one Cal told me. Since my trust in people has always been nonexistent, even with someone like Cal who's been to Portage, I steer Betty onto the off-ramp without so much as a flutter of concern. Unlike humans, technology has never failed me.

Getting out of class a few hours early to cover a baseball game is a nice perk, but it's unsettling to be driving in an unfamiliar town in the middle of the afternoon. Adventure has never been in my DNA—perhaps because I have enough drama at home—and aside from visiting colleges last spring with Ember and her parents, I've barely explored my state, let alone the rest of the country. I follow the turns as they appear on screen, until I'm pulling into a packed parking lot next to a high school that's a blend of modern glass and steel and aged brick. My high school was built in the nineties and still looks fairly new, but it's missing this building's sleekness.

Students dressed in a garish combination of orange and brown walk toward the far end of the parking lot, along with a handful of kids from my school. Instinct tells me that's where the game is. See, I didn't need Cal's directions. Even so, I shoot off a quick text to let him know I arrived safely.

My fingers hesitate over my phone. A good daughter would also text her parents. Gen visited with Mom for a few minutes before I left—I figured if Mom could only see one of us, she'd be happier to see her—but Dad wasn't home yet. Driving seventy-five miles when I've rarely left our tiny town would concern most parents, but it's doubtful Mom knows I'm here and I'm certain Dad doesn't care.

That's not true.

Only because of you.

Eve, they love you.

They love you. I'm the vessel that makes it possible.

You're being dramatic.

Okay, fine. They'd miss me if something happened. But losing you would destroy Mom. And don't say it wouldn't because it's already happened once.

A beat passes, then two.

Satisfied I won that argument, I leave Betty near a light post that stretches high into the sky and follow the crowd.

Last night I read every article written about our baseball team in the past two years, and while my disinterest for the sport has amplified, I'm confident I can write a piece that will make Cal and Mr. Barney proud. Aiden offered to ride together but I shut that down before he could finish his sentence. I won't be able to avoid him at the game, but that doesn't mean we have to sit anywhere near each other.

I flash my press pass to the girl at the entrance collecting tickets and a rush of pride makes me smile. Someday this will be an everyday occurrence. Whether it's on The Hill in D.C. or chasing down a story in another big city, the look of admiration on that girl's face will become so normal I'll stop noticing, only focused on my quest to expose the truth.

My pride deflates when I step through the gates. A story about a baseball game will not be what launches my career. The students filling the metal bleachers look the same as my classmates, but oh so different. While the clothes and hairstyles are familiar, the mix of ethnicities here shames the lily-white cast of my school.

No one pays much attention to me as I find an empty spot on the bleachers behind home plate. There's probably a visitor side where I'm supposed to go—where the other kids from my school are—but I'm the press, damn it, and I need to be close to the action. Boys in fitted uniforms stretch on the field while a wolf-looking mascot runs in front of the bleachers, waving its arms at the crowd. Pockets of students cheer as he runs by, but for the most part, people are on their phones.

Aiden stands near the fence talking to a girl our age, no doubt trying to impress her with his camera's telephoto lens that's in no way overcompensating for anything. He glances at me over her shoulder and I look away. Being on the *Sabre* together does not obligate me to acknowledge him.

Stop. He's not that bad.

He's a fricking Kevin wannabe.

He's just trying to fit in like everyone else.

Doesn't excuse it.

The game starts with a muffled, "Play ball!" from the umpire and the crowd settles in. Our team is up first and while I recognize most of the players, they don't look in the stands. Which is how I want it. The first player hits the ball and sprints to first base, tripping as his foot hits the bag. The crowd groans and he pops up and stands on the base with a smile.

I write "safe" next to his name on my notepad, and for the first time since I started calling myself a journalist, I doubt my ability to do this story justice. Cal offered to answer questions during the game, but I need to prove I'm capable and he's busy with his mom's birthday. The next player swings and misses, then stands there as two more pitches sail by. The umpire grunts and the player jogs back to the dugout.

People watch this for fun?

A couple more players get hits and I'm so bored when the first guy runs across home plate I forget to clap. Rah rah for my school spirit.

Aiden shakes his head at me from his perch near the fence, then goes back to taking pictures.

The energy shifts when the home team is up to bat. A group of boys with their chests painted to spell H-U-S-K-I-E-S waves their arms at the crowd and shout what I guess is their fight song. Parents lean forward as if that'll give them a better view. And a girl in jeans and a loose top, her wavy brown hair knotted at the nape of her neck, sits down next to me.

"What'd I miss?" she asks.

"I'm sorry?"

She nods at the field and rests a foot on the bleacher in front of us. "Who scored for them?"

My eyes flick over my notepad, which is sadly lacking anything resembling a relevant detail.

"You're the reporter for Spring Haven, right?" She pulls out a notebook and rests it on her lap, but it's not a regular notebook. It's a grid filled with rows of tiny baseball diamonds with players' names scribbled down the left side. She taps her pencil on the notepad. "My editor will kill me if he finds out I was late."

I replay the scene when the player crossed home plate. He's in English with me. Cocky but seems nice. "Baker. Jeremy Baker. He's the one who scored."

"Thanks." She makes a note and nods at my pitiful notebook with a friendly smile. "I'm guessing you don't know where everyone else ended up."

A laugh escapes me. "And here I thought I could pass for a sports reporter."

Her knee bumps mine. "No worries, I'll help you out."

As the game progresses, she jots numbers in the tiny squares, drawing lines around the diamonds to show which base each player runs to. When their player scores, the crowd leaps to its feet in a roar and she fills in the square.

"How'd you learn that?"

"My family's really into baseball. My dad played in Honduras before he moved here, and my older brother plays at Western.

Even though I can't play to save my life, I love it." She tucks the pencil behind her ear and angles her body so she's sort of facing me. A calm energy radiates off her, a confidence I try to feel most days but seems natural to her. "How'd you end up here?"

Cal's words form on my lips. "Perfect storm of family birthdays, robotics competition, and prom committee. I prefer political features and social issues, but I'm always up for a challenge."

Something in her eyes sparks at the word "challenge" and the energy between us shifts. Or am I the only one who noticed it?

Gen hovers nearby, but I can't tell if she's judging or simply listening.

A bat cracks against the ball and we both turn to the field as players run from base to base. Aiden moves in my peripheral vision but his focus is on the game. Like mine should be.

The innings slip by as the sun sets behind us. She tracks the game in her official notebook while I write things down as best I can, and somewhere around the fifth inning her knee grazes mine. My belly flips in a way I haven't felt since Lissa and I were partnered for dance lessons in fifth grade gym class.

Did she do it on purpose?

Our shoulders brush. "I'm Mariela, by the way."

The unspoken hesitation that lives inside me fills and expands until the pressure in my chest stretches everything and it feels like I'm going to explode.

Just once.

Please.

Let me have this.

"I'm Gen."

Mariela smiles and holds out her hand. "Pleasure to meet you, Gen."

Thank you.

What have I done?

Her shoulder brushes mine again, more firmly this time, and she taps my notebook with her pencil. "You definitely need my help."

My brows raise in mock disbelief. “I will work magic from these notes.”

“I’m not questioning your magical abilities.” Her eyes lock on mine and her mouth lifts in a small smile. Our energies swirl in the air around us, a gentle push and pull that makes my head spin. “I’m just offering to make it a little easier.”

Touch her.

What?

Nothing obvious, but touch her.

Why?

You said you’re Gen. I want to touch her.

I don’t—

Do I need to do everything here? Touch her notebook and casually stroke her leg.

Stroke her leg.

Mm-hmm.

Fights with Gen can last hours, which will not only distract me from the game, it’ll make things weird with Mariela, who, judging by the uncertainty on her face, might actually want me to touch her.

So I do.

Just like Gen said.

My finger trails over Mariela’s notes. “Do you promise to translate these hieroglyphics?” As I pull my hand away, I let my fingers graze her thigh and linger for a sliver of a heartbeat, long enough to let loose a kaleidoscope of butterflies that flutter inside me, slamming into my lungs and heart and belly and making everything disappear but her.

Told you.

You don’t know anything.

When will you accept that I know everything about you?

A soft smile lights Mariela’s face and the air between us warms. Her gaze drops to my hand, which is safely back on my leg. “I promise.”

What did I just agree to?

The rest of the game is a hazy blur of hits and runs and screaming fans. With each pitch, Mariela inches closer on the bench until it's impossible to ignore that our thighs are touching. The sensations she elicits are familiar to what I feel with Cal, but different somehow. Softer. More intense.

Aiden paces nearby, capturing every play to highlight my magical article, but all I can think is that with one turn of his head, he'll see us.

So you admit there's something to see.

I don't know.

What would you do if he wasn't here?

The question has a multitude of layers. What would I do if Aiden wasn't here right now, or what would I do if Cal wasn't in my life? Or simply, what would I do?

What do you want?

You already know.

Do you need me to make the first move?

I nod, and Mariela raises an eyebrow.

"Deep thoughts?"

"You have no idea."

She smiles and for a moment everything pauses. The game, the conversations around us, my breath—all of it stops. Her eyes are steady on mine and it's like I can feel her pulling me closer. A piece of hair tickles the curve of her neck and my finger twitches.

Do it.

No.

Mariela's eyes drop to my hand as if she can tell what I'm thinking.

Imagination is a funny thing. It can shove you down a rabbit hole, chasing an alternate reality that forever runs parallel to your actual existence, never crossing paths with the life you really live. Conversations and secret glances that never come to be. Phantom caresses that will never escape the boundaries of your mind.

"You're quieter than most of the girls I know." Mariela pulls me out of my head and back to the hard metal bleacher. To this game that has somehow placed her by my side.

My lips curve on their own. "I'm not really into sports."

"What are you into?" She doesn't move, doesn't lean into me or lick her lips or do any of the things Cal does when he wants to kiss me, but I feel it. This tugging from her soul to mine.

"I like to run on the beach. I'm really into politics and want to write about things that make a difference in the world." Saying my dreams out loud makes it feel like they'll really happen.

"And you don't think baseball does that?"

My head tilts as I replay my words, picking apart if I may have offended her. "It does in its own way. But," I touch her notebook again, "I'd have to learn baseball hieroglyphics."

She barks out a laugh. "I've got my brothers to thank for that."

"Do you have a boyfriend?" I say as she asks, "Do you have siblings?"

We both shake our heads, but I guarantee the innocent gesture doesn't make her chest tighten with guilt or silence her heart until the edges of her vision blur.

"Do you have a boyfriend?" she asks.

I whisper, "Not exactly," as the people around us take a collective breath and spring to their feet. Mariela grabs my bare leg just above my knee, her eyes locked on the ball, which sails high above the field as if shot from a cannon. Her fingerprints scorch my skin. Jeremy, the boy from my English class, runs backward toward the fence, never taking his eyes from the ball. Heat races up my leg, pulsing from Mariela's fingers. Jeremy jumps against the fence, pushing himself into the air and stretching his arm to catch the ball, but it bounces off the tip of his glove and lands on the other side of the fence.

"Grand slam!" Mariela shouts, jumping to her feet.

The absence of her hand chills me. I stand.

We're almost the same height.

She laughs. "Tough break. He almost had that."

The players run around the bases while spectators jump and shout and high-five like they're all best friends. That's how sports make a difference. They bring people together and give them a common purpose.

Mariela slaps hands with a guy behind us then turns back to me. Her smile melts my defenses, and I feel raw, exposed. Like she can see through layers of lies that protect my heart. Inches separate us. If someone bumped me our chests would touch.

"Is it over?" My throat feels tight and my lungs ache for a deep breath, but I don't want to move.

"It may as well be."

The scoreboard changes from 9 : 5 to 13 : 5. "I didn't realize we were down by that much." As soon as the words leave my mouth, I realize they could imply one of two things: I'm a terrible reporter and haven't been paying attention, or I'm more into Mariela than I realized and haven't been paying attention. Either way, my notes are shit and I need her help.

"Looks like you're gonna need more than just my notes."

If a guy said that I'd roll my eyes and walk away, but there's no turning away from Mariela. Her green eyes anchor me to the bleachers, and that damned piece of hair lifts in the breeze sweeping through the stadium. And since when does that have an effect on me?

"I think so," I say.

"I'll copy them as soon as the game ends."

So I'm not leaving right away. "Thanks. You have no idea how much this helps."

She gives me a half smile and touches the back of her hand to mine. "I think I do."

The inning ends and Spring Haven steps up to bat.

Mariela leans close to whisper in my ear. "If they don't score eight runs, the game's over." Her breath tickles my neck.

Turn your head.

What?

Kiss her.

Fourteen

What? Here?

It's dark. Everyone's watching the game.

I lean into Mariela until her forehead touches the side of my face. "Thanks. I don't know what I'd do without you." Heat flares in my belly the longer we stay connected, and I pull away before she can. With Cal, I'm always the one in control. But Mariela has cast a spell over me and this new vulnerability has me trembling.

My team gets a couple hits, but no one's able to score and with the third out, the stands erupt and the home team jumps all over each other. Caps fly in the air and someone rushes onto the field with a giant orange cooler and dumps ice and water on the pile of players.

This time I whisper in Mariela's ear. "Don't they still have to bat?"

She shakes her head and her hair tickles my nose. "Nope. Home team always bats at the bottom of the inning. That gives them the advantage if they're losing because they get the final at-bat, but if they're winning, they don't hit."

"Interesting."

People clomp down the bleachers, their footsteps vibrating the structure like a heartbeat. Like my heartbeat. Mariela moves closer to me to avoid getting stepped on. "Do you have to leave right away? If the school was open, I'd make a photocopy, but I need to do it by hand."

I'm an hour and a half from home, it's past dinnertime, and Mom's already covered. "I can stay a little longer."

Her smile sends the kaleidoscope spinning.

The cool night air chills the bleachers, but I barely feel it. Mariela rips a blank sheet from her notebook and gestures to mine. "May I?" Our fingers brush as I hand my notebook to her, and she uses it to support the blank sheet. I rest my hands on my thighs. My pleated skirts are as much a part of my identity as Cal's political tees, but as Mariela scribbles her hieroglyphics, I'm hyper-aware of my bare flesh and how close it is to this girl who's making me feel things I never knew were possible.

The teams pack up their gear and exit the field. Aiden stands at the end of the bleachers, his camera hanging loosely from his neck. He tilts his head and gives me a funny look, but I give him a dismissive wave and turn my attention back to Mariela.

She's quiet as she writes. The air is noticeably colder without the other spectators and goosebumps speckle my legs, but I don't move. I barely breathe. Another piece of hair falls from her bun, transfixing me. Mariela is unlike anyone I've ever met, and while I've always trusted my instincts, I've drifted so far beyond the boundaries of my comfort zone it's nothing but twinkling lights in the distance.

"Are you cold?" She rubs her free hand over her opposite arm and looks around as if only now realizing we're alone.

"A little."

She folds my copy in half and hands it to me with a smirk. "I made a couple notes for translation purposes. Be sure to mention the grand slam."

I laugh through my nose. Our fingers touch as I take the paper, but this time I don't pull away.

Her hand rests on my leg, the same spot as before, except now she's facing me and her movements feel more purposeful. Intentional. Her thumb traces the inside of my knee and my nerve endings come alive. "You've got goosebumps."

"I'll be okay."

"This has been..." she ducks her head, avoiding my eyes. Her hand moves over my leg and we watch it like neither of us is sure what will happen next. She bites the corner of her mouth and traces lazy patterns over my thigh, but these goosebumps aren't because of the cold. "I didn't expect to meet you today," she finally says.

The urge to touch her is impossible to ignore. My hand finds its way to hers, and for a moment she stiffens, like she thinks I'm pushing her away, but I hold her hand more firmly against my thigh and inch closer on the bench. I lean forward, invading her personal space. "This game turned out way better than I expected."

She glances at the empty field before meeting my eyes. "But you lost."

I lift a shoulder in a shrug. "Meh."

The air between us thickens until I can't breathe, but breathing no longer feels important. All that matters is the way the heat from her hand travels through my body, igniting something deep inside me. Her gaze flicks to my lips, and time seems to stand still.

If we're going to kiss, this is the time, but I've never kissed a girl and something's holding me back. Guilt about Cal or awareness that even though the stadium is empty, we're still on display.

Get out of your head and just go for it. It's not like you'll see her again.

Is that my concern? Seeing her later, having her complicate my life?

Do you need my help?

Gen must feel my desperation because my head leans closer to Mariela and tilts so all she has to do is close the distance between us and—

A loud pop echoes in the night air. A startled yelp escapes me and we both jump. I squeeze her hand as the stadium falls into darkness and stars burst across the sky.

"Maintenance guys," she says with a laugh. "Turning off the lights."

We stare at each other in the darkness, then double over laughing.

It feels good to laugh, to shed the tension from the past couple hours. Tears fill my eyes as adrenaline flees my body. "I swear I thought it was a bomb."

"I've been in my car when they turned them off," she says. "But never sitting right underneath." She presses her free hand to her chest. "My heart's racing."

"Mine too." My whispered confession recharges the electricity between us and I dare to touch the piece of hair that's been taunting me. Her eyes close and she turns her face into my hand. Her skin is smooth, more delicate than Cal's or any other boys' I've kissed, and desire sweeps through me so quickly it steals what little breath I have left. She leans toward me and I close my eyes and when her lips touch mine, it's like something inside me loosens.

We pause with our lips pressed together, not moving or breathing or doing anything else that could ruin the moment. Then her hand inches up my leg and her mouth parts. Everything about her is soft. The absence of stubble scraping against my lips is intoxicating and I want to bury my face in hers. Feel every part of her against me.

While one hand flirts with the hem of my skirt, her other hand weaves into my hair, pulling me closer, and I finally allow myself to really touch her. My hand skims her side, hinting at the edge of her breast, then settles at her hip. She breaks the kiss, and I inhale deeply as her mouth travels over my jaw to my throat. The stars shine through pinpricks in the night sky as if protecting us from whatever lies beyond these bleachers, keeping us safe and shielding us from prying eyes. Mariela's hand untangles from my hair and trails over my shoulder until her fingers brush feather-light over my breast, sending heat pulsing through me. Cal's infatuated with my breasts but his caresses never do much for me. But this... Her touch grows bolder and a soft moan rises on my breath to meet the stars. I lift her head and our eyes connect for a moment before I cover her mouth with mine.

As if moving on their own, my hands explore her body while her hand slips under my skirt. Our kiss deepens and the universe spins. It's like I've been reset on my axis, finally aligned to the longing that follows me everywhere I go. I'd always assumed it was my missing twin, but maybe it was this. Mariela's fingers inch higher and my breath hitches when they brush my panties. She pauses, as if waiting for my consent, and I respond by kissing her harder.

My body reacts in a way it never has with Cal. With him it's all about feeling safe. But here, with Mariela, it's about heat and lust and feeling. She's making me want things I've never felt before, and when she pulls my panties aside, I forget everything in the world except her.

We stay on the bleachers until we're both shaking with cold.

"How long is your drive?"

"Hour and a half."

She sits upright. "Shit, Gen! I didn't realize it was that far!"

My heart flinches at Gen's name. So much has happened since that casual lie, I'd forgotten I'm someone else.

"Aren't your parents worried?"

"Probably." My phone's been on silent and Dad texts so rarely I sometimes wonder if my number's even saved in his phone. I check for messages and nearly fall over when I see one from him. "I better write him back."

Her hand rests on my arm as I type. "Are you gonna get in trouble?"

"Nah. They let me do pretty much whatever I want. Home stretch before graduation and all."

She raises an eyebrow. "Ooh, you're a senior?"

"You're not?"

Did I just do something illegal? Please tell me she's not fifteen.

"Junior. So where are you going to college?"

I exhale the momentary panic. The familiar calmness that cocoons me when I think about starting over slows my breathing. "Northwestern."

"Impressive. Let me guess, journalism?" When I nod, she smiles. "Well, I know baseball is beneath you, but I'm really glad you took this assignment."

My fingers lace through hers and a smile, a genuine, from-the-heart smile, spreads over my face. "Me too."

She walks me to my car and after a final kiss with me pressed against Betty's door, she texts me her number and wanders into the night.

Gen's waiting when I start the engine. She doesn't speak, and her unspoken words mix with my guilt over what just happened, filling me with shame. Cal may not be my official boyfriend, but the whole reason I've never committed is to avoid hurting him and I'm pretty sure going to third base with another person counts as cheating.

So now you're a baseball expert?

Just say whatever it is you need to say.

Did you have fun?

You tell me.

What are you getting at?

Since when are you into girls?

I'm not.

Then why did you want to kiss her?

That was all you.

But you wanted her. I could feel it.

Again, you.

You don't think I can tell the difference between what I want and what you're telling me to do?

I think you push it on me when it's convenient.

I don't do that.

The empty roads are too quiet for my racing mind. Gen's silence presses against my chest making it impossible to think about anything but what she did. Or I did. I inhale deeply as I accelerate onto the highway and the heaviness eases. Everything about being with Mariela felt right. The guilt weighing on me is because of Cal, not because a random girl from another school made me feel more alive than I ever thought possible.

Fifteen

I sometimes wonder if I became a writer because of the stories I tell about Gen, or if I'm able to weave her stories because I'm a writer. Her life is so ingrained in mine that sometimes it's hard to know where she ends and I begin.

Or if I exist at all.

Maybe my life is the one that's make believe and no one—

"How was the game?" Cal's innocent question makes me flush from head to toe. I slide my journal into my bag while his finger trails over my knee, giving me flashbacks to last night. To Mariela and the way she touched me.

I swat his hand away.

"Better than I expected. The reporter from the other school helped me keep track of the scoring." Mariela's sheet of hieroglyphics rests on the desk next to my laptop. Thank god she didn't write her number at the top. She texted while I was driving home, and while she could be an interesting distraction until I leave for Northwestern, it's safe to assume I'll never see her again.

Cal studies it for a moment before nodding his approval. "This guy knows his stuff." He sets it back on the desk and leans his head close to mine. "He was just being friendly, right? Should I be worried?"

It'd be so simple not to correct him. To take the easy way out. Let him think the other reporter was a guy and spend the next couple days assuring him he has nothing to worry about, when in reality, Mariela has flipped my world upside-down. It isn't so much the cheating that bothers me—although I am ashamed for breaking Cal's trust—it's how every touch from Mariela felt amplified. Like I've been numb my entire life and suddenly I feel everything.

My forehead brushes Cal's and I force a smile. "He was a she, and she was just being friendly."

This time he flushes. Cal prides himself on being a feminist and his assumption that only a dude-bro could properly score a baseball game hangs between us. His head falls between his shoulders and he grabs my hand. "I'm sorry. You know I don't think that way."

His grip feels clammy and desperate and I have the frantic urge to flee. "Don't worry about it." The last thing I want is to make him feel like he needs to prove his devotion to women's causes—or me.

A new message pings onscreen. My heart jumps, then quickly falls at Willow's name. Our project has become more powerful than I anticipated, and I don't want to think about that right now.

WillowRicha: Hey guys. I attached a couple comps of the flyers. Which one do you like best.

Each version uses the same of Noah's heart-stopping photos, but each has a totally different mood. The background colors and type vary, and while the placement of the pictures is more or less the same, the first has an almost whimsical feel, the second has a cool graffiti-style type, and the third punches me in the chest. It's blueish-black with more straightforward type, but the pictures run off the edge of the page, pulling me in.

I try to ignore the gibberish next to the photos indicating where the text will go. The text I've tried to write but have yet to finish.

Journalist309: Willow, these are fantastic! I like the darkness of the third one but the type is cool in #2.

NoBPhoto: Can you combine those elements?

WillowRicha: Awesome! I can totally do that.

WillowRicha: So Eve, I just need the final copy from you.

Procrastination has never been an issue for me. To be the best you have to chase after what you want, and I want to be the best journalist I can. But this project has made me stumble. We already have the research, but every time I've opened the files to write the copy, perfectionist paralysis settles in. That, and the unceasing fear about what happened to Gen. Maybe she's happy and has a family who loves her, but her face—my face—transposes onto Noah's photos every time I look at them and it's like my brain shuts down.

If I want to be a journalist, I need to turn off my emotions to tell the story. The editor for The New York Times may not have time to worry about my past trauma, she'll just want me to write the piece. I take a breath and slowly exhale. Determination to not be the weakest link in this project has to outweigh whatever anxiety I'm feeling about Gen.

Journalist309: I'll get it to you by the end of the day. I promise.

WillowRicha: Cool beans.

NoBPhoto: Thanks for your hard work Willow.

Irritation crawls over my skin, but I have no one to blame but myself. All they know about me is I'm not delivering my portion of the project. My fingers stroke the keyboard but the apology they deserve stays locked inside me. I'm about to close out of the forum when I get a notification for a private message. Sky's screen name immediately lightens my mood.

Twilight: how's it going?

Her proper use of a question mark is a relief after Willow, even if she seems to have an issue with capitalization.

Journalist309: It's going. We're getting close with our project.

Twilight: us too. it kinda sucks having this

```
project so close to graduation, you know?
especially something so heavy.

Journalist309: Yeah, I know what you mean.

Twilight: everything okay?

Journalist309: Just a lot going on, you know?

Twilight: you wanna talk about it?
```

Most kids are taught to share at an early age—toys, cookies, feelings—but that wasn't my childhood. Instead of letting the other kids play with my toys and telling them when I'm having a bad day, I folded deeper and deeper into myself until they stopped trying.

She seems nice. Just talk to her.

Are you siding with Wes now? About me needing friends?

Gen's silence feels uncertain.

It's good practice for college.

I hate when you use my logic against me.

If it's possible to feel an internal shrug, that's what I feel. I've always relied on Gen's advice, but lately it's felt like she's pushing me into uncomfortable territory. Like she's leading me down a path of self-destruction.

Now you're being dramatic. Just talk to the girl.

I flex my fingers over the keyboard and take a breath.

"Everything okay?" Ember's leaning into the space between our chairs, her brows pinched together in concern.

Gen smiles, then my frown returns. "Just stressed."

"Anything I can help with?"

"Can you write my copy?"

She presses a hand to her chest and her mouth falls open in mock disbelief. "Ms. Future Journalist of the Year needs help with writing?"

This time I shrug in an effort to downplay my frustration. "The topic's hitting a little close to home. But I've promised to have it done tonight so I just need to get over myself and do it."

"Be gentle with yourself." Ember tugs at my sleeve and when I look up, tears shine in her eyes.

My breath catches in my throat and I nod. “I’m trying.”

By seventh grade, the parceling of my life into two columns was as natural as breathing. In the beginning, I simply divided my interests between Gen and myself, but when cliques emerged, Gen elevated with the popular crowd. She continued playing soccer while I joined the newspaper. She went to parties, talked about boys, and was loved by all.

While I hid deeper inside myself, terrified of spilling my secret.

That’s when I became friends with Ember. At first, I wasn’t sure what to think of the quiet girl with a personality too big for her small frame, but I was grateful to have someone who liked me.

Especially as Mom’s personality diverged alongside mine.

Her growing preference for Gen was subtle, and Dad would argue tooth and nail that she loves us equally, but a good performer can tell when her audience prefers one show over another. Especially when you have the same audience night after night after night.

Gen thrived in the attention, and her stories grew more outlandish. It’s exhilarating to both write and perform your work—I can see why some actors choose to also direct. Creating on the fly, making adjustments based on the audience’s reaction, is addicting.

I became so adept at juggling the details of our lives, I didn’t realize my mistake until it was too late. By giving Gen all the fun things, I turned Eve into an imitation of the sorceress from my short story—a bitter shrew who was suspicious of her own shadow. Recognizing my mistake would be punishment enough, but I have to live with it.

The only saving grace was Ember, who stood by my side when other kids teased or taunted about things that only matter in middle school. We became an indestructible duo, and even though there have been times when it’s felt like we were drifting apart, Ember’s heart always stopped me from severing the connection.

Now I couldn't imagine my life without her.

Sky's message sits unanswered on my screen. Maybe it's time to let another person in.

Journalist309: I normally crave distractions from home, but this project has been a lot.

Twilight: is there anything I can do to help?

Journalist309: You probably can't do my share of the work, so maybe just distract me?

Twilight: distraction is my specialty.

We chat until the bell rings and Mr. Barney stands. "We're in the home stretch for your projects. I'm planning to be here late all week if you need my help. And," he smiles as we stand, waiting. "Later this week, if enough of you stay late, pizza's on me."

Whoops fill the room, but their excitement doesn't penetrate my mood. Mr. Barney's earlier warning about the teachers monitoring the forum comes back to me.

Journalist309: Should we switch to texting?

Look at you. Two girls in less than twenty-four hours. What will Joey think?

Shut up.

Twilight: smart. yeah.

She messages her number and I add her to my phone.

me: It's Eve.

Sky: much better.

me: I have to run. Talk later?

Sky: for sure. have a good day!

me: You too!

Cal squeezes my shoulder as I pick up my things and follow Ember toward the door—and beyond his reach. "What do you say? Group date night?"

When I think about the future, I've imagined late nights sitting around a long table littered with pizza boxes and cups of bubbly water while my fellow journalists and I wait for reports from overseas or an update on a political catastrophe. The idea of being part of a group, where everyone respects me for my brain and nothing more, gives me hope that someday things will be better. We've had hints of that under Cal's leadership at the *Sabre* this year, but I have very little hope that the majority of my classmates will come anywhere close to my dream.

"Mmm," Ember says. "Greasy pizza and teenage boys. My favorite."

Cal throws an arm around her shoulder. "Eve will come if you do, so please say yes."

"But I—"

"Yes." Ember's smile is impossible to say no to. She says she understands my hesitation with Cal, but that doesn't mean she doesn't want to see us together as a couple.

"Fine," I say, moving past them into the hall. "I just need to—"

"Stop home, we know," they say in unison as we head to class.

I managed to see Mom for a few minutes before leaving for the game yesterday, but disruptions to the evening routine hurt her, and those minutes didn't feel like enough.

Live a little.

I don't need your permission.

Then stop asking for it.

Cal pauses midway down the hall, falling behind us, and Ember and I turn. "What's up?" I ask.

"Ember, go ahead," he says. "I need to talk to Eve a sec."

She shrugs and gives me a conspiratorial wink. "See you at lunch."

The sinking in my belly should have been enough warning to send me running, but I join Cal where he's leaning against the wall. "What's up?" I ask again.

His hands twist together and his head dips so he's looking at our feet, and that's when I notice the prom poster on the wall behind him.

Nooooo no no no no.

"I know you're not into dates and all that, but," he pauses long enough to meet my eyes. His nervousness is adorable and my guilt makes me want to agree to whatever he wants, but I let him finish. He taps the poster behind him. "I left my elaborate costume at home, but what do you say? Will you go to prom with me?"

Warmth spreads through me, softening the instant rebuff that dances on my lips. I've often wondered why he puts up with me. As Wes said, other girls—prettier girls, emotionally stable girls, girls without a batshit crazy mom and missing sister—would take my place in a second. Yet here he is, subjecting himself to yet another public rejection on the chance I'll dress up to slow dance with him. "You're too good for me."

"What are you talking about?"

"We had an agreement." I inhale, exhale. "No dating."

His eyes close and his chest rises as he takes a deep breath. His face hardens, the soft smile from a moment ago gone. "Is it really so hard for you to believe someone could like you?" The scratchiness in his voice tugs at the part of me that wants to make him happy. To keep him mine.

The bell rings but he doesn't move. Lissa, of all people, appears from around the corner and watches us for a beat before walking the other way, and for a second my sixth-grade self longs for her to look at me with something other than annoyance. Kids scatter down the halls, leaving us alone.

"It's not that," I say. Mariela proved that to me last night. But she doesn't know me—she doesn't even know my real name. Cal knows me better than just about anyone and while he cares about me, it's not enough.

"Then what's the problem?"

"This. Us." I gesture between us before the consequences of what I'm saying register in my brain.

He pales.

I inch closer. "I'm not trying to end things, but you know this'll have to end eventually, right?"

He looks at the ceiling, avoiding my eyes.

My hand rests on his chest. "We're going to schools in different states. It seems easier to keep things simple now so it hurts less then."

"Is that why you've been so hot and cold?" His eyes shine when they meet mine. "Why didn't you say something sooner?"

A pinprick of unease ripples up my back. That's the second time he's mentioned the hot and cold thing, and something deep inside me warns not to ask what he means. So I shrug away the sense of foreboding and give him the answer that will make my rejection easier for him to accept. "I thought it was obvious."

His hand slides behind my neck and pulls my forehead to his chest. The hall is deserted, even the slackers who are always late to class long gone, and the only sound is the thump of his heart. Anxiety creeps from my belly, spreading through my limbs and urging me to escape, to hurry to first period, but I pull in a deep breath and stay tucked in his arms. Cal may not be everything I want in the world, but he's everything I have right now, and I don't want to finish the school year alone. And I definitely don't want to see him with anyone else. Selfishness and jealousy have made people do much worse things, and I've never claimed to be a good person.

"I know prom is juvenile and you're against anything resembling a tradition," he sighs into my hair. "But I don't want to regret not going, you know?" When I nod against him, he continues. "Will you at least think about it?"

"Isn't it in two weeks?"

"Think quickly."

"I'll think about it."

"Ember and Claire are going, so the four of us could get dinner and all that."

A fresh wave of guilt stabs me. I should know this about Ember. I've been so distracted with the competition and keeping Wes from finding out the truth that I've barely talked to her. And Cal. He's trying to make this sound casual, like it's not a big deal, but I've been on the receiving end of enough of his persuasive debates to know this is important to him. If I want to hang onto the only friends I have, I need to suck it up and say yes.

"That would be nice."

He pulls back to look at me. "Really?"

"This is a maybe."

"That's better than no." His head dips toward mine and I close my eyes as our lips touch. Cal's kisses usually rouse a flutter in my belly, but the kaleidoscope stays still and it takes everything inside me not to wonder why.

"Cal told me you're going to prom with Claire!" My smile will never be bright enough to make up for the fact that I've pushed Ember so far away she didn't tell me herself. "I'm sorry I haven't texted. I should already know this."

She picks at her lunch, eyes down. "You've been preoccupied."

"That's no excuse. I always want to be here for you." I reach for her hand and she looks up. "You're important to me and I'm sorry if I haven't made you feel that way."

A spark of anger simmers in my chest and my hand tightens on Ember's. How many times have I longed to hear these words from Mom? Instead, she tells Gen she likes her better, ignoring everything I've accomplished, and I'm supposed to go about my day like everything's fine.

I'm squeezing too hard.

Ember yanks her hand away and rubs her fingers. "What's going on?"

A tremor moves up my arms and I tuck my hands in my lap to hide the shaking. "It's my mom."

Her head tilts, her earlier apprehension gone. "Has she gotten worse?"

What's worse than telling your daughter she'll never live up to her imaginary friend?

Eve, breathe.

My lungs tighten, stopping my breath.

I can't.

You can.

Ember's eyes widen the longer I stay silent. "Do you need me to get someone?"

No one can make this better.

I shake my head, but still my breath won't come.

Count with me. One.

Two.

Three.

Four.

Five.

Six.

"Eve, you're scaring me." Ember's leaning over the table. The edges of my vision blur, but not enough to block out the people staring at us.

Seven.

Gen's voice grows louder, drowning out the whispers that blend with the buzzing in my head.

EIGHT.

Nine.

My lungs expand and a cool breath fills me. Tears burn my eyes, and the trembling continues up my arms until my shoulders shake with the effort to control my body.

Ember stands. "Let me take you to the nurse."

"No," my voice squeaks. "I just need a minute."

She lowers into her chair but sits at attention, like she's ready to throw me over her shoulder and carry me to the nurse's office herself. "You weren't breathing."

"But I am now."

"Eve, you know you can trust me." She touches my hand. After last night, I'm unsure of how my body will react, but her warmth grounds me, pushing away the fear that one day the counting won't help and I'll cease to exist. "What's going on?"

My breath shudders and I slump onto my elbows. "It's everything. Mostly the project. It turns out human trafficking is a bit heavier than I anticipated."

Ember leans closer, lowering her voice. "Is this about Gen?"

Hearing Gen's name beyond the walls of my house feels too personal, like an intrusion, and the defenses surrounding my heart fight to hold firm. To everyone else, Gen is nothing but a tragic memory. If they knew the depths my family has gone to, the diabolical way they've kept her alive, they'd do more than haul me off to the nurse's office.

Tell her the truth.

I can't.

Wanting Ember to believe she's important to me and telling her my deepest, darkest secret are light years apart.

"Yes and no," I say. "Researching all the horrific ways humans treat one another, especially girls, has kind of set my imagination on overdrive."

Gen, what happened to you?

Her silence is an emptiness that expands the ache in my chest.

Ember's mouth turns into a frown, and I hate the sympathy on her face. This is why I don't share. "I bet."

I push my shoulders back and clear my throat so my voice comes out strong, assured. "But I'm proud of what we've put together. I think we have a good chance at winning." And getting out of here that much sooner. I pick up my sandwich and smile. "How's yours coming along?"

She fills the rest of our lunch period telling me about her project and her teammates, and when the conversation drifts to Claire, the knot in my chest loosens a bit more.

I can be normal.

I can be a good friend.

And I can do it all on my own.

Sixteen

Rain clouds darken the sky over the lake, pushing me to run faster on the hard sand. Each step carries me farther from home, but I can't outrun my thoughts. What I told Ember was true. This project, which at first seemed like my chance to escape, might be what breaks me.

Gen has always been a part of me, but over the years the concern about what happened to her lessened and I simply absorbed her existence. As a child, long before I knew I wanted to be a journalist, I'd batter Dad with questions until he sent me to bed.

How come Mom never leaves her room?

Why do I change clothes for her?

Why does she call me Gen?

Now I can't stop imagining the worst about Gen. Wondering if she's dead or alive. Maybe every time my chest hurts, when it feels like my next breath will never come, it's because she's suffering. Twins have a bond that connects them from conception and that doesn't disappear just because the person does. If she were dead, my connection to her would be different, less real.

The wind picks up when I reach the pier. Waves crash over the fog house at the end, putting on a show for the photographers hunkered down near the lighthouse. We could have a hundred storms a year and people never tire of documenting the lake's power, many risking their expensive equipment to get the perfect shot that'll go viral online.

I climb over the white boulders separating the beach from the smooth concrete of the pier, but it feels off. This pier, the lake, is my sacred place, where the waves protect me, immersing me in their depths, but Wes and Cal ruined it. Memories of their presence intertwine around the steel legs of the catwalk, crowding my thoughts until the frustration from earlier sweeps through me.

"Why can't you leave me alone!"

I don't know if I'm mad at Wes or Cal or the combination of their concerned eyes and careful words, but I wish I'd never come here with either of them.

The storm clouds race closer as I head home, their darkness threatening to overcome me. Each step brings me closer to a precipice I've kept locked in the folds of my mind, and my curiosity refuses to back down. As a child I wondered what became of my sister, but as the charade grew more complex, there was no longer room to speculate. Now it's like I've opened a portal that cannot be contained until I learn the truth about Gen and what really happened to her.

A cool wind wraps around me as the first raindrops patter the beach. I pause at the access point to the deserted street and stare out at the water, at the whitecaps crashing over the sandbar. The rain strengthens, mixing with the tears that run down my face.

What happened to you?

Are you okay?

Are you happy?

But like every other time I've dared to ask, Gen doesn't answer.

Her silence squeezes my chest until I can't breathe. Everything I've done to keep Gen real—every lie I've told Mom, all the friends I've pushed away so they don't learn the truth, my unceasing anger toward Dad for encouraging this madness—

coalesces with the rain seeping into my pores until my skin can no longer contain it. I fall to my knees. My fists rage with the fury of the waves pounding on the shore, and I scream until my throat is raw and cannot speak the truth.

A dog barks in the distance and I scramble to my feet, my anger fading with the wisps of fog over the lake. Wet sand clings to my stiff legs and falls into my shoes, but I put one unsteady foot in front of the other.

I blink and I'm on my street. From this distance, with the downpour distorting my vision, our house looks much as it did from Wes's backyard: simple, unassuming, safe. It's only inside that the demons awaken, pulling me to the bottom of my despair where I cannot claw my way to safety.

The water pouring over me slows my pulse until I'm numb to everything except the rhythmic patter of raindrops and the interminable ache in my chest. The fog from the beach lingers in my head and I'm floating, drifting, washing away with the rain. My mind carries me to a quiet space where the incessant questions and screaming and confusion are replaced with a fuzziness that fills me up and makes it impossible to think.

To feel.

To anything.

"Eve?" Wes's truck idles next to me. The storm must have drowned out the sound of the engine. His arm rests in the open window, the rain quickly soaking the sleeve of his t-shirt. "Get in."

"But my house is right there." My hand gestures at the end of the road as if tugged by a string, then falls limply to my side. I keep my gaze trained on his elbow because if I see the pity I'm sure is in his eyes, I won't be able to hold myself together.

"How long have you been standing here?"

Eighteen years. "I don't know."

Metal squeaks as the truck door opens. He's throwing me a rope, rescuing me from my private hell with a light hand on my back. "Come on." He guides me to the passenger side. My legs slip on the cracked vinyl as I climb in, but he anticipates me falling and helps me onto the bench seat. Country music plays softly from the speakers, and when he shuts my door, it's like he turned off the outside world. Despite the shiver running through me, I feel safe.

The truck shifts when he slides into the driver's seat. He pulls a sweatshirt from the bag between us on the seat. "It's not clean, but it's dry." He drapes it over me like a blanket. The oversized hoodie covers half my body and my eyes close.

Safe.

"Want to drive a bit?"

I nod.

He drives to the public beach, back to where I'd just been running. The music stops when he cuts the engine so the only sound is the rain drumming on the roof of the truck. "Are you hurt?"

"Not physically." My voice is hoarse and my throat burns.

"Is it your mom?"

I shake my head. Seagulls dip and weave through the spray of the whitecaps and I yearn to have that freedom, to fly above the water that eases my soul.

"Eve, you're scaring me."

My eyes finally meet his, mine burning from tears, his wide and concerned and trusting. I misjudged him. He's popular because of who he is, not because of any superficial accomplishments. Meanwhile I lie to everyone I care about. "You're the second person to say that today."

"And what did you tell the other person?" His voice is gentle, and he leans against his door, as far away from me as he can get in the cab of the truck. Other girls might be offended he doesn't try to pull them close, but he seems to understand that to earn my trust, he has to give me space.

"Half truths."

"Isn't that exhausting?"

My head tilts. "What?"

"Never trusting anyone enough to be yourself?"

Years of deceptions and disappointment and catty whispers curl into a ball that's bitter on my tongue. It would be so easy to tell him, to unload my truth and let someone else carry this burden for a while.

"Yes," I whisper.

"I don't know what's going on with you, and you don't have to tell me. But I think you need to tell someone." He runs a hand through his hair and watches the seagulls scuttle across the sand. "I barely know you and I can see something's tearing you up inside."

Just open your mouth and tell him.

So I do.

Time slips by as I talk, and the storm rolls to the east. The sun bursts through the clouds, reflecting off the water, brightening the inside of the truck and pulling me from my private hell.

Wes hasn't spoken since I started. The disbelief etched on his face turns to horror as he realizes there isn't a punchline. That this is my reality.

He struggles for words, and I try to anticipate what he'll say. That he's sorry. That it'll all work out. That—

"You know this isn't okay, right?"

"Yeah."

"This is abuse."

"It's not abuse."

His gaze levels on mine. "Well, it's not love."

My finger traces the edge of the window where water pools along the rubber seal. "It started that way." Dad's love for Mom, combined with his grief for Gen, was the catalyst for twisting my life into an unimaginable façade.

"Eve, you can't keep living this way." The sadness in his voice is more than I can handle. Tears fill my eyes and spill over my lashes before I can stop them.

"Do you think I don't know that? All I want is to get away from here. To go to college so I can start over where no one knows the heartbreaking tale of Baby Ellaway and the sister who was left behind."

"People don't think that about you." I raise an eyebrow and he lifts a shoulder. "I'm not saying they don't know, but you've made it pretty clear the topic's off-limits. And it happened so long ago—"

"That no one cares," I finish his sentence.

"I was going to say they don't think about it."

"Same thing."

He pushes his head against the back of the seat and exhales as he stares at the ceiling. "I don't know what to say. This is some serious shit. I don't think you should have to deal with it alone."

You're not alone.

"I'm not alone."

"Does Cal know?"

My head shakes sharply, once left, once right. "No." I take a breath. "I've never told anyone."

My words hang between us. If it's possible, they feel heavier than my confession. The shift in Wes's posture is subtle, but it's like the burden of my secret shifts from my shoulders to his, just for a moment. Because now he carries a sliver of my truth.

"Eve, this is..." He exhales again, searching the ceiling for answers to the unsolvable riddle of my life.

"Too much, I know."

He faces me. "It is, but that's not what I was gonna say. This is too big for you to handle by yourself. Have you ever seen a therapist or something?"

The walls slam up faster than I can take a breath and regret creeps through me. Why did I tell him? He's too good of a person to let this go and my life works best in secrecy. "I don't need a therapist."

"I saw one after my dad left. It's not that big a deal."

Wes Sherman continues to surprise me.

You trusted him for a reason.

He rests his arm on the steering wheel, his gaze holding mine while keeping his distance physically. "What are you afraid of?"

You. Everyone learning the truth. Starting over as Just Eve. Or worse, living the rest of my life as both of us. Just when I think I don't have any tears left, my eyes fill again. My throat constricts around my words, strangling my sarcastic laughter. "How long do you have?"

He opens his hands and gestures at the inside of the truck as if to say, "I'm not going anywhere."

I blink back the tears, swallowing down the rising panic that this moment is the start of another After. "There's a lot about my life that scares me, but when it comes down to it, I don't want anything to happen to my mom. Learning the truth might destroy her. She may be crazy, but at least right now she's happy."

"At your expense."

"They'll put her away."

"So her happiness is more important than yours?"

I mimic his earlier shrug. "I've only got one hundred thirty days left."

He closes his eyes and inhales deeply, like he's considering his next words. Or maybe he thinks I'm crazy and isn't sure how to tell me. "So you're just gonna keep pretending to be your sister?"

"I've been pretending to be my sister for so long I don't know how else to live."

Wes either decides there's no use trying to change me, or he realizes I'm so far gone there's no saving me. We sit in silence, watching the waves as they roll gently onto shore, the earlier storm nothing but a distant memory.

When he pulls into his driveway, the gravity of what I've done settles into my bones. My secret is out. It's only a matter of time before every lie, every mistruth, everything I've done for Gen, escapes the safety of my mind and tramples my carefully plotted life.

Seventeen

"I'm not going to tell anyone."

"You say that now."

"Eve." He touches me for the first time since he helped me into the truck. His fingers grip my shoulder lightly, yet firm enough to make me look at him. "You trusted me for a reason. I swear I won't tell anyone. But I can't promise I'll stop trying to help you."

A smirk lifts my lips, breaking the tension. "Great."

He laughs softly. "You probably need to get inside, right?"

"Yeah." I pick at a crack in the vinyl seat, both nervous to spend more time with this person who knows my full truth and afraid to leave his side. He's the only person who sees me. "Mom's probably worried about Gen. She gets anxious when she's late."

He opens his mouth to speak, but shakes his head instead. "I'll see you later."

"Thanks for the ride. And for listening." I slip from the truck without looking back. I don't want to know if he's watching me, worrying about me, seeing me differently. Confessing doesn't change who I am, it only makes it more real.

With each step toward the house, the weight of the day presses heavier and heavier until I slump in a chair in the kitchen. As soon as I sit, Dad stalks into the room, goes straight to the refrigerator, and pulls out a bottle of beer. When he shuts the door and pauses with his hand still on the handle, everything inside me stills.

"Your mother is waiting for you."

I deflate lower onto the table. "I know."

"Where have you been?"

My hand flicks over my damp clothes. "Running. Got caught in the rain." The little girl deep inside me who doesn't understand why her mom is different from her friends' and yearns for someone who takes her to birthday parties and shopping and on surprise trips for Happy Meals after school pokes her head through my defenses and starts to cry.

Dad hesitates with his still unopened beer. "Is everything okay?"

If he paid as much attention to me as he did the rules of his charade, he'd notice my bloodshot eyes and the sand stuck to my legs, but all he sees is the creature who keeps his precious Michelle coherent.

"Yeah, Dad. Everything's great." I wipe my eyes with the edge of my shirt and glare at him. My emotional capacity surpassed its limit half an hour ago and I can't pretend any longer.

"Why the tone?"

My laughter is bitter, loud. He glances toward the stairs like he's worried Mom heard me.

Let her.

"The tone?" My eyes roll and I laugh again. "Can you not comprehend what it's like to live my life with you pulling my strings?" I flop my hands in the air in front of me like a marionette, then wave a hand at the stairs. "To know that no matter what I accomplish, she'll still love Gen more."

"That's not true."

My hands drop to my legs. "Which part."

He twists off the cap of the beer and takes a long drink. "Your mother loves you both equally." He doesn't deny being the puppet master.

"She told Gen she's her favorite."

His face slackens and he sets the bottle on the counter behind him. "She shouldn't say things like that."

"It's a little late for the shouldn't game, don't you think?"

"I'll talk to her."

The urge to break something pushes me to my feet. Alarm widens his eyes. "And say what exactly?" I take a step forward. "Don't play favorites with the girls?" Another step. "You hurt Eve's feelings?" I reach around him and grab his beer. "You can't like Gen better because she doesn't exist?" My eyes lock on his while I take a sip. The beer is bitter but I swallow it anyways. I rarely challenge him directly, and never so blatantly.

He takes the bottle from my hand and sets it back on the counter. Grips my shoulders. I can't remember the last time we've stood this close. Made physical contact. The frustration in his eyes is familiar, like looking in a mirror, but he maintains control over his emotions. Something I'm still working on.

"I know this is hard, and that it will have to stop. Soon." His gaze flits over my shoulder before settling back on my eyes. "I can't make up for what we've put you through, but—"

"You, Dad. What you've put me through."

His eyes close and he exhales through his nose. "I never meant for it to get to this point. Just keep it together a bit longer."

My head jerks back as if he slapped my face. Because that's how forcefully his words hit me. "What are you saying?"

Is he ending this?

Will I finally be free?

He releases my shoulders and leans against the counter. Takes another sip of beer. "I've been thinking a lot. About you leaving for college. When you were little, I only saw the days and weeks in front of me. I didn't think about the future. About you growing up." He taps his lip with the bottle, watching me. "You're right. This can't go on forever."

My legs wobble and my head spins. Years of longing for him to say these words are no match for hearing them out loud, of seeing the look of defeat on his face. He's aged in the last few years, his rich brown hair now peppered with gray, the lines around his eyes making him seem even more serious than he is. For as much as I begrudge Mom for not seeing me, how long has he slipped beneath my radar?

"Won't ending it break her?"

His head droops. "That's the part I'm still trying to figure out."

We stand near each other for a few more minutes, two people bound by a lifetime of lies, unable to be honest with each other. He takes another drink and gives me a small smile. "I should let you go see Mom."

My mind feels frayed, like I'll disintegrate with one more tug, and I still have to work on my project. "Let me know if..." I look at the ceiling as if the right thing to say is written there. "If I can help." It's an empty gesture, one he shouldn't dare consider. Because as awful as it will be for Mom to have her precious Gen ripped from her a second time, Dad needs to clean this mess on his own.

Upstairs, I knock on Mom's door before entering. She's on the couch, knitting needles clutched tightly in her hands, her show playing on the TV. A thread of orange yarn weaves through the blue square in her lap.

Potholder?

Do people even use those anymore?

"Gen!" The needles clatter to the table as she reaches for the remote and presses pause. "I can restart this episode. It's the one where Joey learns to ballroom dance."

The Joey reference makes me picture Cal trying to dance. He'd probably look amazing in a tux, moving across the hardwood floor with lights twinkling all around him. And I should probably have more of an internal reaction than just thinking he'd be a good dancer. A fluttering in my stomach, increased heart rate, something. But my body accepts this fact as if Mom told me she's knitting a green scarf instead of blue.

It's not a scarf.

She restarts the show and beams at me, and I squat next to the couch and pick up the needles. Anything to avoid the childlike eagerness in her eyes. "I can't stay long. I ran home from practice and got caught in the rain and I'd really like to take a shower." Oh, and I told the neighbor boy our secret. The one we keep to maintain your sanity and would probably get you involuntarily committed if it ever got out.

My legs give out and I collapse onto the couch. Is that what Dad's considering?

There isn't another way.

The room closes in on me as Mom hits play. Canned laughter mixes with the roaring in my head and the pieces of my childhood, our childhood, swirl before me. The hours I've spent curled on this couch next to Mom, the juxtaposition of hatred and pity growing stronger with each passing year. The lies I've woven until the line between truth and fiction is nothing more than a shadow moving across a sundial, marking time by falsehoods and tears and a resentment that's grown so strong it threatens to overwhelm my sanity.

But it's not her fault. Maybe at first, but it was Dad's responsibility to stop playing make-believe for the sake of his remaining daughter. And now he's faced with the decision that probably should have been made eighteen years ago.

"Are you okay?" Mom's voice settles my thoughts and I blink her into focus. She's paused the TV again and bites her lip as she studies me.

Why can't you see who I am?

Because she doesn't want to.

That's not true.

You're not the Green Arrow and this isn't DC Comics. Pulling your hair back doesn't make you a different person. She chooses to see what she wants.

But we're twins.

We're still different people.

Could she be right? All I've wanted is for Mom to realize I'm Eve, but maybe deep down she's always known.

"I—I have homework to do." My legs protest as I push to my feet, but I can't stay here a second longer. My lips are cool on her cheek. "Sorry I can't stay to watch." Then I walk out the door without looking back. Seeing the hurt and confusion that's surely on her face will only make me feel worse, and I refuse to let down Noah and Willow.

After my shower, low voices from Mom's room make me pause.

"That was supposed to be our secret." Betrayal laces Mom's words, and a rush of satisfaction and guilt wars inside me. It sucks when someone you love shows they aren't who you thought they were.

"You have to be careful. You can't play favorites."

"I didn't think she'd tell Eve."

"They're sisters. They talk, they fight, they try to one-up each other." There's a pause, and I picture him running a hand through his hair as he chooses the perfect words to keep her in line. Because that's how he's manipulated me all these years.

My breath catches. Has he been manipulating her as well? Guiding her toward a certain set of behaviors to keep our sadistic household more harmonious?

"The girls are very different and Eve can be sensitive."

"I'll apologize to her."

"Don't do that. Just try to be more careful."

The smoothness of his voice as he instructs his wife how to handle her fondness for her make-believe daughter sends a chill down my back. Words like psychotic and sociopath whip through my mind but I don't know which is the best way to describe the man behind our curtain. The man who might be the most emotionally unstable person in this family.

I back away from the door and take refuge in my room. String a tightrope over my research and tiptoe across. If I keep my eyes forward and my balance centered, I can summarize the horrors of what people do to the vulnerable members of society for my portion of the project. But one slip and I'll tumble down the black hole of my imagination, and I fear that darkness will eventually consume me.

Christiane Amanpour watches over me from the wall, her steady gaze encouraging me to turn off my emotions and focus on the task at hand. Which I do until a comment in the margin of my notes catches my eye. But not because of what it says—it's not my handwriting.

"Did Ember write that?" I ask Christiane. She's the only one ever close enough to see my research, but why would she write—I lean closer—to include local missing children cases in our report?

Christiane's gaze remains steady, unflinching. Just like I need to be. Digging into local cases would make this too personal. I turn the page of my notebook, effectively erasing the comment from my mind. Once I do, choosing which statistics best fit with each photo comes more easily than I expect.

For the first picture, the one with the girl working at a diner: 2.4 in 100 said they were forced to work or do something illegal by someone who received money or something of value for what they did.

The second, with the boy in the alley: 1 in 100 teens said they were given money, shelter, food, or something of value in exchange for sex.

And the last, most haunting picture, the one with a girl on a couch with a couple lurking behind her: over 700 teens in our county say they've been trafficked for sex or work.

It may not be perfect, but it's close, and when I load my work into the thread on the forum, I slump back onto my bed with a mix of relief and exhaustion. Then I see a message from half an hour ago.

`Twilight: is it cool if I text?`

`Journalist309: Yeah.`

If Sky's anything like me, she's got enough homework to choke a horse, so it's doubtful she's still online. My short story is due by the end of the week, so I switch screens and settle in with my sorceress. She stands amid a pile of ash that was once her army. When I left off, her next actions were unclear, but the past twenty-four hours have changed my perspective, which also changes hers. Perhaps she destroyed the men because they aren't what she really wants. Perhaps the handmaid standing in the shadows is the true epicenter of this quest.

My phone buzzes at my hip.

Sky: you busy?

me: Just finished working on my project

Sky: are you doing okay?

This is what happens when you tell people things. They remember, then they expect you to keep talking about it.

me: Glad it's done.

Sky: soooo...

I groan audibly. Here it comes. It was stupid to think Gen wouldn't worm her way into my new friendships. She's part of me and I can never escape her.

I didn't realize you were trying.

Not you. But the specter of you.

Sky: you doing any better than last time we talked?

me: Is it okay if we don't get into it right now?

Sky: sure! sorry if I offended you

me: It's okay. I've just got other things on my mind.

There's a pause, like she's afraid to ask any more questions.

Now you've scared her off.

I count slowly as I inhale.

If I'm going to make new friends, I can't chase them off the second they get personal. Friends ask each other questions.

It's how they get to know each other.

Exhale.

I can do this.

me: I don't want to dump my problems on you.

Sky: try me

Trust has never come easy for me, but in this moment, sitting in my quiet bedroom surrounded by homework, I want to try. It doesn't seem real since I can't see her face or see the judgement or curiosity or disapproval in her eyes, but maybe that's what I need to take this first step.

me: What color are your eyes?

Sky: that's what you want to ask?

me: I'm just curious.

Sky: that was quite a build up to ask about my eyes

me: Making friends isn't easy for me.

A moment passes, then two, then her answer appears.

Sky: brown

Mariela's green eyes flash through my memory, followed by the way they closed just before we kissed.

me: Mine too.

Sky: us and over half the population of the world

me: How do you know that?

Sky: random facts intrigue me

Sky: so what do you really want to ask?

me: Something happened yesterday that I can't tell my friends about.

Sky: and you need an anonymous crisis hotline

Delirious laughter bubbles out of me, eviscerating my grip on this latest secret.

me: Something like that.

Sky: consider this your judgement free zone

me: Thanks.

me: So.

Sweat breaks out over my body. Once I admit what happened I can never take it back.

Kind of like with Wes.

me: The short version: I have a sort of BF but last night I kissed a girl.

Apparently, no secrets are safe today.

Sky: was she the first girl you've kissed?

Kissed, touched, absorbed into my very being.

me: yeah

Sky: which is bothering you? the fact that you kissed someone else or that you kissed a girl?

me: A little of both?

And bothered isn't the right word. More like tossed upside-down so nothing makes sense anymore.

Sky: do you think you're bi?

me: I've never thought about it before.

Sky: you've only dated guys?

Lissa flashes through my mind. Things I wanted back then but didn't know what to call it.

me: If you can call it dating, yeah.

Sky: and what's with the sort of BF?

me: He's sweet and wants to be serious, but I don't see the point.

Sky: maybe it's not the being serious part that's the problem. maybe it's because he's a dude.

I snort. Cal is the farthest from what I'd consider a dude, but she has a point. He makes me feel respected and desired, two vital parts of a relationship, yet I constantly push him away.

me: Maybe you're right.

Sky: it's not a trick question. if you liked the kiss, then I think you have your answer

me: So you think I'm bi?

Sky: it's not up to me. you're the only one who knows how you feel and what you want

me: You should be a therapist.

Sky: did you think I just came up with the ACH?

me: ACH?

Sky: anonymous crisis hotline

me: Ha! Yes, I did.

Sky: nope, I'm a legend around here. my friends say it's like I've got a sixth sense about fixing their problems. I just pay attention to what's left unsaid and poke it

What's left unsaid would fill her brown eyes with judgement and ruin our friendship before it even starts. Besides, I've had enough confessing for one day.

me: Maybe you should be a social worker.

Sky: I've thought about it. it'd be cool to give back to the system that helped me

Sky: my life is practically storybook but not all kids are that lucky

me: Wait. What?

Sky: oh sorry. I was adopted.

me: You were?

Sky: yeah, but I don't want to be a therapist. design is a part of me. I'd rather just help my friends, you know?

me: I get that.

My life experience probably over-qualifies me to be a therapist, but I'd be too afraid to unearth things about myself that are lurking beneath the surface.

me: Well, thanks for listening.

Sky: don't just listen to me. listen to yourself.

Right. Cal.

me: So I probably shouldn't go to prom with him.

Sky: lol. it's just a dance. is yours in your gym?

me: Worse. Community center.

Sky: ha. it's your call. I won't judge you either way.

I repeat her last words to myself. I won't judge you. They give me permission to feel how I feel without worrying about anyone else.

I've never felt so free.

Eighteen

WillowRicha: Eve, this is great!

NoBPhoto: Yeah, seriously.

Journalist309: We did this together. My words are the last thing you see. The photos and layout are what will grab people.

Journalist309: You guys seriously crushed this.

The flyer doesn't look much different now that it has my copy. For as much as I pride myself on my work ethic, I give praise when it's due, and Willow and Noah turned what started as an idea into something powerful that could actually make a difference. Noah's images have captivated me, especially the bottom picture. It's a girl with hair like mine sitting on a threadbare couch. Her hair's hanging in her face, her arms wrapped tightly around her knees like she's trying to make herself smaller. If I squint, the shape of her legs and the curve of her hands resemble mine. Which is the whole point of this project—for our peers to see themselves in the models and realize this kind of exploitation could happen to anyone.

Before this project, I had vague ideas of what Gen's life must be like—assuming she's still alive. But since Noah sent the pictures, this is how I imagine her. Scared and alone, unloved, and doing anything she can to get through the day.

NoBPhoto: High fives all around.

NoBPhoto: So how do we practice for the presentation?

WillowRicha: Can we just take turns reading the flyer.

I swallow past the lump in my throat.

Journalist309: I've got more stats. Want me to write up a script? Then we can take turns reading.

NoBPhoto: Do you have enough info for a script?

Journalist309: Too much.

Not all trafficking involves violence or sex.

Some victims are forced to work while someone else takes their money.

But every 30 seconds, another person becomes a victim of human trafficking.

Sex trafficking is basically a form of modern-day slavery.

Survivor rights include getting prostitution charges cleared from their record.

That last one unleashes an unending nightmare of my body double being forced into sex. I have complete control over what I do with Cal—I can't imagine having sex with a stranger, or someone I'm afraid of, or worse, someone who doesn't care if I live or die.

WillowRicha: Thanks Eve.

WillowRicha: Now for the serious question: what are we going to wear.

For once I don't roll my eyes at Willow's breeziness. Her ability to lighten the mood is like a tether from the abyss of my imagination.

NoBPhoto: We are not wearing matching outfits.

WillowRicha: How else will we find each other. What if we dressed all grungy, like we live on the street.

Then I would literally become my vision of Gen.

Journlist309: I think that might be insensitive. And I'm sure we'll find each other.

WillowRicha: All good. It was just an idea.

Journalist309: I'll put together the script so we can rehearse.

WillowRicha: Just one week to go! I can't wait to meet you both!

"Your story turned out great." Cal's voice in my ear startles me.

After my conversation with Sky Friday night, I spent the weekend finishing the flyers and writing what I hoped was an informative and entertaining account of the playoff game.

He nuzzles my shoulder and guilt prevents me from pushing him away. "I tweaked a couple terms for accuracy, but the story is solid."

"Thanks. I'm not switching to sports reporting, but it was a fun change of pace." My cheeks flush at the double meaning. Fun doesn't begin to cover it. Mariela's text sits unanswered in my phone, a constant reminder of what I did and what I felt. The memory of her hands on my body are like phantoms following me everywhere I go.

"The other piece was great, too. Although I'm not sure how you had the time—"

"What other piece?"

"On local graduation rates. It'll be perfect for the next issue."

Panic sears through me. My pulse thumps in my ears, drowning out whatever else he's saying. I would bet my mother's well-being I didn't write an article about graduation rates. Gen's smile somehow makes its way to my face and I nod until the roaring subsides.

"Have you given it any more thought?"

My mind is too full of everything to discern what he's talking about. "About?"

He exhales and rolls his eyes. "Prom."

"Oh, sorry." I press the side of my head against his as my heart rate slows. My rule against PDA seems stupid since according to Wes, everyone already knows. If we go to prom, the secret will definitely be out.

What's the big deal?

I'm doing it for the wrong reasons.

He doesn't have to know that. Be nice for once.

Inhale, exhale. "I'll go."

His excitement is palpable. His eyes practically sparkle as his fingers tuck a stray piece of hair behind my ear, then trail over my jaw, stopping at my chin. For a second I think he's going to kiss me in the middle of the *Sabre* office, but instead he gives me the softest smile I've ever seen.

My heart flutters, but for all the wrong reasons, and my thoughts rapid fire.

He should not be this excited over a stupid dance.

I'm definitely leading him on.

He would be crushed if he found out about Mariela.

There is no future for us.

But I can't say any of that.

"We'll keep it casual. I'll wear my suit and you can go naked as far as I care."

The corner of my mouth lifts in a smile. "I'm sure you'd like that."

"I mean," his head dips toward mine and I back away, keeping a sliver of distance between us. "I wouldn't completely hate it."

"It can't be that hard to find a dress in two weeks."

"So just wear this." His finger hooks on the hem of my skirt the same way Mariela's did and I resist the urge to push him away. Being with her changed how my body reacts to him. Instead of a mild stirring of affection, each caress amplifies my irritation and trips over my guilt until I can barely look at him.

"I'll figure something out."

A minute before the bell rings, Mr. Barney clears his throat. "I know you're all in the final crunch for the project, but don't forget about your regular assignments." His gaze lands on a couple underclassmen who aren't even working on the seniors-only project, then he smiles at Ember, Cal, and me. The professionals. "I'm hosting a pizza night tomorrow at seven. That should give everyone enough time for practice or games or whatever it is you do after school—"

I nudge Ember. "Or dress shopping?"

Her eyes widen, staring at me, then Cal, and I nod.

"—before putting in some extra hours here at the *Sabre*. I'll need your RSVPs tomorrow morning, so check with your parents if you need to. And as always, be respectful out there."

The bell rings and chairs scrape as everyone stands.

"You said yes?" Ember's smile is fleeting, like she's afraid I'll change my mind. It's the same expression that's been on Cal's face since I said I'd go to the stupid dance.

"Yes, and now I have two weeks to find a dress." We step into the hall, Cal trailing behind us, pretending not to listen.

"What about—" she bites her lip. Several beats pass before she continues. "What about your mom?"

My brows furrow. I realize most mothers live for this kind of thing, but I can't imagine her leaving the house to go shopping. "What about her?"

"Any chance she has a dress you could wear?"

I snort. "What, like in a movie where the thirty-year old dress magically fits, is in style, and ends up being the prettiest dress at the dance? I'm sure she has something like that in her closet between the two hundred sweaters she's knitted." In my eighteen years, I've never seen Mom wear anything except pants, cotton shirts, and the occasional workout gear when she does aerobics—plus the aforementioned sweaters.

Ember shrugs before coming to a stop at her hallway. "You never know. Just ask." Then she heads toward class with a wave over her shoulder. "See you at lunch!"

Cal nuzzles my neck from behind. "This is gonna be great." His hands slide around my waist and all at once my breath stops and my pulse races, but not from arousal.

My body is telling me to run.

How am I going to get through an entire night of hand holding and slow dancing with him?

Just pretend to be me.

You don't think he'll notice?

He's a hormone-fueled teenaged boy.

Touché.

I disentangle myself from his embrace and take a step back. "We're not doing the coordinated thing, right? You're wearing your suit and I'll wear…" I wave at the prom poster on the wall. "Whatever I figure out."

He steps closer until my back hits the wall, his warm eyes focused on mine. "Whatever you want."

What I want is to take back my yes and spend the final days of school with my head down. Going to prom will put me—us—on people's radar, and I don't want the extra attention.

"Thanks, Cal." I slide past him and hurry to class, dread creeping through me.

The following afternoon, Wes is half-buried under the hood of his truck when I get home from my run.

"Car trouble?" I ask, wiping my face with my shirt.

He emerges from behind the hood, a silver tool in his greasy hand and the same cautious smile Cal and Ember had earlier on his face. "How was your day?"

"It was a day."

He sets the tool down with a clink. "How are you feeling?"

I take a step back and narrow my gaze. The grease on his hands looks too precise, and his clothes are too nice to be working on his truck. "Were you waiting for me?"

"I'm worried about you."

"That's not a denial."

This is what I get for telling him.

He's just being nice.

He shrugs and wipes his hands on a dirty rag. Maybe he really is fixing his car.

I jut my chin at the engine. "What's wrong?"

"She's making a weird noise."

My lips curl into a smile before I can stop them. "Is that the technical term?"

He smiles back. "Yep. Weird noise is right before wobbly bit in the car mechanic's manual."

Props for rapid-fire alphabetization.

"So you weren't waiting for me?"

"As exciting as it is talking to you, I do have a life."

A blush warms my cheeks. "Sorry."

"But since you didn't answer, how are you feeling?"

Before I can answer, an unfamiliar pickup truck rumbles around the corner and down our street. Wes drops the rag on the open hood and stalks to the end of the driveway. "Stay there," he calls over his shoulder, and the tension in his tone keeps me from arguing. The truck stops at the end of the drive and a man with scraggly gray hair and grease-streaked arms gestures at Wes. Their voices don't carry, and for once Wes's shoulders aren't relaxed. I stay rooted in the driveway until the man's eyes sweep over me in a way that makes me cross my arms over my chest.

Wes moves to block his view, but doesn't turn around.

Go help him.

He doesn't need my help.

You don't know that.

I approach, my stomach roiling. Wes's face has an expression I've never seen on him. Uncertain, scared, more and more protective as I get closer—

"You should go inside."

"This your girlfriend? My boy has good taste." His eyes are blue like Wes's and it's possible the gray used to be blond, but that's where the similarity stops. The lines creasing his face tell of a hard life and his lecherous sneer makes me regret approaching. But I'm here, so I may as well help.

"Eve's not my—"

I slide my arm through his and Gen smiles. "We're not official, but..." then I give a Wes shrug.

"What do you want?" Wes says it like it's not the first time he asked. "You know you're not supposed to be here."

"PPO expired when you turned eighteen. Besides, I wanted to see you."

A thousand thoughts fly through my head but the ones blazing in neon lights—Personal Protection Order—launch questions I don't have the right to ask.

"Well, I don't want to see you." Wes tightens his arm against mine, and I'm not sure if it's to protect me or reassure himself. "Go."

His dad drops his gaze and the relaxed façade slips for a beat. I almost feel bad for him until he meets Wes's eyes again. "You tell that bitch of a mother she can't keep me away from you anymore."

Wes releases my arm and grips the edge of the open window, peering at the man who my imagination screams is dangerous and shouldn't be messed with. "I made the decision not to see you after you threw me through a wall. The PPO was the police's idea."

My gasp makes them both turn, and for a moment the resemblance between them is frightening. Since I've met Wes, he's been a solid, safe presence, but here, staring down his abusive father, an energy rolls off him that I wish I'd never seen.

They face off for hours or minutes or only a few heartbeats, then his dad brushes Wes's hands off the window and guns the engine. Loose stones erupt behind the truck as he yanks on the steering wheel, carrying him down the street in a cloud of exhaust.

"He seems nice." I immediately bite my lip to prevent anything worse from slipping out, but he gives me a sad smile.

"Nice is not the word I'd use, but yeah. That's my dad."

This moment feels too private, like I've stumbled into a secret Wes never intended to share. "I guess we all have our shit, right?"

He stares at the empty road, rolling his shoulders like he's physically shaking off his dad's presence. "You could say that."

We stand side by side at the end of his driveway, wrapped in a moment that feels bigger than ourselves. Maybe this is what growing up is all about. Maybe we really can be friends. "I need to get inside. See you later?"

"See ya."

My departure feels too abrupt, so I turn, my hand on the front door. "I hope you fix the noise."

He waves a hand. "Thanks, Eve."

I grab a glass of water from the kitchen and go directly to Mom's room. The twists and turns of my emotional rollercoaster over the past couple days feel amplified by the encounter with Wes's dad, but Mom doesn't have the luxury of getting off the ride. If I don't get things back to normal with her, she'll start to spiral.

Her door is ajar, so I push it open and poke my head in with a smile. But she's not on the couch. The TV is off and her knitting rests in its basket beneath the window. Everything seems to be in place. Everything except my mother.

Nineteen

My heart stutters. She's always on the couch, or at least in the vicinity. "Mom?" I step into the room and head directly for the window. Wes's treehouse, which was visible the last time I looked, has hunkered into the new leaves in the tree. "Did she leave?" I rest my hip on the windowsill and face the room as the bathroom door opens.

"Oh, Gen! You're early." Mom wipes her hands on the front of her fleece shirt, her face lighting up as she approaches. "Can you believe how much the leaves have popped in the last few days? Spring is doing her magic."

I return my gaze out the window and try to remember how insignificant this room looked from out there. Like the secrets and lies and heartache were tucked safely in these walls, unable to reach inside the treehouse. My chest starts to tighten so I turn away. This isn't the time to escape. Right now I have to perform.

"I have news." Gen smiles so hard the room sparkles.

Mom's eyes crinkle as she smiles and my heart does a silly pitter-patter. This display of love may be for Gen, but there's something to be said for making someone this happy, even if it isn't real. She bites her lip, waiting.

"I'm going to prom!" Bubbly and happy. Excited. Not a care in the world beyond what to wear.

And maybe if I keep repeating these reminders, they'll actually come true.

She pulls me into an embrace and squeezes. "That's wonderful! With the boy I met?"

A kick to the gut.

"What was his name?"

Punch to the chest.

Breathe, Eve.

Mom cocks her head, her smile fading.

Inhale through my nose.

"Yes, Cal. My boyfriend."

She sits on the edge of the couch and folds her hands on her knees. "What are you wearing?"

I hate the part of me that wishes she would offer to take me shopping, or at least realize I need a dress. But I know better than to hope for things that'll never happen. "I'm not sure. Nothing fancy."

"But prom is meant to be fancy." She taps her chin. "I don't know if you'll like it, but I still have a dress from when I was your age. You're welcome to try it on."

This time my laugh is real. "No offense, Mom, but hot pink and poufy shoulders will never be back in style."

She raises an eyebrow. "Give me a little credit." Before I can stop her, she's on her feet and disappears into her walk-in closet. I've never understood why she needs such a big closet when she never leaves the house, but if I compare all the things I don't understand about my mother, her closet space is at the bottom of the list. Plastic rustles and her muffled voice doesn't quite reach me.

"What'd you say?" I join her in the closet as she yanks a royal blue cocktail dress from the back corner. The skirt flares over a layer of crinoline and tiny rhinestones dance over the bust. Delicate straps hold the dress together. "Mom, that's actually pretty."

She rolls her eyes, and longing nearly knocks me off my feet. These moments should be our normal, not so few and far between that I don't know the person buried beneath her grief. "I knew what I was doing." She presses the dress against her body and sighs. "I don't think I could squeeze into this, but you're in such great shape I'm sure it will look beautiful." She meets my eyes. "If it's not a faux pas to wear your mother's dress?"

The material is a little scratchy, but the silk lining is smooth to the touch. The length is close to what I wear every day, so exactly what I'd pick. "Mom, it's perfect."

"Are you sure?"

"Let me try it on."

I pull my shirt over my head and kick off my running shorts. With a couple tugs, the dress slides over my body, settling nicely on my narrow hips. My gray sports bra stands out like fog rolling over a bright blue lake.

"Okay, so maybe a different bra," Mom teases.

It's like seeing a different person. One who laughs and jokes and can see beyond the walls of her self-imposed prison. The only mirror in her suite is in the bathroom, so I rustle out of the closet to preen at my reflection. Sports bra aside, it does magically fit.

Mom follows me into the bathroom and rests a hand on my shoulder. Our eyes meet in the mirror. "You girls have my teenaged figure." Her finger hooks under the thin strap. "I can adjust this if it's too loose."

My fingers test the resistance and our hands brush. "I'll try it later without the boob compressor."

She laughs, the smile crinkling her eyes. "Are you sure you can't convince your sister to go, too?"

My heart thrills, wrapping around this feeling to hold it for later, then roll my eyes. "It's not really her thing."

"I suppose not." She sighs and gets a faraway look, as if remembering something from long ago. "The night I wore this dress, I thought I was on top of the world. Ricky Meyer was the captain of the basketball team and student body president, and we'd dated since junior year. Even though we'd been on hundreds of dates, prom was like a fairy tale. The perfect end to high school."

Thinking of Mom with another man, even in high school, feels weird. My hands drop to the counter. "I didn't realize you dated someone before Dad."

"Oh, honey. We didn't meet until our late twenties. We both have histories we brought to our marriage."

Did you know this?

How would I?

Gen feels as unbalanced as I do.

Was she afraid of the world back then? Or has her mind always been fractured and just needed one big push to fall over the edge?

"I never thought about your lives before you were married." Probably because Dad never talks about it and Mom, well, Mom exists in a world of make-believe.

She steers me back to the closet with her hand on my lower back. "It's not something parents talk about with their children."

Child.

She unzips the dress and lifts it over my head. For a moment I'm three years old, shortly before Mom shut herself away from the world. We're in a dressing room on a Mommy and Me date while Dad "took Gen" on a father-daughter thing, and I'm surrounded by dresses that would rival a Disney princess's. The crinoline scratches my face and I don't understand why Mom keeps calling me Gen, but she seems happier than I've ever seen her so I smile and pretend to love every moment. Because even at that young age, I knew something about Mom was different and I'd do anything to keep the smile on her face.

I pull on my shirt and it's cold against my skin. A shower would be great, but like that day trying on princess dresses, I don't want to break whatever spell has fallen over Mom.

We watch an episode and the connection between us hums like a current. Questions flash through my mind—about her teen years, her parents, when she first felt her balance slip—but I keep them inside. It's been years since she talked like she has today and I won't be the one who snaps her back to the present. When the episode ends, we stand and she pulls me into a hug.

It feels like love.

The sunset blazes across the sky when I pull into the school parking lot. Cal's car is already here, plus a half dozen others from the *Sabre*. Most of the hallways are dark except for the path to the newspaper office, and the scent of cheese and tomato sauce greets me as I step into the room.

"Eve, thank god." Ember rushes to my side with a half-eaten piece of pizza in her hand and gives me a one-armed hug.

I hug her back, the emotions from earlier lingering. "You'll never believe what happened," I say. She quirks a brow at me and I wave a hand over my midsection. "My mom's dress fits. And it's not awful."

Her jaw drops. "You mean you're officially in a teen rom-com?"

"I'm so extra extra."

She laughs, but her smile quickly fades.

"How's it going here?"

"The testosterone-fest is getting out of control."

Cal and two other writers are in their usual seats, focused on their laptops, greasy paper plates at their sides. But Aiden, Kevin, and a sophomore who's glommed onto them watch us from the back corner.

My eyes narrow at Kevin. Aiden wins the award for inappropriate comments, but he's generally harmless. Kevin is mean. "Did he say anything to you?"

"Nothing more than usual. Mostly shit about Claire."

"Where's Mr. Barney?" His zero-tolerance policy is well-known and usually well-respected.

"Soda run. Pizza place forgot it."

I drop my bag next to my chair and throw Kevin another scowl. Cal smiles up at me as Kevin says, "Trying to make Claire jealous?"

Ember slams her laptop shut and glares at Kevin. “What’s your problem, Kevin?”

The room falls silent, but Kevin smirks like he’s enjoying the attention. “I’m just making an observation.”

“You and your observations need to leave me the eff alone. You already outed me to my parents. What more do you want?” Her voice quivers with anger and frustration and a barely concealed fear only I am close enough to notice. She’s sworn she’ll never forgive Kevin for taking away her opportunity to tell her parents about her sexuality in her own way, when she was ready. Not at the end of an awards ceremony because he was pissed she won the award he wanted.

A protectiveness surges through me and I’m on my feet before I can stop myself. “Back the fuck off, Douchewipe.” The words hover over the room and now everyone’s staring at me, no doubt wondering when I found my voice.

Kevin’s gaze bounces between me and Ember, a satisfied smile declaring that our reactions are exactly what he wanted. “Like I said, just making an observation.” He waves a hand at the room that’s supposed to be our safe space. “Isn’t that what we do here?”

Cal’s out of his chair so fast it falls backwards. “You need to crawl back into whatever hole you came from.”

Aiden sinks behind Kevin, who’s puffed out his chest like a wild animal. Ember trembles next to me, her hand light on my arm.

“Cal, stop. He’s just trying to get a reaction,” I say.

“Looks like I got one.” Kevin’s sneer matches mine.

I don’t back down, and my mind races to catch up with why he said anything in the first place. Ember and I have been friends for years and my entire girl-on-girl history was last week. Which no one knows about. Except—my gaze levels on Aiden. He couldn’t have seen anything. He left long before the lights went out.

But there were a few moments when our hands brushed, or our legs pressed together, or our eyes met for longer than was really necessary. Did he figure out what was happening before I did?

"What set him off?" Ember asks, still close to my side.

"I'll explain later," I whisper before stepping behind Cal. "Hey, just let it go."

"What did he mean about making Claire jealous?" He studies me like he's trying to solve a puzzle.

"If I tried to figure out the intent behind every douchey thing he does I wouldn't be your best reporter and I wouldn't be headed to Northwestern." I press my cheek against his shoulder. "There's a reason we call him a douche. It's because he's a douche."

"Well, I apologize for my gender." He runs a finger over my temple and leans close enough to kiss me. "Can you come over later? I feel like it's been forever."

It's barely been a week, but he is an eighteen-year old male. My lower lip juts out in a Gen-inspired pout while fear of him finding out the truth makes my hands shake. "Shark week," I lie. My tryst with Mariela may have ended when I drove out of the parking lot, but until I figure out what it means, it feels wrong to sleep with Cal.

He scoffs. "You know I like you for more than sex."

"Get back to work!" Mr. Barney's voice makes us jump apart. He sets bags filled with two-liter bottles of soda on the table near the pizza boxes. "Drink up."

"Drink up or get back to work?" Kevin asks. He's perfected the wide-eyed innocence of a kid who sucks up to adults but treats his peers like shit the moment they turn around.

"Quit being a smart aleck," says Mr. Barney.

Kevin holds up his hands, all smiles. "Just following the rules, sir."

"My ass," Ember mutters less quietly than she probably meant to.

Mr. Barney glances our way but unloads the bags without reprimanding her. Perhaps he has a better understanding of Kevin's true nature than I realized.

We grab drinks and pizza and settle in to work. I keep all my documents in folders so the desktop is orderly, but there's a file in the center of the screen.

When I double-click, a box appears asking for the password.

The sensation of a thousand eyes on my back makes me swivel in my seat, but everyone is focused on their own work. No one sneaks a look at me. No one's waiting for my reaction.

I double-click again and am greeted with the same prompt.

What is going on?

My standard passwords don't work. The file mocks, taunts, teases, but refuses to unlock.

Ember pokes me with her pencil. "So?" she asks with a nod in Kevin's direction.

It takes me a moment to remember what she's talking about. "Not here."

"Bathroom in five?"

I nod, then move the file to the corner of my desktop, tucking it in the back of my mind where it's almost hidden.

Almost.

For the next five minutes, I rush to compile the various trafficking stats for my presentation without imagining Gen in each scenario. It goes faster when I shut off the part of my brain that puts her under the control of the sadistic people who force teens to do unspeakable things. Victims are typically kept in line through emotional and physical abuse, so even when they aren't slaving—literally—at their jobs or sleeping with people for money they don't get to keep, each new day brings a fear of what torment awaits them.

After college, when I'm a real journalist covering gruesome stories, I'll need the ability to mute my inner voice, to silence the emotions that threaten to lock me inside myself until the outside world is nothing but a distant memory.

Like Mom did.

Ember closes her laptop, and I hit save and follow her to the bathroom.

"Have fun, girls!" Kevin shouts with a wave.

Ember pushes into the bathroom and whirls to face me. "What," she practically spits on the T, "was that all about?"

"Kevin being Kevin?" My tone is light, but Ember knows me well enough to know I don't ever joke about Kevin.

"Did something happen?" She leans against a sink and her shoulders slump. "Have I been a bad friend and not noticed that he's been a shit to you, too?"

"No! God. If anything, I've been the bad friend." I bend at the waist and peek under the stalls to make sure we're alone. "But that's not what he's talking about. At least, I don't think it is."

She holds up her hands. "Okay, you've officially talked yourself into a circle. Explain, please."

A spark of anger flares in my chest. This is all Gen's fault. If she hadn't pushed me to kiss Mariela none of this would be happening.

Keep telling yourself that.

It was your idea.

But you're the one who enjoyed it.

"Eve?" Ember's dark eyes lock on mine.

"Sorry." I lean against the sink next to hers and cross my arms over my chest in an attempt to contain the confusion writhing inside me. "I'm not really sure how to say this other than to just spit it out."

"Maybe lean over the sink?" She smirks and gestures at the sink. "You know, to spit."

I huff out a laugh. "I kissed a girl."

Her smile drops. "Woah. Who? Where?"

"I thought I was the reporter?"

She rolls her eyes.

"At the baseball game."

"Interesting."

"That's a word for it."

"So, what does this mean?"

"Like do I like girls? I don't know." Heat flares in my belly thinking about Mariela's soft lips and the way her hands felt on my skin.

"I'm assuming Cal doesn't know?"

I shake my head. "We've never said we're exclusive, but I'm not such a bitch that I don't know this would hurt him."

"But you're still thinking about it." When I don't answer, she continues. "I guess you need to figure out what it is you want. If it's not Cal, then maybe you need to let him go."

Not break up with him, let him go. Because my pseudo claim on his heart is preventing him from finding the person who would treat him with the respect he deserves and actually make him happy. "I already tried."

Her head snaps back.

"Wes told me some people think I'm stringing him along." Her eyes widen as Lissa and Audrey flit through my mind and I level my gaze at her. "They aren't wrong, the difference is I've always been clear about our future. He just won't listen." I run my hands over the smooth surface of the sink. "I tried to give him an out and somehow ended up agreeing to go to prom."

"I assumed you weren't into the tradition behind it. I didn't realize all this was going on."

The comment stings. My best friend should not be wondering these details about my life—I should trust her enough to share. At least about my joke of a love life. "Everything I do leads to Cal getting hurt. I'm just trying to minimize the damage."

"If you've been honest with him—aside from this girl—and he still wants to be with you, then you shouldn't feel guilty."

"But I should because of the girl."

"Cheating is cheating. And there are feelings involved. He's definitely going to be hurt."

Keeping Cal at arm's length was supposed to protect him. By avoiding the boyfriend-girlfriend label, I thought my actions wouldn't impact him, but I was wrong.

"At this point, bailing on prom feels cruel."

"It would be fun to share a limo." Her voice is wistful.

I whirl on her. "Cal didn't say anything about a limo! He said simple."

Ember laughs and touches my arm. "I'm kidding. But—" she pauses, drawing me closer. "My parents offered to host the pre-party." Her eyes light up as my jaw drops. "Just snacks and pictures and stuff before we go to dinner."

"With Claire?"

She nods and bites her lower lip.

Tears burn my eyes. This is huge. Since Kevin outed her last semester, her parents have refused to acknowledge not only Ember's sexuality, but the fact that she's in a loving, committed relationship.

"I was as surprised as you. I'm not sure what changed for them. Maybe it was realizing they were going to miss out on prom pictures if they didn't accept that I have a girlfriend."

"This is wonderful. I'm so happy for you." We hug in the middle of the dingy room that's probably witnessed more than its share of tears over the years, and it's not awkward or stiff like with my parents. It's joyful and heartfelt and real. I pull away, a smirk lifting the corner of my mouth. "But no limo."

She laughs, pushing me away to check her eye makeup in the mirror. "We'll drive to dinner in one of our normal cars, enjoy a low-budget meal, then you, me, and Claire can check out the pretty girls in slutty dresses at the community center."

My cheeks flush. "Please don't think I'm terrible for not telling Cal."

"Eve, we all have our crosses to bear. Some days just getting through high school is enough to send anyone to the loony bin. If lying to Cal keeps the last weeks of high school from blowing up in his face, then that's probably the best thing to do."

"Thanks for understanding. And for not judging me."

"I'm glad you trust me enough to be honest. The first time I kissed a girl, I thought my life was over. Even though it felt like the worlds had finally aligned for me."

Yes, exactly like that.

She squeezes my hand. "You'll figure it out. And I'll be here every step of the way."

Guilt threatens to chase away this brief moment of happiness. Ember's always seemed so secure in her identity that when she kissed that girl, I didn't have much of a reaction. Now I realize I should have.

And I should have trusted her about Mariela sooner.

"Thanks, Ember."

"Now let's get back before the douchers think we're having sex in here."

The laughter that bursts from my lungs expels some of the heaviness twisting inside me. Until we return to the *Sabre* office and Cal smiles at me and the pressure in my chest tightens with each beat of my heart. I thought telling Ember would make me feel better, but the trust in his eyes turns my insides to stone.

His knuckle grazes my knee. "You okay?"

Gen somehow pulls a smile out of me. "Girl talk."

His eyebrow quirks. "Do tell."

Gen laughs. "Not on your life."

The rest of the time passes quickly, and when I hit send on the presentation notes, I lean back in my chair and stretch my hands over my head. I've almost turned off the part of my brain that pictures Gen living in a boarded up room in the back of a store, unable to leave or go outside. Has she gone to school? Is she graduating too, or is she an illiterate slave who never sees the sun or has never stared over the lake with her toes in the sand?

I shake my head. Those thoughts need to stay buried, hidden deep enough that they won't interfere with the competition. Because while we still have to practice our parts, we're done. And our project isn't just solid, it's amazing. We're going to crush the other teams.

And I'll be out of here that much sooner.

Cal catches my hand when everyone's leaving. "You sure you can't come over?"

I wave a hand at my midsection and pretend to scowl.

He huffs out a breath. "We can just watch a movie or something."

"What, and cuddle?" Word retraction should really be a thing.

He drops my hand. "Forget it."

"Cal, I'm sorry." He's stalking out the door so I hurry to his side. "Bonus of shark week is it makes me cranky." My fingers slide through his. "Rain check?"

He doesn't smile, but the hardness in his eyes softens. "After prom?"

Nausea rolls through me, but I smile up at him, press my lips to his, and erase any doubts in his mind. "It's a date."

Kissing Cal usually pauses my thoughts long enough for me to regain control, but not tonight. Instead of losing myself in the moment, I'm thrown back to those cold metal bleachers and the girl who flipped my already complicated life upside down.

When his hand slips under my shirt, I step back. "See you tomorrow?" I don't mean for it to come out as a question, but nothing is certain anymore.

He kisses the tip of my nose. "Of course. Sleep tight, Eve."

My phone buzzes with a text but I don't check it until I'm safely inside Betty.

Sky: how's my favorite journalist?

The kaleidoscope slams against my ribcage.

Twenty

"Eve, you look amazing!" Ember's dark hair is loose around her face, a fresh streak of fuchsia complementing the pink in Claire's dress. Ember's dress twinkles in the lights, making the colors shift from blue to silver.

I reach for the fabric. "Are those crystals?"

"Glass beads. Took forever to sew on."

My jaw drops. "You made this?"

Claire slips her arm through Ember's and smiles at her. "She embellished it."

"You continue to amaze me."

Ember steps back from the door. "Come on in. Hey, Cal," she says, peeking around me. He hasn't released my hand since he picked me up, but he also hasn't said much. Dad took the obligatory photos in front of the mantle, but Mom stayed in her room and I didn't have the energy for a creative excuse. "There's drinks on the kitchen counter."

Ember's parents stop talking when we enter the kitchen. "Oh, Eve, honey, you look so beautiful," says Mrs. Chen. Some people look exactly like one parent or another, but Ember is a perfect combination of both of them. Delicate bone structure and eye for detail from her Mom, height and sense of humor from her dad. Mrs. Chen grazes her finger over my long curls and sighs. "You look so much like your mother."

Mom and Dad are older than most of my friend's parents, but when you never leave your hometown, it's impossible to escape your past.

One hundred fifteen days.

"I bet there wasn't a dry eye in your house when they saw you," she says, touching my cheek.

Gen smiles. "There may have been a few tears."

Cal cocks his head at me and I shake him off. Mom never asked where I was, but she did cry when she saw me—as Gen—in her dress before Cal arrived. It's one thing for her to think Gen's dating Cal, but another to get him to play along without telling him the truth. We took pictures in her room, she fussed with my hair, then slipped a twenty in my hand "just in case." My mind boggled wondering where she got the cash, but she was so excited I let her hug me and promised to have fun.

It's easier this way.

Even though she never asked about Eve.

Mr. Chen gestures at the spread on the counter. Bowls of chips and pretzels and a platter of dumplings and mini taquitos surround a punch bowl holding a frothy pink concoction. "Help yourselves." His shoulders seem stiff and his smile's not as relaxed as usual, but Claire's here and no one's head has exploded.

"Who needs to go to dinner?" Cal says, grabbing a dumpling and popping it in his mouth whole.

Ember swats his arm. "Don't ruin your appetite." It occurs to me too late that I should be the one reprimanding him. The one concerned about his well-being, which includes what food he eats and when, but it's like I was born without the gene that makes me capable of showing my friends that I give a shit.

"I'll always have room for Ray's." The greasy hamburger place is an icon in Spring Haven. When Cal promised simple, it was my first request.

"We could have made dinner for you," Mrs. Chen says. Her gaze lingers on the interaction like she's wishing Ember was with Cal instead. Her jaw ticks, but she swallows whatever she's thinking and smiles. "I don't understand how you kids like that place."

"It's tradition!" Ember laughs, pulling Claire against her side.

Her parents exchange a look but Ember's too lost in Claire's eyes to notice.

"We'll just cover ourselves with napkins," says Claire. "Grease so does not go with this dress."

They laugh and scavenge the snacks, oblivious to the tears burning my eyes. Happiness to finally be a part of a group mixes with heartache that I'm not truly one of them, that I never will be, topped with a tiny bit of remorse for leaving them. We're all going away to school, but I'm the only one counting the days until my escape. The only one fleeing.

Cal catches my eye with the last taquito inches from his mouth. "Did you want this?"

Tears blur my vision, but I smile and shake my head. Suddenly that taquito represents everything I'm leaving. The last taquito right now could be the last taquito ever and I'm not ready for goodbyes.

Ember bumps my shoulder as she bites a pretzel. "What's going on?" she asks quietly enough that the others don't hear. "Are you having second thoughts?"

Mariela flashes through my mind like a bullet train, but I let her pass my stop without boarding. "Would you believe I'm getting nostalgic?"

She catches my eye. "Nope."

We both laugh. "Surprised me, too."

"Eat some food before we go eat. I plan to dance my ass off tonight, so calories don't count." She leads me to the table and forces a dumpling into my hand. "This is the perfect antidote for unwelcome nostalgia."

The first bite throws me back to freshman year and the first time Ember invited me over. Her mom made a feast unlike anything I'd ever seen outside a restaurant. Over the years, the Chens always made me feel welcome regardless of my mood and sent me home with leftovers for my parents. They may not understand the full dynamics of my life, but they've somehow always known how to make me feel included.

"Better?" Ember asks.

"I'll miss this." Emotion clogs my throat, making it hard to swallow.

"Oh god." She raises her voice. "Time to go! Dad, you get five minutes for pictures then we're outta here."

We touch up lipstick and check our teeth for food, then gather on the deck off the living room. It's too early for a sunset, but the manicured backyard is the perfect backdrop for tonight. Cal presses the length of his body against mine and kisses the top of my head.

"You look beautiful."

My heart flutters. Maybe I'm not hopeless. "You said that already."

"I plan to keep saying it." He squeezes my hand and straightens next to me. Mrs. Chen fusses with our hair and turns our bodies so we face the same direction. When she smiles, we smile back.

Mr. Chen takes enough shots to fill an album, then Mrs. Chen is hugging us and we're grabbing our purses and piling into Cal's car.

At Ray's, Cal and Claire go inside to order our food, giving me another moment with Ember.

My hands twist in the beaded fabric of my dress. "I'm a horrible person."

Ember reaches from the backseat to swat my hands. "Stop it, you'll rip off the pretties." She rests her cheek against my seat and sighs. "The situation isn't ideal, but the fact that you feel bad means you're not a horrible person."

I shake my head. "I don't think it works that way."

"Sure it does. If you didn't feel guilty, that'd make you a sociopath or something. And," she smiles, "you are definitely not a sociopath."

She has no idea.

Ember pokes my arm. "Hey, tonight will be fun. No one expects you to have the rest of your life figured out. Just enjoy yourself."

But I do have my life figured out. Or at least the big stuff. The relationshipy, touchy-feely part gets more confusing every day. "Easy for you to say." I wave at Cal and Claire, who push through the glass door loaded with bags of food. "You've got someone amazing who loves you."

"You've got that, too." Her voice softens. "You just have to decide if that's what you want."

Claire climbs into the backseat while Cal pops the trunk. "It's about time we all hung out. We should totally do stuff this summer."

Wes shrugs and Gen smiles and I wonder if I'll ever have a reaction of my own. "That would be fun." Unlikely, but fun.

Cal gets in the car and hands me a plastic bag loaded with paper towels and plastic bibs with lobsters on them. Laughing, I pull one out and tie it around my neck.

"You are the sweetest!" Claire shouts. "I know I agreed to this meal, but I considered not eating so I wouldn't grease up my dress." She and Ember tie on their bibs while I hand out paper towels for our laps. The car falls silent as we eat.

A glob of ketchup lands on Cal's bib and I lean over to wipe it up with a fry, but before I can eat it, he looks at me with an expression so tender it makes me want to run screaming from the car. No matter how many times I say we're not a couple, in his eyes we are.

How will he remember me when he's older? As the girl who made him happy in spite of herself, or the girl who trashed his heart and closed him off to future happiness? Because it's going to hurt him when I leave, whether it's at the end of the summer or next week.

"You okay?" he asks, and frustration coils through my belly. I don't want to worry tonight. I just want to eat my three-dollar meal, watch my classmates dance, and get on with my life.

Breathe.

"Yeah, just pausing before inhaling the rest of my burger." My smile doesn't reach my eyes, but he must not notice in the dim light because he leans over to kiss my shoulder. Then steals a fry.

"Hey! Back off!" I shield the rest of my fries and we all laugh.

I can do this. I pretend every day of my life, so I can pretend to have fun with the people who care about me.

That mantra carries me into the community center, which is exploding with rainbow-colored tissue paper, streamers, and balloons. "Is our theme Funfetti?" I ask, but they don't seem fazed by the pair of unicorns flanking the entrance. "No really, what is going on?"

Gen likes unicorns, not me.

Claire arches a brow. "You really don't know the theme?" When I shake my head, a smile lights her face. "It's a Care Bears slash eighties theme. Fun, right?"

"I covered a baseball game so someone could come up with rainbows?" A flush races over my skin as the words leave my mouth. Without this assault of the eyeballs, Mariela would've never sat next to me and changed the way I look at the world.

Cal grabs my hand and gives our tickets to the teachers seated at a table in the lobby. "Come on. If you at least try to have fun, I'll steal a unicorn for you."

Round tables with bowls of rainbow candy ring the perimeter of the room, leaving a large space in the center for dancing. An overly intense DJ bops her head to a Michael Jackson/Madonna remix blaring from the speakers in the corners while half the senior class laughs and dances and acts like this is the only place they want to be.

"I love this song!" Ember shouts before dragging Claire into the fray, but I hesitate near the door.

Cal's smile fades. "You don't want to dance?"

Everything inside me itches to run away, but I can't ruin this moment for him. My hand slips into his and he guides me to the center of the dance floor. If I squint, the sparkling lights make the community center seem almost magical. Like a fairy tale. When Cal's arms cradle me to his chest, my head falls against his shoulder.

"I have to admit, until I picked you up and saw you in your dress, I wasn't sure if you'd come tonight."

I pull back to meet his eyes. "Am I really that terrible?"

"No." His gaze drops. "Just confusing. One minute you're telling me you love me, and the next I'm not allowed to touch you. I don't get it."

"I never—"

Yes, you did.

But—

Just go with it.

I stare at the flower on his lapel. "I know I'm not always the easiest, but you—you're important to me, and I'm sorry if I haven't made you feel that way." They may be the same words I used with Ember, but it puts a smile back on his face.

His mouth dips closer to my ear. "You make me happy, Eve. I'm glad you agreed to come."

The fluttering changes to a panicked canter that doesn't subside until the song ends. We grab a couple chairs facing the dance floor, and as soon as I lean back, Cal's hand finds my bare leg. It's a move he's done a hundred times, but instead of parting my legs beneath the tablecloth and letting him stroke farther up my thigh, every fiber in my being wants him to stop. I shift so I'm angled toward him and cross one leg over the other. His brows furrow, but he doesn't push. Cal never pushes. Instead, he drapes his arm over the back of my chair, proving he's a better person than I am.

When did I say I love him?

Does it really matter?

"I'd ask what's wrong, but I don't think you'll tell me." His voice is low enough that it mixes with the base line of the song, making his words almost impossible to hear.

Almost.

Telling him about Mariela now will ensure my legacy as the girl who ruined prom. Telling him later won't be much better, but at least he'll have this memory. "I'm just thinking about how this chapter of our lives is almost over. These people we've known forever will scatter in a few months and we might never see them again."

"It's not like you to be melancholic."

My shoulder lifts in a shrug. "What can I say, I'll miss a couple of them." I gesture at the dance floor, my gaze settling on Ember and Claire. The song shifts to one from this decade and squeals drown out the music.

He lifts my hand to his lips. "Only a couple?"

Shrugging seems to be my form of communication tonight. "Maybe a few." This is definitely leading him on. Each casual word edges us closer to the inevitable and will only make the breakup worse.

Cal kisses my knuckles before setting my hand back in my lap. I should smile at him, reassure him that I'm happy to be here, but I can't bring myself to do it. Instead, I scan the crowd, careful not to make eye contact with Wes at a table on the other side of the room. But it's too late. He's on his feet and weaving around chairs toward us, the strobe light behind the DJ stuttering his movements until he's in front of our table.

He stops next to Cal and they bro-nod at each other, then his gaze meets mine. His smile masks the concern in his eyes and his shoulders lack their usual ease. "I didn't think you'd be here."

I press my hand against Cal's chest. "He was very convincing." Wes may know how I feel about Cal, but Cal doesn't know Wes and I are friends and I'll be damned if I give Cal a reason to be jealous.

"Good for you, man." Wes guy-punches him in the shoulder, then nods at me. "Can I borrow Eve for a dance?"

My stomach drops. So much for sparing Cal's sensibilities.

Cal shifts away from me as if giving me permission, but he's not smiling. He's also not scowling. He's just... accepting that another guy is asking me to dance right in front of him.

This is your fault.

I know.

If you care so much about his feelings, you wouldn't dance with Wes.

My chair catches on the carpet as I stand, and Cal pulls it out of the way. I press a kiss near his ear and swallow hard. "You're the one I'm going home with." My voice comes out low and scratchy and Cal must take it as the promise it sounds like because he turns his face and kisses me on the mouth. Hard.

Then I'm face-to-face with Wes, surrounded by sweaty bodies as I shift from one foot to the other in my non-rhythmic form of dancing.

"I hope I didn't start anything." His body moves in time with the music but he keeps his distance.

"What's this about?"

"I haven't seen you in a while."

"And you thought now was a good time to catch up?"

"It's just a dance, Eve."

Wes has never made a move or given any indication he's interested in me, but dancing together at prom carries a weight I'd rather not deal with. We rotate and people move, giving me a clear line of sight to Cal. He's watching us without being obvious, and my chest tightens. "He's a good guy and I don't want to hurt him."

"I'm not even touching you."

The DJ chooses that moment to switch to a slow song. "Here's one for all you lovebirds out there," she says.

"I don't think so." I move toward Cal, but freeze. Lissa's standing next to him, touching his shoulder and smiling in a way I used to wish she'd look at me. And he's smiling back at her. He glances my way and something incomprehensible passes between us. A question, a challenge, a look I've never seen in his eyes—at least not directed at me.

Then he stands and follows her to the opposite side of the dance floor.

"Looks like you're stuck with me," Wes says.

Jealousy flares through me, followed by irritation because I did it to him first. I glare at Wes. "Did you two plan this?"

He touches his chest. "Me and Lissa? Give me some credit. She probably saw him alone and took advantage." He gestures at the space between us and raises his brows. "Shall we?"

Frustration seeps out of me but I step closer. He's an inch or two taller than Cal and it's a stretch to rest my hands on his shoulders. He takes one of my hands and holds it out to our side like we're in seventh grade, while his other hand settles on my waist.

"Don't want anyone to get the wrong idea," he whispers. We spin in a lazy loop around the dance floor, never getting too close to Cal and Lissa, who are talking as they sway.

"What do you think they're talking about?" Bitterness laces my tone and I bite my lip. I lost the right to be jealous when I kissed Mariela, then again when I agreed to dance with Wes, but seeing my former crush playing with my current interest's tie is stirring up old feelings I'd rather keep buried.

"You might like her if you gave her a chance."

Gen snorts in my head.

"Been there, done that."

He turns me so my focus is on Ember and Claire, and I shake off the darkness creeping into my thoughts, the constant drumbeat of "he knows he knows he knows" that loops through my head whenever Wes is around. Tonight is supposed to be fun. Wes is my friend. This will only turn into a shit-show if I let it.

"How's your truck?" I ask.

He nods, then looks over my head. "I can't figure you out."

"What's there to figure out?"

He exhales softly, his breath blowing the hair on the top of my head. "You're one of the most self-absorbed people I know—for good reason—and whenever I wonder why I bother, it's like you remember your manners and say something nice."

I yank my hand away and cross my arms, my determination to keep the evening pleasant evaporating into the air around us. "You're the one who decided I needed a friend."

"Don't get mad—"

"Too late."

"I'm just saying, you aren't the easiest person to be friends with."

He's not wrong.

Shut up.

You're the one pushing everyone away.

"Don't do me any favors." Backing away, I bump into the couple behind me. "Sorry." I move around them and burn a path to the exit.

"Eve, wait!" Wes's voice carries over the ballad droning through the speakers, and I feel everyone's eyes on me without turning around. Exactly what I didn't want.

Ember's behind me as soon as I step into the lobby. "What happened?" She touches my elbow, letting her fingers trail down my arm until she grasps my hand. "Are you okay?"

Her touch grounds me, anchoring me to the present, to the mess I've made of my life. "I'm fine. Just making bad decisions and pissing off my friends."

She squeezes my hand. "Not all your friends."

I snort. "The night's still young."

"Do you want to leave?" She glances over her shoulder, and I follow her gaze to where Claire's waiting by the door.

"No, I wouldn't do that to you." Wes's words roll through my mind. "I'm sorry I'm not the friend you deserve, but I'm so glad you're here." I put an arm around her shoulder and hug her to me.

Her free hand cups the back of my head. "Shit got heavy fast."

We both laugh, and when we pull apart, she touches a finger to my forehead. "You need to get out of there and have fun. This isn't the time for overthinking." The music gets louder as the DJ switches to a fast song and Ember looks toward the door. "I owe

Claire at least ten more dances. Come with us…" She trails off and I follow her gaze to the door.

Cal stands with his hands in his pockets, a pained expression on his face.

"Go have fun," I say.

She grabs Claire's hand and must smile at Cal because he gives a half-hearted smile as she passes, but it fades as he meets my eyes.

His sigh nearly knocks me over. "You okay?"

Since when did I become a drama queen?

How much time do you have?

"I was just getting air. It's hard to breathe in there." Especially seeing you and Lissa together.

He inhales deeply, then exhales just as slowly. Calming himself so he doesn't cause a scene? He's done this countless times when I've pushed his buttons at school, but this time a twinge of guilt pricks me. It's like I'm destined to ruin tonight for him.

"You're right. The air is better out here." He holds out his hand. "But there's a dance inside. Come with me?"

My smile is the one Gen gives Mom. Pure and heartfelt and guaranteed to smooth any lingering doubts of my sincerity. The petty side of me wants to ask about Lissa, but that isn't fair. Nothing about this is fair. "Yes."

I somehow follow Ember's advice and stay out of my head for the rest of the night. We dance and jump and laugh and when the final song plays, Ember declares this the night to end all nights.

We drop off Ember and Claire, and when Cal drives us back to his place, I turn off the uncertainty that's followed me since that night on the bleachers. Push away thoughts of Mariela's hands and Lissa's mouth and Sky's mind. Let him unzip my dress and guide me to his bed, where I keep my promise, willing the butterflies to make an appearance.

But they never do.

Twenty-One

"Wish me luck!"

Mom smiles at me from bed. She rarely gets up before I leave for school, and momentous days in my life are no different. "Good luck." She smooths her hair off her shoulders and looks confused for a moment.

My excitement bursts as if she stabbed me through the heart. "The competition."

"Oh, right." The light reaches her eyes too late. She doesn't care. She never has.

"Anyway, goodbye."

Dad's waiting in the kitchen with a smile and a travel cup of coffee. "Knock 'em dead." He hands me the coffee and gives me an awkward hug.

I step out of myself long enough to recognize that at least he's trying. That he knows how important this project is to me, even if he doesn't know the reason I want to win. "Thanks, Dad."

Willow's bringing the printed pieces, and my notes are already in my bag in the car, so I feel oddly empty-handed as I step outside. I send her a text that I'm on my way, then copy the same message to Noah. The sun streaks over the treetops and my pulse accelerates. The day feels full of promise, the soft clouds carrying a wisp of the unknown.

Wes comes outside as I open Betty's door. We haven't talked since prom last weekend and I'm not sure if he's been avoiding me or if the end of the school year has kept him busy, but anticipation for the competition has turned me into a bubblier version of myself.

"Will you ever stop stalking me?" My wide smile makes it clear I'm teasing, but his smile isn't as bright.

"I don't stalk my friends." His face is unreadable as he walks to his truck.

Is he mad or just giving me a hard time? I open the door wider and pause, watching him. I'd apologize if I thought I did something wrong, but I am who I am and that's not changing after eighteen years. Besides, he's the one who made being my friend his mission. He knew what he was getting into.

"Okay, I guess I'll see you."

"Good luck today."

My head tilts.

"I don't live under a rock." This time his smile is the one I've grown accustomed to. Caring and thoughtful and typical Wes. "You can tell me about it on a run later."

A strange calmness passes through me at what he's offering. Not forgiveness, but acceptance. A way to move forward. "I'd like that."

That serenity stays with me as I pick up Ember and we take the back roads to Grand Valley State University. The main campus is only ten minutes from Grand Rapids, the second-biggest city in Michigan, but it's an island amidst farms and strip malls, eons away from the city's skyscrapers and fancy restaurants.

Cal offered to ride together, but I've been avoiding him since prom and chickened out, telling him I needed girl time with Ember. He deserves a clean break but the time never seems right. Every moment in the last weeks of high school feels significant and no matter when we have the talk, I'll be the girl who ruined it for him. Avoiding him is no better, but I have too much on my mind to fully worry about him.

Nervous anticipation keeps us quiet until we're out of Spring Haven. I dig deep for the confidence to not only get through the competition, but win, and settle on a comment Miss Emory made about my short story. Not only did she give me an A, but she said she's impressed with how well I turned off my journalist brain to write high fantasy.

Maybe my brain can come up with a way to end things with Cal without destroying him.

In the middle of farm country, Ember clears her throat. "How are you feeling about Cal?"

"Are you reading my mind?"

She touches my arm. "You seem distracted by more than just the competition."

Tell her who you're really thinking about.

Sky and I have texted every night this week. We've yet to exchange photos—she thought it'd be fun to do the big reveal today—but I already feel like she understands me in a way few others do. Since the first day I found her in the Dr. Seuss thread, something about our personalities has clicked. I don't feel like I have to pretend with her. She doesn't know about Gen, but I trust her in a way I never expected.

But saying that out loud would make it real and I'm not ready for real.

"I haven't talked to him."

You're hopeless.

"How are things with your parents? They seemed cool with Claire."

"They're trying. I guess that's all I can ask for."

This time I touch her arm. "It has to get easier, right?"

She shrugs. "They're trying to be extra extra."

I smile, but don't respond. No one wants parental advice from me.

We arrive at the main campus with minimal missed turns, and an unfamiliar bubble of hope carries me toward the building. Ember pulls me into a hug. "You're going to kill this."

"So are you. Good luck." And I mean it. As badly as I want to win, Ember deserves success as well.

We split up to search for our partners, and a fresh wave of nerves nearly overwhelms me. I'm about to come face-to-face with Sky. The possibility of what her friendship could mean chases away all thoughts of kidnapped sisters and human trafficking and partners who won't use question marks.

Two girls from another school smile at me when I enter the auditorium. "Cute skirt," one of them says. My shoulders stiffen, waiting for their cruel laughter, but they keep walking down the hall. A boy gives me a friendly smile, then another group holds the door to the auditorium for me.

Is this what life is like when you don't push everyone away? The students from the other schools don't know me and instead of going through life angry at the world, they give strangers the benefit of the doubt and assume they're friendly, too.

"Thank you," I murmur, hitching my bag higher onto my shoulder.

A tall boy with light brown hair and thick-rimmed black glasses opens his mouth like he's going to say something, then gives me a puzzled look and heads toward another group of students.

Cal's standing inside the main doors and, almost as if he feels my eyes on him, he turns. My bag suddenly feels too heavy to bear and I let it slide to the floor. On the surface, he looks as calm and collected as always, but his skin is pale and his eyes lack their usual brightness. He watches me for a heartbeat before giving me a small smile.

I move to his side and take a deep breath. The scent of his body wash sparks a thousand memories that speed through my mind like a greatest hits montage, but the longing I usually feel when I'm around him is gone.

"Good luck," I say, smiling in a way I hope speaks only of friendship and doesn't lead him on.

"Can we—" his voice cracks and his eyes close briefly. "Can we talk later? I don't know what I did, but I miss you."

My stomach drops. He doesn't deserve for this to be dragged out any longer. "Want to go for a run later?"

His eyes widen and I realize too late what I've implied.

"Not for that." I nod at the crowded room. "I'm gonna have a lot of energy to burn off after today."

He laughs, but his smile feels forced. "I know what you mean." His gaze travels the room and he bites his lip, a classic deep-thinking move for Cal. He turns to face me, his arm brushing mine, when my phone buzzes.

I slip it from my back pocket.

Sky: just got here.

My stomach flips and it feels like an electric jolt shoots through me.

"I've gotta go. My team is here." It's not a complete lie. Willow and Noah texted when I was on the road to let me know they were here, and I do eventually need to find them. But right now all that matters is meeting Sky.

"I should find my team, too. Good luck." He shuffles away, each step a kick in my gut. He's not fully broken, but I've already damaged him.

Sky: where are you?

Me: In the auditorium. Just follow the smell of desperation.

Sky: haha. parking now.

I stop a girl near the auditorium entrance who looks as nervous as I feel. "Do you know Noah or Willow?"

She smiles. "I go to school with Willow. Do you know Ember or Tim?"

"Ember's the girl with the pink streaks near the back." It's like a spotlight shines on Ember wherever she goes. For the millionth time, I'm hit with a wave of gratitude that she overlooks my insecurities and neuroses and considers me her friend.

"Cool, thanks. Willow's the girl in the purple flowery top." She points at an Indian girl my height with an angular bob that hangs in her face.

My smile is genuine. "Thanks. Good luck."

"You too."

I should go to Willow. We need this time to practice. But Sky's almost here. Before I can make a decision, Willow approaches, a warm smile on her face. "Are you Eve?"

"Yes?" It comes out a question, and before I can declare my no-hugging policy, she pulls me into a hug, and I'm enveloped in vanilla and cotton and happiness. Her warmth softens whatever anxiety I felt about meeting her.

"It's so awesome to meet you! Have you found Noah?" I ask.

"He's the gorgeous one with glasses who looks like he fell out of GQ." She points at the guy with glasses who gave me the weird look minutes earlier. He's not what I expected and yet exactly what I expected. His slim-fit button-down is tucked into equally skinny pants and his hair has the same casual messiness that Cal has perfected. His smile reveals perfectly straight teeth and I'm struck with a stab of jealousy. He already knows Sky. She didn't mention if there was anything more than friendship between them, but he'd be a hard one to resist.

"He's definitely cute."

She purses her lips. "Me-ow. Maybe we should have exchanged photos. I would have stepped up my game."

Laughter bursts out of me, relieving some of the pressure that's been building inside.

Willow raises an eyebrow. "You don't think so?"

"He's not my type." Speaking of which. "Hey, I know we need to practice, but I want to find someone before we get started."

"Ooh, intrigue."

My smile feels shy. "Maybe. We've been chatting and agreed to meet before the competition."

Willow gets a dreamy look in her eyes. "No worries. I've got everything right here." She pats her bag. Her smile is contagious, and I regret every mean thing I thought about her.

"I'll catch up with you as soon as I find her."

Sky: I'm inside.

Me: Are you sure you don't want to find your team?

Sky: ugh, no. That Kevin guy is a loser.

Me: Haha, yeah he is. Sorry you got stuck with him.

I weave around the other excited competitors as I text. Some are already practicing their presentations while others hug and laugh like they're old friends. When I reach the stage, I turn and face the crowded room, and the anticipation nearly knocks me over. This is really happening. I'm finally going to meet Sky. I swallow the fear that my feelings might be one-sided and send her a text.

Me: I'm up front with the yellow rose.

Sky: really?

Me: No. Yellow plaid skirt.

Sky: how very Cher of you.

Sky: you should already know what I look like.

Me: How's that?

Sky: didn't Noah tell you I helped with your project?

Me: No! Even though you're the competition?

Sky: I was one of the models.

Noah's photos flip through my mind, but all the faces are concealed. Each hold their own power but it'd be impossible to identify the model, especially in a crowded auditorium.

Me: How are there so many people in here?

Sky: this feels way too dramatic. and the auditorium is packed!

A group of students block my view of the entrance, so I take a deep breath to calm down. To remind myself she might not feel the same way. Odds are Sky will end up being a great friend but never see me in a different light.

Sweat breaks out over my palms and I bounce on my toes. Maybe I should have gone for a run this morning. Then the crowd parts and a girl with long dark hair like mine and a smile that's as familiar as my heartbeat stops in the aisle.

Her smile slips to shock as the air is sucked out of the room.

I've never questioned my ability to comprehend what's right in front of me, but this doesn't make sense. It's like I'm standing in front of a mirror but my reflection refuses to cooperate. My hand covers my mouth.

My reflection does not.

I blink my eyes but she's moving toward me.

Fuck.

No.

The girl stops.

How is this possible?

I don't know.

Because the girl standing in front of me with an equally shocked expression on her face is Gen.

As in my kidnapped sister.

In the flesh.

Twenty-Two

She steps closer, the confusion on her face mirroring the turmoil ripping through me. "How?" Her fingers touch her lips, almost as if she expects me to mirror her movements. Because while our hairstyles and clothes are different, no one could deny we're twins. "I don't understand."

My mouth opens but words don't come out.

She didn't know I existed.

"Eve?" Her voice cracks, breaking my name in two.

Gen.

Everything about her feels like home. But as she steps closer, eighteen years of worrying and pretending and frustration pulses inside my chest. My breathing stops. No amount of counting will help.

Tears well in her eyes and she's close enough to touch my arm. "Please say something."

Sky.

This is Sky.

The girl from Noah's photo who captivated me. Who looked like me.

The girl I haven't been able to stop thinking about. The one I've been so excited to meet that practicing for this competition became an afterthought.

The girl I hoped felt the electricity through our texts that kept me up long after we said goodnight.

The girl who is my sister.

People are starting to notice us.

My gaze drops to her hand on my arm, and I'm startled by how much it looks like my hand. My arm. I meet her eyes, my tears matching hers, but the impossibility of breathing makes my head roar. The pulsing in my chest grows stronger, drowning out the whispers around us. I stumble backwards until the edge of the stage presses against my spine. She's no longer touching me but the innate connection that binds us despite being separated for eighteen years tells me she's not going to stop trying.

The people around us blur so all I can see is her, my sister, this person who's been apart from me and yet still a part of me, shadowing my every thought, every action, every temptation.

"Eve?" The desperation in her voice amplifies the sensations racing through me. The kaleidoscope of butterflies no longer flutter gently in my belly. No, they are freaking the fuck out, slamming into my ribcage so hard I feel like I might throw up.

"I—I have to go." Our shoulders brush as I push past her and run away away away. Someone shouts my name, but I weave through the bodies that seem frozen in place, confused by the crying girl sprinting toward the exit.

In the hallway, I press pause on my mounting panic long enough to look for Ember, to tell her I have to leave, but she's still in the auditorium. Then the walls start to spin.

Outside, the sun refracts on my tears and the world goes white. My breath comes in short bursts, not enough to fill my lungs but enough to keep me alive. Doubled over, my mind frantically tries to rewrite what happened, to find an explanation other than the one that says the girl I've been talking to, the one I thought I might have feelings for, is my sister. That Gen is alive. More than alive. She's beautiful and happy and funny and someone I'd choose to be friends with. That I chose to be friends with. For so many years, I thought I had to be alone because no one understood me, but my match was out there, living three hours away along the same lake that's always been my solace.

My phone buzzes in my pocket and I blink away the blinding light. A few people linger outside, but no one's followed me out here.

Sky: please come back.

Cal: What happened? Why did you leave?

Willow: Eve! We only have a few minutes left to practice! Where are you.

I thumb out a message and copy paste it to each of them.

Me: I'm sorry.

Then I text Ember.

Me: I had to leave. I'm so sorry. Good luck. Cal will bring you home.

And to Cal.

Me: Please bring Ember home.

I don't bother explaining. As soon as they see Sky, they'll know.

Everyone will know.

Without another look back, I stumble my way to Betty and let her carry me home.

The moments before Sky arrived replay over and over as buildings and farms and oncoming cars pass in a blur. I cling to the excitement that buoyed me the past few days—the anticipation at finally meeting her—and try to shove it into this new reality. But it refuses to fit.

Emptiness expands in my chest until I feel like I'm going to explode.

"Gen, where are you?" My voice is barely a whisper. She hasn't spoken since we saw Sky and her silence feels heavier than anything I've ever felt.

Gen.

Nothing.

I repeat her name as the miles slip by, and with each utterance her appearance shifts from Gen in a ponytail and UVA sweatshirt to the girl in royal blue pants and a striped top who stood before me in the auditorium. I imagine Gen saying, "I'd never wear something like that," but she still doesn't speak.

"Please, Gen, I can't do this without you."

Her presence crushes my chest, and I gasp for breath, fighting to keep control of the car. Gravel crunches beneath the tires as Betty pulls off the road. A cloud of dust fills the rear-view mirror, seeping into my pores until I'm choking, wheezing, sobbing. Flashes of Gen laughing with Mom—talking about her friends and soccer and boys—shine bright like a movie then fade just as quickly, the memories dissolving as if they never happened.

Something seismic changes within me and I don't know if I'll ever be the same.

Betty somehow gets back on the road but skips the turn to my street and instead drives to the state park. To the pier. The sun burns high in the sky, warming the pavement and dancing over the waves in the channel. My phone's buzzed nonstop since I left the competition, so I tuck it into my backpack on the passenger seat. They can live without hearing from me for a little while longer. Couples meander along the boardwalk, oblivious to my need to be closer to the water, and it takes forever to get to the end of the pier where waves lap against the concrete. I want to throw myself onto the ground and let the water wash me away, but the strollers and bikes and general happiness surrounding me give me pause.

The end of the pier is a slab of concrete the size of Mom's room jutting into Lake Michigan. Standing at the edge when the water's calm makes it feel like you're hovering in the middle of the lake with only your thoughts, but unfortunately this sunny Saturday morning has heralded people from all over west Michigan to this exact spot. There's still enough of a chill in the air that only a few boats are out, but that will end as Memorial Day approaches.

I normally don't care what others think of me, but after a few cleansing breaths with my eyes closed, their watchful eyes make the hair on my neck stand on end. Gazing out over the water, I take a final deep breath and start the quarter-mile walk back to land. But I'm not ready to go home. Because once I set foot in the house, everything will become real. Out here, at the edge of the world where the water meets land, I can balance between realities a little longer.

My legs buckle near the lighthouse and I give in to the maelstrom swirling through me. The waves call to me, beckoning me closer. I settle on the rough concrete and focus on the rhythmic movements of a nearby fisherman as he throws the line out, reels it in, and throws it out again. He seems unconcerned with the teenaged girl watching him, too focused on the water to notice that my world is crumbling around me.

He reels in a fish and tosses it, gasping and writhing, at his feet. That's me. I am that fish. Ripped from my world and thrust into an alternate reality where I don't know how to survive.

I push to my feet, but instead of heading to my car, I turn and walk along the beach.

And keep walking.

Gen refuses to speak but I can feel her expanding and contracting in every pore, every cell, every atom of my body. Like we're both afraid to ask what finding my sister means for us.

A sharp pain grips my chest so suddenly I double over. Hands to my chest, I fall to my knees. The sand digs into my bare skin and cool water laps at my skirt, but I can't move.

Ten.

...

Eight.

...

Six.

...

I pause, waiting for Gen to take her turn, but she's hanging from the precipice of my consciousness by a thread so thin that one wrong move could sever it forever. Sever her from me.

And I'm not ready to say goodbye.

A couple with a chocolate lab approach from the south and I stumble to my feet. My breathing is strangled, barely letting in enough oxygen to ease the lightheadedness that moves the ground beneath me, but I force myself forward. The dog rubs against my legs as we pass, and his damp, scratchy fur anchors me. My hand slides over his head and I'm rewarded with a giant tongue on my arm.

"Sorry!" the woman says as her man-friend tugs on the leash. "He loves people."

"It's okay." My voice sounds ragged, like the little breath I've managed to take doesn't want to be wasted on speaking. The dog lunges once more and something resembling a laugh bubbles out of me.

The empty shoreline stretches before me. My legs yearn to run, but I need to prolong my return home as long as possible.

What's going to happen to Gen? My Gen. The Gen in my soul.

And Sky. The expression on her face made it clear she didn't know I exist, at least not in the twins-separated-at-birth way, and I can't imagine what this will do to her. Will she want to meet Mom and Dad? A thought shakes me. What will this do to Mom? Yanking away her beloved Gen after eighteen years could shatter her mind so badly that her fragile grip on reality will never be restored.

Gen whispers through me like a ghost, chilling my legs, my arms, and finally prickling along the base of my skull. But she doesn't speak.

"Please tell me what you're thinking."

But I already know. Because it's how I feel. Angry. Confused. Scared. Happiness should be in there somewhere, but it's buried so deeply beneath everything else I can't find it.

The world blurs until I find myself beneath Wes's treehouse. The wooden slats nailed to the tree call to me, promising respite from everything I'm trying to avoid. My house looms nearby like the climax of a story I'm terrified to finish and I blink against the fresh tears burning my eyes. I'm not ready to see her. To tell her.

The rungs are sturdy beneath my hands and I squeeze until my knuckles turn white and splinters prick my palms. My legs push me up, up, up until my elbows rest on the dusty floor and then I pull myself inside. Ambient light filters between the boards of the walls, and the two chairs still rest near the window facing my house. Exhaustion strikes hard and fast. The scratchy floor barely registers against my bare legs. I'm an expert at pretending everything is okay and I'm a master at ignoring the less-than-perfect.

And this way I don't have to see Mom's window.

My head falls into my arms. The competition should be over by now, the winners announced. A twinge of guilt opens my eyes. Willow and Noah didn't deserve to get screwed out of the competition, but maybe they presented without me. Maybe our work wasn't for nothing. Hope buoys me for a nanosecond before reality crashes into the treehouse. Good things don't happen to me. There's only tolerable misery and utter devastation, with the occasional moment of pleasure to keep me sane. Expecting anything else is guaranteed to end in disaster.

Maybe that's what happened today. I let myself hope a little too much and the universe overcorrected, and now nothing will ever be the same.

A flutter of pressure moves from my belly to my heart, gripping my lungs and throat and lips, squeezing me like a rag until there's nothing left.

Days or weeks or hours pass.

Someone's shouting my name. Deep shadows fill the cramped room, the promise of a sunset peeking through the window. I try to sit up but my arm tingles with sleep and I fall to my side with a thump.

"I'll check the treehouse." Wes's voice sounds far away, but then the ladder creaks and panic pushes me upright. In a matter of seconds, this illusion of security will be ripped from me. I'll have to stop pretending. When his head crests the floor, a mix of dread and relief sweep through me. Wes is safe.

Something unreadable passes over his face when he sees me. "She's here." His voice cracks as he looks through the opening. "Stay there." I avoid his eyes as he pulls himself onto the floor. He leans against the farthest wall and rests his arms on his bent knees.

Does he know? He must, why else would he be looking for me? And who else is down there? I'm not ready for whatever is about to happen, for the chaos waiting below.

"Are you hurt?" he asks.

"That's subjective." My throat is dry and my voice comes out scratchy, like I haven't spoken in years.

A breath of a smile touches his lips.

"I'm physically intact."

He nods as if he's reassuring himself of something. "And the rest of you?"

My shoulder does a perfect casual Wes-shrug. "That remains to be seen."

Relief rolls off him as he exhales. "So..."

I shake my head, stopping him, willing him to give me a few more minutes.

He scoots across the floor until he's by my side in the center of the treehouse. "Eve, people are worried about you."

The intensity in his gaze is too much. Right now, he's the only person in the world who knows the full depth of what's simmering inside me. Who fully understands what finding Gen—Sky—means to me and my family.

"Cal found your car at the beach and..." His gaze drops to the floor and he bites his lip. When he looks at me, his eyes fill with tears. "We thought..." he blinks several times and swallows hard. "We thought you tried to hurt yourself."

Instinct lifts my hand to reach for his but I stop before touching him, dropping my hand to the floor between us. He grabs my fingers and pulls my hand onto his knee, holding tight.

"A lot of people care about you. We'll help you through this."

It's already starting. "I'm not ready," I whisper.

He glances at the opening of the treehouse, presumably to whoever's waiting down below. "I don't think you have a choice."

Tears fill my eyes and spill down my cheeks. Gen, where are you? Gen Gen Gen Gen Gen. A hollowness creeps through my chest, pushing out the remaining oxygen, closing my throat, and replacing my usual longing for a life free from secrets and pretending. If Gen would just say something, I'll be able to breathe. I'll be able to go on.

But not until then.

Wes presses my hand against his knee. The hardness of his kneecap grounds me. He's real. This right here is real.

And Gen didn't speak the last time I was up here. If I want to hear her again, I have to rejoin the real world.

"Who's out there?"

He bites his lip and attempts a shrug, but it lacks its usual nonchalance. Nothing about this situation is normal.

I lean onto my hands and peer through the opening. A police officer stands near the base of the tree, his hands on his hips, ready for action. Ready for me. My brain shuffles through all the reasons the police are involved—missing teen, possible suicide risk—then slams to a stop when I hit the real reason: they located a kidnapping victim. Gen's disappearance is the coldest of cold cases and today she appeared with a smile on her face, prepared to compete for a summer program. Until today, her life has been completely ordinary. Now it will never be the same.

"Do I have to go down there?"

His voice is tentative. "Yeah. I'm really sorry this is happening but—"

I hold up my hand. "Please don't say it. I know finding her is a good thing but right now it's too much." The cop shifts from foot to foot and just as I'm leaning back, he looks up and our eyes lock. In that brief moment, reality seeps into the treehouse, peeling back the roof and prying the slats off the side until I'm left raw and exposed on the dusty floor.

"What can I do?" Wes asks.

"You're already doing it." Has it really only been a month since Wes pushed his way into my life? His refusal to leave me alone was annoying, an intrusion, but now I'm grateful for him. As the only person who knows about my family, there's no one I'd rather have with me. A lump forms in my throat, making it difficult to speak. "I guess you were right."

He gasps and presses a hand to his chest, making me smile. The small pitiful smile of a wounded animal, but a smile. "About what?"

"That I needed a friend."

His foot bumps mine. "You're welcome."

My smile fades. "So, friend, I don't suppose you'll keep me stocked up here so I don't have to leave?"

"I'm not carrying a bucket of piss down those stairs."

My smile flickers back. "That's fair."

He nods at the opening. "Want me to go first?"

"No. I'll go." The reflex to take several deep breaths while my thoughts spin out of control kicks in, but no amount of oxygen will make facing whatever awaits at home easier. One leg drops over the edge. When my toe bumps the first slat, I shift my weight so I'm standing on the board.

Wes touches my hand, which is gripping the floor of the treehouse like it's the only thing tethering me to this safe space. The moment I let go, my life will change.

Your life has already changed.

That's something Gen would normally say, but it's my voice in my head.

"You can do this," Wes says. "You're stronger than you think."

"If you say so." Exhaustion or dehydration or a combination of the two makes my legs shake as I lower myself to the next rung. Closer to whatever waits at the bottom of the tree and in the house and in every corner of my life. When I lower farther, my arms stretch straight above my head and my fingers clamp tighter to the floor.

It'd be so easy to let go, to play trust-fall with the earth.

She's guaranteed to catch me.

Wes wraps his hand around my wrist. "Do you need me to race you?"

I appreciate that he doesn't baby me, that he understands what motivates me. Maybe this friendship thing isn't all bad. "I can do this."

Wes loosens his grip as I release my grasp on the floor, but I forgo falling backwards and lock my fingers around the worn slats nailed to the tree. The letters WS are carved on the top of the next slat, and I imagine Wes choosing the top instead of the side because it's not visible from the ground. The rebellious impulse battling with his need to keep everyone happy. I run my thumb over the mark, over this symbol of a simpler time. Longing steals my breath and I close my eyes. Rest my forehead against the rough bark of the tree. Everything has changed.

Strong hands grip my waist and set me on the ground, and fatigue rushes from my toes to my chin. My knees give out and the hands hold me upright.

"Can you stand?" The cop's blue eyes lock on mine, his jaw tight as he assesses me. He's not much older than me but authority oozes from him.

"Do they know?" I ask him.

He must take my question as an answer to his, because he takes a step back and rests his hands on his hips. "Your father does. He asked that we not tell your mother yet."

In all my fantasies of how our charade would end, I never imagined this day. "Yeah, she's… uhh…" Lost her grip on reality? The swirling mass of uncertainty claws through my mind, ripping through the order I've worked so hard to maintain, but I shove it back into the unknown.

No. Not yet.

Gen, where are you?

"It's probably best if we wait until we know more." The confidence in my voice is all Gen. She may be hiding, but I can feel her and I'll use whatever strength she'll give me.

The floor of the treehouse creaks and we both look up. Wes's feet hang from the opening, and in seconds he's standing next to us.

The cop clamps a hand on Wes's shoulder. "Thanks for your help."

Wes looks at me and the concern on his face nearly undoes me.

Not yet. I clench my jaw and straighten my shoulders.

"I—I guess I'll see you later," he says.

I touch his arm. The words to appropriately thank him don't exist, and I hope he can somehow sense what my touch is trying to say.

He trudges across the yard and the cop nods at my house. "Ready?"

No.

A curtain flutters in a first-floor window of Wes's house, the outline of his Mom slipping into the shadows before I can see her face. See the concern or judgment or fear in her eyes.

The cop has the courtesy to remain silent as we walk around the side of the house and approach the front door. What do you say to a person who just found their kidnapped twin? Congratulations would make sense, but my disappearing act probably made it clear it's more complicated.

He opens the door for me and steps aside.

"Can you wait out here?"

The cop nods, and it strikes me that he hasn't introduced himself, hasn't made an attempt to grab control of this fucked up situation. The name tag above his heart says Vandenberg. Good Dutch name, Mom's voice whispers in my head.

"Thanks."

The front door swings open, and when I step inside, everything feels the same, but different. Like when I returned from visiting colleges with Ember and her parents. The things that identify this house as mine sit quietly in their places, but their essence has shifted and an uncertainty hangs in the foyer, thickening the air until I can practically see the molecules suspended around me.

"Dad?" My voice falls flat at my feet. A faint rustle, clothing on clothing, sounds from the kitchen. The emotions I've carried since this morning slide off my shoulders and I set them in the hallway where I normally leave my backpack.

Stand straight.

If I'm going to have this conversation, the unceasing desperation that threatens to crush me needs to wait.

My insides still and I listen for Gen's voice, but it's like she's shut down.

It doesn't matter. I can do this without her. Being weighed down with her opinion will only make it more difficult.

Dad's sitting at the kitchen table, hands folded in front of him, staring at a coffee cup. He reminds me of the paintings we saw on a class trip to the art museum in Chicago. Pensive, haunted, frozen in a moment that will never be replicated and yet represents a turning point in his life. In our lives. His eyes flick my way but his expression doesn't change.

"Dad."

He looks up. His red eyes seem to have sunk even deeper into his lined face, but a hint of a smile brushes his face. "They found her. They found Gen."

"I know." The confusion on Sky's face will forever be seared into my brain. She never felt the connection that's buoyed me my entire life.

"Do you know what this means?"

There are a thousand answers, a thousand possibilities, but only one repeats over and over in my mind.

I'm free.

Twenty-Three

But, of course, it's not that simple.

The frantic texts from Ember, Cal, and Sky should have clued me in to how freaked out people would be at school, but by Monday morning, I've convinced myself I don't matter enough to cause much of a stir in the high-school rumor mill. Dad said I could stay home, but the last week of high school feels important, and I worry I'll regret hiding from the world.

That illusion shatters the moment I enter the *Sabre* office.

"Stop the presses!" Kevin shouts from his perch on the back table. "Our front page just walked through the door!"

I freeze. My feet, my lungs, the fake smile plastered on my face. My shoulder brushes the door jamb but I can't move. Can't flee.

Gen, help.

Tell me what to do.

"Kevin, enough." Mr. Barney's voice booms from the front of the room, the look on his face daring anyone else to speak. He stands, adjusting his polka-dotted tie. "Do I need to remind you all that we are a team? What is our motto?"

"Be respectful," the room parrots back.

"We do not torment, belittle, or otherwise ridicule our peers. If you have a question for Miss Ellaway, you ask it in a professional manner, and only when she's ready." His eyes lock on mine, but I still can't move. Something passes between us—

an understanding, a flash of sympathy—and he looks back at the class. "And today is not that day," he says.

"But it was all over the news," Kevin argues. "I'm not saying anything we haven't already heard."

"One more word and you're out."

My heart pounds in my ears, blocking out Kevin and Mr. Barney and the rest of the staff, cracking the barrier that's shielded me from what I haven't been able to admit.

That Gen is alive.

Gen is Sky.

Sky is my sister.

I should be happy, ecstatic, crying tears of joy. She hasn't been trafficked or tortured or killed. She's been living three hours away in Traverse City and is funny and charming and while she may not be how I imagined her to be, she is my other half.

The girl I allowed to creep into my heart and started to like as more than a friend is my sister.

Ember appears at my side. "Come on." She leads me to my seat between her and Cal and eases my bag to the floor. Cal's gaze catches mine and a hundred emotions pass between us, but this isn't the time. Ember pulls out my laptop and sets it on the table in front of me. "Don't listen to him. People don't care as much as he says."

I wish she was right.

Cal touches my arm and together they anchor me to the chair and get me through the first hour of this unfamiliar reality. At home I could pretend it wasn't happening, even as the police murmured for hours with Dad in the living room, as they told him about the daughter who'd only been missing outside the walls of our home. But now it's like the Band-Aid has been ripped off and the open wound in my soul is gasping for air.

Mr. Barney catches my eye before launching into a recap of the competition. Sky's reaction when she saw me plays on a loop. Did she really not know I existed? Did she never feel that tug of longing that's been a part of me my entire life?

Despair threatens to overtake me.

Swallow me whole.

Everyone claps and Ember stands and gives a shy wave. “Thanks, everyone. All the projects were incredible and I’m really excited for the internship.”

Guilt drowns the rest of my emotions. Ember won and I didn’t know. When she sits, I slip my arm through hers and lean my head close. “Why didn’t you tell me?”

“It didn’t feel important after…” she waves her hand at the empty room. “Everything.”

“But this is important. You deserved to win.” The jealousy I expect never surfaces, only sadness that she’ll be gone for a month this summer while I’m still here. Whatever here means. I squeeze her arm. “You’re so extra extra. With exclamation points.”

A small smile flits over her lips. “My team was pretty extra.”

“And I completely abandoned you.”

“It’s okay.”

“It’s not. My life shouldn’t supersede yours, no matter how fucked up it is.”

She presses the side of her head against mine, a silent forgiveness or acceptance or understanding, and I block out the rest of the room until the bell rings.

Kevin gives us a wide berth as we leave, and if anyone else hoped to talk to me, Ember and Cal keep them from getting too close. But they can only protect me for so long.

Conversations stop as I walk through the hall. Eyeballs track my movements as if my body has become a magnetized beacon promising sensationalized fodder that’s sure to keep them salivating until graduation. People don’t forget about kidnapped babies, they merely tuck away the memories until they crawl from their hiding place, destroying everyone who worked so hard to keep them in the past.

“Come on,” Cal says, guiding me through the crowd, his hand gentle on my elbow. For once I let him be the boyfriend he wants to be, to protect me from something too big for him to battle. When we reach my class, he pulls me against his chest and for the first time since Saturday morning, I feel safe. Like maybe I can get through this. Then the whispers around us grow louder and the illusion shatters.

"Thank you," I whisper into his shirt.

"Can I see you later?"

I'd love nothing more than to burrow into his cocoon and never leave, but I can't. "We're having a family night tonight. Can we meet tomorrow?"

His finger traces the side of my face. "You know I'm here for you."

"I know."

By lunch I've tuned out everything around me. Ember's waiting at our table, a grim expression on her face. She starts to stand as I approach, but quickly sits on the edge of her seat. "I wish I could do something."

"I'm sorry I ditched you on Saturday."

She waves a hand, dismissing my apology. "How else are you supposed to react when your long-lost twin shows up?"

A hint of a smile touches my lips and tears burn my eyes. "I don't know what to do," I whisper.

"How can I help?" She reaches across the table for my hand and squeezes. "I can't imagine what you're going through, and I don't know what you need, but I'm here for you."

The warmth of her skin reminds me this is real. For a second, the murmurs around us come into focus and the curious gazes of my classmates make my skin crawl. Then I blink and they fade into the background.

I squeeze her hand back. "Thank you. I'm not one hundred percent sure what happens next." I swallow the other thoughts that yearn to trip off my tongue, like why hasn't Gen—my Gen—spoken since Saturday? I can still feel her with every heartbeat, every breath, every hesitation before I speak, but she won't tell me what she's thinking. "We're planning to tell my mom tonight."

Ember pulls back and cocks her head. "Wait, she doesn't already know?"

Too late I realize that of course my mother should already know her missing daughter has been found. She should've been the first person I called and there would be tears and laughter and plans for a joyous reunion. But all I can think about is how this might destroy her. "It—it's complicated."

She bites her lip as if afraid to say anything else.

My head sinks into my hands.

Gen, tell me what to do. Please.

Desperation claws at my throat, masticates my words, devours my thoughts, threatens to swallow my breath until there's nothing left of me but flesh and bone.

"I don't know what to do," I say again.

"Try to focus on the immediate. Right now, you've got fifteen minutes to eat your sandwich, so unwrap it."

I do.

"Now take a bite."

The lack of saliva in my mouth makes it difficult to chew, but I force down one bite, then another. It sits like a rock in my gut and after a few more bites, I set it back on the table.

Ember smiles. "Good."

I meet her eyes. "I—I can't believe she's been this close the whole time."

Dad and I took a day trip to Traverse City before I started preschool—one of many adventures he took us on "to give Mom a break"—but all I remember is throwing stones in the bright blue water.

Two separate times.

So I could change outfits.

That was one of the first photos Dad manipulated so it showed two of us. Me and Gen.

Was she living there then? Could we have been mere blocks from her home while we forced a gaiety that would never exist in our family?

"Have you talked to her?"

My hair covers my face. "She's texted. I haven't replied."

"Don't you—" she pauses. Takes a breath. "She's probably freaking out. Can you imagine finding out you'd been kidnapped?"

My entire life has revolved around the shrapnel of Gen's disappearance, and while I've certainly wondered what happened to her, in most scenarios I pictured her suffering and alone. From what I can tell, Sky has had a normal life with parents who love her.

"No, I can't."

"I think you should reply to her."

"I know." My thumb traces the crust of my sandwich. "But what do I say?"

"You'd already been talking, right?"

"Yeah." A simple word that conceals so much. I'm grateful I never told Ember about my confusing feelings for Sky and how finding out she's my sister has amplified those feelings from oh-my-god to what-the-holy-hell.

"Maybe just ask her how she is. If I were her, I'd be desperate to hear from you."

The kaleidoscope stirs and I want to rip out my belly, throw it across the room, and stomp on it for betraying me. "You're probably right."

"How's it been at home?"

When a mad scientist's universe begins to crumble, he either lashes out at the world or retreats to his lair. Despite being the mastermind behind my dual lives, Dad's never had much of a backbone and this latest revelation has exposed his true colors. After our non-talk Saturday night, he only emerged from their room long enough to assure me Mom doesn't know about Gen.

"About the same."

Ember's jaw drops. "How is that possible?" Then she reaches for my hand. "I'm sorry, that was insensitive. I just mean..."

"It's complicated," I repeat.

The rest of the day is cut short when I'm called to the principal's office. Ms. Wirth has always been a sympathetic character, the type of person who claims to care about us and actually backs it up by remembering inane details about our lives. She's leaning on the front of her desk when I arrive, a cup of coffee in her right hand and a worry stone in the left. Her sad smile confirms why I'm here.

"Have a seat, please." She gestures to one of the cushioned chairs to the side of the desk and sits in the other. Once I'm settled, she takes a breath before speaking. "I heard what happened at the competition. After all these years..." she takes another breath and continues working the stone. "How are you doing? Is there anything I can do to make this easier?"

Yeah, mute the assholes whose whispers have followed me all day. I give her a Wes shrug. "Not really."

She sets the cup on the desk and reaches for the armrest of my chair. Not close enough to touch me, but reflex pushes me back. She moves her hand to her lap. "Have the kids been rough?"

Tears prick my eyes and I blink them away. "They aren't saying anything that isn't true." But that's not what's made me numb. The rest of the story will come out in days or hours or minutes. A reporter could be putting the final touches on the article right now and people will find out about the freak who's been walking these halls alongside them.

"Would it be easier if you stayed home for a few days? I could arrange for your teachers—"

"No." My voice is stronger than I feel. I take a breath to soften it. She's only trying to help. "We're so close to graduation. I just want to finish classes and be done."

One hundred two days.

Her lips pull into a firm line. "Okay, but promise you'll let me or another teacher know if you need us to intervene."

I nod and Gen smiles and Ms. Wirth escorts me out of her office. It's midway through fourth period, the halls are quiet, and suddenly being here is too much. Without stopping at my locker, I head for the nearest exit and step into the sunshine.

Betty carries me to the lake. I don't get out of the car but roll down the windows and let the spring air sweep over me. Crews are uprooting the slatted snow fences meant to prevent the beach from blowing away during the harsh Michigan winter, tossing them into the back of their trucks, while bulldozers level out the sand that drifted like snowbanks over the past few months.

In Spring Haven, this is the official start to summer, even though the calendar insists it's over a month away. People stroll near the shore but keep their distance from the water. It may look like almost-summer but two months ago this was a scene straight from the north pole and the water won't warm up until July.

Gen, why won't you talk to me?

Her weighted silence wraps around me. If a non-sentient being were capable of physical touch, this would be her hug. Like she's telling me it'll be okay. Or that even if it's not okay, she'll always be here for me.

If I'm going to get through another day, I have to believe her.

Telling Mom we found Gen will undoubtedly break her beyond repair. For as many times as I've longed for a mother who sees me for me, not the persona I've created for her, a fierce protectiveness urges me to keep her safely hidden in her room. To shield her from the reality that's threatening to sweep me away with the lake's current.

My eyes close and I turn inward, listening for Gen. I can almost hear her whispering that nothing good will come from this.

Then I remember Sky's confused face—my face—in the auditorium. How can finding my twin be a bad thing? Life is about balance, and perhaps being reunited with my sister will counter the damage to Mom's psyche.

Seagulls glide on a breeze above the bulldozers, watching for treasures unearthed by their unyielding blades, but where they see hope, I only see the decaying underbelly of a part of life that was never meant to see sunlight. Some things are better left buried.

When the crews load the last fence into a truck, I drag my gaze from the mesmerizing rhythm of the waves and head home.

Dad's waiting for me in the living room.

"Are we really telling her?"

"Do you see another way?" He's paler than normal and scruff lines his usually clean-shaven face. "The police are reopening the case. They're going to want to talk to her."

"Is she even capable of that?"

His head hangs from his shoulders. "I don't know."

A thousand replies tumble over each other, all blaming him for creating this madness. "You should have tried harder."

"I've tried as hard as I can."

"I mean with therapy. She needed help. She still needs help."

He doesn't answer.

Regardless of whose fault this is, it's our reality and it's being ripped apart at the seams. His feet are heavy on the stairs, each step bringing us closer to the climax of our story like a train screaming into the station, brakes squealing in protest.

He knocks lightly on her door and I follow him inside. Canned laughter greets us, a discordant soundtrack for the scene we're about to play.

She's knitting on the couch and looks surprised to see Dad. "Larry, what are you doing home?"

Her lack of awareness of the world stuns me. Did she not feel the seismic shift that happened between her daughters? Isn't there supposed to be an invisible connection between a mother and her children, a sixth sense that sends a shiver through your body, alerting you that something major has happened? But maybe that's what drove her over the edge. The certainty that her daughter was out in the world without her—alone, afraid, and unloved.

"Where's Gen? I finished her blanket." She holds out the blue and orange square and only now, with it spread over the coffee table in front of her, do I realize it's UVA's school colors.

The punch to my gut happens so fast it steals my breath. Of course she made Gen's first.

"I'm starting yours tomorrow."

As if tomorrow will ever be the same.

Dad settles next to her on the couch and takes her hand in his, while I slide down the wall near the door. "Michelle, we need to talk to you."

Her eyes sparkle with a light that rarely comes out. Either she's nervous and doesn't want us to know, or she's genuinely pleased to have us both here. "That sounds ominous."

"It's important."

She nods, her trusting gaze bouncing between the two of us. "Where's Gen? Shouldn't she be here too?"

My stomach clenches. No good can come from this.

Dad clears his throat. Takes a deep breath. Grips her hand more tightly. "Remember when the girls were babies?"

"Oh, they were just the most beautiful girls. Remember everyone said that?" She smiles at me. "I couldn't have been more proud."

The brighter she smiles, the deeper he sinks into himself, like their emotions are inversely connected. My heart tugs with the urge to help, to make this easier for him, but this isn't my charade to unravel.

"Do you remember the day—" his voice cracks. "The day I took them to the park?"

"I was so tired." She smiles, but it fades for a moment as she studies me on the floor. "You girls were so much work. If one of you napped, the other was awake. Those early months were a blur." The lines around her eyes soften as she glosses over Gen's kidnapping.

Dread slithers up my throat, dragging with it every instance of hurt and resentment and frustration that shaped me into who I am.

Dad clears his throat. "Michelle, do you remember when the police came?"

A tremor moves through her and she flinches. Closes her eyes. "They were awful. Said awful things."

"I remember."

I've only heard the story a handful of times, and only when tensions between us reached an apex and I refused to continue his game. Dad fed me the truth in small enough morsels to keep me going, and each time I rebelled, he fed me a little more. Because what father wants to tell his daughter he's the reason her sister is gone?

But in this room, that truth never happened.

He drags a hand over his face and meets my eyes. I hold his gaze, urging him to continue. "Michelle, this is important," he repeats. "Something has happened. Something good."

She straightens the knitting needles on the coffee table and sets the blanket and balls of yarn in the basket by her feet. Her smile seems hesitant and her fingers shake as she rests her hand on Dad's. "Then why the doom and gloom? I thought someone died."

The heaviness in my chest nearly pushes me through the floor. Blood roars in my ears, putting more and more distance between me and the voice I long to hear.

Gen, please say something.

I need you.

You can't be gone.

The weight expands through my body until I feel paralyzed. My arms fall to my sides, the soft carpet dampening the thump as my hands hit the floor.

"No, no one died. Quite the opposite, in fact."

"Well goodness, Larry. Why the theatrics?"

His eyes close as he takes a deep breath and together we balance on the edge of yet another Before and After. "Michelle, they've found Gen."

Her eyes dart around the room. "Then why isn't she here?"

"I know this is confusing. I thought I was doing the right thing."

She looks over his shoulder at me, then stands. "Eve, can you make sense of this?"

Why did I go along with him? All these years I convinced myself I was merely his puppet, but while he may have started this pretense, I'm complicit in his lies.

We watch her, waiting for our creation to short-circuit, but she merely paces the room, her hands knotted against her stomach. She stops in front of me and touches my arm. "Eve, where is your sister?"

I'd like to think I'm strong enough to do the right thing, but who's to say what's right anymore? My hand covers hers the way it has a thousand times and she smiles the smile she usually only gives Gen. For a second it feels like everything will be okay. "I'll go get her."

I barely register the look of horror on Dad's face as I slip into the hall.

Don't think about the consequences as I step into Gen's room.

Practice my smile as I put on her UVA sweatshirt and pull up my hair.

Then return to Mom's room to say goodbye.

Twenty-Four

The *Sabre* office is quiet when I arrive and the interminable weight on my chest eases. This place of facts and truth calms me, and I feel like I have an iota of control over my life.

Mr. Barney sets down his tablet when he sees me.

My bag drops with a thud on the floor in front of his desk. "Thanks for coming in early to meet me."

He nods and gestures at the chair behind me. "Pull up a seat."

Take a breath.

Channel Christiane Amanpour.

Lean on my years of shoving aside any emotions that might get in the way of reporting my story.

The chair squeaks on the floor as I sit. "First, I want to thank you for defending me yesterday. All of this has been..." Impossible, devastating, overwhelming. "Surreal."

His normally jovial face grows serious, his brows furrow, and lines form around his eyes. "I can't even imagine." After a pause, he continues. "But I don't think that's why you asked to meet early."

I shake my head. "If I want to make it as a journalist, I'm going to have to write stories that are difficult for me. That hit close to home. So," my jaw ticks and I look him in the eye. "I'd like to write the article on my family. For the *Sabre*."

He leans back in his chair on an exhale. "Are you sure that's a good idea?"

"I don't trust anyone more than I trust myself."

"That may be true, but isn't it an active investigation?"

Wes shrugs for me and Gen turns on the charm while I push down the bile churning in my stomach. "I'd rather set the record straight. People are going to talk and at least this way the whispers will be true." My thumbnail traces a groove on his desk. How many students have sat here before me, confessing their soul's darkest secrets or begging for leniency? "It feels fitting to have it in the last issue. So I can go out with a bang, so to speak."

He drags a hand over his jaw the way Dad does when he hasn't shaved. "I can do that. Do you want to work with Cal, or directly with me?"

"You. Thank you." This betrayal feels worse than what I did with Mariela. Cal knows we were never exclusive, but rejecting his help as an editor cuts to the core of who he is.

"He's going to wonder why."

"I'll make him understand."

Footsteps shuffle in the hallway and a moment later Cal steps into the room. His reporter's eyes make quick inventory of the situation as he moves past us to his desk.

"But not now," I whisper so only Mr. Barney can hear. He nods, and I move to my regular seat.

Cal watches me, eyes curious.

"We were just talking about the deadline for the final issue."

"It's in three days."

Three days to write the hardest story of my life. Three days to figure out how to explain my secrets to everyone I know. Three days to keep pretending. "Yeah."

"How are you doing?" he asks. "I was hoping we could talk yesterday but I know things are probably crazy."

The word is like a dagger in my chest. That's what everyone will call me. Or if not me, Mom. And Dad for orchestrating it all. I fall into my chair but keep a smile on my face. Gen may be refusing to speak, but she's still helping me when it counts. "Can we talk about it later? I can come over tonight."

Despite the panic, trails of elation and giddy anticipation flit through me. In one week, I won't have to schedule around Gen's special time with Mom. She was so confused last night that Dad gave up trying to get her to understand, but as the investigation continues, the charade will have to end.

I know I should text Sky, but the pieces of her personality have yet to meld with how I've imagined her, and I'm not ready for her to be real. To be better than my Gen. Because it's one thing for people to like the Gen I created, but what if they like Sky better? From what I know of her, I like her better, so it's only natural the rest of the world will too.

The others arrive as I'm imagining a life as just Eve.

Mr. Barney and Cal run us through the deadlines for the final issue and my thoughts drift to Mom. Will she find a foothold with a different Gen and somehow rejoin the world, or will her mind fully break?

Cal's gaze finds mine and I shut off those thoughts until hours later when I'm tucked on the couch in his room.

"I'm worried about you," he says. An empty seat cushion divides us, but his long arm rests across the back and his fingers tangle in my hair. I skipped my run and drove here so we could study, and my skirt feels like more of an invitation than my usual running clothes. I feel more exposed than when I'm in this room naked after my shower. His hand drops to my bare leg and trails lightly over my skin.

"I just want to get through graduation."

"What were you and Barney talking about this morning?"

Lying seems pointless. He's going to find out, and better to hear it from me now than when the final issue comes out. "I told him I want to write the story about my family. About Gen." Her name catches in my throat and I reach for the water on the low table in front of us.

Concern creases his brow and his fingers stop moving over my leg. "Do you want my help?"

A transparent glass of water makes a poor shield, but I press it to the side of my face anyway. The coolness calms me, settling my thoughts. "I already asked Mr. Barney." Through the glass his jaw clenches. I shift so my body's facing him and the movement makes his hand slide to my thigh. A different kind of need simmers inside me. A need to be seen. Despite the skepticism on his face, I cover his hand with mine. "We're both too close to this to be objective. Having someone who's not emotionally invested will be good."

His face relaxes, but his eyes are still serious. "I guess I get that."

The glass clinks on the table as I set it down, then I move closer. My skirt hitches farther up my legs until it's barely covering me, and the emotion in his eyes shifts to something I'm more familiar with. Something I can control. With one hand he sets his books on the table while the other travels the rest of the way up my leg. His mouth grazes my ear. "I wish you trusted me."

Guilt and a weird sense of obligation push me closer to him. Hurting Cal may be inevitable, but it doesn't have to happen today. "I do trust you. More than anyone else." Wes smiles in my mind and I shoo him away. He may know the truth, but he doesn't know me like this. Want me like this. My hands explore Cal's body and he pushes me back on the couch. His mouth is warm, familiar, and I return his kiss with an energy I haven't felt in days.

We don't bother moving to his bed. Afterwards, once I've put my clothes back on and am reaching for my books, he pulls me onto his lap and wraps his arms around me.

"I thought I was losing you." His admission twists in my hair, his breath warm on my neck. "You've been so distant, I thought..." he trails off, either afraid to speak the words aloud or not yet able to voice his concern.

My body relaxes into his in a way it only does during sex. My duplicitous life has made it impossible to let my guard down, but maybe I've been wrong to keep Cal from getting too close. His trust and loyalty have never wavered and all he's gotten in return is a girl who uses her body as a reward. Exhaustion settles through me, starting in my belly and creeping through my arms and legs. I'm so tired of lying. Cal tightens his embrace, interpreting my physical reaction as a response.

"I kissed someone else." The words are out before my brain grasps the consequences and it's too late to reel them back in.

His body stills, the confession thickening the air around us. Seconds tick by. His breath quickens, his heart thuds against my ribcage. One hand drops from my side. "Is that why you're always insisting we're not exclusive?"

I'm not sure what I expected, but it's not this flat, emotionless question that skips the unnecessary details and cuts to the meat of the story. His journalistic tendencies lead him straight to the Why—not Who, What, When, or Where—and a tiny part of me hopes he won't ask the more obvious questions.

"It wasn't planned, and it was only the one time. And it has nothing to do with my fear of commitment." Plagiarizing the words he's thrown at me a hundred times feels like a cop out. "But I've felt guilty ever since, which shows you mean more to me than I thought."

He drops his other arm and somehow puts distance between our bodies even though I'm still on his lap.

This is why I don't share with people. Nothing is coming out right.

"So I'm supposed to be happy about this?"

My head drops and my hair hangs in my face. "No. I was a jerk. I'm just trying to be honest with you." But I don't know if I'll ever be fully honest with him. Telling Wes about Gen was a moment of weakness I'm not eager to repeat. That part of my life will be over in a matter of days, so telling Cal now will only make things harder when I leave at the end of the summer.

"Did you sleep with him?"

"Her. And no."

His lips tighten into a thin line. I know him well enough to see the questions flipping through his mind like an old-school

Rolodex, but he holds them inside. After what feels like an eternity, he asks, "Why are you telling me now?"

"Because you've been nothing but amazing and I hate lying to you."

"Do you feel better?"

Quite the opposite. The guilt that's followed me since the night I met Mariela amplifies as he withdraws further inside himself. "No. But I haven't been fair to you."

He slides a hand under my legs and moves me off his lap. "I think you should go."

"Are we…" Over? Fighting? On a break?

"The offer still stands to help, but I need time to wrap my brain around what you've done."

"Okay." I dump my books into my bag and hesitate in front of him, unsure if physical contact is still allowed. I finally settle with touching his arm. "I'm sorry for hurting you. That's the one thing I never wanted."

He nods once, his lips still tight, his eyes unreadable.

Outside, I sit in the driveway for a minute before starting the car, absorbing the past hour and committing the details of his house to memory in case I'm never invited back. We've been heading for this moment since we first kissed, the inevitability of our demise as certain as Mom's inability to crawl out of her mind's defenses and join the real world. Cal will get past this and go on to be an editor in a big city, far away from Spring Haven and the memories of the girl from senior year who never wanted to break his heart but did anyways.

I can only hope my future holds something equally promising. The college countdown has given me something to look forward to—especially on the days when it feels like I'll never escape the horrors that have defined my life—but there are moments when I fear all my hard work will be for nothing. That no matter how far away I run, or how many stories I weave, I'll never fully leave this life behind me.

A single porch light greets me when I get home. Wes's house is equally quiet, so I hurry to my room to work on the article, but when I flip on my bedroom light, a gasp escapes me and I jump back. Mom's standing at my window, looking out at the backyard, seemingly unconcerned with the fact that she hasn't set foot in my room in nearly a decade.

My words somehow make their way up my scratchy throat. "Mom, what are you doing in here?"

She turns, the hint of a frown playing on her lips. "Gen never came home. Do you know where she is?"

The weight of Gen's silence buckles my knees. I catch myself on the dresser, then stagger across the room and sink onto my bed.

"What's wrong?" The bed squeaks as Mom sits next to me. She pushes the hair off my face and peers into my eyes.

This isn't the first time she's expressed concern for me, but this is the first time it's happened in my room. The darkness that lurks beneath Gen and her lies whispers to milk Mom's attention while I can. To take advantage of this crack in her 2007 bubble and let her mother me.

A heavy sigh pushes me against her. "It's been a long couple days." My phone buzzes in my pocket but I ignore it. Nothing is more important than this moment, right now.

Her fingers work through a snarl in my hair before resting against my cheek. We're a mother and daughter in an after-school special, chatting about the latest teenaged drama. She hesitates for a heartbeat, like she's debating what to say, and concern flickers across her face. "Anything I can help with?"

Lightness fills me, inflating every cell and pushing away the doubts that threaten to ruin this moment. Right now she is everything I need her to be. This clarity may last a few minutes or a few hours, and it might never happen again. I will it to swallow me whole so I can save this feeling for the days when the darkness wins. My arm slips through hers and the heat from her body calms my racing thoughts.

Mom. This is Mom.

"I had a fight with Cal. I did something stupid, and today I told him and—"

"I thought Gen was dating Cal?"

Fuck.

Walls slam around me, between us.

Seventh-grade Eve grasps at the threads connecting us.

No! I need more. I'm not ready to lose you.

But the moment has already shattered. Mom slips into her shell so quickly it's as if the past minutes didn't happen, and as the vacant expression returns to her face, I'm left wondering if it really happened. Our arms are still linked, but my lapse of judgement splintered our tenuous connection. Her everyday smile brightens her blank eyes, and she looks around my room as if seeing it for the first time. "I can't remember the last time I was in here."

"Let's get you back to your room. I bet a new episode is about to start."

We stand, and she touches my face with the same gentleness as before. Everything inside me stills and I struggle to keep my breath calm.

Why can't you see that I'm Eve AND Gen?

"Will you send Gen in when she gets home?"

Her words are a thousand needles in my eyes, my throat, my chest. Sharp pinpricks that burst the hope that ballooned inside me, leaving burning tears and a lump that makes it hard to breathe. "Sure."

Her lips brush my cheek with a practiced coolness, then she returns to her lair, unaware of the shrapnel she's left in her wake.

The pieces of me lie scattered on the carpet alongside my earlier enthusiasm to write the article. Determination flickers deep inside me, a faint glow that barely warms me. Passion can only get you so far. It'd be so much easier to give up. To let Cal or one of the other reporters write whatever they think is my real story while I drift into oblivion.

I flop onto my bed and my phone pokes me, reminding me of the unread text.

Sky: are you there?

This is how I've imagined conversations starting with my sister. Not "how are you?" or "please talk to me," just a simple status check before launching into whatever drama takes priority that day.

Me: Yeah.

Sky: I feel like I'm losing my mind.

Guilt pushes me into a sitting position so my back is against the wall. I've been so wrapped up in what finding Gen meant for me and my family I haven't truly considered what it's doing to Sky. The disruption to my life is light years behind the truth-bomb that exploded in her face. At least I knew she was missing.

Me: Is there anything I can do?

Sky: can I call you?

Before I can answer, she texts again.

Sky: I hate the phone too but this is too much to type.

Me: It's okay. We can talk.

My phone buzzes and her name displays on the screen. I never assigned a photo to her contact and, for a second, I'm tempted to put Gen's selfie as a placeholder. The hair might be wrong but the face is the same. I answer on the second ring and she starts without a greeting.

"I keep wondering if it's true. If I was really kidnapped like the police said. But I saw you. I've seen your picture. We're obviously sisters. Twins."

Her words roll over me, a familiar blanket that until now I've only heard in my head. In the weeks we were chatting, we never spoke. Would I have recognized my voice in hers if we had? Either way, this outcome, this moment, feels preordained.

"You really had no idea?" I ask.

She sniffles, and I imagine her in a room like mine, sitting against the wall, our poses mirrored even though we're separated by almost two hundred miles. "Sometimes I'd feel this, I don't know... longing. Like something was missing." She laughs, a small pitiful sound that makes my heart ache for her. "I just figured I wanted a boyfriend."

The voice in the back of my mind checks that box.

"Do you think this is why we felt a connection?" she asks.

"Maybe." Did the universe push us together, or is this the type of coincidence you read about in books but feels too fantastical to have actually happened?

"I have so many questions," she continues. "My parents are a mess. The adoption agency told them I'd been abandoned at a fire station."

Another box checked off. Maybe she'll answer every unknown that's haunted me since childhood without me having to say a word.

"Now the police are saying I'm the infamous Baby Ellaway." Her breath shudders into the phone. "What's this been like for you?"

How do you summarize your life in a sentence? While editors typically write the headlines, Mr. Barney has had me practice with my stories, drilling the basics into my head. To the point. Action verbs. Hit the emotion. And the fewer words the better. "We've never recovered." My eyes close and I imagine her doing the same. "I was too young to remember you, but you've always been a part of me." I can't tell her about Mom. About what we've done to her. What we've made her believe. "The missing puzzle piece that would put our family back together."

She inhales sharply.

"What?"

"We sound alike."

A smile softens my face. And not a fake Gen smile meant to put the other person at ease. This is an Eve smile. "I noticed that too."

"Can I ask you a question?"

"Of course."

She hesitates, and I can feel her uncertainty in my soul.

"You can ask me anything."

Her voice comes out a whisper. "When is our birthday?"

My heart stutters. She's gone through life without this most basic piece of her identity. "March 9."

"They were close. The hospital guessed March 17."

"I can't imagine not knowing."

She laughs softly. "I guess we both have a lot of unknowns we can finally get answered."

The Gen I created confronts this living, breathing person on the phone. My sister. In my mind, they dance around each other like rival gang members, knives in hand, one a fully-formed figment of my imagination, the other a shadowy creature with too many empty spaces. Twins share DNA, so in theory, we have a million things alike, but I've made us have more differences so I could keep the stories straight.

A desire to know every detail about Sky wraps around my heart. Is she right-handed? Athletic? Popular? And the darker things. About her mind. Does she struggle like Mom? Does she long to leave her hometown and start over someplace new? Does she use people to make herself feel better?

My gaze travels to the hall and I picture her purple bedspread. "What's your favorite color?"

"Green. Yours?"

"Blue. Do you like to run?"

"I run on the beach whenever I can."

Warmth spreads through me.

"Favorite food?" she asks, and I relax onto the pillow. We go back and forth, sharing details we should know innately but were stolen the day she disappeared. With each answer, the threads that have stretched and twisted—always yearning for something I could never have—grasp onto something real. Tangible. Something I can count on.

She is not your sister.

My pulse jackhammers, and the hollow weight that's followed me since Saturday fills until I can't breathe. The warmth evaporates, sending chills through my body.

What?

This... imposter... is not Gen.

I know this is confusing, but it's her. I saw her. Sky is Gen.

She can't replace me.

But—

I won't let her.

Twenty-Five

A cold case nearly two decades old...

A school project ripped open a cold case...

No one could have imagined that a school project would reunite a missing child with her family, ripping open a cold case long forgotten by everyone except the Ellaway family.

My head falls back, but my bedroom ceiling holds no answers. The article doesn't have to be Pulitzer-worthy, but perfectionist paralysis grips me so tightly I can barely get past the opening paragraph. Which is silly because they'll read it no matter how it starts. The final issue comes out in two days, which means I need to turn this in by the end of the day so Mr. Barney can give feedback.

Across the room, my phone buzzes with another text. Most of the senior class is celebrating the end of the school year with a bonfire, and Ember has texted so many times I threw my phone off the bed so I wouldn't be tempted to answer. I've promised to show up for graduation and that's the last time I plan to see most of those people.

Plus Cal's there and I don't want to ruin his night.

With a mouse click, I switch screens to the police report of Gen's kidnapping. The detective handling our case didn't want to share the files with me, but Mr. Barney helped clarify a few rules about the press's access to cold cases and the files were emailed to me within hours. As for the current investigation, Sky filled in enough details to make the article well-rounded without worsening her newfound notoriety.

Sky Emerson grew up an only child in a loving family in a small house steps from the East Arm of Grand Traverse Bay. She knew she was adopted, but the adoption agency's story that she was abandoned by her mother at a fire station was far from the truth. In reality, Gen Ellaway was kidnapped from a park while sleeping next to her twin sister. We may never know why the assailant chose Gen, but that decision set their lives on an irreversible path that led to the two sisters finding each other almost eighteen years to the day since they were torn apart.

While the Ellaways wondered what happened to their daughter, Sky flourished. A graphic designer, she works for her school newspaper—the same as her sister. They also share a love of running on the beach. Beyond that they're still learning what they have in common.

My eyes roll so hard it hurts my head. No one beyond our families cares about this. They'll read the story because they're salivating for the details of the biggest scandal to hit Spring Haven in years, but finding Baby Ellaway is nothing more than a juicy story to whisper around the bonfire until the minutiae become so warped they no longer resemble the truth.

While we're left to put back the pieces of our lives.

Both Spring Haven and Traverse City police have interviewed the adoption agency, but the original files were never digitized. The only details are the ones shared with the Emersons: Baby Jane Doe, estimated to be two months old, was left at the fire station under the Safe Haven statute, which permits children to be turned over to authorities without prosecution. Hindsight insists

the police should have investigated this infant more thoroughly, especially since it was only one month since Baby Ellaway had been kidnapped less than two hundred miles away, but Baby Jane Doe was put into the foster system and quickly adopted by the Emersons.

The lack of an investigation feels too simple. Gen's disappearance made regional news. If the police had done their jobs, my entire life would have been different. Mom would be whole. And I would have had my sister.

Do you really wish that?

With a roll of my shoulders, I push Gen away.

So you only want me when it's convenient for you? Now that you have your precious Sky I'm supposed to just go away?

Why can't I have you both?

Her silence makes my heart ache.

I continue reading.

Sky never knew she had a sister, an identical twin who thought of her every day and never imagined she'd find her—especially not through a school project. As the sisters get to know each other, they ask that the public respect their privacy.

Moving forward, the Ellaway and Emerson families have many hard truths to overcome. But they also have something else—hope for a future that only holds happiness.

...a future full of happiness.

... a future that's both hopeful and filled with love.

Maybe Mr. Barney can fix the last line. He'll tell me if it needs work. I hit save, then switch to my email and send it to him before I can second-guess myself. Sky asked to see it so she knows what's being said about her, so once it's approved, I'll send it to her as well. I just hope she doesn't think I'm exposing her more than she already has been.

A car door slams outside, followed by a knock on the front door. I tiptoe across the hall to peer out Gen's window, and just as quickly hurry back to my room. The detective is probably here for Mom or Dad, but sooner or later he's going to want to talk to me, and I'm not ready.

The sun sits low in the sky but there's still enough light for a run. My running clothes feel like a second skin as I slip out the front door, past the unmarked cruiser, and glide down the street.

The lake welcomes me, her waves pounding the shore with a ferocity normally reserved for winter. Like things have built up to the point that she can't hold it in anymore. No matter what's going on in my life, this will always be where I feel whole. My legs stretch over the sand, each step carrying me farther from the detective and his questions and the chance that he'll learn more than we want him to.

When I return to our street, the car is still in the driveway.

Wes would probably let me hide in his house, or I could sneak around back to the treehouse. Or I could be an adult and face my fears. The wind picks up, cooling the sweat on my skin and sending a shiver through me. Volunteering information and answering questions are two very different things. As long as I keep my answers brief and stay focused, I can avoid lying to the police and prevent them from learning the full truth.

The door creaks when I step inside. Multiple voices carry down the stairs and my heart stops. They're in Mom's room. Which means they see the pictures. Her confusion about Gen has probably already convinced them she needs to be taken away, but instead of running upstairs and protecting her, I go to the kitchen and get a glass of water.

Sit at the island.

And wait.

Twenty minutes pass before footsteps sound on the stairs. Dad spots me in the kitchen and something unspoken passes between us. He looks defeated, like he can't carry the guilt of his lies much longer. I nod, and he turns to the detective and the officer standing behind him.

"Do you need to talk to Eve while you're here?" Even though I gave him the okay, his words feel like a betrayal.

The detective pokes his head into the kitchen and nods at me. "I think we've got enough for tonight. We can schedule it for another time."

Gen smiles over my glass of water. "Can't wait."

Dad walks them to the front door, then reappears in the kitchen.

"How'd it go?" I ask.

He sinks into the chair next to me and buries his face in his hands. I've seen a lot of emotions from my father over the years, but I've never seen him this hopeless. This scared. His skin seems to hang from his body and the gray streaks at his temples have multiplied overnight. For the first time in my life, I feel the need to protect him.

"Not well," he finally answers. "They saw the pictures. And your mother... She was very confused. It didn't take a rocket scientist to figure out something else is going on."

The air stills around us until it's so thick I can't breathe. My fingers go numb against the glass and I set it down with a clink. My heart races and pauses, galloping and slowing until the roar of my pulse is all I hear.

They know.

And soon everyone will know.

My feet find the floor and I carry my glass to the sink. Dad's saying something else and I turn to face him. Shake my head to clear the buzzing that's drowning out everything else. "What?"

"When should I tell the dectective you'll talk to them?"

How about never? "Can it wait until after graduation?"

"Eve, this is an active police investigation." He doesn't need to say the rest. As a journalist, I understand the urgency during an active case, but as the girl holding all the secrets, I want to stall as long as I can.

"Tomorrow after school."

He nods, ending the conversation. Because what else is there left to say? Dad's rules that began when I was a kid no longer apply. Everyone's talking about Gen.

Soon they'll know Mom never leaves her room.

And unless Dad knows something he's not telling me, my special time with Mom is over.

After my shower, I reply to Ember so she knows I'm alive and tell her I'm going to bed. She replies with a flurry of photos from the bonfire, mostly of her and Claire looking happy, like they have all the time in the world. Longing grips me for the briefest of moments, but it's not a longing to be part of that group. It's a longing for something I've never had, and now fear I never will.

An email from Mr. Barney is waiting for me when I wake up.

Eve,

Other than the last line, the story is perfect. I hope you're okay that I tweaked it for you. It'll run in the last issue tomorrow. Nice work.

I hope your family can find peace.

Mr. B.

I had my first story published in the *Sabre* my freshman year and the jittery nerves before a story comes out have never waned. But this is different. The panic racing through me isn't concern over a typo or a snide comment from an underclassman—this is fear. Because the police know the truth and it's only a matter of time before the rest of the world finds out.

And they'll not only learn I've been lying my whole life, but the final story of my high school career will be proof that when given the chance to come clean, I lied again.

School buzzes with the excitement brought on by the end of the school year. Kids whoop and laugh down the halls, hugging people they've barely spoken to all year, while I feel like a zombie. Gen smiles for me. Lifts my hand to wave at people I'll never see again. When a boy from my history class wraps an arm around me and squeezes, Gen laughs. "People have lost their minds," I say to Ember, who's laughing alongside me. The difference is her laugh is real.

The day passes in a blur. Ember buoys me with tales from the bonfire and anticipation for her internship, but it feels self-indulgent. Today marks a different kind of ending, one that will change the trajectory of my entire life. After school the police will learn the truth. The Gen I've held in my heart will be set free, making room for Sky and freeing me to live the life I've always wanted.

So why do I feel like I'm losing Gen? An unbearable sense of loss wraps around me, hollowing my heart and coloring what are supposed to be the happiest days of my life with a bleakness that even the brightest sun can't penetrate.

A cruiser sits in the driveway when I get home, the engine idling. Dad's waiting in the foyer when I open the front door. The detective from yesterday sits in the arm chair in the living room, a glass of water on the coffee table in front of him on a coaster I've never seen. I follow Dad to the couch and flinch at its stiffness. Since Mom never leaves her room, Dad and I float between the kitchen and our bedrooms. The living room has always been a showpiece, something to tell visitors we're just like them. I don't think the flatscreen TV is even plugged in. The couch squeaks as Dad sits and I lean back.

Take a deep breath.

One.

Two.

Three.

This is normal. Detectives always interview me after school.

Four.

Five.

Which is worse? Betraying your mother or erasing your sister?

Six.

Seven.

The breathing isn't working. Spots dance in the air and everything feels muted, detached, like I'm floating out of my body and watching this scene from the corner of the ceiling.

"I'm Detective Ramos. Thank you for meeting with me." His smile is not unpleasant, and his dark hair has the same peppered streaks as Dad's, but there's a seriousness in his gaze that pins me to the couch. My head nods dumbly and my gaze flicks to Dad, but he seems as shell-shocked as I am. "I know you and your family have been through a lot in the past few days, and I appreciate your help getting answers." He flips open a notepad and balances it on his knee.

My journalistic brain latches onto this detail. Does he have a detective shorthand to document what I say, or does he already know enough of the truth that interviewing me is just a formality?

"Could you tell me how you met Sky Emerson?"

Sky.

Gen.

Sky.

My sister.

I clear my throat, but it doesn't make it easier to breathe. "We met on the forum for our project."

"And you weren't aware of her true identity?"

My head tilts at his accusing tone. "It's a forum. We used screen names. Hers is Twilight. I'm Journalist309." He glances at Dad and my eyes roll on their own. "Have you seriously never heard of screen names before?"

His pen scratches in his pad. "No need to get defensive. I'm on your side here."

Heat flares through me. "Sure feels like it." Was he like this with Mom? She's not strong enough to withstand an interrogation, to understand that the detective's piercing glare is intended to intimidate but doesn't mean she did anything wrong. Questions for Dad whip through my mind, but now's not the time to ask. If the detective thinks the scene in Mom's room is an act and we're all in on it, I need to be careful what I say.

"When was the first time you met Miss Emerson in person?" he asks.

My mouth falls open and Dad clamps a hand over my knee.

"Eve, he needs to hear your version of the story."

"Then maybe he should let me tell it."

Detective Ramos leans back in the chair and waves a hand at me. "By all means."

I mirror his position. The armrest is stiff against my side but I force my limbs to relax. "We started the group project a little over a month ago. At first I only chatted with Noah and Willow, my partners, but there were public rooms where everyone could get to know each other." The detective's brow grows heavier with every breath, making sweat prickle my palms. Nothing about my friendship with Sky is suspect. "We started chatting a few days after the project started, then switched to texts."

He leans forward. "Why did you switch to texts? Were you trying to hide something?"

Dad crosses an ankle over his knee. His posture is mostly relaxed but the tightness in his shoulders confirms he's pissed. "Do you have teenagers?"

Detective Ramos smiles. "My girls are barely out of diapers."

"Give it another ten years and you'll understand."

The detective rolls his neck before returning his attention to me. "Please continue."

"We did nothing wrong."

"I didn't say you did."

"But you're implying it." My jaw clenches and I gesture at him with a flick of my wrist. "Everything about you implies I'm guilty of something. Do I need to remind you that I'm the one whose sister was kidnapped? And I'm the one who found her?" My chest constricts and the spots from earlier punctuate the air between us.

He holds up his hands, elbows on his knees. "I think we got off on the wrong foot. You have no need to be defensive."

The spots fade and a shaky breath fills my lungs. "Sky and I are friends. The fact that she turned out to be my sister..." My gaze drops to his scuffed shoes. "I'm still trying to wrap my brain around it."

"We all are," Dad says.

"Have you talked to Miss Emerson since Saturday?"

My back straightens and alarm pulses through me. "Am I not supposed to?"

Detective Ramos holds out his hands as if to placate me. "Eve, my goal here is to get the complete story. Of course you're allowed to talk to your sister."

"Okay, sorry." But anger heats my blood. When you've been raised to hold a secret so closely no one ever questions, to choose every word with a surgeon's precision, it's impossible to turn it off because a man in an ill-fitting suit says it's okay.

"Do you have plans to see her?"

I shake my head.

Dad rests his hand on my leg. "We've talked to the Emersons but haven't made plans for a reunion yet."

My heart nearly leaps out of my chest and that damn kaleidoscope stirs. "You've talked to them?"

"Of course. But we're—I'm not sure if Mom is ready."

Understatement of the year.

Detective Ramos clears his throat. "The press might want to be there when you meet."

"Not happening," I say at the same time Dad says, "I don't think that's the best idea."

The detective shrugs. "It's a small town. People like to know the details. I'm just trying to prepare you for what's to come." He flips to a new page in his notebook and glances between us before setting his gaze on Dad. "Mr. Ellaway, could I have a moment alone with Eve?"

My pulse jackhammers like I just sprinted on the beach.

Dad leans forward as if he's going to stand, but hesitates on the edge of the couch. "Why?"

"I have a few questions I'd like to ask Eve privately." Not a single muscle moves as he delivers this statement. No tick above his eye, no clench of the jaw. Nothing to clue me in as to what he's thinking.

Dad rises on shaky legs and moves toward the kitchen. "I'll be in here. If you need me." If he's trying to say something telepathically, the message disintegrates before it reaches me.

I face the detective and take a deep breath to calm my nerves. Repeat, "I haven't done anything wrong," over and over in my head until he speaks.

"Eve, this situation with your mother and father, the circumstances of your upbringing," he drags a hand over his face and in that moment his armor cracks. He's no longer a badass detective but the father of two little girls, staring at a future he never imagined for his children. "I think it's important that you seek counseling so you can move past the abuse—"

A deafening silence drowns out the rest of his words, like all sound has been sucked from the room. My heartbeat echoes in my skull, bouncing off the walls and windows and smooth planes of his face, which has stopped moving. Abuse. The same word Wes used when I told him my secret. Is that what this is? Not just a charade to help Mom, but something that could actually have consequences? A fire sparks deep in my belly, igniting my veins until I can barely breathe.

"What about my dad? Will he be punished?" My voice sounds hollow, like I'm shouting from deep within myself. "He destroyed two lives."

His lips move and I shake my head.

He frowns.

They move again and the pressure in my head lessens with a whoosh. A cabinet closes in the kitchen and the faucet turns on, then off. A chair squeaks.

"Unfortunately the legal system can't do much since you're eighteen and no one witnessed the alleged abuse."

Mom did.

"Witnessed?" Anger flares hot, burning the tumult from my mind. "Do you need me to go upstairs and pretend to be Gen for you?"

His jaw clenches, the muscle popping against the stubble on his cheek. "I'm not doubting the abuse. It's just hard to prove and the prosecutor may not want to touch a case they don't think they can win."

"So that's it?"

"You can file a civil suit, but it's not an easy road. And it would be very public." He leans forward, elbows on knees, and I imagine him talking to his daughters. Teaching them to stay away from bad people like my father so they don't end up like me.

He did this. It's all his fault.

But he only did it because he wanted to help Mom.

And what about you?

Me. Eve.

Detective Ramos sighs. "You have to do what's right for you."

But not just me. What's right for our family.

And taking Dad from Mom would destroy her.

Twenty-Six

The detective's words echo in my ears the next day as the *Sabre* office hums with last-day-of-school energy. Mr. Barney stands at the front of the room, copies of the final issue in his hand.

"I want to tell you how proud I am of each and every one of you."

"Even the douche canoe?" Ember whispers, and I smile.

"You should be proud of your hard work. Your dedication and the extra hours you've put in—especially the early mornings—will serve you well in the future. And for you seniors, excellent work with the final project. Only one of you will be heading to GVSU this summer—" people pat Ember on the back. "But the rest of you..."

I shift closer to Cal and rest my hand on his thigh.

He jumps at the contact. He's always been the one to initiate anything when we're in public, and I'm not sure if I'm even allowed to touch him, but the nostalgia pumping through the school has indeed made me melancholic. This chapter of my life will be over in a matter of days, but part of me wants to hold onto that connection a little bit longer.

He hesitates before covering my hand with his and for a few minutes the rest of the world fades away. The impending destruction barreling toward me, threatening to rip my world in half, pauses because of this boy. I lace my fingers through his and my breathing grows easier.

A few minutes before the bell, everyone gathers around the table in the center of the room, hugging and laughing, and it hits me that this is The End. I'll be part of a different staff at Northwestern, but my identity as a journalist will be on hold for the next few months. Desperation to hang onto this moment tugs me to Cal's side. I reach for Ember and pull her close, too.

"What's up, chickadee?" Ember asks, wrapping an arm around my waist and resting her head against mine.

"I guess it's hitting me that this is the end."

She touches my cheek and makes a mewing sound. "I knew deep down you cared about this place."

"The place, yes. Most of the people? Questionable."

We laugh and Cal squeezes us both against his chest. "Great job on the article, Eve." He smiles, but it doesn't reach his eyes. "I would have helped, but I get why you went to Barney instead."

Will I ever find someone—guy or girl—as accepting as Cal? Or a friend as amazing as Ember? "I'm gonna miss you both."

"Hey," Ember pulls back to look me in the eyes. "We're not going anywhere. The internet has guaranteed we will remain friends for the rest of our lives."

The rest of our lives seems like an unfathomable concept when each second is a drumbeat bringing me closer to the world finding out the truth. I'm not dense enough to think Ember and Cal won't support me, but this casual ease might be gone forever.

The bell rings and eyes track us through the hall.

Track me.

Rumors carry an excitement because the truth is uncertain, but a printed story makes it fact. It's what I love about journalism, but it's also what's filling me with the urge to drop my bag and run from the building. To keep running until everyone forgets me.

Ember slips her arm through mine. "Hold your head high. You have nothing to be ashamed or embarrassed about."

If only that were true.

The morning drags by, each tick of the clock drowning out the chatter in my classes.

They'll. Know. The. Truth.

Over and over, until I'm almost relieved when a sharp inhale sounds across the hall before lunch. It starts with a low murmur, then the frantic whispers and gasps grow louder as the story is passed from phone to phone.

"Her mom sounds nuts."

"Did you see the pictures?"

Their comments slither through the air, worming into my brain and wrapping around my lungs until I can't breathe. My article didn't have pictures, which means the media got hold of the story.

"She pretended to be her?"

No no nononononononononono. Panic jolts through me on a current, stretching and tearing my insides, torching my nerve endings in a desperate attempt to escape. Sweat beads on my upper lip and my hands lock on the edge of my locker. If I don't move, if I don't look at them, it won't be real.

You knew this would happen someday.

But why today?

Now you really get to go out with a bang.

Everyone knows.

My recurring nightmare has come to life. I close my eyes against the whispers. Despite the battle raging inside me, goosebumps prick my cool skin and a rhythmic humming blocks out their words. It takes me a moment to realize it's my phone buzzing at my feet. There's no need to look. I can guess who it is. What they're saying. Or asking. Because it's what I've feared for as long as I understood the depths of our depravity. Dad and I led Mom down a wormhole from which she'll most likely never recover. We've lied to everyone we know and it's too late to take it back.

I try to run, but bodies block my escape.

"Did you really do this?"

"How did you keep it secret?"

"Are you crazy?" The last comment comes from a girl from my English class whose past attempts at conversation fell on deaf ears. Or perhaps crazy ears.

Tears burn my eyes and everything slows. It wasn't supposed to end like this. I'm supposed to cut ties with them at graduation, leave them wondering about the girl who never spoke, who left Spring Haven for college and never looked back. Now the story is out of my control.

I push through them, my vision blurry. Curious contemplation turns to hungry stares, their need to feed on the gossip of my life drawing them too close.

Someone calls my name but I can't look. Can't look at any of them.

They stop short of touching me, like I'm contagious. They get near enough to taunt, jeer, ridicule, then step back before they're exposed to whatever contagion made me the way I am.

Instead of heading to the cafeteria, I end up in the *Sabre* office. The door's unlocked, the lights off, but when I slip inside, the air feels different from this morning. The energy that charged the halls simmers here, but it's softer, like a heavy blanket dampens the full impact of what's happened.

I'll just stay here for a few minutes.

My phone continues to buzz so I pull it from my bag.

Dad: The press found out.

Ember: I'm here for you.

Ember: We can skip out if you need to.

Cal: Are you okay?

Ember: Don't come to the cafeteria.

Cal: I'm worried about you.

Mariela: Who ARE you???

Sky: why didn't you tell me?

I slump against the wall beneath the windows. Press the side of my face against the cool cinderblock wall. This is happening too fast. When I dreamed of being free from the lies, I imagined it on my terms once I was far away from the people I grew up with. Now I'm trapped in the room that's always been my sanctuary, the heart and soul of this school. I want nothing more than to hide in my room until I leave for college, but first I have to get out of this building.

Me: I'm in the Sabre office.

The minutes feel like hours until the door creaks and Ember steps inside. After a quick scan of the room, she eases her way around the tables until she's crouching in front of me. She rests her hand on my knee and the concern on her face nearly undoes me. This is what it's going to be like from now on. Everyone who I'd kept safely in the dark now knows the real me, the person who's deceived them and made them believe she was a different person.

"What can I do?" Ember's voice is soft and her unshed tears shine in the dim light.

"I don't know."

"We're worried about you."

They're already talking about me as if I'm the freakshow at the circus. Only except for the bearded lady or man with a tail, I'm the girl who pretends to be two different people.

"Who's we?"

She shifts so she's sitting next to me, staring out at the empty room instead of into my eyes. "Me, Cal, Claire." A pause. "Wes."

"What are they saying?" Part of me wants to take back the question, to keep myself suspended in this in-between state, never knowing the full weight of the whispers that could hold me down and make it impossible to move on.

"People are confused. It's a lot to take in."

"A little too extra extra?"

She snorts, a gentle puff of air that diffuses the tension in my chest enough that I can breathe. "Do you want to leave?"

I nod, my head thumping against the wall.

"Do you need me to drive you?"

My head rolls to the side so I'm facing her. "No. You can't miss the last day of school because of me."

She shrugs. "Eh. I'm pretty much checked out at this point."

I grab her hand and she squeezes. "Ember, I'm not ruining the last day of high school for you. My life will still be a disaster in a few more hours. Help me get outside and we can see each other later." My voice sounds strong, assured, and for a moment I think she buys it.

Her shoulder presses against mine. "I know you're full of shit, but I'll help smuggle you out."

My heart fills with an unfamiliar emotion: gratitude. She must have a million questions, but she's helping me first. "Thank you."

She pulls me to my feet and leads me to the door, then sticks her head into the hallway. "It's as clear as it's gonna be."

We take a step into the hallway, and she stops so suddenly I bump into her. The nearest exit is at the end of the hall, but my locker is closer to the cafeteria, where half the school lingers over their final bland sandwich and slice of greasy pizza.

"Skip your locker," she says. "We can get your stuff when no one's here."

My forehead drops against the space between her shoulder blades. "You don't know how much this means to me."

"I think I have an idea."

The fact that she understands I need more time proves I made the right choice texting her. Cal would have pestered me for details that I'm not ready to share. I press my hand against her shoulder and she squeezes my fingers.

"Can I come over later?"

My instincts urge me to push her away. To insist I don't need help. But that would be another lie and I'm tired of lying. "Sure."

"I'll text when I'm on my way," she says. "Now go."

Her gaze burns into my back as I hurry down the hall, followed by the unspoken questions that have to be whirling inside her. But those will have to wait.

Outside, the sun shines and birds chirp and the world continues spinning on its lopsided axis. I take a deep breath as I cross the parking lot and step into my new After.

Twenty-Seven

I skip driving by the beach and head straight home. The fewer chances for people to see me, to recognize me, the better. No cop car sits in the driveway, and no lights burn in the kitchen. No one's expecting me for hours, but something pulls me upstairs to Mom's room. The door is ajar, and I peek through the opening. Mom's folding laundry on her bed and this snapshot of domestication nearly undoes me—until I notice the news playing on the TV behind her. In my eighteen years, I've never seen her watch anything other than Friends. Does she somehow understand what's going on, or is it a complete fluke that the day our lies burst into the world, she happens to get tired of her BFFs?

"Eve, you're home early!"

I startle, hitting my head on the edge of the door. Pain shoots through my cheek but I brush it aside, focused only on keeping her attention on me and away from the TV. "School let out early. Do you need help?" Sweatshirts and leggings tangle together in the basket on the bed, and a fresh wave of alarm rushes through me.

She never does my laundry. I make sure of it. Because if she did, she'd notice Gen's lack of dirty clothes.

I reach for Gen's UVA sweatshirt. A spot of blood—my blood—stains the hem of the sleeve.

"I wish she'd told me that was there," Mom says with a frown. "Now it's too late to get out."

No hint at why she's strayed from her usual routine.

"Gen doesn't always think about how her actions affect other people." The words slip through my filter and hang between us. I've criticized my sister in front of Mom as often as I've seen her watch the news.

Which has switched to coverage of an accident on the highway. Sports should be next, followed by weather. There's only ten minutes left in the broadcast and unless they do a human interest piece at the end, we should be safe.

"Are you two fighting again?"

Again?

"Gen seemed worried about Cal, and since you mentioned him the other day, I thought maybe..." she trails off and my mind races to fill in the gaps, to recall what I could have possibly said that made her think I'm stealing Cal from Gen. My lies are usually catalogued neatly in separate compartments, ready for when I need them, but it's like a tornado came through and uprooted each falsehood, exposing them for what they really are.

"No, everything's fine."

One of Dad's favorite movies defines fine as freaked out, insecure, neurotic, and emotional. Based on that definition, everything is most definitely fine.

She sinks onto the bed and clutches a pair of Gen's leggings to her chest. "I can't believe my baby girls are graduating from high school."

"Are you coming to graduation?" Sometimes a thought appears fully formed in your mind, and that's how I decide I only want Dad at graduation if he brings Mom. Whether by choice or Dad's manipulation, Mom has never attended a school function and this is a way to force Dad's hand, to make him prove he has my best interests in mind.

"Your father and I talked about it, but I haven't decided. It's been so long since I've been out..." she trails off, her hands twisting the leggings round and round, and the question I've held back since I was old enough to know better bubbles to the surface. Before today there was always more time, a day in the future when I could hear her version of the story, but that window of opportunity is about to slam shut.

I take a breath, and on the exhale put voice to the words that have worn a groove in the tip of my tongue. "Why don't you leave the house?"

Her head snaps up and her eyes widen. "I—I don't know."

Not what I was expecting.

"Life hasn't turned out the way I anticipated." She sighs as if she's the one holding back what she wants to say, then her lips curl into a smile. "But I'm so grateful to have you."

My heart swells until it feels like it might burst, even though deep down I know neither of my parents will see me graduate.

"Both of you," she continues.

The disappointment that's become as much a part of me as breathing sweeps away any hope of her understanding what we've done. "Well, it'd be great if you can go to graduation, but I understand if you can't."

She tosses the leggings in the basket and reaches for my hand. "Life doesn't always go the way we want. Then again," she nods at the TV, which is playing a commercial, "sometimes it does. Look at Ross and Rachel. Even after they had Emma, we thought they'd never get back together. But they did. And Monica found her happy ending. They all did."

Comparing my life to a nineties sitcom isn't the most helpful advice, but she's trying. "Thanks, Mom."

Movement on the TV catches my eye. A photo of two girls flashes onto the screen. At first glance it looks like an ordinary picture, but the desperation from earlier crawls its way up my spine when the camera zooms in on my face in duplicate. It's the same photo that hangs near the window. Did a cop take it while pretending to look outside? Or was he imagining what it would be like to spend every waking minute in this room when the impulse struck to violate her basic rights? The sound on the TV is too low to hear the report, but the anchor's brows are creased and her pretty mouth frowns as she speaks.

The story is spreading.

I need to protect her.

I lean over the clothes and brush a kiss on her cheek to keep her focused on me. "You don't have to decide now."

"It's in a couple days, right?"

Only a couple more days before I'll never have to see my classmates again. "Yeah." The end credits roll and I stand. My head feels heavy and my legs wobble as if I just finished a run. "I'll see you later."

Reminders of how we've lied to Mom are everywhere. The pictures, Gen's room, the separate wardrobes. And the lies. All the lies. They pile on top of me, suffocating me. It's still hours before Dad will be home, but I can't spend another minute in this house.

The treehouse beckons me. Wes's car isn't in the driveway, so I cross the yard and climb the ladder without looking back. Just a few more hours, then I'll face reality.

An old beanbag chair sits in the corner like it's waiting for me. I flop into it and my butt hits the ground, but it's still better than the floor or the tiny chairs. Exhaustion creeps through my bones, curling me into the fetal position. It'd be so easy to let unconsciousness take over, to keep my head down for the next couple months, then escape to college and never look back.

Instead, I pull out my phone and text Ember.

Me: I'm in the treehouse behind my house. Bring snacks.

Me: Please and thank you.

The other unanswered messages taunt me. As much as I want to block out what's happening, avoiding my friends will only prolong the inevitable.

I reply to Cal first.

Me: I'm home. I'm okay. You deserve an explanation but I need time.

We've barely spoken since I told him about Mariela, but the truth—everything I've kept from him—colors every conversation we've ever had. The tenacity that drew me to him is the same trait that will make it impossible for him to let this go, and he won't leave me alone until he hears the truth for himself.

Sky is next.

Me: I didn't know how to tell you the truth. Finding you was a shock. I didn't know if you were even alive, and then to find out I already knew you—I'm still sorting out what this means.

No amount of explaining could ever make her understand, but I hope this is a start.

Dad's straightforward message—the press found out—stares at me. The coldness that wraps around my heart when Gen takes over feels familiar, safe, and I skip his message without replying.

Mariela's message is the only one left. We never talked after the night of the game, and I'm okay with that, but guilt pricks me for using Gen's name. I keep my reply truthful.

Me: I don't know.

Fatigue comes swiftly. My head drops onto the dusty canvas and stuffing from the chair puffs into the air. As I close my eyes, my phone dings.

Sky: it means we're sisters. nothing else matters.

Warmth spreads through my chest, pushing away the emptiness that threatens to overwhelm me. No matter what happens, we're sisters, and no one can take that away from us again. A tingling on the back of my neck chills me. I burrow deeper into the beanbag, but before I can fall asleep, a creak sounds below the treehouse. I hold my breath, willing the person to go away, but another board creaks under their weight and a moment later, Wes's head emerges through the opening.

"We have to stop meeting like this." My voice croaks but it earns me a smile.

He pulls himself inside and sits with his legs dangling through the opening. "Technically, this is my property."

We could banter until Ember arrives, pretending everything is normal, but it's taking all my energy to keep my eyes open. "I assume you heard the news?"

"Yeah. And I gotta say, I'm a little sad I'm not the only one who knows your secret anymore."

"You knew it wouldn't last."

"True, but I kinda hoped. For your sake." His voice is too soft, his eyes too compassionate. I need the Wes who gives me shit and doesn't treat me like a wounded baby bird.

"Do me a favor and don't mention to Ember that you already knew."

He looks around the cramped room. "Okay?"

"She's on her way here."

He nods.

"She's my best friend. It's going to be hard enough to get her to understand without also being upset that I confided in you."

He runs his fingers along the rough floorboards near his legs. "And what about Cal?"

"Let's assume you shouldn't tell anyone that you knew. But he's not coming here." The longer I put off talking to Cal, the harder it will be. Unless he decides my lies are too much for him and he cuts me out of his life for good. Then I won't have to explain.

"Got it." He swings his legs, and a memory of twelve-year-old Wes comes into focus. We had a sixth-grade track and field day where they forced kids to run fifty-yard dashes, attempt long jumps, and throw metal balls into the grassy field. Wes was always an active kid, but a broken arm landed him on the bench for most of the day, legs swinging like they are now.

"How did you break your arm?"

His head snaps up and he touches his arm on reflex. "What?"

"In sixth grade. At the track and field thing. You couldn't participate because of your cast." A darkness passes over his face—the same darkness that haunts me—and I immediately regret asking.

"You met him."

A surge of energy pushes me into a sitting position, grateful for the distraction from my own problems, but the look on his face drowns that feeling in guilt. "I didn't mean to pry."

He waves a hand between us. "Nah, you've seen the worst."

Meaning his dad. I bite my lip and wait for him to continue.

"Dad left not long after that. He didn't usually hit us—he just yelled—but something set him off and he threw me against a wall. Kept me out of soccer that spring."

"I'm really sorry."

He shrugs, and the familiar gesture gives me hope that maybe I can get through my trauma, too. "We all have our shit, right?"

We fall into a comfortable silence, each lost in our thoughts, until plastic rustles beneath us. He quirks a brow at me and I smile. "Supplies."

He moves his legs so he's lying on the floor with his upper body hanging through the opening. "Hand it up," he says, and a moment later he's setting a bag filled with sodas and snacks next to me. "It's creaky, but it'll hold you."

Ember's squeal makes me smile. Despite her thin frame, she's not athletic, and climbing a janky ladder up a tree is not on her list of fun things to do. But she's doing it for me.

Wes shifts into a crouch to help her up, and then my best friend is stretched out on the beanbag next to me, pulling me into a hug. We don't hug often, but she somehow knows this is what I need. To feel safe. Loved. Despite everything I've done.

"Thank you for coming," I murmur into her hair. "And for the snacks."

She tightens her arms for a second, then relaxes and pulls back so she's looking me in the eyes. "You've always been there for me when I needed you, and now I'm here for you. That's what friends do."

Wes clears his throat. "Well, I'm here for the snacks. Whatcha got in here?"

The bag rustles and I smile. My greatest fear came to life today and these two—my friends who before now have barely said more than hello to each other—have somehow made it a little less awful.

"Pretzels, chocolate, sugar," Ember says. "Crisis basics."

Wes opens the bag of pretzels and starts eating, and my focus drifts back to Ember. Her eyes search mine as if she's unsure how much she can say in front of him, but instead of answering, I let my head fall against her shoulder.

"New clubhouse rule," I say. "No talking about the elephant in the room."

"I didn't know we had rules," Wes says. Ember shoots him a look and he tosses me a pretzel. "No elephants. Got it."

"Do you remember," Ember says, "how far away graduation felt when we started high school? Now it's less than a week away and I feel more uncertain about the future than I did then."

I wind a piece of her hair around my finger. "You're going to Kendall fricking College of Art and Design, and you're going to turn the design world on its head."

Her shy smile tells me I hit close to home. "What about you, Wes?" she asks. "Was high school everything you expected?"

He launches into stories about soccer and playing for Hope College in the fall, and the cadence of their voices lulls me into a space one step up from sleep. My eyes close and Ember strokes my hair until the only thing in my head is this exact moment in time.

And then nothing.

It's dark when I wake up. Fog muddles my brain, and I feel trapped between unconsciousness and a reality I don't want to face. In my dream, the world was closing in on me. No matter how fast I ran, the shadows inched nearer. Then I was falling, falling, falling.

Next to me, Ember's putting wrappers back in the bag as Wes climbs down. She tosses him the bag, then nods at me. "Ready?"

My head shakes on its own. "This was the best slumber party I could ever hope for."

She tips an imaginary hat at me. "I aim to please. But we can't stay here."

"I know."

She nods at the opening in the floor. "After you." Probably to make sure I don't barricade myself inside.

Wes stands beneath the creaky ladder, ready to catch me if I fall.

And as I climb down the tree, I'm no longer afraid. The coming days won't be easy, and I'll probably wish I never left this treehouse, but the only way to regain my independence is to get through this next chapter.

And I finally feel like I'm ready.

Twenty-Eight

Twisted Family Lives in Lies.

Reclusive Mother Deceived by Family.

House of Horrors in Our Backyard.

The last headline feels like a stretch, but people don't know what to make of the Ellaway family. Of me. The national media picked up the story while I was singing Kumbaya in the treehouse with Wes and Ember, and now there's no escape. Everyone knows the truth.

When you've lived in a boiling pot your whole life, you don't realize the water's peeling off your flesh until someone points it out, and then that rawness is all you feel. Each ragged breath is another reminder that while we've found Sky, I'm losing Gen.

I swipe my phone closed and toss it on the bed.

Graduation is in an hour, and while I've been tempted to skip the ceremony, I want my classmates' final memory of me to be me holding my head high as I cross the stage, not bolting out the side door of the school. Today represents the official end of my high school career and everything I've longed to escape, except now the media—the group I've wanted to be part of since I could first string a sentence together—has betrayed me. Tarnished the one thing that's kept me focused.

There's a beat inside me, one that's always preceded Gen sharing her opinion, but her voice remains quiet. The emptiness growing inside me builds, hollowing my belly so I constantly feel a dropping sensation, like when you think you're at the bottom of the stairs but there's still one left. The reflex to catch myself has me grasping for anything solid.

"Good luck today." Mom's voice at my door makes me jump. She grips the doorframe as if it's the only thing keeping her grounded, and her smile is tentative, uncertain.

"Thanks."

"You look nice."

I've worn this skirt and top combo a hundred times, but the white Chucks are new. "Thanks," I repeat.

She glances over her shoulder and my heart aches for her. Dad tried to explain that Gen isn't here—that she never was—but when you're a family of frauds, even your deceptions are flawless. Now Mom's trying to make sense of something that can never make sense.

"Are you coming to graduation?" She's already given the answer, but the part of me that still longs for an ordinary mother can't let go of the hope that someday, maybe today, she'll surprise me.

She picks at the wooden doorframe with her fingernail. "I would. I—I want to. But..."

"It's okay, Mom. I get it."

When she looks up, tears shine in her eyes. "Do you? Because I don't."

Frustration blooms in my chest. When I dreamed of ending the lies, I never considered that we were merely shifting the ways we protect Mom. Gen may be gone, but Mom's confusion will always be here and the outlines of a new future play in front of me. Of careful visits and guarded phone calls, always wondering if today will be the day she finally snaps.

"I—I can't do this right now. I have to get to school."

Her gaze drops to the floor and she nods.

"I'm sorry."

"No, it's okay." She shakes her head, pauses for a moment, then turns around and heads back to her room.

Or so I thought.

When I go to the bathroom to finish my hair, Mom's sitting on Gen's bed, gently rocking back and forth with the UVA sweatshirt clutched to her chest.

The world has already established I'm a horrible human being, so I barely flinch as I keep walking.

Dad's waiting downstairs in a pair of dress slacks and a button-down, his hands knotted at his waist.

"Seeing me off?"

"Eve, please reconsider."

My shoulders straighten and a confidence I don't feel pushes up my chin. "I told you. You're only welcome if Mom comes too, and since that's not happening..." Wes shrugs for me.

"Why are you doing this?"

I step closer. The scent of his aftershave tickles my nose. "Are you more upset that you can't come to my graduation or that your pawn is fighting back?"

His mouth opens, closes. Then he inhales deeply before reaching for my shoulders, but I step beyond his grasp. "You know going outside... going to the school. It would be too much for her."

Of course I do. Worrying about my mother's well-being is a reflex, but I need to do this. To prove to Dad—and to myself—that from now on, I control my life. "Just be glad I'm not pressing charges." He doesn't need to know it's not an option.

I leave him standing in the foyer and walk out the door, alone.

A pair of news vans idle in the street but I keep my eyes focused on what lies ahead.

"Eve Ellaway."

Ember whoops from the second row on the football field, her smile as bright as the sun beating down on us. Today would be better with her next to me but the school insisted on alphabetizing us.

A few people in the audience snicker as I cross the stage and accept my diploma from Ms. Wirth, who seems like the only person outside of my circle who's happy to see me. When we shake hands, she holds it long enough to make a fresh wave of sweat break out over my back.

Just let me off the stage so I can climb back into my hole.

After the ceremony, Cal catches me at the edge of the field, a hopeful expression on his face. "Eve." My name is enough to make heads turn, but he either doesn't notice or doesn't care. His mother hovers nearby and from the expression on her face, she'd love nothing more than a chance to save my soul.

Cal steps closer and I tilt my head up to look at him. At the start of our non-relationship, I often wondered how it would end. Would he fight for me, or walk away without a second thought? Looking into his eyes now, grief flirts with guilt. Part of me is sad this has to end and feels bad for ever dragging him into my life. But it's better to cut him loose.

He bumps the toe of his white Chucks against mine. "Nice shoes." His smile fades the longer I don't speak. "I have something for you."

"We're doing gifts?" My voice squeaks. My heart races. Why does he have to be so sweet, even after everything I've done?

He pulls a tiny unicorn from his pocket and holds it out in the palm of his hand like he's presenting the crown jewels.

My fingers brush his hand as I take it. "Is this from prom?"

He lifts a shoulder. "I promised I'd steal you a unicorn if you had fun." Then he takes a breath and dread pushes away all other emotions. He loves words as much as I do and the determination on his face screams that he's rehearsed this. "I know you're dealing with a lot right now, and I'm sorry you felt like you couldn't trust me. But I'm not ready to say goodbye. You're important to me, more than you probably know. You make me look at the world in a different way and make me believe in things I probably shouldn't." He nods at the unicorn in my hand. "You're my unicorn. I know you don't want to be an us, and you're probably going to insist this is the end of the road, but I think that would be a mistake."

"But this is the end of the road."

His jaw ticks.

I want to feel his warm skin beneath my fingers one last time, but I keep my hands clenched at my sides.

"Why do you refuse to be happy?"

"Why do you refuse to let me go?"

"So this is it." He waves a hand at the people lingering in the grass around us. "Here. Now."

A tiny piece of my heart calves like an iceberg falling into the ocean, and the little voice in my head whispers maybe I should keep him a little longer. Just through the summer. I push the voice down so deep it might find where Gen is hiding and give him a Wes shrug. "I'm sorry, but I think it's for the best."

Then I walk away before I can change my mind.

Sky texts to congratulate me, but I haven't replied to her since the treehouse. The warmth that envelops me when I think about having a tangible sister is cut short by the darkness buried deep inside me. I want her in my life, but something won't let me. It insists I'm better off alone, unable to hurt anyone else with my lies.

I just wish I believed it.

Twenty-Nine

JUNE 5

IS IT POSSIBLE TO BE TRAPPED IN LIMBO WHILE YOU'RE STILL ALIVE? GRADUATION IS A FADING MEMORY, BUT IT'S STILL MONTHS UNTIL I CAN FULLY ESCAPE. THE WORLD KEEPS SPINNING ROUND AND ROUND AND IT'S LIKE I'VE FALLEN INTO AN ALTERNATE UNIVERSE WHERE EVERYTHING STANDS STILL.

EVERYTHING EXCEPT THE ONE THING I WANT TO STAY THE SAME.

—EE

Thirty

"Is this really the only option?"

Dad exhales and it's like he leaves everything inside him on the kitchen island. "It's been almost a month. She's not coming around."

"What did you think would happen when she learned the truth? You had to have known it would end badly." Even though I've dreamed of the day I can write The End on our sick charade, now that we're here, I'm scared for Mom. I'm scared for all of us. What will happen to our family? Her damaged mind has trapped each of us in different ways, but part of me wishes I could change it all back. Just for a little longer.

He buries his face in his hands. "I didn't think. How could I have imagined this—" he gestures at the kitchen as if the answers lie in the tiled backsplash. "What it would do to her."

Years of frustration and anger and pent-up accusations bubble in my chest. And I finally don't hold back. "That's what it all comes down to, isn't it? You didn't think. You saw an easy solution to your fuck-up and you've ruined all of our lives."

His head sinks lower in his arms. "You don't think I've told myself that every day for the past eighteen years? Regretted not insisting she stay in therapy when Gen was first taken? Going along with her delusions was the easy way out and now it's too late to stop."

Anger simmers beneath my skin. "But a mental institution?"

Dad lifts his head. His eyes are wet with unshed tears and the grimace on his face deflates my fury. "You're leaving for school in less than three months. I can't do this on my own."

This. My mother has been reduced from the object of our deception to a burden who makes our lives miserable. Because of our actions. Gen's urge to please everyone and make them happy bumps against my frustration. It'd be so easy to agree, to appease his guilt and let him live the rest of his life free from the woman he destroyed. But I can't let it go that easily.

"Don't make me feel guilty for going to college and living my life. This has always been my plan." I pace the room, unable to stand still any longer. "Did you know I've been counting the days until I can leave? Until I can put this freak show behind me and just be Eve?"

If it was possible to fold inside yourself, I think he would. "I know this has been hard on you."

"Hard? Dad, you trained me to be two people! To divide my life into two versions of myself until I don't know where I end and she begins. Now that we've found Sky, I don't know how to make sense of anything." I move closer so he feels the full impact of my words. "How do you think it makes me feel knowing that even after everything that's happened, Gen is still Mom's favorite?"

His head snaps back. "I talked to her... she promised she'd be more sensitive."

My eyes narrow and a scowl smears my face. A growl rumbles deep in my chest, but I hold it back with a shaky breath. "It's obvious where her preferences lie. Even after you talked to her."

"Parents aren't supposed to play favorites." His watery eyes spur my rage. How dare he feel sorry for himself after everything he's done.

"Yeah, well, there are a lot of things parents aren't supposed to do." Tremors travel up my arms, crawl over my shoulders, and wrap around my throat. When I was small, Dad told me playing this game with Mom would make her love me twice as much. I did everything he asked because I wanted to be a good daughter. Wanted the extra love. Now I'm stranded on an island while the most important people in my life drift away in the only boat.

Rather than begging for them to turn the boat around, to find another way to keep Mom sane, I walk away, unable to look at him another second. But I can't completely let it go. "At least now you can stop fake-reading Gen's book."

"What?"

I face him. "The bookmark. I know you move it so it looks like she's reading."

There's a beat before he speaks, a hesitation that reaches between us and slowly squeezes my chest. "I've never done that."

"What?" Everything goes still. Silent. Then a dull roar gains momentum until my pulse thunders through my body.

"I only go in there to vacuum." His words barely register over the screaming in my head. "I always thought it was nice how you decorated her room and made it feel lived in."

This doesn't make sense. If he isn't—then who?

An answer wiggles through the chaos in my mind, pushing each terrifying thought out of the darkness.

You.

Me.

The ground shifts beneath me and I grip the wall to keep from falling. From tumbling deeper into the unknown. The room spins, leaving trails of questions like vapor in the air.

What does this mean?

Did you know?

Am I as crazy as Mom?

This doesn't change anything.

A shuddering breath strengthens me as Dad approaches.

"Are you okay?"

I brush past him and stumble on the stairs. Focus on the carpet that's been flattened by years of weary dread and obligation. What else don't I know?

Empty memories ricochet through me. The article I didn't write. The password protected file. Telling Cal I love him.

Dad's talking behind me but all I can hear is the memory of Gen's voice insisting Dad is lying, that it's another mistruth in his twisted game. I imagine her smiling like it doesn't bother her—because nothing bothers her—and desperation to have her back nearly turns me inside out.

But what if he's not lying?

A single sob escapes my throat, then I shove these new feelings deep down where she's hiding and climb the stairs.

When I go to Mom's room, she's sitting on the edge of her bed puzzling over the neatly folded piles of clothes. It's not unlike the day I helped her with the laundry, except now she's packing to go away without fully understanding where she's going, or why.

"Can I help?" I ask.

Her lip trembles when she looks up. "I don't want to leave. I like it here."

Despair tangles with my anger. For all the times I've wanted to scream at her, to make her see I'm Gen and Eve, none of this is her fault. Her mind wasn't strong enough to handle losing her daughter and she coped the only way she knew how. The fault lies with Dad, who chose to follow Mom into her alternate reality rather than fighting to do the right thing, the thing that could have saved her, even if it was harder. She doesn't deserve any of this.

Pain rips through my heart, slicing through me and spilling tears down my face. "I know, Mom. But this will help you."

"Help me with what? I have everything I need right here." Her voice cracks as her gaze travels over the room—over the TV, her knitting, the manipulated photos—before meeting my eyes. "Your father and you girls are my world."

My selfish desire that she acknowledge there's only one of us—at least here in our home—refuses to die. "You can take your friends with you. And I'm sure they'll let you knit." But maybe they won't. They assured us Mom won't be with anyone dangerous, but knitting needles could cause serious damage in the wrong hands.

"It won't be the same."

On that we agree. Nothing will ever be the same.

I help her pack, tucking her knitting supplies into a separate bag in case they turn them away. We say goodbye with a final awkward hug, my heart cracking a little more as she strokes my cheek. "I'll miss you."

"I'll miss you, too," I say automatically.

Instead of retreating to the treehouse like I'd planned, I go to Gen's room.

Pull the UVA sweatshirt from the bottom drawer.

And go back to say goodbye once more.

Mom's still on the bed, bags on the floor, a somber expression aging her beyond her sixty-two years. I drum my fingernails on the door to get her attention and she springs to her feet.

"Gen. Oh, Gen." She crosses the room and pulls me tight to her body, her breastbone rough against my chest. "I don't want to leave!" Sobs wrack her frame and I hold on as if I'll never let go. My tears loosen the dam holding everything back, but if I don't keep it under control I might drown her here in her room. My fingers stroke her hair and the detached part of me wonders where I learned how to comfort her. To keep her here in the present. Certainly not in this house.

When her crying slows, I guide her to the couch, where we sit angled so our knees press together. Her hands splay over mine and she doesn't bother wiping the tears from her face.

"Promise you'll come visit."

The kick to the chest knocks the breath from my lungs. I shouldn't have come back. I should have left it at my first goodbye and gone to college feeling sorry for her and the cruel hand life dealt her. But now the desperation in her voice is burned into my memory, a permanent reminder that she prefers the daughter I made up. Eyes closed, I bite back the hurtful replies dancing on my tongue and level my voice. "I'll do my best."

She shifts closer, wraps a thin arm around my waist, and rests her head on my shoulder. "I don't know how to get through the day without you and your sister. You girls are my everything."

I tilt my head against hers. "Focus on getting better so you can come back to us." How many lies does it take to completely destroy a person? As far as I know, there's little hope she'll be released in the near future. And when she does come home, I won't be here.

And neither will Gen.

She lifts my hand to her lips and sighs.

"You'll get through this, Mom."

A shudder passes through her, sending shivers through my body. Was this what it was like inside her womb? Feeling everything she feels as if it's happening to me. Wanting what she wants. Craving love from someone who doesn't exist.

She sighs against my neck. "I hope so."

A knock at the door makes us both turn. Dad has one foot in the room, one hand on the doorframe. He takes in my appearance as quickly as he takes a breath. "Michelle, we need to go."

Her grip on my hand tightens, sending a ripple of panic through me.

"Mom, you can do this. You're stronger than you think." Not all lies are bad. Some build you up until you find the strength to stand on your own. I gently untangle our hands and push to my feet. When she rises, I give her a final hug. "I'll miss you."

"I'll miss you, too."

Dad gathers her bags and steps into the hallway. "Come on, Michelle."

It feels wrong that her life can be carried out of the house in two suitcases. When I leave for college, I plan to fill Betty until I can't see out her windows. Without thinking, I grab a framed photo from the dresser. I was eight or nine and very into Harry Potter, based on the outfits in the picture. "Mom, take this too."

Dad shoots me a look and I pull it to my chest. "You know she can't."

Because having a manipulated photo of her imaginary daughter will detract from her therapy to undo eighteen years of damage.

Mom reaches for the frame. "Just one can't hurt."

This is how it starts. One little lie. A slight alteration of the truth.

Dad drops the bags and takes the photo from her. "I'm sorry. They said no family photos."

That's not actually a rule, but in Mom's case they made an exception.

Fresh tears brim her eyes and her lower lip trembles. "Then let me get one last look at you." She presses a hand to each of my cheeks and studies me until I start to squirm. Then she kisses my forehead and steps back.

And doesn't insist on a final look at Eve. At me.

"Bye, Mom."

Dad leads her down the stairs and out the door and off to never-never-land. Emptiness turns me inside out and too late I rush to Gen's window. My life may have been a series of performances with Dad pulling the strings, but Mom was always there, not just as my audience, but an enthusiastic participant who devoured every tale I wove. Dad's already backed out of the driveway but I catch a glimpse of Mom's hand pressed to the passenger window, her long hair shielding her from the world she's worked so hard to forget.

I sink onto the bed, my head in my hands, as the final curtain falls. "I could get through this if you would just talk to me." My voice gets lost in the corners of the room. The anticipation of the heaviness in my chest that comes when Gen's thinking makes me feel light-headed. Hollow. And still she doesn't speak.

"Do you have something better to do?"

Sky's face flits through my mind. It's been weeks since I've texted her, and we haven't spoken since the awkward day she and her parents joined Dad and me for lunch. The Emersons said they understood why Mom stayed home, but I recognized the confusion on Sky's face. Despite the bumpy start, our connection was almost tangible, an electric current that leapt over the table and bound us together, and while we promised we'd see each other soon, my silence has made that impossible.

Not that she hasn't stopped trying.

"She won't replace you," I say to the room, but that's not true. My stomach pitches to the floor. There's only room for one sister in my heart. I can't have them both.

"Yes, we met, but she had to see Dad. I haven't talked to her since then."

Gen's silence is worse than the pain of losing her. Because I can still feel her. She's here, she's just refusing to speak.

I sink to the floor and a scrap of paper peeks at me from under the edge of the bed. It must be from when I trashed her room. I turn it over, and Gen smiles back at me. My heart stutters. This proves she's still here. She's mad and punishing me for wanting something more—someone else—but she hasn't disappeared.

"Gen, I'm sorry. But what was I supposed to do?"

A hint of a whisper drifts through my mind—You were supposed to choose me—but it's impossible to know if it's Gen or my own imagination filling in what I want to hear. My fingers dig into the carpet. If I close my eyes, I can imagine the soft fibers caressing my flesh are strands of her hair, that the bed frame pressing against my side is her hip bumping mine. This room is Gen and she's begging to come alive, to live outside these walls and experience the world for herself.

"Then why won't you talk to me? Ge-e-e-e-e-e-e-en!" My scream echoes off the walls, reverberates through my skull, stripping my throat until it feels raw.

But she doesn't answer. Her silence feels like a death.

I crawl on all fours to the dresser and pull myself to my feet. Stare at my reflection in the mirror. At Gen. Her hair's coming loose from her ponytail, her eyes bloodshot, her skin puffy from crying. But that's not what makes me pause. The fury in her gaze nearly undoes me. Like she can't stand to look at me.

"Gen, I'm sorry."

She cries with me, her lower lip trembling while her eyes search mine for some explanation of how this got so fucked up. Then the tears stop and her glare pierces through me, splitting me in two.

Panic turns me away from the mirror. Everything in this room screams betrayal. If I'm to believe Dad, it's my own mind that's betrayed me, but I don't remember putting any of these things here.

I grab the alarm clock from her nightstand and with a scream that comes from the bottom of my soul, slam it into the mirror. Glass shatters onto the dresser and tiny splinters pepper my bare feet, but Gen's still watching me. Taunting me. I rake the clock over the shards until only the upper corners cling to the wooden frame and I can no longer see the look of disdain on her face.

The clock drops to the floor but the fury inside me is just getting started. I attack her bed, pulling tugging yanking until the sheets cover the broken glass. My fingers sink into her feather pillow—we're allergic but it doesn't make much difference in here—the sharp quills poking me through the flimsy fabric. With another scream, I rip the pillow at the seams, sending feathers into the air. The volume in the room drops as feathers drift around me, their downy softness silencing my cries.

But I'm still not finished. The last time I destroyed Gen's room I was hurt by Mom's inability to see me for who I am, but this is like a purge. If I'm going to move on without Gen, like she so clearly wants, I need to remove every piece of her from my life.

Nothing is safe from my wrath. Clothes pile on the floor, the remaining pictures ripped from the walls, and with one deep breath, the lamp explodes against the inside of the closet.

"Still not enough," I pant.

As if on autopilot, I cross the hall to Mom's room. To her crafting drawer. Find the shiny scissors that as a child were strictly forbidden. My breathing slows, filling my lungs and reenergizing my blood to give me the strength I need.

Leggings fall in strips at my feet. Bedding is rendered useless. Curtains become scarves. When it seems there is nothing left to destroy, I set the scissors on the dresser and tug the UVA sweatshirt over my head. My fingers hesitate at the sleeve with my blood, this physical reminder of what Gen and I share, then the blades slide up the sleeve, mutilating the thing that has always felt the most like Gen. I pause as the scissors close around the UVA logo. Maybe I should keep this one reminder.

You're so weak. Finish what you started.

My inner voice sounds so much like Gen that I close the scissors without another thought. The U lands among the debris at my feet, the VA still in my hand, and I stumble back as if I'd cut the letters from my own chest. This feels too final. I grab the U and press the two pieces together. One memento of our lives together is okay.

My rage slips from my body on an exhale and my legs tremble. She's truly gone now. Erased from our family more thoroughly than she was eighteen years ago. I tiptoe around the broken glass to the door, but one final burst of adrenaline rocks the dresser, pushing it forward onto the pile of Gen on the floor.

Gen wanted to leave. Now she can.

For the first time in my life, I am truly alone.

Thirty-One

JULY 8

I SHOULD HAVE KNOWN THAT WHEN THEY TOOK MOM, I WOULDN'T BE FAR BEHIND. THERAPY IS A FAR CRY FROM BEING INSTITUTIONALIZED, BUT IT FEELS LIKE A SENTENCE, NONETHELESS. MY ENTIRE EXISTENCE HAS BEEN A LABYRINTH OF LIES, STACKED HIGHER AND HIGHER UNTIL THE TRUTH IS NOTHING BUT A BLUR IN THE DISTANCE. THE DAY I FOUND SKY—GEN—I TUMBLED FROM THAT PRECIPICE AND HAVE YET TO HIT THE GROUND.

WHO DECIDES WHAT'S NORMAL AND WHAT'S NOT?

ONE WORD DOES NOT DEFINE ME ANY MORE THAN SISTER OR JOURNALIST OR RUNNER. I AM THE SUM OF ALL MY PARTS AND A DIAGNOSIS FROM A DOCTOR WHO DOESN'T KNOW ME DOES NOT CHANGE WHO I AM.

—EE

Thirty-Two

The sun blazes high in the sky, sending sweat running in rivulets past my sports bra and down my bare back where it pools at the waistband of my shorts. I prefer to run early in the morning this time of year, both because of the July heat and because the pasty-white tourists sunning themselves all over the beach—my beach—make it nearly impossible to maintain my pace. But my morning runs have been bumped to the afternoon three days a week because my therapist decided that's how often I need to see her if I want to be "better" before leaving for school in forty-seven days.

As if an hour every other day can fix eighteen years of conditioning.

She's not terrible, but she waves my diagnosis like a white flag whenever I resist whatever mental calisthenics she has planned for that session. Using phrases like "let's unpack how this makes you feel" makes me want to rip the flags from her hands and shred them like I did Gen's room. But that's what landed me here, so instead I stare at her flags, trying to reconcile her words with what I know about myself.

Dissociative disorder unspecified.

Unspecified, like I'm too fucked up to fit into one of their checkboxes, so they've lumped me with my two personalities and brainwashing and evidence of amnesia into the uncategorizable category.

Plus C-PTSD and a little anxiety tossed in for flavor. But who wouldn't be anxious growing up knowing that when your sister was stolen, it could have been you? Or that your mother decided life is better in her cocoon, screw the rest of the world.

As for the disorder, I'm not sure if I buy it. Yes, I talk to my sister—or I used to until she vanished two months ago—but twins do that. They communicate in a way regular mortals cannot, and while I haven't gotten to that point with Sky yet, we're working on it. I'm just not ready to see her face to face.

The dissociative part makes me a little uneasy. My ability to be two different people, to completely compartmentalize my emotions, has been necessary because of Mom. If I reacted every time she inadvertently said something hurtful I'd never get through the day, let alone the past eighteen years. So, while my therapist says it'll take over a year "to learn the appropriate coping skills and accept my trauma," I'm not convinced.

I sidestep a pair of toddlers flinging wet sand over their heads and settle into a steady pace. This stretch of beach edges million-dollar homes and while the law states anyone can be here, the homeowners chase away anyone who tries to set up camp, which makes it perfect for running. My stride lengthens, my breathing deepens, and my thoughts fall away. Right now, it's nothing but the gentle lapping of the waves and the cry of a distant seagull. No pushy doctors or rediscovered sisters or parents who've never given me what I so desperately wanted.

The crowd thickens closer to the pier. Rather than slowing to a walk, I turn around a quarter mile early and maintain my pace. When I hit the people-free zone, a runner in the distance starts to look familiar.

Then he waves.

I'm debating running past Wes without stopping, but as he slows, my therapist's voice tells me to spend more time with people. A lazy smile brightens his face, even as he rests his hands on his knees to catch his breath.

"Wondered if I'd ever see you out here again."

I mirror his stance and take a deep breath. "I mostly run in the mornings."

He taps his chest. "Evenings. Working landscaping. In the mornings."

That would explain his arms. He's always been in good shape, but soccer players tend to have long, lean muscles. Wes's biceps have doubled in size since we first met.

My smile lacks Gen's confidence, but it's my smile. "This is pretty much my life."

He straightens and runs a hand through his damp hair. "You've had a lot going on."

"Yeah."

"I'm guessing you don't want to talk about it."

"It feels like that's all I'm doing." He quirks an eyebrow and I tap my chest. "Therapy."

"Ahh." He stretches his arms over his head and gazes out over the water. "Too bad you can't have your sessions out here."

The fact that he understands what the open water means to me touches me in a way I can't explain. But maybe he's the same way. Surely I'm not the only one who finds solace in the ever-changing water.

"You want company for the run back?" he asks.

My reflex to turn him down and bury myself in my mind wiggles its way in front of the polite responses my therapist has taught me, but I push it back and force another smile. "As long as you promise not to talk until we're home."

His smile calms my breathing. "Deal."

Maybe I can do this friend thing after all.

Later, when I'm safely tucked in the treehouse, I text Sky.

Me: You should be proud of me.

The cobwebs along the ceiling dance in the summer air swirling through the cramped space. For as much time as I spend up here, it still looks uninhabited—the only sign of life a candy wrapper gathering dust beneath the cobwebs. The same two chairs are shoved against a wall and the bean bag chair, which I'm currently sitting in, is positioned beneath the window to take advantage of the breeze.

Sky: very proud. tell me why.

Me: I let Wes run with me today.

Sky: baby steps

Me: Actually we were running pretty fast.

Sky: haha groan

When I first started therapy, I hinted at how exhausting it is to tell someone every single thing about yourself, and Sky has kept the conversation light ever since. I'm grateful we can just talk. That I don't need to change the topic to avoid questions or feel like I'm somehow letting her down when I've already let down everyone else I care about.

Sky: I just got back from the beach. it was hot and crowded. remind me never to go in the middle of the day.

A smile curls my lips and warmth radiates from my heart through my body. It's moments like these, when the connection between us is obvious despite our physical distance, that I feel like maybe everything will turn out okay. That my diagnoses won't define me, and my future isn't already determined. That my sister and I can still have the bond I've longed for my entire life.

Me: It was the same for me. Tourists suck.

Sky: it's funny we both live in touristy places.

Sky: have you ever been here?

My stomach drops. Right after the competition, Sky insisted we see each other and didn't relent until the disastrous day with her parents. She let up when Mom was committed, and I thought she was okay with our current situation, but our nascent connection says she wants more.

Me: Just when I was a kid. We didn't really travel because of Mom.

Sky: right. sorry.

I already know she's only been to Spring Haven the one time, and I'm at a loss how to move the conversation away from what feels like dangerous territory.

Me: That's why I'm so excited to go away for college.

Sky: you could come visit.

Our texts come through at the same time. My comment about college negates the argument that I don't want to travel, and with Mom locked away and my lack of a social life, I have zero excuses not to go. Other than I'm terrified to see her.

The hesitation that consumes me whenever I think about seeing Sky again is like the anticipation before a first date, when you're afraid it can never live up to your expectations. The complicated feelings that stirred the butterflies when we first met have gone into hibernation, and our conversations always leave me in a better mood, so what am I afraid of?

Sky: never mind

Me: Sorry. I'm just not ready.

Sky: but it'll be harder when we start college.

She's going to the same design school as Ember, which is its own level of weird, and even though she'll be closer to Spring Haven while at school, I'll be in Chicago.

Sky: please. before the end of summer?

Me: I don't understand the rush.

Sky: my whole life I've felt like something was missing. now I know what it is and I want to make up for lost time.

Sky: *who

Sky: *you :P

Me: I'll try.

The tension in my chest eases like it always does with her. It's only when I get trapped inside my head that everything spirals and it feels like the world might crash over me, destroying everything I love and swallowing me whole.

Thirty-Three

AUGUST 3

THE CALENDAR SAYS TWENTY-TWO DAYS, AND YET IT FEELS LIKE THE DAY I GET TO REINVENT MYSELF IS SLIPPING FARTHER AND FARTHER AWAY. MY THERAPIST INSISTS MEDICATION WILL HELP ME "FIND MY BALANCE" AND CONTROL MY THOUGHTS, BUT I'M AFRAID IT'LL MAKE ME STOP FEELING. THIS AGONIZING EMPTINESS GEN LEFT IN HER PLACE IS BETTER THAN NOTHING. IF I STOP MOURNING HER, I MIGHT FORGET HER AND THEN I TRULY WON'T BE ABLE TO LIVE WITH MYSELF.

BUT I DON'T SAY THIS IN THERAPY. MUSCLE MEMORY DISPLAYS GEN'S SMILE AND WES'S SHRUG AND EVEN EMBER'S CASUAL OPTIMISM SO MY THERAPIST THINKS I'M GETTING BETTER. THAT I'VE MOVED PAST THE "UNFORTUNATE EVENTS OF MY UPBRINGING" AND AM READY TO START OVER.

WE DON'T TALK ABOUT GEN.

OR SKY.

ONLY EVE.

AND IT'S EXCRUCIATING.

—EE

Thirty-Four

"How's your Mom?" Ember's sitting behind the counter at the mini-golf place where she's working the last few weeks of summer. Her black and purple hair contrasts sharply with the light blue polo shirt she's forced to wear and a trail of sweat runs down the side of her face. The rickcty fan overhead pushes hot air around the cramped room, the repetitive clicks of the motor lulling me toward sleep.

"I don't know how you do this."

She purses her lips at my non-answer and rolls a golf ball between her hands on the counter. "It's a job. It's the only place that would take me for the month after my internship and they let me read when no one's in here."

A little boy screams near the replica of the pier before throwing his club against a boulder.

"But you have to deal with that."

"It builds character, right?" The ball rolls off the counter and bounces against her bag. "So, your mom. Have you seen her?"

I could keep putting her off, but Ember deserves the truth. Her loyalty never faltered after everything came out about me and Gen, and she's one of the few people I don't want to push away. "Dad and I visited a couple days ago." She waits out my pause, chin resting on her fists. "It was weird. A nurse came in a few times while we were there, but aside from that it was like any other time I've seen her."

"Does she..." Ember grabs another ball and rolls it back and forth. "Does she seem to be getting better?"

The doctors insist it'll take years to unravel the labyrinth of her mind. To get her to a place where she can accept that the Gen she's loved for eighteen years isn't real. "She seems the same to me."

"And what about you?"

Wes shrugs for me but Gen's smile refuses to surface. "Therapy is therapy."

Her gaze drops to the counter like she's avoiding my eyes. "What did they—did they say what..."

"My diagnosis?"

She nods, and a piece of my heart breaks for everything she's endured for me.

"Dissociative disorder. Unspecified. And anxiety and C-PTSD."

"And that means what exactly?"

"The technical explanation is I have two personality states." Everything inside me freezes as my words glide into her ears and worm into her brain and alter how she thinks of me. Her face shifts from concern to horror to something unrecognizable, something dark and unfamiliar. Another Before and After. Then she blinks and the Ember I know is back.

"Like multiple personalities?"

"That's what they tell me." My gaze drops and my therapist's words feel like marbles in my mouth. "She thinks it was caused by prolonged and intensive persuasion. Basically, Dad brainwashing me for years."

Her head snaps up and I meet her gaze. "So this is his fault? Shouldn't he be punished?" Anger brightens her eyes while tears burn mine and I thank whoever for the millionth time that she's on my side.

"Yes, but the law makes it hard. And I don't know if I want more attention than I already have."

She smiles, a hesitant curl of her lips. "There is a limit to how extra extra someone can be."

Would she still joke if she knew the rest of it? My brain refuses to accept Dad wasn't involved with Gen's room, and I don't know if that's the diagnosis or normal disbelief because nothing about this is normal. "They've given me a referral for someone near campus, but I don't know..."

She drops the ball in the basket and grabs my hand. "Eve, it's important that you keep going."

"I don't see the point. I found my sister. My mom's getting the help she needs." Dad barely speaks. Gen's room looks the same as when I trashed it. I've pushed away the boy who would've done anything for me. "What's there to talk about?" Even now I can't relax. Can't let go of the fear of slipping up, of what will happen if I let go and just be myself.

"I worry about you. PTSD is no joke. And this is a lot to deal with, especially when we're going away to college."

"That's a good thing. I get to reinvent myself." Although my dreams of living in obscurity are unlikely with the amount of press our story received, especially since my journalism classmates will be the ones most likely to follow the news.

"Is that really what you want?" Ember's voice is soft, uncertain. Very unlike her.

"What do you mean?"

She picks at a groove in the counter. "I don't know. It's just, I like who you are, and I hate that you think you need to change." Her eyes meet mine and a rush of emotion grips my heart. Will I ever find another friend who gets me the way she does?

"I'm going to miss you," I say.

She laughs and wipes a tear from her eye. "I wasn't fishing for a compliment."

"I know, but it's true." My forearms rest on the counter and I lean closer to her. "Besides, didn't you hear? I'm cured."

She snorts, and my breath catches as I remember my conversation with Sky.

"I do have a consolation prize for you."

She cocks her head.

"Sky's going to Kendall, too."

"Interesting."

"So when you miss me, you can just stalk her and get your fix."

Her eyes widen. "Or, you know, I could just become friends with her."

"But not best friends."

She holds up three fingers in a salute. "Never. That would be beyond extra extra." Her lip catches between her teeth. "Speaking of Sky, have you seen her yet?"

A thousand excuses tumble over each other, but Ember will see through all of them. "No."

"Eve, she's your sister. You can't push her away." I both hate and love that Ember knows me so well.

"I'm not ready."

"Will you ever be?"

Before I can answer, the mother of the screaming boy hurries through the open doorway. "Hi! Sorry. I need another orange ball."

Ember's shoulders straighten as she digs an orange ball from the basket. "What happened to the first one?"

The woman has the decency to look embarrassed. "My son hit it in the bushes, and we can't find it."

Ember hands her the ball. "Which bushes?"

She points out the door. "The ones along the fence. Sorry!" she calls over her shoulder.

Ember's shoulders slump. "Feel like digging a ball out of the bushes?"

"You have to find it?"

She taps the logo on her polo. "One of the perks of the job."

"People suck."

"I choose to believe she tried to find it. Parents can't control what their kids do."

Her words knock the wind out of me. I can blame Dad all I want for putting me into this situation, but I chose to go along with it. I'm the one who portrayed my kidnapped sister so flawlessly that not only did Mom believe she was real, she loves her more. It's my fault Mom might never accept Sky as her daughter or believe that the Gen she adores was essentially my imaginary friend. And no amount of therapy is going to change that.

It takes Ember a minute to realize what she said. She reaches for my hand again. "Hey, I didn't mean..."

"But you're right."

She takes a deep breath, and I watch her choose which words to say next. "I think you need to see Sky. Maybe that's how you can start to fix all this. Start to heal."

"You might be right."

Nothing will fix Mom, but I owe it to Sky to try.

Thirty-Five

AUGUST 13

I NEVER THOUGHT I'D SEE THE DAY
I'D HAVE TO SAY GOODBYE.
TO BID FAREWELL TO ALL YOU ARE
AND NEVER TELL YOU WHY.

MY WORLD'S COMING UNRAVELED,
SHATTERED, SPLINTERED, FRACTURED, FRAYED.
THE PIECES RIPPED ME OPEN,
TEARING YOU AWAY.

THE WORLD'S GONE MAD AROUND US
AND NO ONE ELSE CAN SEE,
THAT EVEN IF YOU'RE GONE FOR GOOD,
I'LL NEVER BE JUST EVE.

—EE

Thirty-Six

“Dad, stop being weird.” He’s peering through the window in the front door like a kid waiting for the ice cream truck. “She won’t be here for another ten minutes.”

He moves away from the door and joins me in the living room. We’re in the same seats as when the detective interviewed me, and while the circumstances are completely different, the anticipation is just as crippling. I want to see Sky, I do, but my desire to get to know my sister battles with everything I’ve lost and what I plan to leave behind in a few weeks, and I don’t know where she fits.

When I invited Sky to visit, she insisted we hang out with Dad, but I don’t plan on staying here long. The house has felt desolate since Mom left; soulless since Gen went quiet. I should be grateful I still have Dad, but he’s another reminder of what I’m trying to leave behind. The detective reminded me that I could file suit against Dad, but it would have only prolonged our misery, and nothing the courts could do to him would change anything about our past. About what we’ve done. I’m as complicit as he is.

In my weaker moments, I worry what this house will do to him after I’m gone, but I push those fears down deep where they can’t hurt me.

A car door slams outside and we both straighten.

“I’ll let her in,” I say.

Sky stretches in the driveway, the wind blowing her hair around her face. I take a deep breath as she approaches, then hold it when she stops and turns toward Wes's house. A smile spreads across her face—my smile—and she shakes her head. I don't need to hear her voice to know she's correcting Wes for thinking she's me. Despite the different taste in clothes, we're impossible to tell apart.

The front door creaks as I open it, and her smile broadens. She bounds the rest of the way to me and engulfs me in a hug before I can stop her. She smells like apricots and mint and joy. Her chest squeezes against mine and I swear our heartbeats sync.

"Thank you for finally agreeing to this!" She releases me and nods at the open door. "Is he inside?"

"Yeah. Come on in." My voice is thick with unexpected affection for this person who is both a stranger and my other half. She waits for me to step inside and follows me into the living room.

Dad rises from the couch, his thumbs worrying into fists at his side. "Sky, it's so good to see you again." He moves around the coffee table and there's a moment of hesitation before she steps into his arms and rests her head against his chest in a way I haven't done in years. A burst of something—Jealousy? Possessiveness?—flushes my cheeks and I settle onto the end of the couch while they have their moment. He asks about her drive and leaving for school in a few weeks, and they chit-chat about the storm rolling toward us over the lake.

After a few minutes, she stands. "Could I use the bathroom?"

Dad and I both jump up, our lack of manners a glaring admission of how infrequently we have visitors. "It's at the top of the stairs," he says. "Eve will show you."

A flutter of panic makes my hand shake. She can't go upstairs. She can't see our rooms. Specifically, Gen's room.

A smile that's not my own works its way over my face. "This way!" I take the stairs two at a time and close Gen's door before Sky reaches the top. "Bathroom's here. I'll be in my room." I point at each door and retreat to the safety of my bedroom for what feels like the last time.

The seconds tick by as I stare out my window at the treehouse. To the only place I feel safe these days. Our home has been invaded by police and flipped inside out by reporters, and even though Sky is technically family, her presence here puts me on edge. Like she could somehow chip away at the tiny shred of security I feel here.

"Is this your room?"

Who else's would it be? The thought flits through my head, trailing a vehemence so strong I fold inward, searching for Gen. She's here. I know it.

"For all my life." My voice sounds fake, but Sky doesn't know me well enough to tell the difference. I smile and wave my arms at the walls, at this private piece of me that only a handful of people have ever seen. Her eyes travel over the posters on the walls, the books stacked on my desk and dresser, and finally a picture of Ember and me from prom. Her gaze lingers on the poster of Christiane Amanpour and she raises a brow.

"She's my hero."

She nods. "I've got a poster of Paul Rand in my room."

This time I raise my brow.

"He's like the god of logos and all things graphic design."

"Cool."

Sky looks closer at the prom photo. "Didn't she win the competition?"

"Yeah. That's Ember. My best friend." The words sound juvenile, like we're in grade school, and I'm trying to make the new girl like me. "Practically my only friend," I confess.

It's on the tip of my tongue to mention that Ember's going to Kendall, too, but I'm not ready for them to become friends. For me to be replaced.

Her head tilts as she assesses me, but I don't feel scrutinized like when Cal would try to figure me out. With him I felt like a puzzle scattered across the floor, the most important pieces lost beneath the couch, never to be found. Sky's gaze implores to understand, not criticize. "I bet it was hard to have friends around, huh?"

I nod, and she moves to the window. Her presence in my room confuses my entire being. Part of me wants to make up for lost time and learn everything about her, while another part feels like I should automatically know these things because we're twins. Isn't that how it works? The bond formed in the womb should be impenetrable.

"The treehouse belongs to the neighbors, but Wes lets me hang out up there." Can she infer what I can't say out loud? That I no longer feel safe in my own house and am counting the days until I leave.

Her shoulder brushes mine. "I've always wanted a treehouse."

"Want to go up there?" As soon as I say it, the weight lifts from my chest. Yes, get her out of the house.

But when we climb the ladder and settle into the chairs, I still feel lopsided.

"Have you been to the lake?"

Her wistful smile doesn't reach her eyes. She twists her fingers in her lap, her gaze on the dusty wooden floor. "This is weird, right?"

I exhale so loudly she looks up. She feels it, too. "Yes."

She presses her hand to her cheek and finally looks at me. "My therapist says it'll take time for me to accept what happened to me. And that I shouldn't expect us to be best friends overnight." She leans forward so her elbows are on her knees, her face closer to mine. "But we're sisters. Twins. We should feel a... connection, right?"

Relief swells through me as she struggles to speak her truth. "You don't?"

"I mean, a little. But not like I expected."

My fingers twine through hers before I realize I've reached for her. I'm terrified there will be a jolt of something more, an awakening of the kaleidoscope that's laid dormant for months, but there's nothing but a casual comfort that feels like home. Or what home should be. "It's the same for me. I've wondered and worried and dreamed about you for so long, and now that you're here, I keep thinking there should be this unbreakable bond that transcends the physical world."

The corner of her mouth lifts. "You're definitely the writer in the family."

Family. My insides still for half a heartbeat, then I fling her hand away with a laugh.

She laughs along with me.

Okay, maybe we can do this. "So do you want to go to the lake?"

She nods, then follows me through the yard and back into the house. Dad's reading his tablet on the couch, and the normalcy of the scene catches me off guard. He isn't brooding or fretting, he's merely spending a Saturday afternoon relaxing like he's probably always wished he could. He looks up and smiles when he sees us.

Us.

"We're heading to the lake. I want to show Sky what it looks like farther south."

Sky laughs next to me. "I'm sure it's completely different."

"Well, you don't have a pier, so that part's unique."

Dad rests his tablet in his lap and glances out the window. "Be safe. The storm should be hitting in the next hour or so."

"We will," we say together, and it's like someone presses pause on the room. Sky and I lock eyes and something inside me that's never quite fit falls into place. She touches my arm, the surprise in her eyes mirroring how I feel. "I'm glad I came," she says.

A different kind of pressure fills my chest. With Gen there was always a hesitation, an uncertainty that put me on edge. This feels warm and inviting. A lot like Sky. "Me too."

Outside, wind pushes the trees high above us. Clouds blot out the sun, but it's still warm, the cool air of the approaching storm yet to reach us.

"Do you want to drive to the pier or walk?" I ask.

She follows my gaze to the treetops, hands on hips. "How far is it?"

"A couple miles. Only a quarter mile to the beach."

Her hands drop to her sides. "Let's walk."

Wes's car turns onto our road as we walk down the driveway. My stomach pitches. Through all this, he's given me no reason for concern, but I'm not ready to be Gen and Eve with other people. Not yet.

"I met him earlier. I think he thought I was you."

"I guess we'll have to get used to that, huh?"

She bumps my arm with her elbow. "Guess so."

Our hands lift in a wave as Wes pulls into his driveway, but we don't stop. "See you later?" he calls out the window.

"Sure." He should know it's a lie, should understand I'll need time to process today.

We're quiet until we reach the access point to the beach, then Sky drops to her knees, running the sand through her fingers. After a moment, she looks up at me, her cheeks reddening. "Just saying hi."

Whitecaps dot the surface of the lake, pushing the water so high up the shore we'll either have to walk barefoot or walk in the soft sand. With a silent look, we kick off our shoes and let the rough water wash over our feet.

"This is more like it," she says. "I prefer to run barefoot. It makes me feel like I'm part of the lake, you know?"

My breath catches. Every revelation seems to set off a reserve of emotions I didn't realize were simmering beneath the surface, making me hyper-aware of each breath, each beat of my heart. "I do."

The red fog house at the end of the pier stands proudly in the distance, the bright color a shock against the darkening sky. Waves nip at the concrete, but people dot the length of the pier, oblivious to the danger.

"Are you sure it's safe to go out there?"

"As long as the waves aren't crashing over the end, we should be okay."

She accepts my word as gospel and a hesitation hangs between us as we walk. An empty feeling I'd always associated with Gen—like when you finally get rid of the hiccups—sweeps through me, its tentacles stretching from my fingers to my toes.

I break the silence. "Whatever you need to say, just say it. I won't judge you."

She gives me a side-eye. "Safe space, huh?"

I shrug. "We should be able to be honest with each other, right?"

"Yes." Her lip catches between her teeth and another minute passes before she continues. "I was just going to say something stupid about the competition. I still feel so bad that I let my team down."

I never asked her about her project. Her team didn't win, but I assumed they presented along with everyone else. "What happened?"

"They said I went into shock after seeing you. Completely shut down." She tilts her head forward so her hair covers her face. "You took off and wouldn't answer my texts. I didn't know what was going on and there was no way I could present." She pushes her hair over her shoulder and gives me a small smile. "I'm the most outgoing of our group, so I was supposed to do all the talking. Kevin fumbled through it, but we most definitely did not win."

"I'm so sorry."

Her hand grabs mine and she stops so she's facing me. "Don't ever apologize for being my sister. I don't think there's a way I could have found out the truth that wouldn't be shocking, you know?" I nod dumbly and she smiles. "The competition wasn't the end of the world. It was the beginning."

An energy passes between us where our skin touches, an understanding that goes deeper than anything I could ever explain. My gaze drops to our hands.

"You feel it too?" she asks.

Tears spring to my eyes and I can't breathe past everything I want to say.

"Let's keep walking." She takes the lead, carrying the conversation. The cadence of her words wash over me until a question pierces through the fog. "Which one of us is older?"

"You are by four minutes."

"I've always wanted a little sister." She puffs out her chest and laughs, and the lightness that seems to follow her seeps into my pores. Gen has always been suspicious, even devious, but Sky is everything that is good in the world. Being around her makes my future feel less uncertain, like maybe I don't need to leave every part of myself behind when I go to school.

When we reach the pier, we pause in front of the sign with the picture of two boys our age who drowned decades ago. It's here to warn tourists about the dangers of the lake, but people barely glance at it before trusting the thin slip of concrete that juts into the fierce waters.

"They died here?" Sky asks, her hand trailing over the weathered sign.

"Yeah, before we were born. Kids jump off the pier when it's nicer out." On sunny days, when the water's calm and it feels like summer will never end, dozens of teens pack the center of the pier, jumping in groups, the crazier ones showing off with flips. To outsiders it looks reckless, but we learned instinctually which part of the pier is safest, the knowledge passed down through generations of locals the way butterflies know to migrate south for the winter. We know which parts of the pier have rocks lurking beneath the surface and when the water's too rough to go in. No one who grew up here would dare go in today, which is why it's practically deserted. "It's usually only tourists who fall in."

"Have you jumped off?"

"A few times in middle school, but not recently."

"I'd love to come back when it's nicer. It sounds fun."

"I'd like that."

When I gave Gen a personality, it felt natural for her to be social, the one with all the friends. Her bubbly nature carried me through more than a few situations, but Sky's optimism and general outlook on the world makes it feel fake. Like maybe I can deal with life without Gen's help.

A bearded man with a camera slung around his neck passes as we step onto the pier and gives us a stern look. "You girls be careful out there. She's getting angry." His hiking boots leave wet footprints and the scent of cigarette smoke trails after him.

"That was creepy," Sky says.

"It's pretty standard. People here usually look out for each other."

"Traverse City is like that most of the time, but we don't have this." Her arms spread out wide. The towns along Lake Michigan have the same sugar-sand beaches, but only a few have piers. Walking along the concrete makes it feel like you're stepping into another universe, especially on days like today when the wind whips the waters into a frenzy.

Waves break against the metal lip that wraps around the structure, splashing high into the air and splattering all around us.

"Are you sure you want to go all the way out?" I ask. "We'll probably get wet."

She holds up her shoes and smiles. "I won't melt."

We continue toward the end, pausing on the raised ledge of the lighthouse at the midway point. Water surges over the concrete as if we weren't here, determined to claim everything in its path and leaving puddles dotting the surface, mirroring the darkening sky.

While most people would feel nervous out here, my heart rate calms. Being this close to the lake centers me like nothing else. But not everyone feels that way. "We can turn back."

Sky faces me. Strands of her hair blow across her face and the excitement I feel is reflected in her eyes. "Heck no. This is awesome." She steps off the ledge directly into a puddle and kicks her leg, splashing me. "Come on!"

Her giggles are contagious, and by the time we reach the fog house, I've forgotten everything but this moment. Sharing this place with my sister—my actual sister—is unlike anything I could have imagined, and knowing she appreciates it as much as I do makes the years of suffering feel like a distant memory. Like something I had to endure to arrive at this point in time. We tiptoe through the standing water alongside the fog house and when we emerge at the end of the pier, Sky gasps.

"This is unreal."

Waves roll toward us, threatening to swallow the pier whole. Seagulls swoop and dip near the whitecaps, their cries sending chills up my spine, followed by a hint of the familiar hollowness that was a part of me for so long I didn't realize it was gone. "Stay against the building."

Sky gives me a mischievous smile, tosses her shoes against the foghouse, and moves closer to the edge. A set of waves that look like they could carry us away roll toward us, undulating and cresting until they hit the edge of the pier in a magnificent splash. Sky squeals as water thunders around us, jumping back from the edge but still not joining me along the concrete wall.

"Sky, come back!"

"I've never seen anything like this!" Her hair swirls around her face and sticks to her neck and shoulders, while her wet shirt clings to her body. But she still doesn't back away.

My hair probably looks the same but right now my only concern is my sister. Raw fear pushes away the anxiety that has dominated my thoughts all summer. I can't lose her again. "Sky, please." The wind inhales my plea, tossing it out among the waves that have grown even taller.

"Eve, get over here!" The joy in her smile is everything I've wanted. The water's vehemence dances in her eyes and exhilaration flushes her cheeks a deep pink. She holds out her hand and I step closer. When our fingers connect, the heaviness in my chest that's been missing for so long crashes through me so quickly that I stumble. She grabs my wrist, keeping me on my feet, and a fury unlike anything I've known burns through my veins.

This imposter does not get to slide into our lives after eighteen years.

Gen!

The ferocity of the waves matches the rage blistering through me.

You said you wanted to move on, to remove her from your life.

Sky is my sister. She's not an imposter. She's you.

You can't have us both.

Sky's hand tightens around mine, a shimmer of fear darkening her face. "We should go back."

I try to nod but my body doesn't respond. A wave crests a foot over the pier, pushing us back from the edge, but Sky's grip doesn't loosen.

"Eve?"

"You'll never replace me. You've been in our lives 87 days. I've been with Eve her whole life!"

Sky's face pales. "What?"

A bolt of lightning cracks through the darkening sky. A wave sweeps over the edge and Sky's feet go out from beneath her. She slips in the water washing over the pier, her pink cheeks paling as her hand slips from mine.

Everything inside me stills.

"Eve!"

Her outstretched hand—so much like mine—reaches for me to save her.

I lean forward.

Push instead of pull.

She pitches forward, arms flailing as she tumbles into the mouth of a hungry wave.

For a moment there's nothing—no storm, no danger, no feeling—then her head breaks the surface, and she screams.

"Eve! Help me! Please!" A mask of terror contorts her face as she gulps for air.

She's almost close enough to reach.

Her arms thrash as a wave surges toward the pier and I inch closer.

Our hands could connect if I stretch a little farther.

It's better this way.

My hand extends from my body and our fingers brush, but the wave collapses, slamming her head into the metal edge of the pier. In a moment so breathtakingly clear it will forever burn in my mind, her face goes slack and she sinks beneath the water.

No scream.

No final breath.

Just gone.

Gen, what did you do?!

It's better now.

No!

Lightning splits the universe in two, cleaving straight through my heart. Waves pound all around me and I stumble toward the safety of the wall, shedding the person I was before, the other half of my soul.

Footsteps.

Running.

Screams.

Discarded shoes on the wet concrete.

Rain turns to salt as everything inside me empties onto the pier.

Men in slick black suits.

Shouting.

More bodies disappearing into the waves.

Sky's lifeless body being pulled from the water.

The world collapsing on me.

Can't breathe. Need to breathe.

One.

Two.

Three.

The counting in my head keeps time with the compressions on Sky's chest.

Four.

Five.

"Miss?"

Rough hands on my shoulders.

"Do you know her?" Face freezing as he looks at me, looks at her. "Oh shit."

"Eve!" Dad's hands on my arms.

How did he get here?

"Where is your sister?"

"I—I tried to pull her back."

"What?"

"She was too close to the edge." I point at the spot where my sister was erased from my life, but the lake is gone. "The waves." Where did the waves go?

A bright light shines in my eyes.

"She's in shock."

"A witness said you tried to save her."
Her fingers were so cold.
Are even colder now.
It was Gen who snapped.
Not me.

My world flipped when Sky appeared, and now, I'm trapped in a spiral that can only have one ending.

Thirty-Seven

AUGUST 25

THE DAY HAS FINALLY ARRIVED. I DON'T REMEMBER WHEN I STARTED MY COUNTDOWN, BUT I'M LEAVING THIS MAUSOLEUM OF A HOUSE AND THE TOWN THAT KNOWS MY EVERY SECRET, AND I DON'T KNOW WHEN I'LL BE BACK. NOSTALGIA TICKLES MY SENSES, THREATENING TO WEAKEN MY RESOLVE, BUT THIS IS WHAT I WANT. TO LEAVE IT ALL BEHIND. TO BE RID OF THE DOUBLE-SPEAK AND HIDDEN JEALOUSY AND WHISPERED CONFUSION THAT'S BECOME THE CORE OF MY BEING.

NOW I GET TO START OVER.

BECOME SOMEONE NEW.

THE REAL ME.

Dad knocks on my door and I snap the laptop closed. "We need to get on the road." The bags under his eyes melt into the scruff on his cheeks, and his shoulder slumps against the doorframe like it's the only thing holding him up.

"I'm all set." I grab my backpack from the foot of my bed and take a final look out the window. Wes left for school a week ago to start training with the soccer team, and the treehouse has already heard my silent goodbyes. I texted Cal, but he's moved on with Lissa. Fate finally dealt him a kindness and they're both going to the University of Michigan on the east side of the state, where I'm sure they'll fall in love and have babies and change the world.

Ember's gone too. We made plans to see each other at Thanksgiving, but that promise felt fuzzy, her words placating. The tears in her eyes were real, but the hesitation between her words left me unsettled.

Dad turns off the light and I try to smile. To put on a brave face. Anything to slow the rising panic that's drowning out whatever Dad's saying over his shoulder.

My gaze drifts over Gen's room. A bright comforter anchors the bed along the wall, her orange and blue knitted blanket folded at the end, but the rest of the room is bare. No pictures, no clothes, no details to mislead the outside world. The living room is the only space that actually looks lived in. Dad spends most of his time in there since Mom went away, choosing to avoid the room that entombed the woman he loves.

We step into the morning, the sun reflecting off the roof of his car. Betty rests in her normal spot, patiently waiting until I can take her with me. My heart clenches. I'll miss her the most. She mirrors the rising sun as boldly as Dad's car and I shield my eyes, unable to look any longer.

My suitcase rests next to my knitted purple and white blanket on the backseat, and travel cups of coffee await in the center console. My leaving is probably hard for Dad, but he's fulfilling his role as puppet master to the very end.

Memories flicker through the trees as we drive through town. The route I ran to the beach, the restaurant where we ate before prom, the drawbridge connecting Spring Haven to the rest of the world beyond the river. A sense of relief pushes away the past when we reach the highway, and I finally close my eyes.

Gen doesn't speak. Whatever she has to say was lost that day on the pier.

The world blurs into shape when we exit the highway. Skyscrapers dot the horizon, white puffy clouds daring their spires to stretch higher, to puncture the sky and let darkness consume us. The harsh sun burns my eyes, and I slink lower into the seat, welcoming the darkness simmering just beneath the surface.

"Just a little farther." Dad's voice sounds mechanical, like it's coming through the radio, not from the shell of a person next to me. The past few months have hollowed him, annihilating his personality and washing away whatever qualities once made him a man. The person my mother fell in love with. My father.

Some days I wonder how things might have ended if I pressed charges, but spending the rest of his life atoning for his sins should be enough. His personal torment is better than anything the justice system could have decreed.

He turns down a tree-lined street and before I can fully wake up, pulls into a parking lot in front of a two-story brick building. The engine goes silent and a chill races over my skin. We're here. It's actually happening.

"It'll be okay," Dad says, but I'm not sure if it's for his benefit or mine. "Leave your things for now."

My hands shake as I open the door and follow him along the uneven sidewalk to a metal door. A door that says keep out.

Or stay in.

Thin wires crisscross the glass in the narrow window, and years of shoes and who-knows-what have scuffed the base of the door, revealing a mottled rainbow of paint colors. A faint buzzing murmurs between my ears as Dad swings the door open.

It'll be okay.

Dad tells my name to the woman who greets us. The lobby is a smear of pale blue walls and green-flecked tiles and fake leather furniture. The walls splinter into hallways lined with closed doors, dividing the building into orderly rectangles. The greeter leads us down one of the halls to a room with an open door. Next, I'm sitting on the edge of a bed with a scratchy blanket and Dad's telling me he'll get my things. The single window has the same razor-thin wire running through it. There's no treehouse in the distance, but there are trees and what looks like a small garden.

The greeter hovers in the hallway until Dad returns empty-handed.

"Where's my stuff?"

Dad's eyes flick to the greeter, who turns to me with a gentle smile.

"We're checking in your belongings. Ted will bring them shortly."

My shoulders straighten. "Like a search?"

She clasps her hands in front of her, causing her uniformed shirt to bunch around her breasts. "Standard procedure with all our girls."

A tremor starts in my fingers and winds its way through my body until I can no longer sit still. But the small room holds me tight, and Dad and the woman block the exit. I pace circles around the confined space, my hips brushing the bed, the nightstand, the single wooden chair, and she moves closer.

"You'll meet with Dr. Kolb shortly, then group starts at eleven. Say your goodbyes with your father and we'll get you when it's time." She rests a hand on Dad's arm and a look of sympathy passes between them.

Sympathy for him or me, I'm not sure.

Anger slides around my heart, slowing my breathing and blurring the edges of my vision. But Dad doesn't wait for me to explode. He crosses the room and pulls me into his arms, the familiar scent of his soap making me homesick in a way I never expected.

"Eve, I wish it hadn't come to this, but it's your best option. And who knows, maybe after some time we can talk about Northwestern again."

Northwestern.

My dream.

My future as a journalist fades with each ragged breath, with each wail echoing in the hallway. I nod against his chest so he'll think I understand. But it's everyone else who doesn't understand. What happened on the pier wasn't my fault. I tried to save Sky. It was Gen who couldn't handle her being in my life.

Dad releases me and I drift back to the bed. "When can I call?" he asks the greeter.

"In seventy-two hours."

He makes a show of looking at his watch as if he's locking that detail in his brain, but I know he's doing whatever he can to divert the attention from himself. Because me being here is the culmination of his actions and no amount of bumbled goodbyes will change that.

He touches my cheek and years of practice keeps the smile on my face. "I put a notebook in your bag so you can still write."

"Thanks."

"No writing devices for seventy-two hours." The greeter's voice has a calming effect, but her words set off alarm bells in my head and panic in my chest. This is real. A judge agreed with the police that I was somehow responsible for Sky's death and now I'm trapped in this cinderblock labyrinth indefinitely.

"Oh," Dad says.

Our eyes meet and years of rage and confusion rush to a boil, then back to a simmer just as quickly. As he fidgets in front of me, a sense of clarity pushes away everything else. He no longer controls me. I may not be where I hoped, but the chance to rewrite my story still rests in my hands. The doctors or whoever's in charge may think they know me, but the others are a blank slate.

I touch Dad's arm and Gen smiles one last time. "I'll talk to you in three days."

The greeter closes the door behind them, and I'm left alone in the soulless room with pale blue walls and a scuffed linoleum floor. My new home. Wind sways the trees outside and their familiarity reinforces my determination. I'm in control now. I choose who I am and what people think of me. Counting down the days until I left for college was really a countdown to the day I could step out of Mom and Dad and Gen's shadow and truly become myself. And that day has arrived.

Before long, I'm shuffled to an office where a white version of Mr. Barney skirts around the same questions the police asked, informs me of the rules here, then, after skimming a folder with my name on the flap, sends me back to my room. I lay on the bed until there's a knock on the door.

A guy not much older than me steps into the doorway with my bags. He sets them at the foot of the bed and smiles. "I'm Ted. Group's in five minutes in the Blue Room. I'll show you where it's at."

"Is everything here blue?"

He cracks a smile. "Pretty much." He leads me down the sterile hall, his sneakers squeaking on the tiled floor. When I dreamed of college, part of that dream was how I'd decorate my dorm room, and specifically my door. But here the doors are unadorned. Nothing covers the walls except miles and miles of pale blue paint. We round a corner and Ted steps into an open room with picture windows overlooking a different garden. Pairs of women stroll the grass, and it all feels a little too perfect.

Ted points at the chairs arranged in a circle. A dozen girls about my age fill most of the chairs. "Grab a seat. I'll bring you back to your room after Group."

No one looks up when I enter, so I take an empty seat next to a girl with brown hair with a faded purple streak. A woman standing near the window takes the chair opposite me and smiles.

"Ladies, we have a newcomer today." She nods at me, her soft gaze penetrating through my remaining panic, reminding me why I'm here. "Would you like to introduce yourself?"

My tongue feels heavy but my breath comes easily. This is the day I've waited for. The past is finally in the past and the future is whatever I make of it. My gaze bounces over each girl, my smile willing them to listen.

To hear me.

I take a breath and on the exhale say, "I'm Genevieve."

Author's Note

Writing about mental health can be tricky. Showing a character's struggles without relying on offensive stereotypes or making them a caricature of a diagnosis is a challenge, and I hope I've served this story well.

I worked with two mental health professionals to make sure Eve was both believable and sympathetic, despite how unlikeable she could be. (No, you weren't supposed to like her.) Together we discussed the plausibility of a person enduring the type of psychological abuse that Eve experienced, combined with her parents' history of mental illness, and what that would look like for a person. My intention with this story was to get inside the head of a girl who had the odds stacked against her before she was old enough to have a say, and then show how she found a way to survive despite those odds.

Book Club Questions

1. Throughout the book, Eve struggles with the feeling that her friends and family prefer Gen over her. In what ways does Eve's mom show her preference?

2. Eve chooses to give Gen the social life to help keep track of her stories. What does she miss out on by making that decision?

3. How does the Eve's secret being exposed compare to Ember's sexuality being revealed against her will?

4. Can you imagine a situation like the Ellaways' that would lead you to make a decision like Eve's dad did?

5. Gen lives inside Eve's head and keeps insisting that she wants to "go outside," while Eve relies on Gen to help her through uncomfortable situations. Were there any times in the book where you felt Eve and Gen traded places—where Gen was the person on the outside and Eve was trapped in Gen's mind?

6. What do you think it means when Eve introduces herself as Genevieve at the end of the story? While the ending isn't happy, do you think her life worked out the way she wanted?

Acknowledgements

When Eve's story first came to me, I didn't believe I was a strong enough writer to do her justice, so she simmered in the back of my mind while I wrote and published other books. When I did start this book, it took a lot out of me—so much so that I landed in the ER with a panic attack. Close friends asked if maybe I should set Eve aside, but I knew I couldn't. Once I got into Eve's head, I couldn't let her go. Much like Gen.

This book is the best I've ever written, and also the most difficult. I hope my effort comes through in the pages. So many people played a role, from moral support to talking through plot points to urging me to hurry up and publish.

Beth Larsen, MSW, for helping me determine if dissociative identity disorder can be caused by both environmental and genetic factors (and loaning me her copy of the DSM-IV), and Heiddi Zalamar, LMHC, for helping me craft a believable character living with the mental illnesses I bestowed upon her. Any mistakes I made with Eve's diagnoses and behaviors are entirely mine.

My posse of writing friends, for their endless encouragement and empathizing when my doubts threatened to overwhelm me. Sara Carlson, for believing in me and my writing and sending the perfect gif for every occasion. Nancy Matuszak, for challenging me to a new editing process that served this story in ways I couldn't have figured out on my own, and for your tireless encouragement through the YEARS of working on this book.

My newer writing friends, whose excitement for this story gave me the boost I needed to shift from editing to publication.

All the Kickstarter supporters, whose pledges allowed me to give Eve the launch she deserved. Special thanks to Tony Ham for always being younger than me and never letting me forget it.

My grandmother, who read an early draft shortly before she died, for her unabashed amazement at the stories my brain dreams up. My mom, Judy Hooyenga, and her sisters, Susan Barajas and Karen Dionne, for your tireless support, encouragement, and enthusiasm—especially when my own waned.

And finally, my husband Jeremy, for feeding me, making me laugh, and distracting me when I needed it. Your love and support is everything.

Keep reading for the start of Flicker, *the award-winning first book in Hooyenga's* The Flicker Effect *trilogy.*

chapter 1

Sunlight pulses across the dashboard—light, dark, light, dark—and catches the dust dancing on the imitation leather.

My eyes stutter, but I blink it away. My heart jumps around in my chest. I stroke the grainy piece of cement stuck between my back teeth with my tongue. The orthodontist swore he got it all, but that was as true as his promise that it wouldn't be uncomfortable.

Uncomfortable. Right.

A tingling sensation pricks the tips of my fingers. I press them together, watching the blood shift beneath my skin. The tingling turns to those sharp needles that remind me of anything but sleep.

I press harder and my toes start tingling too. What the hell?

The dancing on the dashboard gets faster. The trees here are taller, straighter, and the sunlight strobes through the branches. My breath catches and a sudden heaviness pushes me deep into the seat.

I glance at Mom but she's concentrating on the road, humming along with golden oldies or whatever the hell it is she listens to, oblivious to the fact that something very weird is happening to her daughter.

To me.

I close my eyes. The heaviness lifts. Too much. Now I'm floating and—

"But Mom, I'm fine."

Mom crosses the kitchen and leans against the counter. "Biz, you're going. The dentist said your face will change if you don't get braces. Your entire face could look different..."

A sense of déjà vu slams me over the head. I've had this argument. Next Mom is gonna grab the stack of mail that Dad left on the counter and toss it in the basket.

She does.

"Biz?"

The words tumble out of me. "Mom..." The déjà vu doesn't lift. This isn't a memory. I'm not in the car anymore.

I've gone back to yesterday.

~~~

Find all of Melanie's books at melaniehoo.com, and sign up for her newsletter at melaniehoo.com/hoos-letter.
~~~

About the Author

Multi-award winning young adult author Melanie Hooyenga writes books about strong girls who learn to navigate life despite its challenges. She first started writing as a teenager and finds she still relates best to that age group. When not writing books, you can find her wrangling her Miniature Schnauzer Gus and playing every sport imaginable with her husband Jeremy.

Author website: melaniehoo.com
Email: melaniehooyenga@gmail.com
Facebook: facebook.com/MelanieHooyenga
Instagram: @melaniehoo
Threads: @melaniehoo
Newsletter: melaniehoo.com/hoos-letter

Melanie Hooyenga
PO Box 554
Grand Haven, MI 49417